FICTION GOU
Gould, Leslie
Adoring Addie

062013

Adoring Addie

Center Point
Large Print

Also by Leslie Gould and available from
Center Point Large Print:

The Courtships of Lancaster County
Courting Cate

**This Large Print Book carries the
Seal of Approval of N.A.V.H.**

The Courtships of Lancaster County
Book 2

Adoring Addie

ת૦ઍ

LESLIE GOULD

CENTER POINT LARGE PRINT
THORNDIKE, MAINE

The text of this Large Print edition is unabridged.
In other aspects, this book may
vary from the original edition.
Printed in the United States of America
on permanent paper.
Set in 16-point Times New Roman type.

ISBN: 978-1-61173-751-6

Library of Congress Cataloging-in-Publication Data

Gould, Leslie, 1962–
Adoring Addie / Leslie Gould. — Center Point Large Print edition.
pages cm
ISBN 978-1-61173-751-6 (Library binding : alk. paper)
1. Amish—Fiction. 2. Large type books. I. Title.
PS3607.O89A65 2013b
813′.6—dc23

2013006591

For Kaleb,

oldest son of mine,
full of intelligence and creativity,
truth and design

Behold, I make all things new.

Revelation 21:5 KJV

He that hath the steerage of my course,
direct my sail!

William Shakespeare,
Romeo and Juliet Act I, iv, 112–113

Adoring Addie

Chapter 1

 so

My parents were positive I'd met my future husband. They expected me to marry Phillip Eicher, the bishop's son. And soon.

"He's coming over tomorrow, for the barbecue," my mother said, perched on one of our mismatched chairs at the end of the table, her plump hand gripping a pen that hovered over her notebook. She spent most of her days there, writing lists, giving orders, and babying her bad knee. "He wants to talk to your *Daed*—at least that's what his mother told me."

"Oh." I wiped my sweaty palms down my just-starched apron.

A smile spread across her round face. "We'll have a wedding to plan soon."

"*Mutter*, please." I'd always called her *Mutter* and my father *Daed*, the more formal terms, rather than the familiar *Mamm* and *Dat* that my *Bruders* called them. She seemed to prefer it. I don't think my father cared.

Mutter continued speaking as if she hadn't heard my plea. "That's why you shouldn't go today. We want the barbecue tomorrow to be—"

I strode out of the kitchen, my basket of hand-quilted potholders in my arms, hoping she'd think I hadn't heard her. I'd already compromised by waiting to go to the farmers' market until after I'd cleaned the breakfast dishes. It would be nearly eight o'clock, long after the market opened, by the time my cousin Hannah and I arrived.

As I turned the corner into our large living room, a space big enough to host our entire church, my brother Billy came sliding in his stocking feet across the polished floor. His eyes narrowed under his dark bangs, partially pushed up on his sweaty forehead. He carried a gallon jar of pond water and plants in one hand, while his other flew around in an attempt to keep his balance. Still, greenish water sloshed over the rim.

A grin spread across his face as he veered toward me.

I swung the basket around to my hip and stepped sideways.

It didn't matter.

He plowed into me anyway.

I managed to stay on my feet, but the basket landed on the floor, the jar on top and tipped sideways. The murky water soaked my pot-holders that *had* been bound for the market.

"Billy," I cried.

"My tadpoles!" he yelled, falling to the floor,

12

stomach down, his ten-year-old body flailing toward my basket.

I righted the jar, which had a few inches of water remaining, and began picking through the potholders, rescuing the slimy creatures.

"What's going on in there?" Mutter called out.

The tadpoles flopped this way and that. I rushed from one to the next, pinching each one tightly enough to hold on to it but not enough to damage, dropping them back into the green slime.

Billy crowded in too and began shaking out the potholders and tossing them onto the floor, his brown eyes wide.

"Addie?" Mutter yelled.

"Just a minute."

"Nell!" Mutter called to her younger *Schwester*, who'd been holed up in the sewing room off the kitchen since breakfast. "Would you see what's going on?"

"I think we got them all." Billy grinned.

"One more." I plucked the tiniest tadpole from the black border of a potholder still in the basket and dropped it into the jar. "Take them back and let them go." I spoke firmly. "They've been traumatized enough."

"*Ach*, Addie," he groaned.

"Take courage and do as I say. Quickly." I thought of him as Billy the Brave. At ten, although *dabbich*—clumsy—he was still eager to help and please, but he also stuck up for others, including

13

me. "And take Joe-Joe down to the creek with you so he's out of Mutter's way." I scooped up the potholders.

Billy slid to the staircase, called for our littlest brother, the youngest of us seven children, and then headed to the front door to put on his boots. He tended to keep them there to avoid Mutter in the kitchen.

I lifted one of the wet potholders to my face and sniffed. I couldn't help but frown at the swampy smell.

"What happened?"

I lifted my head to *Aenti* Nell's round face and alarmed expression. She was short, a little squat, and had still-dark hair, the same color as Mutter's was a few years ago before it turned gray, but a kerchief partly covered Aenti's head instead of a *Kapp*.

I held up the wet square. "Billy." That was all I needed to say.

"I figured." Her brow wrinkled. She continually brought me comfort in a *Haus* full of chaos. "I have some potholders you can take."

I shook my head. "I think I have ten that didn't get wet. I can try to wash the others." Maybe they would dry in Hannah's buggy on the way to the market.

"You won't have time to iron them. You're leaving soon, *jah*?" She picked up the basket.

I nodded.

"Addie!"

"Go talk to your Mamm," Aenti said. She led the way, with me right behind her. Mutter was all eyes as Aenti Nell traipsed through. Obviously my mother had guessed the situation.

"Looks like you aren't meant to go," she said.

I shook my head. "I still have enough to sell." Barely.

"No, fate has spoken."

I shook my head. I didn't believe in fate—especially if Billy was involved. Unfortunately, my mother did. Many Plain people looked for signs from God to help them make a decision—my mother did that too. But she took it a step further, believing in a fate that, when it came to our family, seemed to dictate a path of endless woes.

Mutter pushed her chair back from the table. "Besides, the list of chores is longer than I thought. You won't have time to finish all of them if you go to the market today."

I didn't respond. I'd been looking forward to going to the farmers' market with my cousin for the last two weeks.

She crossed her arms, her pen still in her hand. "And what about dinner?" Mutter was so used to my taking charge of our household it seemed she felt lost without me.

"I'm cooking tonight," Aenti Nell called out from the sewing room. "Remember, Laurel?"

Mutter shook her head. "I guess I forgot."

My Aenti's voice grew louder as she stepped back into the kitchen, the basket in her hands. "And maybe she'll see Phillip."

That stopped my Mutter for a moment.

"You should be on your way." Aenti Nell transferred the basket to me. It was fuller than it had originally been. Plus, all the potholders were now tucked inside sealed gallon-sized bags. "I'll clean up the floor."

"*Denki*," I whispered. "For everything."

"Just make sure and tell me who all you see." Her eyes twinkled in anticipation. "And all you hear." She patted my arm, turned on her heel, and headed back to the sewing room. Just because she spent most of her days at home didn't mean she didn't want to know every last bit of Lancaster County gossip possible. As a *Maidel*—a woman who'd never married—she seemed to find her joy in other people's lives.

"What about your chores?" Mutter said to me as she stood and shifted her weight to her good leg.

"I've been working all week." I'd cleaned, polished, weeded, cooked, and baked. All that needed to be done were the finishing touches for the gathering we hosted each year just after mid-July. I'd already told Mutter, three times, everything was under control, regardless of what her latest list contained.

"Laurel, let her go." Aenti Nell stood in the doorway to the sewing room, her arms crossed.

16

"She does so much around here. She deserves to have a little fun."

Mutter placed both her hands on her wide hips. "But I need her here."

"I'll help today."

I mouthed "Denki"—again—to Aenti Nell, and then wrapped one arm around Mutter in a display of affection rare for our family, giving her a quick half hug. She'd been more anxious than usual lately, fretting over this and that, but especially the barbecue. And Phillip Eicher.

"Everything will work out," I said. "You'll see."

She squeezed my arm. "Go on, then." A faint smile, mixed with a hint of resignation, lingered on her face.

I turned and stepped toward the living room, wanting to be on my way before another disaster struck. Hannah hadn't arrived yet, but I wasn't going to stay in the house and take any chances Mutter would change her mind.

"Timothy will pick you up," Mutter added.

"Jah, I know." I grabbed my lunch pail from the corner of the table as I passed by. She'd told me four times already, at least. Timothy was on his *Rumschpringe*, his running around time. He was twenty and had a 1993 bright yellow Bronco. I told him it looked like a yellow jacket strapped to a set of wheels and that he drove it like he was out to sting everyone else on the road, but he didn't think that was funny.

"Come straight home," Mutter called out.

"Of course," I answered. Where else would I go?

Joe-Joe sat by the front door, struggling to pull on the second of his rubber boots, his towhead bent toward the floor. He was fair, like me, although his hair was much lighter than mine. He'd turned seven a month before but seemed younger. He was short and slight for his age and still easy to carry. And during the summer, when he was tuckered out from trying to keep up with Billy, he took a nap in the afternoon. He was sweet as pie, cute as a June bug, and cuddly as a puppy. I thought of him as Joe-Joe the Jewel because I valued him so much, and from the time he was born I'd longed to have a half dozen just like him.

"Where's Billy?" Joe-Joe asked as I set the basket beside him and yanked the boot on for him.

"He's outside, waiting for you," I said. "Come on." I stood, balanced the basket on my hip, and tousled his blond hair. He smiled up at me, his dimples flashing across his face.

"Grab your hat," I said as I opened the door.

He obeyed, resting it on his head at an angle as we stepped onto the porch. Even though it was morning, I could feel the coming heat of the day. The initial thrill of summer had grown old as July grew hotter and more humid. We were due for a storm—and soon.

Joe-Joe skipped across the worn planks, dragging me down the steps. I'd asked Timothy to paint the porch several times, but he hadn't. I'd ask Danny, who at sixteen was far more reliable than Timothy.

In the distance, I heard the clippity-clop of a horse—most likely Hannah's—pulling a buggy down our lane.

Billy stood at the edge of the trees, the jar in his hands, bouncing from foot to foot as he waited.

"Keep Joe-Joe with you," I called out to him.

"Jah," he answered.

My youngest brother zigzagged across the green lawn, his arms twirling in circles, but then he turned and waved at me, a smile as bright as the summer sun on his face. He laughed and then took off after Billy. They would spend the day in the willow trees along the creek, and in and out of the sycamore grove that bordered *Onkel* Bob's property. My Bruders' boots would be off in no time, and barefoot they'd catch more tadpoles, salamanders, and marsh periwinkles.

They lived a childhood I'd only dreamed about—one I'd watched my other Bruders experience too. I was sure I loved the outdoors as much or more than any of them, but what I experienced when it came to nature was mostly in our garden, from spreading the heaps of chicken manure—*Misht*—used to fertilize it to weeding the mammoth plot. At least that work allowed me to be outside.

Now that I was older, though, instead of wishing

for a childhood of romping through the trees, I longed for a husband, a marriage, and a child of my own as sweet as Joe-Joe. I longed to be out from under Mutter and her lists and worries and talk of fate. Everyone knew I was anxious to marry and leave my parents' home. And most days I thought if Phillip Eicher was my ticket then so be it. But on other days a nagging sensation plagued me. It was on those days I wasn't entirely sure how I felt about Phillip.

And this happened to be one of them.

"Come on!" Hannah yelled from her buggy. "We're running late."

I hurried across the lawn toward my cousin. As much as I loved them, I was desperate for a break from my family—if only for a few hours.

As Hannah drove away from our farm, I shifted on the bench and peered through the rear window of her buggy at our old white Haus, growing smaller in the distance.

I'd been raised to honor my parents. I'd never done anything but please them. The closest I'd ever come to not obeying was ignoring Mutter's request for me to stay home today.

If Aenti Nell hadn't intervened, I likely would have given up on going.

Aenti Nell and my cousin Cate both said I had a gift for managing a house. My parents never acknowledged it though.

That was another reason I longed to start my own family. I wanted to share my hopes and dreams with someone who cared. I wanted to partner with a man who would listen to me. With someone who valued me for who I was.

The buggy rounded the first curve, and the Haus fell from view.

"Addie?"

I faced my cousin. "Jah?"

Hannah's dark eyebrows waggled at me. "Whatcha thinking about?"

I shook my head.

She giggled, her pure white Kapp bobbing up and down, a stark contrast to her dark, dark hair and olive skin. She took after my Mutter's side of the family, while I, with my blond hair and fairer skin, took after my Daed's. Hannah also took after my Mutter in that she tended to be either very happy or very sad—rarely in between—and also solid in her shape, although she was an accomplished horse rider, and that kept her in good condition.

Today Hannah was happy. She grinned. "Who ya thinking about?"

"No one," I said, a little too forcefully, confused by my doubts.

"That's not what you were saying last week." Hannah held the reins lightly.

"Ach," I sighed. "How do I know . . . for sure? Day after day. Week after week."

"Well, if you're worried about him, don't be. Molly says Phillip is as serious as can be about you."

Molly Zook was Hannah's best friend and rivaled Aenti Nell when it came to knowing the juiciest gossip in Lancaster County.

Hannah leaned toward me. "And why would you have any doubts? He's the perfect catch."

That was just it. Phillip was the perfect catch. It actually made it harder for me to be sure how I felt about him.

"I know your parents like him a whole lot better than they did Mervin Mosier." Hannah giggled as soon as she said his name.

The thing was, Mervin was a wonderful-*gut* young man, although my parents certainly didn't seem to think so. Last year they had, out of character, allowed me to go kayaking with a group of *Youngie*, including him, his twin brother, and my cousins, Cate and Betsy, on my father's side, whose family farm bordered ours. But when Mervin showed an interest in me, Daed cited a decades-long rift between the Cramers and the Mosiers and forbade me to see him again.

As we passed my Onkel's farm, I waved at Cate as she hung wash on the line, her dresses flapping in the breeze alongside her husband's shirts. Her Dat, my Onkel Bob, had been married to my Daed's younger sister. But she had died when Betsy was a newborn. Onkel Bob stayed on good terms with my Daed, and we remained close.

As much as I appreciated my cousins, our families didn't have a lot in common. Their family was small. Ours was large. They had a business that catered to the *Englisch*, which meant they were much more comfortable with ideas outside our community. That was reflected in Cate's speech and what she read, plus she used modern office equipment every day and managed the crew of workers when Onkel Bob had meetings.

But that wasn't why I admired my cousin more than any other woman I knew. I admired her because she was a loving daughter, Schwester, and wife, but still she was very much her own person, and somehow she'd managed to find a husband who appreciated that.

I wanted what Cate had found.

Hannah interrupted my thoughts again. "Phillip plans to buy the farm near his parents' place, jah?"

"Oh really?" I hadn't heard.

"And he's hoping to get a loan from his district to finance the purchase." Hannah leaned toward me again. "There are advantages to being a bishop's son."

Phillip's Daed was the bishop of the next district over from us, the one Onkel Bob and his family belonged to, but Bishop Eicher had a good reputation all around the area, and many, many people highly respected him, including my parents.

"Who told you about the farm?" I wedged

my hands under my legs, flat against the bench.

Hannah's voice rose in volume over the *clickity-clack* of the horse's hooves. "Molly. She says he plans to marry soon." Her dark eyes danced. "He says it's official, you're his *Aldi*."

We had been courting, so it was no surprise he considered me his girlfriend. Still, today, the term made me shiver.

"Ach, Addie. He's so tall and handsome."

He was.

"And capable," Hannah added.

"Jah." He longed to farm a place of his own—that I knew.

"So what's the problem, then?" She glanced my way, her dark eyes concerned.

I sighed. I'd already told her, but she hadn't been listening. I asked it again, slowly, "How do I know, for sure, that he's the right one?"

She chuckled. "If you figure it out, let the rest of us know. Okay?"

I shook my head. She met more men—from Pennsylvania, Ohio, and even Indiana—over one weekend of Youngie parties than I'd met in my entire life. "But I haven't gone out with anyone else," I said, "except just that once with Mervin. What if there's someone else out there who's the right one?"

She sighed. "Ach, Addie. Don't think about it so much. It's not as if you have a say in the long run anyway."

I sank back against the seat. "What do you mean?"

"You have to marry someone who is Amish, whom your parents approve of, who lives somewhere close. The man can't be a Mosier. And your Dat would prefer a farmer, jah?"

I nodded. What she said was true.

"In that case, consider Phillip the catch of a lifetime." She scooted up on the bench, urged her horse to go faster, and changed the subject. As she prattled on about the party she'd attended last Saturday night, I thought about what she'd said. Did I really have so little control over my own life?

To the right an Englisch farmer was baling his hay, and as Hannah turned the buggy onto the highway, the warm breeze, boosted by the force of his tractor, sent a cloud of dust our way. We both turned our heads. To the left a young Amish boy herded a group of cows across a pasture, and ahead, alongside the road, an older girl propelled a scooter with her foot.

"There's a party tonight. Want to come?" Hannah pulled farther to the right to let a car pass.

"I have too much to do," I answered. "I barely got to come along today."

Before we reached Paradise, the market came into view.

Hannah turned the buggy onto the side road. "How long until the wedding, then?"

"Hannah!" It wasn't our way to speak so openly.

"Oh, come on, Addie." She slowed the horse. "Everyone knows it's what your Mamm and Dat want—and we all know you'll do as they say. Besides, you want to marry and leave home, jah? And soon?"

I didn't answer.

"You'll come to love Phillip. By the time you marry, you'll know for sure." She didn't wait for my response. "Just wait and see."

I craned my neck to see who was at the market—not wanting to think about, let alone discuss, my future.

The booths sat on the corner of the Zooks' farm, all manned by Youngie—and more girls than guys, who were more likely to be working in the fields or holding down regular jobs on a Saturday morning.

With its inventory of vegetables, fresh-cut flowers, plants, breads and baked goods, jams and preserves, handwork, wooden planters, and homemade food, it attracted mostly weekend tourist traffic.

As the buggy bumped over the rutted road, Molly waved from the center of the market, a bouquet of herbs in her hand. Tall and fair, with hair lighter than mine, her face lit up like a lantern in the night. Molly Zook was hard to miss.

She had begun overseeing the market on her parents' property in the middle of May, two months earlier. The Zooks ran a nursery stock business. They had transformed their family farm through the years, field by field, into rows of trees and shrubs. It was no secret the bust in the building boom had affected their profits. In hopes of supplementing their income, Molly's father had planted flowers in a couple of fields the last few years, but her parents were older than most and obviously struggling to keep up with all the work on the farm. The boys in the family had moved away from Lancaster County and the older daughters were all married and had families of their own. Only Molly and her little sister, Bea, still lived at home.

It seemed Molly aimed to bring in more income to the family through the market. She was the sort of girl who always had a new idea. Her enthusiasm alone could carry a project.

Hannah and I would be sharing Molly's booth, and I, no doubt, would be picking up all sorts of bits of gossip Aenti Nell would love to hear.

Molly pointed at something beside her, blocked by a pole and canopy. I craned my neck as Hannah pulled the buggy into the pasture behind the booths, bringing the subject of Molly's smile into clear view.

Phillip Eicher, at six foot four, towered above everyone else in the market. He lifted his straw hat from his head, showing his dark bowl-cut hair, and waved at me with vigor.

● ● ●

The mouth-watering smoke from sausage grilling, mixed with the smell of freshly baked pretzels and pungent herbs, greeted us along with the first sunflowers of the season, buckets of snapdragons, and containers of dusty pink lilies as we reached Molly's table.

Her blue eyes sparkled. "Look who's here." She swept her arm wide, gesturing toward Phillip, as if I might be surprised.

He'd placed his hat back on his head and now had his thumbs hooked around his suspenders. His white shirt was neatly tucked into black pants.

"Hello," I said to him as I placed my basket on the tabletop. "What are you doing here?"

"I'm on my break." He tipped his head toward where the smoke was billowing out of a barbecue, a row beyond us. "I already got something to eat." Then he smiled, slightly. "And I was hoping to see you."

My face grew warm as I arranged the potholders on the table. He stepped toward me, and for a moment I thought he might comment on my work—or Aenti Nell's, to be exact—but he didn't.

"I have something to tell you." He leaned toward me, placing his palms down on the table. I was always surprised at how clean he kept his hands considering his work.

I raised my head, my heart rate increasing. "Oh?"

"There's a farm close to my folks' place," he said. "I've been talking to the owners." He stopped, as if waiting for my reaction.

I wasn't about to tell him Hannah had told me. I smiled and then said, "Go on."

"The soil has to be the best in the county. Even better than your Dat's. And the barn is in good shape, although it does need a new roof."

Hannah and Molly leaned against each other, their Kapps touching, watching us. They were quite the contrast in height, coloring, and personality too—and yet they complemented each other perfectly. Every time I saw them together, I couldn't help but wish I had a best friend. That's why I wanted a husband who would listen to me, who would be that friend.

Phillip's voice grew louder. "And the chicken coop is larger than your Mamm's, almost as big as my parents'. The Haus is old but adequate." I'd never seen him so animated.

I stepped to the back of the table.

He took a deep breath and then said, "What do you think?" His biceps bulged against the sleeves of his shirt as he crossed his arms.

I met his gaze. "It sounds fine, just fine."

"Well sure," he said. "You'll want to take a look-see." He grinned. "No need to worry about that."

The nagging sensation began to spread.

Before I could speak, he continued, "The garden

plot there used to be huge, as big as at your place, but now it's just for two people. But I was thinking we could enlarge it and raise enough extra to sell." He looked around. "Maybe here. You could be in charge of that."

I choked out, "Sure."

He chuckled. "You aren't afraid of extra work, are you?"

No words came—I simply shook my head.

"Well," Phillip said, a happy look on his face, "I should get back to work." The place he hired out to was a half mile up the road. "I just wanted to tell you about the farm." He grinned a second time. "Because the owner said I could give you a tour—next week."

Hannah and Molly shifted again, this time toward a commotion down the row of booths.

"I'll have to see if that will work with Mutter's schedule," I said to Phillip. But who was I fooling? We both knew it would.

My attention drifted to the loud voices, certain they were familiar. I shaded my eyes against the morning sun. Sure enough it was Mervin Mosier and his twin brother, Martin, at the end of the row, eight or nine booths away from us. They were wearing matching mauve shirts, suspenders, black pants, and straw hats over their sandy hair. Plus aviator sunglasses.

"Genuine Amish hope chests," Martin called out to an Englisch couple passing by.

"Custom-made and personalized," Mervin interjected. "And we're not joking."

"Or pulling your leg!" Martin boomed.

They grinned at each other, and then Mervin's voice rang out loud and clear. "You'll also find mantels, bookends, and trivets too."

I stepped to the side of Molly's table to get a better look. I could see a fireplace mantel, although I couldn't make out the details, and beyond it were several chests. Phillip joined me, stepping close enough so that I could smell the scent of his Mamm's strong lye soap on his skin.

"Made by our cousin—who is new to Lancaster County, straight from Big Valley," bellowed Martin.

Hannah giggled.

"What's their cousin's name?" I asked, impressed by the woodwork I could see and also by Martin and Mervin's tribute.

Phillip crossed his arms.

"Ask Hannah." Molly elbowed my cousin. "He wouldn't leave her alone at the party last week-end."

"His name is Jonathan. His family's moving back from Big Valley to take care of his grandfather." Hannah wrinkled her nose. "He's cute and nice and all, but when I told my Mamm and Dat about him they said he's like all the Mosiers, that his family is trouble and to steer clear." She

31

pointed toward a figure wearing a black hat. "That's him."

All I could see was his back, his suspenders crossed over his back in an X. His blue shirt was untucked and bunching up around his waist.

"Too bad about the rift between our families." I crossed my arms.

"Jah, but it's okay." Hannah shrugged. "If I was going to court a Mosier it would be Mervin, not Jonathan." She grinned.

"Why?"

She shrugged again. "Jonathan's too much of a dreamer. Kind of a sap. Besides, he didn't have much of a plan for his life." She grinned again. "Not like Phillip does, anyway."

Instead of responding to Hannah, Phillip smiled at me and nodded. "Jah, I do have a plan. A good one." Phillip stepped even closer to me, bumping my arm with his. "What time should I arrive tomorrow?"

"Well," I said, "around two. Any sooner and we'll put you to work."

"I'd like that," he said.

"I was just kidding." I didn't want him to come early. "See you then." I knew my voice lacked enthusiasm, but Phillip didn't seem to notice.

He strode off down the aisle between the booths, saying hello to Martin and Mervin as he passed. The two turned their heads toward me.

Hannah and Molly watched Phillip go.

Molly sighed and turned toward me, her index finger intertwined in the tie of her Kapp. "I hope you're grateful," she said.

"For . . . ?"

She tilted her head, gave me a scathing look, and pointed to Phillip just before he turned at the end of the row, by one of the vegetable booths. "You—any of us—could do a whole lot worse."

I must have grimaced, because she said, "Goodness, Addie. Get off your high horse and give him a chance. He might not be the brightest . . ."

My face reddened. "It's not that." It wasn't as if I thought I was too good for him. It wasn't that at all.

Molly grabbed a sprig of rosemary and held it to her nose. "What's bothering you, then?"

"How do I *know?*"

She shook her head. "Know what?"

"If he's the right one."

She twirled the rosemary. "You don't ever *know.* You *decide.* And then you train him."

Hannah laughed, and I couldn't help but smile, but I couldn't take what Molly said seriously. First of all, she wasn't married. Second of all, I'd been trying to train members of the opposite gender my entire life—I wasn't sure I wanted to do that in a marriage too.

Before I could think of what to say to Molly, an older Englisch woman stopped at my table.

Grateful for the interruption, I turned my attention toward her. She quilted too, and we chatted as she chose five potholders to buy.

After the Englisch woman left, Molly sat down beside me, crushing the sprig of rosemary in her fingers, sending a pungent pine scent into the air. "Sorry if I said more than I should have."

"No, it's fine," I answered. I wasn't opposed to hearing her opinions.

"So if you're not set on Phillip, why don't you come to the singings? You might meet someone new."

"Jah," Hannah said. "And to the parties too. Kids from all over have been coming. There are all sorts of good-looking guys."

I wouldn't mind going to the singings, but I wasn't interested in the parties, and besides, I wasn't sure I wasn't set on Phillip. No more than I was sure that I was. "We'll see" was all I said.

The next couple of hours sped by as the day grew warmer. Molly peddled her herbs, selling out of her gigantic dill, her silver-edge lavender, and all of her flowers in the next couple of hours. Hannah sold her half-pint jars of strawberry jam, which seemed to be the perfect size for the tourists. I didn't need to do much to pitch the potholders; Aenti Nell's work sold itself, and by noon over half of them were gone. All three of us fanned ourselves with folded newspapers Molly had brought to wrap herbs in.

The dust from the field grew thicker as more and more feet pounded over it, and the line at the lemonade stand a row away from us grew longer and longer.

Several times, I glanced toward the booth Martin and Mervin had been at, but I didn't see them or their cousin again. Molly walked around the market several times and came back with bits of gossip. She said Mervin and Martin hadn't left. Instead they'd parked themselves by the food booths.

The sausage had been tempting me all morning, but I pulled out my ham salad sandwich from my lunch pail, the same one I used to pack for school, and shared half of it with Hannah.

After that the day grew lazy as the heat hung over the pasture and settled under the tarp where we sat. Thankfully, the traffic of tourists stayed steady and kept me awake.

After a while Mervin stopped by our booth to chat, but soon Martin yelled at him to help him out at their cousin's booth.

"Jonathan took his buggy to get more hope chests," Mervin said, twirling his hat in his hands. "They've been selling like hot cakes." He turned and ambled up the row. A crowd of customers awaited him. Martin motioned for him to hurry and Mervin quickened his pace, but just a little.

Sometime after three, the rumble of an engine

caught my attention. It sounded like Timothy's, but he was an hour early.

I stood, ducking out from under the tarp. Sure enough, his Bronco was cruising down the side road along the market.

I sat back down.

"Timothy?" Hannah asked.

I nodded, wiping away the trickle of sweat at my temple.

"Maybe he's going to look around for a while," she said, a tinge of sarcasm to her voice.

"Unlikely," I said. "He's come early for some reason."

Hannah groaned.

"What?" I asked.

"Maybe he's looking to take care of some unfinished business."

That didn't sound good. "Such as?"

"Mervin and Martin. He had a falling out with them at that party last weekend. He'd been talking to their cousin Tabitha."

"Who is she?" I'd never heard of her.

"She lives on the other side of the county—her mother is Mervin and Martin's Daed's sister. She came over to help out with their grandfather, until Jonathan's parents move here for good."

"Oh."

"Timothy had been drinking, and Mervin and Martin told him to back off."

My face grew warm.

Hannah continued. "When Timothy left, he shouted he'd get even."

"Oh dear." I snatched up my lunch pail and dropped it into my basket. Timothy didn't take kindly to being bossed around, and even less so when he'd had too much to drink. He was sure to be vindictive. I gathered the potholders that hadn't sold, slipped them into a plastic bag, and put it in the basket too. Then I grabbed my money box, took out the wad of cash I'd earned, slipped it into the pocket of my apron, and dropped the box in the bottom of the basket, where Timothy wouldn't see it. If he did, he'd realize I'd earned money and ask to borrow it.

When we were young, Timothy and I had been close. He'd even had a pet name for me—Toad. But by the time he turned sixteen he'd turned against me. He'd always teased me, sure, and that I didn't mind. It was the mean streak he developed once he started partying that I couldn't stand. He criticized and bullied. Made fun of me and others. Always put himself first, even though we'd been taught the exact opposite. He'd always been a little moody, but the last few years he'd changed into a troublemaker.

As a child I thought of him as Timothy the Terrific. Now he was Timothy the Terrible.

"I'm going to go tell him I need to go home—now." I gave Hannah a quick hug and stepped out from under the tarp.

Timothy, who was wearing jeans, a torn gray T-shirt, and a baseball cap over his dark-brown hair, stopped behind the crowd gathered around Mervin and Martin's cousin's booth.

"Hey!" Timothy called out as he jumped up and down.

At the sound of his voice, Mervin froze with a trivet in his hand.

As Timothy yelled, "Hey!" a second time, Martin spun around.

I started to walk toward them, but Hannah grabbed my arm. "Don't," she said. "Let them figure it out."

A couple with two little girls, each wearing braids, stopped at our booth. The husband picked up a jar of Hannah's jam, and the mother asked to see my potholders. I took a sampling out for her, and she said she'd take ten, which left me with only two unsold.

As I made change from my pocket, I could make out Timothy's voice but not his words.

"What's going on over there?" the woman asked, turning toward the commotion, a daughter hanging on either side of her.

"I'm not sure," I answered.

She directed her attention back at me as I handed her the bag of potholders. "Have you seen that young man's hope chests?"

I shook my head.

"They're masterpieces. I ordered one for each of

my girls. Wish I'd had something like that growing up."

I nodded. So did I. Not having been given a chest—*Kashta*—of my own was one of the biggest disappointments of my childhood.

"We're hoping to order one of his mantels sometime," the husband added. "His work is incredible. I've never seen anything like it."

The group that had gathered around the booth started to disperse—thanks to Timothy, I was sure. I grabbed my basket and started toward my brother, who now stood with his feet spread apart, pointing his index finger at Martin. Timothy towered over both of the twins, looking exactly like the bully he was.

Mervin stepped in front of his brother as Martin shifted his foot forward. I couldn't see what happened next, but Mervin stumbled backward, probably shoved by Timothy, and then fell with the trivet still in his hand over one of the chests on display, crashing into the mantel behind it. The upper piece shifted.

Martin darted forward, lunging for the top piece, just as Timothy shoved him too, sending him flying into the booth, straight at the mantel. The whole thing toppled over, followed by the sound of splintering wood.

Chapter 2

ᔕᕮᔕ

I froze in the middle of the pathway. I'd seen Timothy stir up trouble plenty of times but never destroy something of value. How dare he? He'd been intentional about shoving both Mervin and Martin into the mantel. Now it lay in ruins.

"Come on," Timothy called out, running toward me, his baseball cap flapping in his hand, a wild smirk on his face.

He flew past me as Martin struggled to his feet and took off after Timothy, his head now bare. I put my basket down and shoved my hand into my apron pocket and took out my rubber-banded wad of money.

As Martin reached me, I grabbed his arm. "Take this," I said, shoving the bills into his hand. "And tell your cousin I'm sorry. Timothy—"

"—is a creep." Martin tried to pull away from me.

I held on tight. "He can be, jah," I said. "But going after him is only going to make things worse."

"You shouldn't have to pay for what he's destroyed." Martin took the money anyway.

"He'll pay me back." Somehow. Someway. I'd see to it.

Martin nodded at me. "See that he does." He held the money up. "This should help Jonathan —at least he wasn't here to see it happen." Martin told me good-bye and headed back to the booth.

I followed him. Mervin was trying to lift the mantel, but Martin told him to leave it as he showed Mervin the money.

"Denki, Addie," Mervin called out. "That will help. With our grandfather ill and Jonathan's family not farming here yet, he's supporting the family."

In the background Timothy revved his Bronco and then honked the horn.

"You'd best go." Mervin stepped out of the booth, his eyes sympathetic.

"Jah." I picked up my basket. "Please don't try to retaliate," I said. "It isn't our way." I couldn't help pointing it out, even though Mervin knew it as well as I did. We'd been taught that since we were babies.

"Maybe you should talk to Timothy about that," Mervin said.

I nodded. "I will. And to my Daed."

Martin snorted. "A lot of good that will do."

My face grew even warmer.

The horn blared again.

Feeling defeated, I gave a half-hearted wave to

41

the twins, called out a good-bye to Hannah and Molly, who'd retreated back to their tables, and cut across the flattened pasture to Timothy.

"They're jerks," he said as I opened the back door and put my basket on the seat.

"They're not." I climbed into the front of the yellow jacket on wheels, feeling as if I were part of a hive gone wild. "Even if they did tell you to keep away from their cousin. Tabitha, right?"

He scowled at me. "I don't know who you're talking about."

"Hannah told me."

Timothy stared straight ahead, but venom filled his voice. "Then she's full of it."

I shook my head.

Timothy gripped the steering wheel tighter. "And so are all the Mosiers. Always have been."

"Don't say that."

"And the one that does the carvings? He's the biggest loser of all."

My anger with my brother neared the boiling point. "How would you know?" I fastened my seat belt, glared at Timothy until he fastened his too, and then stared straight ahead. "Besides, you're the one who instigated it."

He gunned the car, spinning out as he sped toward the highway. "No—the Mosiers started it years ago."

I knew my parents didn't think highly of the Mosiers, but I had no idea what was behind the hard feelings. "What happened between our two families?"

"You don't know?" He had a smirk on his face.

"No, I don't." And I was pretty sure he didn't either.

"Well, I'm not going to be the one to gossip about it. And don't ask Mamm or Dat. It will just make them mad."

I'd ask Aenti Nell. "Regardless of all that," I said, "I heard you'd had too much to drink last weekend. And you were definitely the instigator today. You should apologize . . . and stop this nonsense." I stared straight ahead. "I gave the twins money to cover the damages. You'll have to pay me back."

He let out a snort. "I wasn't the one who knocked over that stupid mantel. And you didn't ask me if I wanted you to pay for it."

"I'll talk to Daed about it, then."

He snorted again. "Good luck with that. He doesn't care." He turned left instead of right at the stop sign.

"Where are we going?"

"By Sam and George's."

I sighed. Our older Bruders were renting a trailer from an Englisch family down the road. I hadn't seen it yet . . . and had no desire to. "Is that why you came early?"

"Nah, Mutter wants you home."

"Why?"

"She's worried about the barbecue tomorrow."

Her anxiety was definitely getting worse.

Timothy accelerated on the straight stretch.

I grabbed the door handle as my heart pounded. He hadn't had an accident—yet. I couldn't fathom why not.

His phone rang, and he fumbled it out of his pocket.

"Let me get it," I said.

He ignored me again, answering the call and holding it against his ear.

I could hear George's voice, asking where we were.

"Five minutes away," Timothy answered.

"We're not staying long," I shouted so George could hear.

Timothy ignored me, said good-bye, and plopped his phone in the console between us.

I wiped my forehead with the hem of my apron and pointed the car's vents toward my face, trying to maximize the little bit of air coming out.

I'd have to tell Aenti Nell about the broken mantel to explain why I didn't have her money. I'd tell Daed about what Timothy had done, because someone needed to put my brother in his place, and as much as I wanted to, I knew whatever *I* said wouldn't make a difference.

Daed was the only one who could make Timothy stop, but my brother was right. Daed didn't seem to care about my Bruders' wild ways.

Although my family was more isolated than my cousin Cate's, when it came to the Rumschpringe time, my parents were far more lenient than some—when it came to the boys. My Daed ignored my Bruders' vehicles, late nights, and grumpy mornings. My parents were too tolerant, mostly denying my Bruders' shenanigans. I guessed Daed had been on the wild side as a Youngie too, and that's why he put up with it.

When it came to anything concerning the Mosiers, Daed bristled—like when he thought I was interested in Mervin and forbade me from seeing him. He definitely had a part in the mysterious rift between the two families.

Hopefully though, learning Timothy had destroyed someone else's property would get Daed's attention.

The Bronco bounced as Timothy turned onto a dirt road. Over a knoll, a trailer house came into view beside a scraggly oak tree. My two other older Bruders were rebellious, but not like Timothy. Samuel, the oldest, was almost twenty-five, unmarried, and still not a member of the church, which I was sure bothered my parents, but they kept quiet about it. He'd always been easygoing—too much so. He wasn't a leader, and Timothy had him wrapped around his little finger. There were times when I thought of my oldest sibling as Samuel the Simple.

George was next. At twenty-two, he had an

Amish girlfriend, Sadie, and I hoped he would join the church soon and settle down. He was quick to laugh, plus kind and giving. I thought of him as George the Generous.

Timothy turned into the driveway of the trailer and parked next to George's old blue truck. He opened his door. "Coming in?"

"No." I stared straight ahead, my seat belt still in place.

"Get off your high horse, Addie," he said, climbing out of the car.

I didn't answer, but when George bounded down the wooden steps and flung my door open, I couldn't help but reconsider. He grabbed my hand, his deep brown eyes twinkling.

"Addie! Come see our place." He wore his dark hair so cropped no one would guess he'd grown up Amish. At just under six feet, he was the shortest of my Bruders but the most muscular. They were all as strong as teams of oxen, broad like my Daed, although none of them were quite as big as he was. All were built for farming and barn raisings, although currently, Samuel and George were picking up shifts at a shed manufacturing business.

George was my favorite of my older Bruders, and I missed him—even though I didn't care to see the dump he now called home. For him, though, I unfastened my seat belt and headed up the steps. Timothy was already inside, taking three cases of beer from Samuel. I was tempted to say something—Timothy wouldn't be of legal drinking age until his next birthday—but held my tongue.

"Ach, you two," George said. "Do you have to do this in front of Addie?"

Samuel nodded at me, flicking his long brown bangs from his eyes as he did, but didn't answer. Timothy ignored George, flexing his biceps as he hoisted the cases against his chest.

"I'll give you a tour," George said, leading the way into the living room. I had to squint coming in from the bright sunshine into the small cavelike room. Brown carpet that looked as if it hadn't been cleaned since the trailer came off the assembly line covered the floor. There was a large TV on the far wall, an old couch, and a straight-back chair—that was all.

I followed George into the kitchen, where a lone card table sat pushed against a wall. Dirty dishes filled the sink, and the garbage, in a plastic bucket, overflowed with fast-food bags and containers.

"Want to see the rest?" George asked.

I shook my head, imagining the two messy bedrooms down the hall. "We best be going."

George's voice had a hint of teasing to it. "Don't you want to stick around and help tidy up?"

"I have enough to do at home," I answered, straight-faced.

"Jah." His tone was serious now. "I know."

I smiled at him and patted him on the shoulder. "Denki," I said, "for showing me around."

Timothy and Samuel had gone outside. The back of the Bronco slammed shut as I started for the door.

"See you tomorrow," George said, right behind me, giving me a pat on the shoulder when we reached the tiny porch.

"Jah," Samuel answered. "We wouldn't skip the barbecue, not for anything." They hadn't been coming around the house much lately, but I knew they wouldn't want to miss the annual gathering of relatives and neighbors.

Samuel turned to Timothy. "Have fun with those Mosiers tonight."

Timothy tossed his keys in the air. "Want to join me?"

"Maybe . . ." Sam glanced at George, who shrugged. Sam turned back to Timothy. "We'll see."

I descended the steps and climbed into the passenger seat, slamming the door, hoping Timothy would get the message. He chatted a few minutes longer and then climbed into the car. "Want to go tonight?" he asked.

"No." I wasn't that desperate to get out of the house.

"I might need you to stop me from hurting a Mosier," he teased.

"I really am going to tell Daed about what happened today."

He glowered at me. "Haven't you ever heard of sibling confidentiality?"

"You went too far this time. Daed needs to know."

"I told you he won't care."

"I think he will." True, Daed wasn't fond of the Mosiers, but he was as nonresistant as any Amishman. He wouldn't want Timothy destroying property—and certainly not hurting anyone.

"He'd never admit it, but he dislikes the Mosiers even more than I do."

I looked out my window as Timothy turned onto the highway. My one outing with the Mosier twins, Mervin in particular, is what motivated Daed to push Phillip Eicher my way. At that point, he—or maybe it was Mutter needling him—decided not to leave my destiny in my own hands.

My parents would never meddle in matters of courtship with my Bruders the way they were with me. Maybe if I had Schwesters, they wouldn't be so focused on whom they wanted me to marry. Then again, maybe they would.

Back when I was little I'd wished I'd been born a boy, because their work seemed like play. As I grew older, I tolerated my work a little more. Some of it I even enjoyed—the quilting, the baking and cooking, and the gardening. The bigger I grew, the easier the cleaning and laundry and sewing became too. But the boys still had more fun, always together, horsing around in the pasture, racing the buggies, and throwing each other into the pond. I worked mostly alone unless I was quilting with Aenti Nell. I enjoyed her company, but most of our conversation centered on relatives and neighbors, while I longed to talk about ideas and feelings.

It wasn't as if I saw the boys and Daed discussing anything important though. Sure, they talked about their work, but their conversations tended to be about which boy did which stupid thing out in the field.

I wanted a *Mann*, a husband who would listen to me and talk with me about things that mattered. Who would include me in his plans. I wasn't sure if Phillip Eicher was that man, but perhaps I hadn't given him enough of a chance.

Timothy pulled out to pass a pickup and then stepped on the accelerator as an SUV sped toward us. It was big and black and barreled down the road. I braced my feet against the floor and took a deep breath, terrified it might be my last.

Timothy yanked the car back into his lane at the last second. An overwhelming sense of helplessness spread through me. I'd just been dependent on Timothy, someone I didn't trust, for my very existence.

As my fear subsided, the helpless feeling transformed into a sense of hollowness.

Whom could I trust?

Ten minutes later and nearly home, in a shaky voice I managed to say, "I'm not going to ride with you anymore. I'm going to tell Mutter no from now on."

"What are you talking about?" He stared straight ahead.

"That near accident."

"Ach, that was nothing." He scowled toward me. "You need to get over yourself. Life is more than just about what you want. It helps the family for me to give you rides."

I didn't respond. Life had never been about what I wanted. I wasn't pitying myself—it was simply the truth. And the Amish way. We were taught from the time we were little children that we're not the center of the world. But somehow Timothy hadn't gotten the message.

He turned down our lane, speeding along too fast but slowed as he neared our Haus and pulled along the far side of the cow barn, where Daed allowed him to park his car. Billy and Joe-Joe came running toward me, shouting my name as I climbed from the seat, pulling my dress from the back of my sweaty legs.

Both boys had mud streaked across their faces like war paint. Joe-Joe held a tabby kitten with both his hands, while Billy held a calico in each of his. Billy stumbled over a rock but caught himself before he fell. The cats squirmed in his hands, and he held on tighter.

I grabbed my basket from the back and started toward the boys.

"Go put the kittens back," I said. "They need their Mamms."

Joe-Joe frowned.

"And then come in the house for some lemonade. It's so hot—you probably need a drink, jah?" I added.

He smiled at that and followed Billy toward the barn.

As I rounded the corner, Mutter called out for me from the back steps.

Then Daed stepped out of the cow corral. At six and a half feet he was a near giant of a man, solid through and through. A fringe of gray hair showed under his hat and his matching beard flowed down his chest to his belly. "You're late," he said to Timothy. "Come finish the milking." Then he called out to Billy. "Get back in there and help Danny."

In no time, the little boys hustled back from returning the kittens, and Joe-Joe took my hand, pulling me toward the Haus as Billy obeyed Daed and skipped off to the barn.

"Sure you don't want to go with me later?" Timothy called out to me.

I ignored him.

"Where you going?" Daed asked Timothy as he reached the barn door.

"Out," Timothy answered. "Later."

I pulled away from Joe-Joe and told him to go ahead. "He's looking to pick a fight with the Mosiers," I said to Daed as I held the basket in front of me.

Daed looked from Timothy to me and then back to Timothy. He shook his head. "No fighting, son—you hear? Sure, some things can't be fixed, but you let those be. You understand?"

I glared at Timothy. "Like a mantel?"

He shot me an angry look.

"What's this all about?" Daed took a step toward Timothy.

"He broke a mantel Jonathan Mosier made. I gave all the money I made today to Martin and Mervin to help pay for it."

His bushy eyebrows shot up. "Jonathan Mosier . . . Would that be Dirk's son?" It was as if Daed hadn't heard the last part of what I'd said.

I shrugged. "He's Martin and Mervin's cousin."

Daed took a deep breath. "Did you pay for it, son?"

Timothy's eyes narrowed.

"I just told you, *I* did," I answered. "Although I'm sure I didn't pay enough."

"Pay her back," Daed ordered.

Timothy nodded, with no trace of his earlier bravado.

"Addie, come here," Mutter called out. Joe-Joe was beside her now, trying to hold her hand.

As I approached, she whispered, "What were you telling your father?"

"It's nothing."

Her voice grew louder as she spoke. "You were talking about the Mosiers. Did those twins do something?"

"No."

"I knew I shouldn't have let you go."

"It's nothing to do with me. Honest." I passed her, shifting the basket to the side and taking Joe-Joe's outstretched hand, pulling him alongside me into the Haus.

I sniffed, but all I could smell was the lemon scent of the polish I'd put on the wood floors the day before. Aenti Nell hadn't started dinner. I stopped in the middle of the kitchen, sliding the basket onto the tabletop. There was leftover chicken from the night before, unless they'd eaten it for lunch.

"Addie." Mutter limped through the back door. "What's going on?"

"Dinner," I answered. "That's what's going on—or not." I'd so looked forward to a break from cooking that I couldn't stop the disappointment in my voice. I opened the refrigerator. The chicken was gone.

Mutter sat down in her chair.

Aenti Nell cleared her throat from where she stood in the doorway to the quilting room. "I lost track of time."

"I see." I placed my hand atop my Kapp, as if the gesture might keep my emotions in check. Clearly it was time for me to take charge.

Mutter picked up a pair of pants, stabbing her needle into the fabric. "The *Mansleit* will need to eat soon."

The menfolk would eat when the food was ready.

I'd put two pounds of cooked hamburger into the freezer the day before, so I could make a quick spaghetti sauce. I poured Joe-Joe a glass of lemonade and then told him, as he downed it, "Go get me four jars of tomatoes—one at a time —and an onion from the cellar."

He drained his glass, handed it to me, and started toward the basement door. "After you do that I'll tell you what to pick from the garden."

We had lettuce, spinach, and radishes ready to use, and I'd baked bread the day before.

Aenti Nell picked up the basket. "How many potholders did you sell?" she asked as I pulled the sealed bag of hamburger from the freezer.

"Nearly all," I said. I motioned for her to come closer to me, and as I turned toward the sink, lowered my voice so Mutter wouldn't hear. I explained briefly what happened as I plopped the plastic bag of hamburger in the sink and ran warm water over it to defrost it.

"Ach, Addie, that's a shame," she said. "For you." She shook her head. "That Timothy. I hate to see this grudge get passed down to the next generation."

She seemed genuinely sad.

"Jah," I said. "It's a sorry predicament."

She nodded, a wary expression I hadn't seen before settling on her face.

I lowered my voice even more. "So what is this grudge all about anyway?"

Aenti glanced toward Mutter, a worried look on her face, and whispered, "I'll tell you later."

I nodded and said, in a regular voice, hoping to cheer her, "I saw Molly."

"Oh." Aenti Nell brightened. "Any news?"

"Nothing you don't already know."

My Aenti smiled.

"You should see Molly's rosemary though. It's the best I've ever seen. She sold out of nearly everything except for her parsley and sage. I meant to bring some home." We grew herbs but they weren't nearly as robust as Molly's. "Hannah had sold almost all of her jars of jam when I left."

I gathered the pots and pans I needed for the sauce and pasta as I talked. Daed wasn't fond of spaghetti and salad—he said it barely filled him up—but it was the best I could do on such short notice.

Joe-Joe came up the basement stairs with the tomatoes, one jar at a time, and then the onion, making a special trip just for it. I asked Aenti Nell to chop it. She took the remaining potholders into the sewing room and then returned to help me.

I handed Joe-Joe the garden basket, and he headed outside. I started the sauce and told Aenti Nell about the food at the market and then put the water on to boil for the spaghetti. Next I set the table around Mutter as I told Aenti Nell about the jam Hannah had made.

I stopped at the sound of heavy footsteps on the back steps. The men, I presumed, were early.

The door swung open, and Billy stepped through first, a grin on his face. Behind him was Phillip Eicher.

Mutter perked up at the sight of him. She started to stand, but he quickly told her there was no need.

"Won't you stay for supper?" she gushed.

I stood statue still, watching Phillip. He'd changed into a clean white shirt and pants. And shoes instead of boots. He held his straw hat in his hands, and his bangs fell in a perfect line across his forehead.

"Denki," Phillip answered, looking at me. "I'm happy to stay, but I'll go out and help finish up the milking." Molly and Hannah were right—he was a good catch. I could do much worse.

"Oh, stay here," Mutter replied. "Cap has plenty

of hands out there." Then she paused and added, "Unless you want to speak with him about something."

Phillip smiled. "When he has the time."

My face grew warm. Usually, in our community, the young man didn't speak with the girl's father before he'd spoken with her. Perhaps he planned to speak to me tonight.

I spun back toward the sink. The odd sensation lodged below my heart and pushed upward.

I turned my attention back to dinner. Now that we had company, I would need to come up with a dessert, but I didn't have time to make anything before we ate. I decided to pilfer a plate of cookies from the dozens I'd made for tomorrow.

Phillip sat down on the other side of the table, where he could watch me. "I drove by the farm on the way here." He hooked his thumbs around his suspenders. "The sunflowers along the fence are already as big as dinner plates. And the corn is up to my shoulders, I'm sure. . . ." He hadn't been much of a talker before, but that seemed to have changed.

Now it seemed as if he couldn't stop.

It was the first time Phillip had ever stayed for dinner. He was the youngest of ten, so although meals with his family used to be a big event, for the last few years it had just been him and his parents. I couldn't imagine his mother, even when her table was full, putting up with any nonsense from her children.

Meals at our house were far from orderly. It wasn't that my Mutter purposefully put up with the nonsense—she just didn't know how to stop it. And although I did my best, I couldn't seem to rein the boys in either, at least not entirely.

Before Daed had a chance to lead us in our silent prayer, Billy dumped his pocket of rocks onto the table. Daed sent him outside with his collection until the prayer was finished.

Billy ate silently when he came back, and for a moment all was calm, but then Timothy started in about the Mosier boys. Phillip gave me a questioning look. I shrugged in return.

"Addie is too friendly with them," Timothy said, looking at Mutter. "You shouldn't allow her around them anymore."

"You're the one who invited me to the party tonight," I shot back. "Don't you think they'll be there?" I'd never been so contentious before, not in front of my parents anyway—and certainly not in front of company.

"Addie!" Mutter said.

"Don't worry, I'm not going. I'm just pointing out that Timothy isn't making any sense."

"Of course you're not going." Mutter had her gaze on Phillip now. "She never goes to those things."

Under my breath, I whispered, "Obviously

what's good for the gander isn't for the goose."

"You don't go to those parties either, do you, Phillip?" Mutter asked.

He squared his shoulders. "Not anymore."

"How about you?" Timothy said to Danny. "Are you going with me?"

Danny placed his fork on his empty plate—he'd inhaled his dinner in record time—and looked up but didn't speak. He pushed his straw-colored hair back from his forehead, showing the streak of white where the brim of his hat kept the sun from his face. Having recently turned sixteen, he was just entering his Rumschpringe. He was the quietest of my Bruders and the most reliable. I thought of him as Danny the Dependable.

Finally, as he glanced from our father to our mother, he said, "Jah."

"That's fine," Mutter answered. "As long as you're up first thing in the morning."

"Don't go," I said to Danny. "Stay home and help me get ready for tomorrow."

He wrinkled his freckled nose and said, softly, "I'll get up early, I promise, and do whatever you need."

Joe-Joe nudged me, a grin on his face. "I'll help," he said, and then began twirling his spaghetti on his fork, sending sauce splattering in all directions.

"Stop," I said.

I'm certain he meant to obey, but instead he lost

his grip on his fork, sending it clattering to the floor. He scooted down and, dropping to his knees, reached under his chair.

A moment later, he chirped, "Oops!"

That got my attention.

"Got it!" he said.

Thinking he meant the fork, I expected him back on his chair, but one glance his way and I saw he was still rooting around on the floor, grabbing at a plastic container.

"Oops!" he exclaimed again.

A frog jumped onto his chair. Joe-Joe's head popped up as Billy scrambled to the floor, nearly knocking over his chair.

I lunged for the frog, but it slipped between my hands onto the table.

"What's going on?" Mutter squealed.

I didn't bother answering her. It was obvious to all.

The frog leapt again, this time into the quarter-full bowl of spaghetti sauce. Timothy began to laugh as Joe-Joe lunged forward, his hands landing in the bowl. Somehow he managed to grab the frog. He pulled out a tomato-red blob, a triumphant expression on his face, until a half second later the frog managed to wiggle away again.

Billy scurried around the table, most likely to rescue the frog, but I grabbed at it again and somehow managed to hold on this time. Billy bobbled the plastic container from the floor, I plunked the frog into it, and Billy secured the lid, full of good-sized holes.

"Go set it free," I said.

Billy nodded, his face solemn.

"No," Joe-Joe wailed.

"Don't you want it to live?" I asked.

"Jah. With me," he answered, tears filling his eyes.

I shook my head. "God didn't make frogs to live in our Haus."

Billy headed toward the back door, and seemingly resigned, Joe-Joe wiped his hands across his face, painting his skin with sauce, and started to sit back on his chair.

"Oh, no you don't," I ordered. "Straight to the bathtub."

As he left the table, I looked around at the others. Timothy was still laughing, although quietly now. Aenti Nell nodded in approval. Phillip frowned, his forehead wrinkled under his dark hair.

"It's usually not like this at mealtime. Is it, Addie." Mutter glanced from Phillip to me.

I shrugged. It usually was.

Daed continued shoveling spaghetti into his mouth as if nothing had happened.

Mother turned back toward Phillip. "Tell us about the farm you're hoping to buy."

Timothy groaned and Danny asked to be

excused as Phillip directed his attention to my Mutter, beginning his description with the barn.

I pushed back my chair.

"I'll do the dishes. You take care of Joe-Joe," Aenti Nell said.

"Denki."

As I headed down the hall, Phillip kept talking.

A half hour later, when I returned with a pajama-clad Joe-Joe at my side, all my Bruders—and Phillip—were gone.

Certain he was out talking to Daed, a wave of panic overtook me. Light-headed, I leaned against the table.

"What is the matter?" Mutter asked from her place at the table.

I stammered. "Where . . . where's Phillip?"

Aenti Nell turned from the sink.

"He said he'd see you tomorrow," Mutter said. "He's off to help his Daed move some hay before dark, so he didn't have a chance to talk with your Daed either."

Relief washed over me as I exhaled slowly. "I need to talk with Daed tonight."

"Whatever for?"

"I think maybe Phillip thinks I've agreed to something that I haven't—not yet anyway. . . ." My words trailed off as the look of horror on Mutter's face grew.

"Adelaide Cramer," Mutter barked, "don't you

even think of rejecting that nice young man. You will never, ever find a more suitable husband."

Aenti Nell stepped from the sink toward us, holding her wet hands in the air, and said, "Schwester . . ."

"Stay out of this," Mutter snapped at her. "We don't let you live here to meddle in our business."

Horrified, I called out, "Mutter!" Aenti Nell didn't deserve such treatment.

"Don't you get sassy!"

"Addie," my Aenti whispered, "your mother's right. It isn't my business. I shouldn't have—" She turned back toward the sink.

Mutter shifted in her chair and asked me, "What's gotten into you all of a sudden?"

"I need more time is all . . ." The odd feeling beneath my heart expanded.

"I know what you want. A husband. A home. Children. What every woman wants."

"Jah," I said. She was absolutely right. "I'm just not sure how to know for sure who that husband should be."

"I haven't seen any other suitors coming around." She spread her arms wide. "Have you?"

I was only eighteen—well, nineteen in less than two weeks. And sure, I'd been anxious to marry and have a place of my own, but . . . what was the rush?

My mother's voice softened. "Addie, it's normal to question these things. But that's what making a commitment is all about. It's a decision." She motioned for me to come sit beside her, and I obeyed. Now she was whispering. "Believe me, you don't want to end up like Nell. Life would have been much easier for her—and all of us—if she'd married years ago. Instead—"

"Laurel." Aenti Nell spun around from the sink. "Don't."

My mother stared at her sister for a long moment, and then, with Aenti Nell still watching us, widened her eyes and nodded at me, as if my aunt's reaction proved Mutter's point.

But I had no idea what, exactly, she meant. I stood and began putting the food away, telling Joe-Joe to go brush his teeth.

"Billy needs to get to bed too," Mutter said.

"Jah," I answered. And then I needed to clean the bathroom so it would be usable tomorrow and clean the kitchen and sweep after Aenti Nell finished the dishes. In the morning I'd need to fix breakfast, make the coleslaw, bake the rolls, and marinate the chicken Daed would barbecue later in the day. Then slice the watermelon and make the date pudding. Maybe Mutter had been right —maybe I shouldn't have gone to the market. Maybe I should have stayed home and worked.

Joe-Joe took my hand, turning his face up toward mine, showing the sprinkling of freckles across his nose. "Will you read me a story?"

I was tempted to say no because of all I had to

do, but honestly, putting Joe-Joe to bed was one of my favorite parts of the day.

"Jah," I answered. "Go pick one out." He scurried into the living room straight to the basket from the bookmobile while I stepped outside to call Billy into the house.

Mutter was wrong. Phillip hadn't left. He and Daed, with Billy running circles around them, were standing in the driveway next to Phillip's buggy, deep in conversation. My heart raced until Daed pointed to the field of corn and I realized they were talking about the crops.

Beyond them, in the distance on the lane by the patch of sweet peas, stood a man I didn't recognize. His head was held high, his hat back, and he appeared to be looking at the fading sky. Maybe he hoped to see the first star. Or perhaps he was whistling at the birds bedding down in their nests in the poplars that lined the lane. His profile was toward me, nearly silhouetted against the setting sun. In the dim light, his hair, what I could see, appeared to be the color of the summer moon.

As if he sensed me watching him, he glanced my way and smiled. Then he turned and strolled up the lane.

I stared after him until Phillip caught my eye. He waved. I responded, quickly, and backed into the house, pulling the door shut behind me.

Chapter 3

෨෨

Like all communities, Plain people have our fair share of dysfunctional families, a term I'd learned from my cousin Cate. Just a week ago she mentioned she'd been reading about middle children, who typically long for more attention, and how some are pleasers and others are terrors. I was pretty sure she had me and Timothy in mind.

"The terrors take too many risks," she'd said, "and the pleasers not enough."

I thought she was on to something though, at least as far as I was concerned. I *was* a pleaser. I'd been trying to please my parents my entire life, feeling as if I needed to win their approval. But no matter what I did, it was never enough. I couldn't measure up to what they wanted or, for that matter, what God wanted.

Still, all I knew to do was keep trying.

But it was funny how Cate's passing comment got me thinking and, looking back on it, had even inspired me to go to the market against Mutter's wishes. It was also the reason I began evaluating how I felt about Phillip. Was he truly what I wanted? Or was my motivation in courting him to please my parents?

As I dressed at five o'clock the next morning, I found myself wondering about taking risks. It wasn't the norm for an Amish girl to take any at all. We lived protected lives—going from our Dat's home to a husband's. We might go on a few outings, but it wasn't as if we went rock climbing or parasailing or bungee jumping or anything. I couldn't imagine, exactly, what a true risk would look like in my life. More so, I couldn't imagine my parents ever letting me take one.

Our family came across to others as pretty normal. But I knew better—although I was far too loyal to discuss it with anyone. Mutter was depressed. And Daed had possessed an awful temper when we were all younger. He seemed to have mellowed with age, but I remained leery of his anger and still tiptoed around it. I found myself constantly monitoring Mutter's moods as well.

I stepped out of my room determined to prepare a good breakfast to get everyone off to an extra-positive start. As I hurried down the stairs, through the living room, and into the kitchen, I hoped for as little chaos as possible on the one day, aside from when we hosted church, we were on display to our community. At least half of the families in our church district would join us, along with Mutter's relatives—minus my grandmother, who was visiting a widow friend a county over.

Only Onkel Bob's family on my Daed's side would be in attendance, but still that was a big crowd of people.

For some reason Mutter and Daed kept hosting the barbecue even though it seemed they enjoyed it less and less each year. They thought others were judging them because none of their sons had joined the church—and most likely they were right.

Mutter sat at the table, scribbling down one of her lists. She wasn't much of a morning person and only nodded at me in acknowledgment.

"*Guder Mariye*," I said in return as I put the water on to boil for coffee and then took the bacon from the refrigerator.

I didn't mind she was quiet until she had her coffee. I relished the stillness of the kitchen while Daed and the boys did the milking.

The breeze blew through the open windows above the sink, along with the concert of the mooing cows. The morning light cast a peachy glow through the first floor of the Haus, brightening the wood floors, which felt cool against my bare feet. The rooster crowed in the distance, followed by the chirping of blue jays in the elm in the courtyard.

As I lined the largest cast-iron skillet with the bacon and mixed up the batter for pancakes, I thought about our Haus, which had been passed down from generation to generation in my Daed's family for nearly two hundred years. The L shape formed a courtyard in the back that had been paved with bricks and filled with plants and flowers. An elm tree grew just off of the court-yard on the lawn, shading the side yard and providing a climbing structure for my brothers.

One of the six upstairs bedrooms, which just happened to be mine, had a small balcony—awfully fancy for a Plain house. Years ago, my three oldest brothers had slept in the room, but after they began sneaking out of the house by transferring themselves from the balcony to a trellis and then dropping down to the courtyard, my parents moved them to a different room. I was the one they trusted with the balcony. And I validated their trust, over and over. Never had I even stepped out onto that balcony. Just as I had never crossed them or disobeyed—until questioning my feelings for Phillip last night.

The scent of the coffee mingled with the sizzling bacon, creating one of the most comforting smells in the world. I poured Mutter a cup, added cream, and put it on the table in front of her.

Next I turned the flame on under the griddle and added blueberries from our garden to the batter as an extra treat.

"Oh, Addie." Mutter craned her neck from the table. "You shouldn't waste the berries on us. We should serve those this afternoon, to our guests."

"The little boys can pick more," I said, stirring the batter lightly. The bushes hung heavy this year. She knew that.

I worked quietly, spooning batter onto the griddle, turning the bacon, then flipping the pancakes. After I took the first batch off the griddle, Mutter pushed the list she'd been writing toward me.

"These are the chores that have to be done this morning," she said.

I skimmed the items. She hadn't included anything we hadn't discussed the day before.

"Make sure and wear your purple dress," Mutter said. "It goes so well with your eyes."

I'd slipped on a work dress for the morning. I'd change later, before our guests arrived.

Joe-Joe tiptoed into the kitchen, bleary-eyed and still in his pajamas. I gave him a hug and directed him to the table.

As I spooned more batter onto the griddle, Danny traipsed in through the back door.

Before I realized Daed was behind him, I asked, "Where's Timothy?"

Danny shrugged as our father marched through the kitchen into the living room. A moment later, he yelled up the stairs, "Timothy! Get down here. Now!"

"What time did you get home last night?" I asked Danny.

"I don't want to talk about it," he answered, stifling a yawn.

"Where's Billy?"

"Feeding the chickens."

I dished up the bacon and then flipped the second round of pancakes. "Watch the pancakes," I said to Danny. "I'll go get Billy." I headed out the back door, happy to be outside. Daed would be ready to pray in just a minute.

Billy wasn't in the chicken coop.

I called out his name as I headed toward the barn.

"Back here!"

I rounded the corner. There he stood, inspecting a can of beer. "What's this?" He held it up to his nose and made a face.

"Is it empty?" I asked.

He nodded, shaking the can as he did. "Oops," he said, as liquid splashed onto his hand. "Not quite."

The ground was littered with cans—the same brand that Samuel had given Timothy the day before. I thought they were for the party, and perhaps some of them had been, but it looked as if Timothy had a fair share on his own. No wonder he couldn't get out of bed for chores.

"Those," I said, "aren't for you. That's for sure."

Billy dropped the can and it bounced off a rock, clattering against the concrete foundation of the barn. "Are they Timothy's?"

"Probably," I said. "But they shouldn't be. He's too young."

"But Samuel and George are old enough, right?" Both were old enough, and it was clear Samuel had taken to drinking, but I liked to think George didn't drink, though I didn't know for sure.

"Right. Kind of." I sighed. "Regardless of how old they are, they're stupid to drink this stuff, especially so much at once." One or two might have been fine, but by the looks of it, Timothy had gone overboard. "Let's go in for breakfast. Timothy needs to clean these up."

"I can do it," Billy said, grabbing a second can.

"No. Leave it. It's Timothy's mess—he needs to take care of it."

He still had the can in his hand as Daed came around the corner with a feed sack. "Bag these up," he said, thrusting it at me.

Billy the Brave stepped in front of me. "Addie said Timothy should do it."

"He's not feeling well."

I frowned.

He pushed the sack toward me again. I took it as I said, "Timothy's going to hurt himself or someone else if he doesn't stop."

"At least he was drinking here." Daed crossed his arms. "And not driving."

I shook my head. Sure, it looked as if he'd been drinking here, but there was no way to know he hadn't been drinking and driving too.

"Look." Daed's eyebrows came together as he wrinkled his brow. "Boys will be boys."

I grimaced, clutching the sack tightly.

Daed turned to Billy. "Go back to the house."

Billy tossed the can he'd been holding against the side of the barn, stumbled backward, and took off at a run.

"Our boys aren't that different than others. What they're going through is as common as dirt." My father, like most men his age, had a collection of odd sayings. "Not all Youngie are so foolish. That's why your Mamm and I are thankful for Phillip Eicher," Daed said, motioning toward the dozen cans. "He's hard working and doesn't run around."

"About that," I said. "I really need to talk with you—"

"Later." Daed turned away from me. "After the barbecue. We have too much to do until then." He strode off, stretching his stride with each step.

I flung the sack open and began picking up the cans, turning my head away from the smell, painfully aware of my ambivalence about Phillip. What if he was my only chance at marriage? It wasn't that I wanted to push him away—I just wanted to slow things down. There was nothing wrong with that.

When I finished picking up the cans, I stashed the sack in the back seat of Timothy's car. By the time I reached the kitchen, everyone was finishing up with breakfast. All that was left was one pancake and a half piece of bacon.

I washed my hands at the kitchen sink, using the lavender soap I'd made last fall, the sweet smell washing away the stink of the beer. I hoped Daed wouldn't have time to talk with Phillip today either, not before he had time to listen to me at least.

One blessing of the day would be not having to worry about the Mosier boys and Timothy. There was no way Mervin and Martin would be foolish enough to show up at our barbecue—or so I thought.

The hickory smoke from Daed's barbecue filled the courtyard and blew in through the open kitchen window. I picked up one of the coolers of lemonade and started toward the back door, telling Danny to grab the second one.

"Bring the bowl of blueberries," I told Billy, nodding toward the table.

He did, tilting it precariously.

"Careful now," I said.

He righted it and followed Danny through the door as I held the screen wide open. Joe-Joe traipsed along, a stack of napkins in his hand.

Mutter sat on a lawn chair in the courtyard, under the canopy Daed had bought the year before. Nan Beiler, whom my Onkel Bob seemed to be courting, sat beside her. Nan was Mennonite and wore a printed dress, noticeably different from our Plain colored fabric, and a rounded Kapp instead of a heart-shaped one. She drove the local bookmobile, and because most Amish were big readers, nearly everyone in our area knew her.

Danny and Daed, with Billy and Joe-Joe's help, had set up the tables and benches from the church wagon. Since it was an off Sunday, and services had been at a neighbors' farm the week before, it worked out well.

My cousin Cate and her husband, Pete, were walking toward us from the creek, where they'd cut across from Onkel Bob's property. She carried a bowl in her hands, and Pete carried two folding lawn chairs. Joe-Joe took off toward them, swinging his arms around and around and twirling the napkins as he did. I was relieved when Cate snatched them from him before he let go.

Beyond them, by the horseshoe pit, stood a young man I didn't recognize. Unless . . . I squinted into the afternoon sun. Was he the man I'd seen the night before? I couldn't be certain from so far away.

I forced myself to stop staring and put the cooler of lemonade on the table and then took the bowl of blueberries from Billy. Cate smiled as she neared me, waving the napkins in one hand and lifting her bowl higher in the other.

"I brought potato salad," she said. "Pete's Mamm's recipe." She took off the lid and put it on the table and then met my gaze with her deep blue eyes. "You look tired."

I yawned, on cue, and then laughed. "Just a little."

"I imagine you've been working hard."

"I'll rest tomorrow."

She smiled. "Right . . ." She nodded toward my dress. "Purple is such a good color on you," she said. "And the black apron—now, that's a good idea."

I soaked in her compliments but focused on the practical one. "Jah, I figured a white one would be dirty in no time."

I scooted Cate's bowl to the right to make room for the trays of sliced watermelon that were still in the kitchen and then changed the subject. "Is Betsy coming?"

"I think so."

Betsy was expecting a *Bobli* soon. Cate had laughed when she told me, saying it was a wedding trip pregnancy for sure, although Betsy and her husband, Levi, had only traveled as far as his parents' farm, where they'd been ever since.

"How's she doing?"

"*Gut*," Cate answered. "Tired—and a little nervous, I think. But overall, fine."

I wondered if it was hard on Cate, who was six years older than Betsy, to have her little Schwester having Onkel Bob's first grandchild. Of course I'd never ask her. I did step back and try to evaluate, slyly, if there was any chance Cate might be expecting, but she appeared as thin as ever.

I hoped she and Pete would be blessed with a Bobli of their own soon.

Cate stepped over to Mutter and Nan, and Pete wandered over to Daed and Onkel Bob, who hovered over the barbecue. They hadn't started the chicken, yet all three were intent about something, probably the state of the burning coals.

My Aenti Pauline, one of my Mutter's Schwesters, and her family arrived next, minus her husband and Hannah. "Owen's taking care of one of the horses." Aenti Pauline's family raised both standard-bred and quarter horses on their farm. "And Hannah spent the night at Molly's, although she may come later."

I couldn't help but envy how free my Aenti Pauline was in letting Hannah have a life of her own. I'd never spent the night at a friend's house, not even at the homes of my cousins.

A few minutes later both of my Aentis met me in the kitchen and, under Pauline's lead, helped me carry out the rest of the food. As Daed put the meat on the grill, Betsy arrived with Levi, who directed her to a lawn chair right away. Plain dresses did a good job hiding a pregnancy, but it was obvious Betsy was due soon, both by her size and by the way she walked.

A minute later Mutter rose to greet Phillip and his parents, who were walking toward the gathering from where they'd parked their buggy in the field. The breeze caught Bishop Eicher's long white beard, sending it off to the side. He grabbed it with one hand and his hat with the other. Patty Eicher, the bishop's wife, was nearly as tall as her husband, thin as a rail, and all business. Phillip's face brightened when he saw my mother limping toward him. I decided to let Mutter welcome them. I would greet them later.

Timothy and Danny were flirting with a group of girls from our district. I searched the crowd for the young man I'd seen earlier—and probably last night—but when I couldn't find him, I turned my attention back to my Bruders, calling out to them to put out the rest of the benches. Timothy ignored me, but Danny got busy right away. As I glared at Timothy, I saw a movement in the bushes by the creek.

Two heads popped up, both wearing sunglasses. I didn't react, not wanting to alert Timothy.

"It's almost time to eat," I called out, waving my hand at Timothy and the girls, who wore flip-flops, white Kapps, and pastel dresses—mint green and baby blue, light pink and lavender, as if they'd been freshly dipped in Easter-egg dye.

Keeping an eye on Mervin and Martin as they darted in and out of the brush, I gathered Joe-Joe and Billy around me, readying them for the prayer, but before Daed started it, Samuel, George, and Sadie arrived. She wore a dark blue dress and was as petite as George was brawny. She was a shy one and stuck to his side.

It took a few minutes for everyone to settle down again and for Daed to start the prayer. A minute into it, when we should have all had our eyes closed, Joe-Joe stirred. I peeked as he pointed toward the creek.

Not lowering his voice, despite the fact that we were in the middle of the silent prayer, he asked, "Who's that?"

Mervin and Martin both froze for just a moment and then disappeared behind the willow tree. That's all it took for Timothy, followed by Samuel, to bolt after them.

Daed took his time with the prayer. Perhaps he sensed something going on and figured the longer everyone had their eyes closed the better, although I kept my eyes wide open. Timothy and Samuel disappeared behind the brush, swishing foliage and tree branches as they bounded down the trail. I could only imagine what Timothy, with Samuel's help, would do once they caught the twins.

Finally Daed ended the prayer with an amen and headed toward the barbecue. Out of the corner of my eye, I saw Phillip and his parents talking with Mutter. I waved to him as I walked by and hurried on toward my father. "Did you see Timothy and Samuel take off after the Mosier twins?"

Daed, tongs in his hand, shrugged his shoulders, but an expression of concern covered my Onkel Bob's face.

"You have to do something," I said to Daed.

"Ach, Addie, such as the tree is, such is the fruit." Daed's sayings were downright annoying at times. "Besides, I'm too old for that sort of thing." He tugged on his beard with his free hand.

"You have to stop them! Not join in."

"Oh, well now . . ." Daed squinted into the distance.

"Come on, Cap." Onkel Bob grabbed Daed's arm. "Let's go."

Daed could put me off, but he couldn't ignore his brother-in-law. He put the tongs down on the edge of the barbecue and ambled off after Onkel Bob, looking like the giant of a man he was, seemingly unaware of what his sons were capable of as he continued to tug on his beard.

I matched his stride. "They headed toward the creek."

Phillip stepped toward me, his hat in his hands. I waved. "I'll be right back."

"Addie!" Mutter stood by her lawn chair, leaning on the arm of it.

"In a minute," I called out. Joe-Joe and Billy rushed toward me, each taking one of my hands and slowing me down some. Ahead Danny fell into step behind Daed and Onkel Bob. George stayed back with Sadie—at her urging, I was sure.

"Go over to Cate." I let go of Billy's hand. "And take Joe-Joe with you."

"Ach, Addie," he said. "Why can't we watch?"

"Because there won't be anything to see." I passed Joe-Joe's hand to Billy and gave him a push toward Cate, who stepped out to meet them, and then I began to jog. I ducked beyond the poplar tree, and by the time I was a few steps down the path along the willows, I could hear Timothy's voice.

"You know they have this coming!"

I pushed through the branches. Daed and Onkel Bob, with Danny behind them, stood on our side of the creek, while Timothy and Samuel stood on either side of Mervin and Martin on the other bank. The twins each had their hands up around their faces but not as if they might throw a punch—more like they were hoping to protect themselves.

"No one has anything coming," Onkel Bob said. "Come on, Mervin and Martin. It's time to eat. We want you to be our guests."

I couldn't help but smile at the appalled expression on Timothy's face.

Onkel Bob looked toward my Daed, who cleared his throat and said, "Jah, come on. We don't want any trouble."

"Samuel and Timothy, step aside and let our guests pass first." Onkel Bob took a step toward the creek. Mervin and Martin had worked for him for a couple of years but had quit to help run their family farm a few months ago. Still, I knew they respected Bob Miller as much as anyone in the county.

Timothy, red to the tips of his ears, stepped backward, and Samuel, who looked a little bored, stepped to the side. Mervin, followed by Martin, crossed over the rocks that made a makeshift bridge. Onkel Bob stuck out his hand as they neared the bank and pulled them, one after the other, to the shore.

"Denki, Bob," they said in unison once they were both safe. Then they followed him up the pathway. When they reached me, they both nodded their heads. Daed passed next but didn't look at me. Then came Danny, who gave me a smile. I fell in step behind him, but in no time Timothy was at my heels.

"Way to go," he hissed.

"Knock it off." I began marching, passing Danny on the straight stretch.

When we reached the pasture, the eyes of all of our guests were on us until, as if they just realized they'd all been staring, everyone directed their attention elsewhere. Everyone except for Mutter and her two Schwesters. They stood frozen.

"Our guests who just arrived will start the food line," Onkel Bob called out, gesturing toward Martin and Mervin. "Fall in behind them. Let's eat!"

It was then I noticed the stranger again, standing on the edge of the crowd closest to the volleyball net, behind a group of boys around Billie's age. At a closer distance, I was certain he was the young man I'd seen the night before.

His hat sat back on his head, showing thick, sunny hair that needed to be cut. He stood tall with his arms crossed, an amused look on his face and a relaxed air about him that impressed me. His dark blue shirt bunched at his waist around his suspenders.

His shoulders were broad, but he wasn't solid like Phillip. Instead he had a lanky strength to him, a fluidity that made him appear at ease. As I passed by, he winked—or perhaps he had something in his dark blue eyes.

Had he been standing there earlier when I flew by? Perhaps he found the whole episode amusing. I suppressed a smile. It would be funny, if it didn't involve my family.

I hurried on by, stopping next to Cate and the little boys.

"Who's the stranger?" I whispered to her.

"I have no idea." She held Joe-Joe's hand as she spoke. "He must have come with someone," she added.

I scanned the crowd for Timothy. He stood at the edge of the trees, arms crossed and face red, staring at the mystery man.

Chapter 4

ಬಜ

Joe-Joe and Billy grew anxious to eat, so I reminded them we needed to wait until our guests had gone through the line. I took them toward the shade, but Mutter called us all over to where Phillip stood beside her, his hat in hand.

"What was going on over there?" Phillip asked.

"It's a long story." I turned toward Mutter. I certainly wasn't the one to explain any of this.

Mutter said, "I think my boys were surprised to see the Mosier twins is all."

"Is all?" I mouthed to her.

She jerked her head back, as if shocked at my retort.

Aenti Nell waved at me from the food table. "You're already running low on coleslaw," she said, gesturing to the middle of the table. "And get some more chow chow too." That was a popular relish with pickled green tomato, cabbage, and bell pepper. "And keep the baked beans coming!"

"I'll be right back," I said, thankful for an excuse to escape.

When I returned with a metal bowl full of

coleslaw, Phillip was in line. "I'll eat over by the willow," he said. "Meet me there."

I gulped, which he probably took as an affirmative nod.

As I worked refilling the other salads, the baked beans, and the rolls and then putting out the cookies, pies, date pudding, and cakes, the stranger moved a little closer, all the while keeping his eyes on me. I would have felt self-conscious, but he looked so innocent, so harm-less, and so open, that I wasn't. Nor did his gaze offend me.

When Cate and Pete, with Joe-Joe and Billy with them, started through the line, she asked me to join them.

"I'll be right there," I said, holding up my hand and then heading toward the stranger, who had planted himself by the tool shed.

"Are you going to eat?" I asked.

"May I?" He turned toward me, his blue eyes smiling.

"Of course," I said, thinking I smelled a hint of pine. His arms were crossed, his hands resting on his biceps. I couldn't help but notice the tendons stretching toward his long fingers and the stain of varnish on his nails.

He looked around for a moment, his eyes landing on Mervin and Martin, who sat near Daed and Onkel Bob as they turned pieces of chicken on the barbecue. Timothy sat with Samuel beyond the willow tree, farthest away from every-one.

"Denki," he said.

Before I could say any more, Aenti Nell approached, calling out to me in a raspy voice. "Your mother needs to talk with you."

I kept my tone low and even. "Now?"

She nodded, a serious expression on her face. "Come along."

I gave the stranger a little wave and then followed my Aenti.

My mother reached out her arm but didn't touch me as I stepped to her side, even though I extended my hand. "Phillip's over there all alone," she whispered.

"Jah," I said. "I'm going to fill my plate and join him."

"*Gut.*" She glanced over her shoulder. Phillip's father stood by Daed and Onkel Bob, and his mother sat a few feet away. I wondered if she could hear us.

Mutter continued whispering. "Talking to other young men isn't wise—especially when everyone is watching." She nodded her head in the direction of Phillip's mother as she pursed her lips.

"I'm going." I stepped toward the tables, not wanting to endure any more of her chastising.

I filled my plate, strolled toward the willow, and knelt next to Phillip, who had already finished eating. Tucking the skirt of my dress behind my knees, I slipped down to a sitting position, determined to engage Phillip in conversation that steered clear of the topic of us, as a couple. The longer I could avoid any talk of that, the more likely I'd be to sort out my feelings.

Before I could speak, Timothy called out to me, but I ignored him. He and Samuel then left their plates by the willow tree—most likely for me to collect—and headed toward the edge of the lawn to the volleyball net. George and Danny had already finished eating and were batting the ball back and forth, while Sadie sat on the grass and watched.

Mervin and Martin continued to stay close to Onkel Bob.

"What was your favorite dish?" I asked Phillip, nodding toward his plate as I scooped up a forkful of potato salad.

He waved his hand away from it. "Oh, I couldn't say. It was all good enough."

"Good enough?" My hand stopped in midair.

"Not as good as my Mamm's," he said, now brushing his hands together as if cleaning them.

"Oh?"

"It's just . . . I mean . . . I think . . ." he stuttered, as if he realized he'd put his foot in his mouth. "It's just not what I'm used to."

"Oh, of course," I said. "I know your Mamm is a good cook. There's no reason to be embarrassed." I wouldn't hold an unintended remark against him. I took the bite of Cate's salad.

Before I'd even swallowed, Phillip began describing the corncrib on the farm near his parents'. Relieved by his chatter, I finished my entire meal without having to answer him once.

"I hope to buy some hogs," he said. "But you won't have to worry about them," he said. "I'll be in charge of all the livestock. You'll just tend to the house. And the garden, of course."

I nodded as he spoke, half listening. Some newlyweds I knew worked together on their farms, before their children arrived. I turned so it still appeared my attention was on Phillip, but instead I kept an eye on the stranger, who was standing back by the tool shed, eating from the plate in his hand.

Beyond him, Mutter said something to Aenti Nell, who then rose and wandered over to the young man and spoke with him for a moment. He said something that made her laugh, and then he leaned toward her, as if listening extra carefully in a concerned way. When she left, I turned my head toward Phillip, who now suggested he might raise sheep also, depending on the price of wool. Without interrupting, I took his empty plate.

When he stopped to take a breath, I said, "Go get a piece of pie. I need to start cleaning up."

After I retrieved my Bruders' plates and the

dishes of guests along the way, I started toward the kitchen.

On my way back, Aenti Nell motioned me over to where she, Mutter, and Aenti Pauline were sitting in lawn chairs and eating.

"What did he say to you?" Aenti Nell whispered, nodding her head toward the stranger, who was now sitting with his plate not too far from where Phillip and I had been.

"That he would go through the line in a bit. Which he did. What did he say to you?"

She smiled, showing her dimple, and shook her head.

"What?"

"I'm just surprised he's sticking around is all."

"Why shouldn't he be?"

My Aenti tilted her head and squinted at me. "Why are you being difficult?"

"I'm not."

Her eyes widened, and then she threw back her head a little and chuckled. "You don't know who he is, do you?"

I shook my head, puzzled, but stopped as the pieces came together. My eyes must have shown my realization.

"Jah," Aenti Nell said. "It's Dirk's Jonathan." She nudged me with her plump elbow. Identifying a person by their father was common to my Aenti's generation.

I couldn't help but smile.

90

"All of this is upsetting your mother though. She wants someone to tell him to go home."

I stepped back. "Not me."

"Me neither." My Aenti's eyes sparkled. "I haven't had so much fun in a long time. Besides, your Dat said she—and Timothy—should leave him be." She lowered her voice even more. "Anyways, it's time they all got over this nonsense. Don't you think?"

I agreed. But considering how determined Timothy was to keep the grudge going, it would take more than the adults ignoring the rift to put an end to it.

Aenti Nell sighed.

"What is it?" I asked.

"Oh, nothing."

I shook my head. "It's something. Tell me."

The tone of her voice softened. "It's just that he looks so much like his father."

"Aenti?" I tried to catch her gaze. "What are you saying?"

"Ach, it's nothing. Just an old woman's memories."

"You're not—"

She held up her hand. "Enough of this. We need to clean up."

"You wait. I'll get started in just a minute . . ." I searched the grounds. Jonathan stood back from the tool shed now, in the shade, out of view from Mamm. Phillip sat by the willow again, eating a piece of pie. I could imagine the monologue running silently through his head.

After I took my collection of dirty dishes to the kitchen, I darted back outside and behind the group of girls from our district, heading toward the shed.

When I reached Jonathan, I couldn't think of anything to say except, "Can I help you with something?"

He removed his hat. "I'm looking for someone," he said.

"Oh?"

"A girl."

Ach, he'd come to the barbecue hoping to see Hannah. He'd been enamored with her the weekend before at the party. He didn't know her parents had forbidden her from seeing him. It all made sense now. I decided to play dumb. "Oh?"

"Jah, I have something I wanted to give her."

With a tease in my voice, I asked, "So, it's a certain girl you're after?"

He nodded.

My voice serious now, I said, "She's not here."

"How do you know?"

"I'm her cousin."

"Ahh," he said.

I was having fun. Hannah had been right. Jonathan Mosier did seem like a bit of a sap. "She may be here later, if you want to stick around."

"Denki," he said. "I think I might." He put his

hat back on then and grinned at me. Sap or not, I found him handsome.

I waved and then walked back behind the group of people gathered around the elm tree so Phillip wouldn't see me, circled all the way behind the barbecue back by the half barrels overflowing with red geraniums and blue lobelia, and dashed into the kitchen through the back door.

I found myself thinking about Jonathan as I scraped the plates into the slop bucket, wondering what he'd brought for Hannah. It had to be something small. Not one of his carvings. Not even a book or a card. Something that fit in his pocket. We didn't wear jewelry, so it couldn't be a ring or a bracelet.

Phillip had never brought me a single thing in all the times he'd come to call. Not even a flower.

Why hadn't I asked Jonathan what he'd brought for Hannah? I mulled over the possibility of speaking with him again as I stacked the plates, while Cate took out another tray of cookies. Maybe Hannah was right about Jonathan being a dolt, but he'd come looking for her, carrying a gift.

Maybe he wasn't a pushover. Maybe he was sweet. And caring. He certainly seemed kind, even in the way he'd chatted with Aenti Nell. Maybe Hannah would change her mind once she realized his goodness.

I ran the hot water and squeezed in the soap. When bubbles formed, I submerged the plates and began scrubbing. By the time Cate returned, followed by Betsy and Nan, dishes filled the rack. Betsy lowered herself onto a kitchen chair, propping her feet on another one, as Nan and Cate began drying.

"I wish the Bobli was here already," Betsy said.

"Jah," Nan said. "So I could hold it." She pushed back a strand of fine blond hair and grinned.

Cate whispered to me, "She's going to make a good *Mammi*, jah?"

I nodded but didn't say anything out loud, not wanting Nan to hear me. I would have liked to know what my Onkel Bob's intentions were as far as marrying Nan and making her a grandmother, but of course I wasn't going to ask. For years Nan and Cate had been friends due to my cousin's devotion to the local bookmobile. Then a year ago last spring, Nan and Onkel Bob had met. They seemed smitten with each other, even though she was Mennonite.

I wiped at the sweat gathering on my forehead with my wrist and then dropped my hand back into the dishwater.

Nan edged in beside me. "Go on outside," she said. "Let us clean up."

"Ach, no. You should be out visiting."

Betsy laughed from the table. "We're old married ladies." She was all of eighteen, almost nineteen. "You should be out there with the young men. With Phillip, jah?"

"Nan's not an old married lady," I said. "Maybe she'd like to be outside with Onkel Bob."

They all laughed, but then Cate gave me a sympathetic look, most likely in regard to Phillip.

"Go on out," she said. "Pete took him over to the horseshoes."

"Denki," I said, giving up my position at the sink to Nan, intending to check on Joe-Joe and Billy but knowing I'd be looking for Jonathan too.

Mutter and Aenti Pauline were still sitting in the courtyard in their chairs under the canopy. In most families, the matriarch would be in the kitchen supervising clean up, but not in mine.

I avoided Mutter, circling wide. I didn't see Jonathan and decided to head toward the creek to check on my little Bruders. They were with a gang of other boys, running barefoot along the trails, beating down the grass and brush even morc. Joe-Joe had watermelon juice on his chin, a streak of mud across his face, and scratches along his arms. When he saw me, he took off galloping after a group of older kids.

I popped back up out of the trees and brush into the pasture on the other side of the willow tree, shading my eyes to see the volleyball game at the far end of our yard.

Mervin and Martin were playing, along with a

group of Youngie, all barefooted, opposite my Bruders.

"Come on," George called out to me. "We need another player." Sadie was still sitting off to the side, obviously not intending to play.

I started to decline until I saw Jonathan next to Martin—and Phillip nowhere to be seen.

When I reached the game, the players had rotated a turn, and Jonathan stood nearest the net on the left side. I slipped off my flip-flops and stepped to the position opposite him on the other side of the net, and then glanced from one brother to the next. Danny seemed as relaxed as ever, positioned in the middle of the players. George stood to his right and grinned at me. Samuel stood to Danny's left and although he didn't smile, he was no longer seething. That left Timothy in the middle of the front, across from Martin, a scowl on his face.

Cate had told me one time that Native Americans used the game of lacrosse to train their warriors and sometimes they even played against another tribe to settle a dispute, instead of going to war.

The Amish didn't believe in wars. Or even disputes. And certainly not in settling a conflict through a competition. Or so we said.

Mervin stepped back to the server's spot, tossed the ball into the air, and slammed it across the net. Timothy hit it so hard I didn't think anyone would attempt to return it, but Martin did, sending it skyward and over the net with a bump. I positioned myself under it, sending it back. Jonathan volleyed straight at me with a smile on his face, and when I returned it close to the out-of-bounds mark, he lunged for it but missed, rolled onto his back, and popped up grinning, holding his hat in his hand.

George headed back on our side to serve as a familiar voice called out, "Do you have room for one more?" It was Phillip.

"How about two more?" Pete walked behind Phillip.

"We get Pete," Martin called out.

That left Phillip on our side. He stepped in between Timothy and me, forcing me over, a position away from Jonathan.

Jonathan stepped back as if alarmed, a goofy smile on his face, as Phillip squared his shoulders.

George served the ball straight to Mervin, who bumped it back over the net in my direction. Under normal circumstances, I could have returned the ball easily, but having Phillip beside me made me nervous, and I lifted my right forearm as I bumped it, sending it off at an angle. Phillip lunged past me, trying his best to save it, but it landed out-of-bounds before he could.

He took a deep breath as he stepped back and then blew his breath out, sending his bangs upward.

Next, Martin served the ball and it came straight to me again, but before I could hit it, Phillip stepped in front of me, crashing the ball down on Jonathan, who set it back to me. Again Phillip slammed it over the net.

Obviously he didn't trust me to hit the ball myself.

Jonathan returned it again, but over my head to Danny, who didn't have a chance to hit it either because Phillip took a giant step backward, lobbing it over the net, this time to Martin, who sent it spiraling off into the pasture.

"Ach," Pete called out, "that was quite the volley."

"Jah," I answered.

Mervin glared at Phillip and said, "He's so mighty for a tender thing."

I blushed, afraid I might be the "tender thing" he referred to.

"Too boisterous also," Jonathan added.

Mervin nodded as George served again. Jonathan returned it to me, but again Phillip stepped in front of me. I stuck out my bare foot, hoping to teach him a lesson, but he deftly maneuvered around me without seeming to notice my intent and bumped it high in the air toward Timothy. He slammed it across the net to Jonathan, who returned it again, this time to Danny. He set it high, to the center, in the perfect position for Phillip to spike it back over the net.

Which he did, straight to Martin, who missed it entirely. Timothy and Phillip high-fived.

Jonathan turned toward Mervin and said, "We'll get it next time."

"You might," his cousin said. "But I think my chances are done." He sighed.

I couldn't help but think that Mervin referred not to the volleyball, but to love, which had soured him. He'd cared for Betsy. Then me. Both times he'd been rejected. Now he thought I loved Phillip. I couldn't help but feel for him.

Phillip clasped his hands and stretched his arms over his head, cracking his knuckles as he did.

Mervin rolled his eyes at Jonathan, and I stepped away from the net, guessing I wouldn't see any more action. I was right. Every time the ball came close, Phillip lunged in front of me. Jonathan made a face each time.

Finally I slipped away, wiped the sweat from my brow, grabbed my flip-flops, and headed toward the willow, stopping under the weeping branches, where I could watch the game without being seen.

A couple of minutes later, as Timothy and Martin disputed a play, Jonathan slipped away too. As the disagreement escalated, Phillip began looking around, his face beet red, toward the yard and then toward the tree. I turned quickly and scampered down the path toward the creek, a sense of hollowness overtaking me.

A moment later, I heard footsteps behind me. I

turned, afraid Phillip had followed, but it was Jonathan, smiling as he flew down the steep trail and then stopped by my side at the water's edge.

"I'm Jonathan," he said. "Mosier."

"Jah, I know," I answered.

"And you're Addie Cramer's cousin." He grinned. "But I don't know your name."

I took a step backward. "Addie's cousin?" What was he talking about?

He tilted his head. "Jah," he said. "That's what you said. Earlier."

I shook my head, trying to understand what he was saying. "I said I was Hannah's cousin." I closed one eye. "You were looking for Hannah. Right?"

He laughed. "No, I'm looking for Addie."

"Oh," I said.

He dug in one pocket, pulling out a piece of folded paper. "That's not it," he said, digging in the other. "I have something for her."

My face grew warmer by the second. "For me?"

"If you're Addie."

I nodded.

"Oh." His blue eyes sparkled. "I'm happy to have that cleared up." He smiled and pulled an envelope from his other pocket. "Here it is," he said, handing it to me.

As I took it, the flap came open. Inside was money. "What is this for?" But as I asked, I knew. It was the wad of money I'd given Martin. "Ach,

I can't take it back." I forced it into his hands.

"It was kind of you—really." He held the envelope between us as he spoke. "But I fixed the mantel. No one owes me any money." He stepped toward me, slipping the money into my apron pocket. I shivered at his closeness. He smelled of wood, mixed with the earthiness of the soil, the marshy creek, and the freshness of the trees all around us.

"Denki . . . if you're sure."

He nodded.

My hand fell to my pocket. "Was it you last night? Walking down the lane?"

"Jah," he answered. "I thought I would return the money then, but when I saw your family had a visitor I decided to wait."

I blushed, turning my head toward the sound of the little boys shouting at each other downstream.

"Look." Jonathan pointed at a dragonfly flitting by and reached toward it as Phillip called out my name. Jonathan's finger moved from the dragonfly to pointing to the field above the bank where Phillip's voice came from. "Shall we?"

I shook my head and whispered, "I'd rather not."

His finger switched directions, pointing across the creek. "Care to come with me?"

I nodded, a sense of excitement welling up inside of me.

Phillip called out again, but his voice was

farther away—going toward the little boys downstream.

Jonathan grinned and motioned for me to follow as he hopped to the first stone and then to the second.

I matched his surefootedness. A toad croaked back the way we'd come and then another dragonfly flew by. The willow leaves ahead shimmered in the shadows.

"What's up there?" He nodded toward the far bank.

"Trees. And then my Onkel's farm." There was a path between the two properties, a route far shorter than taking the lane.

He kept going, up the trail with stairlike steps from the roots of the trees wound into the bank. When we reached the grove, he took my hand, his rough skin against mine, sending a shiver down my spine.

He stepped between the trees, pulling me along. "Sycamores," he stated.

I nodded, dodging around a mosquito. "My great-grandfather planted the trees."

He ran his hand along the puzzlelike bark. "Probably to stop erosion along the bank, jah?"

I shrugged. I hadn't given it any thought, even though it was one of my favorite spots on the farm.

He dropped my hand and leaned against the tree, both palms flat, supporting himself. "The wood is soft but works great for accents—and for drawers, little boxes, that sort of thing." He stepped back and looked straight up into the tree. "I'd guess these are a hundred feet tall or more. Sometimes sycamores are hollow. Animals often make their home in them."

I stepped two trees over and pointed to the base. Jonathan joined me.

"And little boys. My Bruders have a fort in this one."

He squatted down, shuffled inside, and then called out, like an owl, "Who, who," sending an echo up the tree.

A moment later, he stepped back out with Joe-Joe's bow, made from a willow twig, in his hand. "It looks like your Bruders have a lot of fun."

I nodded. "They play Settlers."

"Did you play here when you were little too?"

"Some." I smiled. "I suppose I'm the one who taught them to play Settlers, on a rare lazy Sunday afternoon."

"Really?" He extended the bow to me, but when I reached for it he took my hand again. "I used to play that when I was little too."

"With your siblings?" I asked, liking the way my hand felt in his.

He shook his head. "Sometimes with my cousins, back when we were young and they came to visit."

"Martin and Mervin?"

"Jah," he said, focusing on my eyes. "They mentioned you recently."

I blushed again.

"It was all good," he said, a hint of teasing in his eyes. "Especially from Mervin."

Determined not to blush again, I said, "They've been good friends to me."

"So you don't hold to this so-called grudge?"

I shook my head as he placed our hands palm to palm, as if together we were praying.

He cleared his throat. "I know you have a lot of Bruders. . . ."

I nodded.

"And you're the only girl."

I nodded again.

"They must all appreciate you very much." He pressed his hand more firmly against mine.

"Actually . . ."

A voice called out, "Adelaide! Your Mamm wants you!"

I hesitated a moment and then said, "That's my Aenti Nell."

"Jah," he said. "I met her earlier."

"Now!"

"I'd better go."

"Stay," he said, his fingers curling around mine.

"I can't," I said, pulling away.

"Can I see you again?"

"Come now!" Aenti Nell shouted, her voice sharp.

Jonathan loosened his grip and I slipped my hand from his.

"Later?" he whispered.

I nodded as I stepped away and then rushed back down the trail, across the creek, and up to where Aenti Nell stood under the willow tree.

"Where have you been?"

"The sycamore grove."

"With?"

I didn't answer but started off toward the Haus at a brisk pace. "Where's Mutter?"

Aenti Nell struggled to keep up with me. "In the kitchen. With Phillip's Mamm. They want to talk with you."

Chapter 5

నవ

Mutter said she simply wanted me to put away the food, instead of Aenti Nell and Aenti Pauline, so I would know where it was the next day for leftovers, but the way she and Phillip's mother watched me as I worked, I was pretty sure it was more than that. They wanted to keep me in their sights.

At one point, when I noticed they were both staring at me with puzzled looks on their faces, I realized I was humming as I stacked the containers of leftover salads in the fridge. I stopped immediately.

"Go on now," Mutter finally said, motioning toward the door. "Phillip was looking for you earlier. We can finish up." I knew that meant she could sit at the table while my Aentis did the work, but she was the oldest of the Schwesters, and they seemed fine following her orders.

Patty pursed her lips together, making her face appear even thinner than it was as I hurried out the door.

I glanced around for Jonathan as I strolled across the courtyard. Onkel Bob, Danny, and George collected the tables. Cate, Nan, and Sadie gathered the lawn chairs. Betsy leaned against Levi as they walked toward their carriage. I hurried my steps, catching up with my cousin, and gave her a quick hug. The next time I saw her she would likely have a little one in her arms.

I turned toward the horseshoe game, where Phillip, Pete, Samuel, and Timothy played. The volleyball game appeared long over, and Mervin, Martin, and Jonathan were nowhere in sight. They must have gone home. I had no desire to spend any time with Phillip Eicher, at all. So I turned back to help Cate and Nan with the chairs.

But by the time I reached them, Phillip was jogging to catch up with me. "There you are," he said.

Cate watched as I told Phillip hello and then added, "I'm going to help with the chairs."

"And I'll go help your Dat." He grinned. "I need to talk with him."

I glanced that way. Onkel Bob and Bishop Eicher stood by the grape arbor, appearing as if they were just finishing their conversation. Daed, George, and Danny each hauled a table toward the church wagon.

Phillip lumbered over to the stack of tables and grabbed two, one under each arm.

"What's that all about?" Cate whispered.

I put my hand to the side of my face and met her kind eyes.

"Is it what it appears to be?" she asked.

"I think so." I choked on my words.

"But you're not sure?"

Unexpected tears filled my eyes. "How am I supposed to *know* if Phillip's the right one?"

Cate took my hand and pulled me behind the tool shed. "If you have doubts, then he's not."

I took a deep breath and dabbed at my eyes, stopping my tears before any escaped.

"I saw you with Martin and Mervin's cousin," Cate said, her voice low.

My face grew warm as I wondered who else had noticed us.

"Do you care for him?" The kindness in Cate's voice helped me relax, a little.

"I only just met him today."

"And?"

"He's different . . ."

Cate raised her eyebrows.

"It's as if he sees me. Do you know what I mean?"

She nodded. "Jah, I know exactly what you mean."

"But he's interested in Hannah."

"It didn't look that way to me." Cate smiled.

"But perhaps he goes from girl to girl. I'm just the next—not the last."

"There's only one way to find out," Cate answered.

"And he's a Mosier. . . ." I looked toward my Daed.

"All the more reason to get to know him. Perhaps the two of you can finally put an end to all the nonsense."

I doubted that but didn't say so.

Across the way, the horseshoe game must have ended, because Pete and Samuel started toward us. Bishop Eicher opened the back door to the house, probably intent on fetching his wife. My immediate hope was that all the Eichers would go home, the sooner the better.

Billy's voice came from near the willow tree. "Addie! Joe-Joe's hurt." It wasn't a panicked declaration, more of an everyday occurrence. Cate sensed it too, because she said, "Go on." She smiled and added, "And take your time."

I headed toward the creek, slipping back down the trail into the world of my little Bruders.

"He's on the other side of the creek."

By the time I reached my youngest brother, he'd stopped crying, but his eyes were red, and muddy tears were smeared across his cheeks.

"What happened?" I asked.

"I fell," he said, pointing to his ankle.

I knelt beside him and felt up and down his foot and leg. His ankle was slightly swollen, but that was all. "Can you stand on it?"

He tried and could.

"Take a step."

He did.

"You probably twisted it," I said. "Let's put it in the creek to soak for a few minutes."

I sat on a rock with Joe-Joe in front of me. He dangled his foot into the water, leaning back against me as he did, tucking his head against me. His fine hair tickled my chin. I turned my face, placing my cheek atop his head, breathing in his sweaty little-boy scent, mixed with mud and creek water. Billy wiggled onto the boulder beside me, resting his head on my shoulder.

That was where Phillip found us, at the edge of the creek. "Could we talk?" He leaned toward us.

I looked up at him, doing my best to soften my expression. "Perhaps another time?"

"Sometime soon?" He straightened, crossing his arms as he did.

I nodded, the tears welling in my eyes again. The thought of talking with him, seriously, terrified me. I didn't want to hurt Phillip. Or my parents. But if Cate was correct, then he wasn't the right one for me.

"Okay." A look of uncertainty crossed his face. "I'll see you soon."

I felt sorry for Phillip as I waved at him with my free hand, holding on to Joe-Joe with my other. My little brother felt so relaxed against me I checked to see if he'd fallen asleep. He had.

Phillip started up the trail as Billy began telling me about his day, but the sound of whistling on our side of the creek interrupted him.

"Who is that?" I asked. None of my Bruders— or Daed—whistled much.

"Maybe it's Pete," Billy offered.

Sure he was right, I called out a hello.

The whistling stopped, but the footsteps continued. In a moment Jonathan was beside us. He held a piece of wood in one hand, another tucked under his arm, and a knife in his other hand.

"Ach," he said. "Just who I was hoping to see." He winked at me as he handed Billy one of the pieces of wood. It was a small branch, stripped of wood and shaped like a bow.

Billy held it up. It had notches in each end, tied with the string, and the handle had his name carved on the end.

"Because the little guy's asleep, I'll give this to you." He handed Billy the one with *Joe* carved on it.

"Denki," Billy said.

"Do you need some help?" Jonathan motioned to Joe-Joe.

I'd carried him plenty of times, but getting off the boulder was going to be tricky.

"Denki," I said again, lifting Joe-Joe as best I could into Jonathan's open arms. "Go put these in your fort," I said to Billy, handing him the other bow. "You can show Joe-Joe in the morning."

Billy took off running, and by the time we'd crossed the creek, he was back at our heels. Jonathan carried Joe-Joe effortlessly, but by the time we reached the end of the trail, Billy had surged ahead of us. I knew not to ask my brother not to tell Mutter and Daed about the bows—that would only encourage him to do it for sure. On his own, he might or might not. I couldn't be sure.

"Just as far as the willow," I said to Jonathan.

He nodded as if he understood.

"When can I see you again?" he whispered, his mouth brushing against my ear as he passed Joe-Joe into my arms.

I couldn't help but smile as my heart beat against the weight of my brother. "Tonight," I whispered back.

"*Wunderbar*," he responded, a smile forming on his lips.

After I'd tucked Joe-Joe and Billy into bed that night, I sat out in the courtyard by myself, positioned so I could see both the back of the house and the lane. The sun had set, but the lingering light of dusk illuminated the yard and side of the house.

A breeze blew through the elm tree, playing the leaves like chimes.

I glanced to the second floor of the house. A lamp shone in the window of my parents' room. I hoped Jonathan would show up—but not until after my parents put out their light.

A lone bat flew above the roof and then out toward the field. A mosquito buzzed close to my ear. Another landed on my arm. I smacked it and flicked it to the ground. In an instant I began to itch all over. I looked toward the lane. No Jonathan. I considered going for a walk, but what if he came to the house while I was gone?

Besides, I didn't want to get eaten by mosquitoes. As I stood, the light in Mutter and Daed's window went out.

As the dark of night fell, I headed to the back door, stepped into the mudroom, slipped off my flip-flops, and made my way through the dim kitchen. Maybe he wasn't coming. Maybe he'd changed his mind and had gone to Hannah's house instead. I tiptoed through the living room and then up the stairs, clutching the railing as I pulled myself along.

When I reached the landing, I opened the little boys' door. The full moon that had risen on the far side of the house cast enough light through their window that I could see they were both fast asleep. Joe-Joe slept with his sheet wound around his legs. Both of Billy's arms were flung above his head, and his mouth hung open.

I carefully closed their door. I didn't need to be quiet for their sakes—they would be fast asleep until morning—but I didn't want to disturb Mutter. When I entered my room I stood still, listening for my parents' voices. Some nights I could hear them through the wall, although I'd never been able to make out their words. Sometimes Mutter would cry and Daed's tone would grow frustrated, but even then I couldn't tell what they were saying.

So far tonight—probably worn out by the activity of the day—they were quiet.

I lit my lamp beside my bed and sat atop the sunshine-and-shadows quilt I had made last year. It was for my hope chest, the one I didn't have, so I put it on my bed instead.

All of my other hope-chest items were in a hamper on my floor, which was the only element of untidiness that existed in my otherwise completely ordered space.

113

Neither Mutter nor Aenti Nell ever came into my room, so they didn't know I didn't use the hand-me-down hope chest my mother had given me.

It had been hers.

And I didn't want it.

Not using it was the most rebellious thing I'd ever done—until I talked to Jonathan at the picnic and encouraged him to come calling tonight.

My dresses hung on pegs across the room. A three-drawer bureau, to the side of the French doors, held all my other clothes. The top was bare except for the only added decor in the entire room—a canning jar filled with cosmos, the white, pink, and fuchsia flowers bending downward.

My parents' door opened with a creak. Sometimes Mutter couldn't sleep and wandered the house. I'd so hoped tonight wouldn't be one of those nights—but it seemed it was.

I ventured to my window, and although I was tempted to step out onto my balcony more than I'd ever been before, I didn't. Jonathan was definitely late. Even though we hadn't specified a time, we both had to get up early in the morning.

I valued punctuality in a person. It was one of Phillip's qualities I appreciated.

After another ten minutes, sure Jonathan wasn't coming at all, I retreated back to my bed and pulled my nightgown from under my pillow just as the hoot of an owl interrupted the still night. I sprang to the French doors and flung them open. Sure enough, Jonathan was waiting in the courtyard, below the branches of the elm tree. Without stepping out, I waved and then motioned for Jonathan to wait over by the willow tree, away from the Haus.

I didn't want Mutter to see him through the kitchen window.

I turned off my lamp, slipped down the stairs, and started for the front door, guessing Mutter was in the kitchen.

Daed's voice coming from the archway startled me. "Out for a stroll?" He had a bowl in his hand.

Speechless, I nodded.

He smiled. "Tell Phillip hello."

I pursed my lips.

"You have my blessing, Addie." He grinned. "Lighten up. We couldn't be happier about the two of you. I told Phillip that today." He held up the bowl. "And by the way, the date pudding is delicious. Best you've ever made."

I smiled at him, although I doubted he could tell in the darkness, snatched up the pair of flip-flops I kept at the front door, and slipped out. I felt like a cheat—but not enough to tell him the truth or, worse, not go. It was the first time I'd ever deceived my father.

And the first time I'd ever taken such a risk.

I fled the house and hurried around the side. At

least Timothy had left for the evening and wasn't drinking behind the barn. And I didn't think he'd taken Danny with him.

The full moon shone above the willow, illuminating the tree and Jonathan. Glancing back once to make sure Daed hadn't followed me out the door, I hurried across the lawn.

"What a night," I said as I reached Jonathan, barely aware of the mosquito that had landed on my arm. I swatted it away.

"Jah." He gazed at me, his eyes full of emotion.

My face grew warm at his intensity.

He held out his open hand to me. On his palm was a thin piece of wood the size of a bookmark. "It's for you."

He'd etched a simple *Engel* in the wood, her face turned upward, her wings spread wide. I closed my hand around it. "Denki. It's beautiful," I said, running my finger over the carving. I slipped the bookmark into the pocket of my apron.

"Want to walk?" He put out his arm, and I took it, placing my hand in the crook of his elbow.

He reached for my hand, locking his long, strong fingers through mine. The warmth of his rough skin sent a shiver up my spine. With each step we took along the ridge above the creek, feelings surged inside of me that I didn't know existed.

Jonathan threw his head back. "Look at the night sky," he said. "Isn't it stunning?"

It was.

Jonathan pointed to a lone pine towering above us to the right. "God gives us all we need. Beauty. Clothes. Food. All we need to have a relationship with him and others. And the assurance he is always present."

I'd never thought of God's provision that way —nor had I heard anyone talk the way Jonathan did. Under the canopy of the night, I felt a peace I hadn't experienced before.

He added, "Everything to sustain life comes from God."

I shivered. Jonathan pulled me closer, brushing his head against my Kapp. "Ach, Addie," he said. "I don't think I've ever felt such joy."

If Phillip had said such a sappy thing, I would have cringed. But coming from Jonathan it sounded real.

We walked in silence for a moment, stepping into the orchard, under the gnarly branches of the apple trees laden with green fruit. As we reached the other side, I asked about his grandfather.

He said the old man's health was failing, although he still seemed full of spit and vinegar and wild ideas. "He let the farm work go and didn't ask my Onkel or cousins to help. And didn't hire anyone. He didn't plant any crops in the spring. He's always had his head in the clouds, but it seems to have gotten worse." He sighed. "My father tells me I take after him."

Jonathan patted my hand. "Enough about me. What's it like to be the only girl with all those Bruders?"

I gave him the short story of my immediate family, then mentioned Onkel Bob, Cate, and Betsy—and then my mother's family.

"They seem to be the ones holding on to the grudge," I said.

"Speaking of," Jonathan said, "what's that all about anyway?"

I stopped walking. "I honestly don't know."

Jonathan turned toward me. "Because my parents have never talked about it—I didn't even know about it until Martin and Mervin told me. But when I asked my Dat tonight, he got angry and told me to stay away from 'all those worthless Cramers.' "

"He hadn't said anything about it before?"

He shook his head. "Nothing."

"That surprises me."

"Why?" Jonathan put his hand on my shoulder.

"I thought both our families held the grudge equally."

"That's just it," he said. "Just because my Dat hasn't talked about it doesn't mean he doesn't carry it. He doesn't talk about much."

"My Daed has hard feelings, for sure. And so does my Mutter and her family. But my Daed's brother-in-law wants it to end."

We started walking again, our hands still joined.

"Jah," Jonathan said. "Mervin and Martin both said your Onkel Bob is a good man." He stopped abruptly, both talking and walking, and then cleared his throat. "I didn't mean that your father and Bruders aren't."

"Ach," I said, pulling him along. "You're right. They're all good men. It's just the ones in my immediate family aren't as wise as Onkel Bob." I explained that he'd been married to my Aenti, Daed's sister, who died when Betsy was born, when I was just a baby.

My paternal grandmother helped Bob with the girls until she died years ago, and my parents always seemed to respect Bob. "However," I said, "my mother is critical of Cate, and of others in the community. It seems to be her way of trying to build herself up, by pointing out the flaws of others."

"I think that's pretty common," Jonathan said.

I nodded. But not acceptable. "What's your family like?" I asked.

"Very small compared to yours."

"Oh?" I suspected his siblings were all younger than he was.

"I'm an only child."

I wasn't sure how to respond. That was very rare for an Amish family.

"I had a Schwester once, for a few days."

"I'm sorry. What happened?" I stared at him by the light of the moon.

"She was my twin, born after me. During the

119

pregnancy there was no indication there were two babies, at least that's what my grandfather told me. They only heard one heartbeat, and my mother wasn't unusually large. It was the last day of January, and the roads were bad when she went into labor. The midwife arrived late. My Mamm labored too long. I weighed eight pounds when I was born. But my Schwester weighed only two pounds. My Dat told me once I'd hogged all the food." He shook his head, sadly. "Worse, my delivery injured my Mamm, which probably cut off my Schwester's oxygen and also prevented my parents from having more children."

I squeezed Jonathan's hand as compassion filled my heart. Not only did he not have any siblings, but it also sounded as if he'd been blamed for it, at least by his father.

He smiled at me. "It's sad, I know. I wish my Daed had more children, particularly more sons, to focus on."

"Why's that?"

"I'm a big disappointment to him." His voice was matter of fact. "I've never measured up to what he hoped for."

"What are you saying?" I couldn't comprehend why any father wouldn't be pleased with Jonathan.

"Mostly that he wants me to farm, and I want to be a carpenter."

"But you're so good at what you do."

"He doesn't think it has much value." We

reached the field with the downward slope beyond the orchard. He chuckled. "You keep changing the subject to me. I want to talk about you."

Before I could protest, he asked, "Who was that guy playing volleyball today? The one who called out your name when we were down at the creek."

I groaned. "That's not talking about me."

He stopped walking again at the edge of the orchard. "Phillip, right?"

I nodded, stepping beside him.

"Are you courting him?"

"He and my parents think so."

"But you don't?"

I took a deep breath. Three conversations with Jonathan, plus Cate's insight, had convinced me. I knew for certain. "Phillip's not right for me." Not once had I felt for him any of the emotions that nearly overwhelmed me now as I stood beside Jonathan.

"I'm so glad to hear you speak honestly."

"Denki," I answered. "There's no reason not to, jah? If I know he's not right for me, I shouldn't pretend." Inwardly I groaned. Somehow I'd have to make it clear to Phillip, sometime soon.

Jonathan leaned toward me. "Nor should I pretend when I know who is right for me, jah?"

My eyebrows arched as I spoke. "And who would that be?"

He beamed, his eyes dancing. "Who do you think it is?"

I stepped backward. "But how can you know so soon?"

"I know."

I tugged on his arm, urging him to walk again. He obliged. "What about Hannah?" I asked. "I heard you wanted to court her."

He answered in a calm voice. "I was interested in her, jah. I *thought* she might be a possibility. But I *know* with you."

"How do you know?"

With the most sincere look I'd ever seen, he said, "How could I not know?" He kept his eyes on me as we walked, his face still bright from the moonlight. "And how about you? You said you know Phillip isn't the right one. Any chance you know that I am?"

"Would you think ill of me if I did?"

"Would I expect something entirely different from you than me?"

I pulled him to a stop in the hollow of the field and met his eyes. "Would you?"

"Of course not."

Feeling awkward, I said, "Perhaps we're both being too rash." I took a few steps in the direction of the Haus.

Jonathan caught my hand. "Perhaps you speak too soon."

I avoided his gaze. "So you believe in love at first sight?"

"Maybe not everyone is as blessed as we, but

jah, in this case I do." He touched my chin. "You can't tell me you're not feeling something special."

"I can't?"

"Something you've never felt before?"

My face grew warm. "Jah, but I don't have any experience in these sorts of things."

He cocked his head. "I thought you would have had lots of suitors."

"My Daed is rather particular."

"But he approves of Phillip?"

"Jah."

"But he wouldn't of me?"

"That's right."

"Because I'm a Mosier?"

"For starters, jah." I had no idea what Daed would think of Jonathan if he wasn't a Mosier, but I think he'd agree with Jonathan's father—that farming was a better vocation for an Amishman than woodworking, especially when his business seemed to cater to Englischers.

Jonathan's expression turned sad as he took my hand and led me down toward the creek. My awkward feeling disappeared, replaced by a sense of hope.

I slipped my flip-flops off, feeling the cool mud on my feet. "Your family makes no difference to me though—I'd feel the same about you no matter what your name."

"Denki. I feel the same about you," Jonathan said, pulling me along. "But maybe we can change things, jah? Bring our two families together?"

I wasn't sure how we'd do that.

"I'm a passionate person," he said. "I like to have a cause. As my old boss used to say, 'Be the change.' "

I liked that.

"Are you in?"

I wasn't sure what difference we could make, but I answered, "Jah, I'm in."

He reached across me then, his palm out. It took me a minute to register what he was doing—a high five, something my Bruders did at times, although never with me. I put my palm up, and he bumped it with his. I liked the feel of his skin against mine.

"Here's to change," he said, grasping my hand in his, curling his fingers around mine for the second time that day.

We walked that way for a moment, until we reached the bank, but then a firefly darted by, and then another one flitted upstream toward the house. Jonathan dropped my hand and, laughing, chased after a third one with me following close behind, stumbling now and then on the uneven ground, the mud squishing between my toes, giggling as I batted a cattail along the creek. My surging emotions, the beauty of the moonlight, and the fairylike fireflies all welled up inside of me alongside the pure joy Jonathan had spoken about. I felt it too, for the first time ever.

In a few minutes the fireflies disappeared across the creek and Jonathan stopped, waiting for me to catch up. He took me in his arms and held me tight. I wrapped my arms around him, holding my flip-flops out from his back.

The joy inside me swelled until a sob rose up alongside it.

"What's the matter?" He lifted my chin.

"I'm just so happy." I swiped at an escaping tear.

He laughed again and hugged me tighter, his body against mine, and yet the gesture seemed innocent enough. It didn't seem as if he had any of the ulterior motives Mutter had warned me about. He seemed to simply want to hug me—and I wanted to hug him in return.

Finally he pulled away, saying, "I should get you back home."

I nodded.

He motioned for me to climb the trail first, which I did, and he followed behind until we came out under the willow. Then we walked side by side, holding hands.

"There are so many things I want to know about you," he said. "Starting with . . . when's your birthday?"

"July thirty-first."

"Just ten days from now. . . ." He paused, then asked, "And your favorite color?"

"The underside of a willow leaf," I answered.

"Ach," he said. "A pale, shimmery green."

I nodded.

"Favorite story?" he asked.

"That's a hard one . . . I'd say 'Baby Moses.' I love his sister's faith."

"I like that one too," he said. "Mine's 'Jonathan and David.' "

"But Jonathan dies."

"Jah." His voice was serious. "But he was a faithful friend." I imagined that was something that came easily to this Jonathan too. He paused for a moment and then asked, "Favorite food?"

I laughed. "Anything I don't have to cook."

It took him a moment to think on that. "Ach, sounds as if that doesn't happen often."

I nodded.

He continued. "Favorite day of the year?"

"The first snow—when everything is new."

"Jah, I like that too," he said. "And that night, especially if the stars are out, I go for a long walk. There's nothing as enchanting in all the world." He stopped. "But my favorite day of this year is today."

I turned my head.

"The day I met you," he whispered.

He was silent for a moment, gazing into my eyes. Then he spoke at a normal volume. "I'd get baptized for you in a heartbeat. And join the church in two."

"Ach, don't say that." Many Youngie made

those decisions based on wanting to get married. But we'd only just met.

"Sure, I'd do it first for God, but you'd be the second reason."

Unsure of what to say, I didn't answer, but the truth was, I felt the same.

Once we reached the pasture, Jonathan led me toward the lane, away from the house. "Just a minute more," he said.

But as he spoke lights from a car appeared coming up the lane.

"It's Timothy," I said. "We should wait until he goes in."

We stepped behind a poplar along the lane, into the north field.

Jonathan pulled me up against the back of the tree. "How about a kiss?" he teased.

I shook my head. I knew it was too soon.

"A holy kiss, then." His eyes danced, as they had before.

I smiled, nodded, and turned my cheek to him.

He kissed it tenderly, his lips soft against my skin. A jolt surged through me.

As he leaned back, the lights from the Bronco passed by. I turned toward them.

Timothy sat in the passenger seat; I craned my neck to see who was driving.

"Danny!" He didn't have a license, not even a permit. Too late, I noticed Timothy's window was down. I darted back behind the tree.

I suspected that Timothy reached his foot over and stomped on the brake by the screech from Danny. I heard the yank of the emergency brake next, and then Timothy stumbled from his Bronco.

He slurred his words. "Ach, Addie, who're you with? Phillip?"

Jonathan started toward the lane.

"Don't," I pled.

He stepped out from behind the tree anyway. Calmly, he said, "She's with me."

The other door opened, and Danny turned off the lights of the Bronco and climbed out, leaving the engine running. "Come on, Timothy. Let's go." Danny, bright-eyed and alert, stayed on the other side of the vehicle.

"Go? There's a Mosier on our property. With our Schwester."

I exhaled and stepped out from the trees too. "Jonathan was on his way home."

"Hiding behind a bunch of trees like a sissy isn't 'on his way home.' "

"Come on, Timothy." I stepped forward and took his arm, turning my head away from the boozy smell of him, which was worse even than the collection of beer cans behind the barn. "We can talk about this in the morning."

He yanked away from me toward Jonathan, his movements jerky. "I want to talk about it now." My brother's cloudy eyes alarmed me.

Jonathan took off his hat and held it over his chest. "I care about Addie," he said. "A lot. I'll do anything I can to make the rift between our families end."

Timothy harrumphed, turned toward the house, and pointed his finger. But then he gasped.

Coming toward us was a figure wearing white, appearing as an apparition. Timothy stepped backward. I shook my head. It moved too quickly to be Mutter. It had to be Aenti Nell.

But I wasn't about to tell Timothy that—not when he was trembling at my side.

A moment later she gave herself away as she called out, "Addie!" As she got closer, it was obvious she was wearing her nightgown with a thin white blanket wrapped around her. "Are you out here?"

"Go," I said to Jonathan. "Now!"

He hesitated. By his response to Timothy, I knew he wasn't afraid of my family. I hoped he knew he'd be doing me a favor to leave though, before the situation became unmanageable.

"Are you sure?" He looked from me to Aenti Nell, who had stopped in the middle of the lane.

"Positive."

"Tomorrow, then?"

"Jah."

"Good night. A thousand times good night." He slipped away.

Timothy shook his head. "He's a coward."

"You're a fool," I retorted.

I turned to Danny and said, "Park the Bronco."

He got back in the vehicle and turned on the lights—fully illuminating our aunt, who jerked her head to the side in response to the bright beams—and drove off toward the barn.

"Why did you take him with you again?" I asked Timothy.

"He wanted to go."

"More likely you wanted someone to drive you home." I wanted to shove him. I was sure he'd fall over.

"Addie!" Aenti Nell called out again. "Get back in the house. You've been out long enough."

I marched toward her with Timothy weaving at my side.

"Where's Phillip?" she asked.

I shrugged.

Timothy snorted but then stumbled. I caught his arm and squeezed hard as I held him up, straining against his weight, deciding I didn't want him to fall after all. If he hurt himself, it would be up to me to nurse him. He found his footing and began to laugh.

Aenti Nell's face turned sour. "Off to bed with all of you." She marched back toward the house, the corners of the blanket streaming out behind her, leading the way.

I struggled along with Timothy until Danny

reached us. "I didn't know you'd gone out," I said to him.

"Ditto." He took Timothy's other arm and we dragged him across the lawn and up the back steps and into the kitchen. Aenti Nell must have gone straight to bed.

"I'll take him the rest of the way," Danny said.

"Denki." I stopped at the sink for a glass of water. As I drank, a wisp of a cloud floated in front of the moon. Then an owl hooted again. I peered out the window. Jonathan stood in the middle of the courtyard, blowing a kiss.

I blew a kiss back and then whispered, "Good night. A thousand times good night." Had I only just met him? Had it only been one day?

By the time I reached my room, Timothy and Danny were bumping around in theirs. I relit my lamp and ran my hand over the smooth surface of Mutter's hope chest.

I'd asked for one for my thirteenth birthday—the only thing I'd ever requested—and when Daed hauled her old hope chest into my room, I'd said I didn't want it.

It was the only time I remember voicing any disappointment, and the way Mutter reacted ensured I'd never do it again. She'd lambasted me about my selfishness for weeks. Joe-Joe was just over a year. Mutter was still exhausted. How dare I expect her and Daed to shop for me at such a time?

I'd kept completely quiet after that about anything I wanted. I'd tried my hardest to be the daughter without any needs or wants. I'd done my best not to add an ounce of extra stress to my parents' lives—until tonight.

A light knock sounded on my door. "Addie?" Danny's voice barely carried through the wood.

I jerked open the door.

Danny stood with his shirt untucked and his suspenders hanging to his knees. He ran his hand through his straw-colored hair as he spoke. "Timothy says he won't tell if you don't."

"It's a deal—as long as he doesn't make you drive him home again."

Danny shrugged. "It's better than him driving home."

"What if you'd been stopped?"

"I wasn't." He stifled a yawn.

We'd both be up in another four hours. "Get to bed."

I closed the door and stepped to my French doors. Jonathan was walking across the pasture toward a shortcut through the fields, his head tipped toward the night sky. I imagined him whistling as he walked, soaking in the moonlight, enjoying the night air.

How I wished I were at his side.

Chapter 6

ͷ

Mutter came into the kitchen earlier than usual, a smile on her face, and handed me a list of chores for the day. I skimmed it. They were all tasks I'd planned to do anyway.

"Get me a cup of coffee, would you?" She settled into her chair.

I poured cream first, then the coffee, and put the cup on the table in front of her.

She glanced toward the sewing room. "Is Nell up?"

"Not yet," I answered. "But she should be soon." I sounded as cheery as I felt. Even though I'd barely slept, I'd never felt better.

Mutter caught me smiling a moment later.

"Happy?" She gazed at me over the rim of her coffee cup, her eyes unusually bright.

"Jah," I answered.

"Do tell." Her eyes sparkled.

I shrugged. "Maybe later." I turned back to the hash browns and increased the heat, hoping Mutter wouldn't ask any more questions. She'd be sorely disappointed if she did.

Danny came in first from the milking, bringing in our full bucket, followed by Billy.

"Go wake up Joe-Joe," I said to him. "Tell him we're about ready to eat." I flipped the hash browns again and pulled the French toast and slices of ham from the oven, where they'd been warming.

Daed clomped into the kitchen next. "Where's Timothy?" he asked, looking straight at me.

I shrugged. "I thought he was out with you."

Daed stomped through the kitchen. A moment later he bellowed up the stairs, "Timothy!" It was becoming a familiar pattern. "Get down here right now!"

I stepped to the archway to the living room as the pitter-patter of little feet descended the stairs. Knowing it was the little boys, I stepped forward and motioned to them to come to me. They scurried around Daed, and Joe-Joe clutched my skirt as he reached me.

Daed yelled up the stairs again.

"Go sit down," I whispered.

Daed shouted for Timothy a third time. Again there was the sound of steps on the staircase. This time it was Aenti Nell, adjusting her kerchief. She shot Daed an annoyed look and shuffled past him.

"Timothy!" Daed boomed.

The ceiling shook above the living room. Perhaps Timothy had fallen out of bed. Both Daed and I looked upward. The ceiling shook again as Timothy stomped across his floor. Then there was a hop, probably as he pulled on his pants. A moment later he started down the stairs. In a few moments he appeared, buttoning his shirt.

"You overslept," Daed boomed. "Again. We were depending on your help."

Timothy didn't answer.

"Son." Daed blocked the bottom of the stairs. "Were you out drinking last night?"

"Not that I remember."

Daed let him pass. I rolled my eyes, which Timothy must have seen because he glanced back at Daed and said, "Why don't you ask Addie what she was up to last night?"

I hurried into the kitchen to dish up breakfast as Daed answered, "No need."

Timothy snorted.

"What's that supposed to mean?" Daed followed Timothy to the table as I extinguished the heat under the hash browns.

"Ask Addie."

I turned around and sent Timothy a scathing look. At the table, Danny shook his head, a look of disgust on his freckled face.

"Jah, she's not the saint you all think she is." Timothy took his place at the far end, next to Mutter, who still had a smile lingering on her face.

"Ach, Timothy," she said. "She's courting. You

don't know what that's like yet—but we're fine with her being with Phillip. They need to get acquainted before they marry."

I directed my attention back to the hash browns, flinging them onto a platter with the spatula, frowning at the blackened mess.

Timothy snorted again.

I flipped the hash browns over so the burnt part wasn't visible.

Daed poured himself a cup of coffee. "What exactly are you saying, son?"

I put the platter on the table and sat next to Joe-Joe.

"Ask Addie." Timothy leaned back in his chair, his arms crossed, his foul breath so bad I could smell it across the table. It was ten times worse than the night before.

Daed sat in his chair. "What's your brother talking about?"

I froze.

"Addie?" Mutter leaned forward.

"You were out last night, jah?" Daed scooted his chair forward.

I nodded.

"With Phillip, jah?" Mutter's voice rang high.

I shook my head as the hollow feeling returned.

"Who with?" Mutter's tone fell.

Paralyzed, I struggled between being the person my parents wanted me to be and the girl I felt so keenly last night when I was with Jonathan, the Addie I wanted to be. My hands shook in my lap, and I couldn't meet my mother's eyes.

Joe-Joe scooted onto his knees, turning his face up to mine. "Jonathan. Right? I hope so because I really like him." He looked from Mutter to Daed. "Billy said he gave us each a bow when I—"

Mutter interrupted him. "Addie!" She struggled to her feet, her hands on the table, her cheeks red. "How could you?"

Joe-Joe reached over and put his chubby hand on mine, whispering, "Why is she mad?"

I squeezed my youngest brother's hand, trying to communicate that he'd done nothing wrong, as Daed put his face into his hands and dug his thumbs into his beard.

Aenti Nell stood and said, "Now, now. Everyone calm down."

I appreciated her gesture, but I didn't think my parents even heard her.

I nodded at my Aenti, took a deep breath, and then found my voice, still holding on to Joe-Joe's hand. "Jonathan is good and kind." I tried my best to stay calm. "And he wants the grudge between our families to end. So do I. Even though we don't even know—"

"That's not the point. He's not Phillip." Daed was on his feet now, towering over the table.

"Exactly," I answered.

"Go to your room." Mutter pressed her hands

hard against the wood. "Right now. Don't come down until we tell you to."

I glanced at Daed. I'd never been sent to my room in all my life, for heaven's sake, and here I was nearly nineteen.

Daed nodded. "Do as your mother says."

I let go of Joe-Joe's hand, pushed back my chair, locked my eyes on Timothy, and left the table.

Billy grabbed for me as I passed by. "I'll go with you," he said.

"No, stay here."

Joe-Joe whimpered.

"Quit your crying!" Daed barked.

Billy scampered around the table and put his arm around our youngest brother, allowing me to flee.

As I reached the living room Daed said, his voice still gruff, "Let's pray."

The smell of breakfast teased me, and I could hear shrill voices and the scrape of a chair against the wooden floor below, probably Aenti Nell as she got up and down to refill the platters.

I sank down onto my bed. The morning breeze floating in through the open French doors brushed against my face, causing me to shiver.

I'd been the compliant child all these years, doing everything my parents asked. No wonder they expected me to marry Phillip without questioning them. But now I knew I couldn't. I would have never dreamed it possible to come to love someone in one day, but I had. I loved Jonathan.

I'd always been so practical. So obedient. So pragmatic. It wasn't like me, I knew, to stand up to my father. Or fall in *Lieb* in a day.

No wonder my parents didn't know how to react.

Perhaps if I explained how I felt to them, told them I'd been wrong to go along with the idea of courting Phillip when I wasn't sure, all along, if I loved him.

There was a shout followed by Daed yelling, "Joe-Joe!"

Then the scraping of more chairs against the floor. My guess was my youngest brother had toppled over his milk.

I could make out muffled sobs, then Mutter's sharp response of "Stop that. Now."

I cringed.

Aenti Nell's soothing tones came next. I held my breath. A few minutes later footsteps fell across the kitchen floor and then the back door slammed. I stepped to the French doors and peered through a pane. Daed marched across the lawn to the barn, his shoulders hunched and his stride long. A moment later Danny followed, but as soon as he reached the middle of the yard he turned toward my bedroom and held up his hand, as if in despair.

That was my dependable brother—loyal as possible under the circumstances.

I leaned forward and mouthed, "Things will work out." I wasn't sure if he could read my lips or not but he nodded his head and headed toward the barn.

Retreating to my bed, I couldn't imagine it would be long until Mutter sent Aenti Nell up to retrieve me. The kitchen needed cleaning. And I had to do the laundry, a chore that no one but me tackled anymore. I should have already put the work clothes to soak, but I hadn't gotten it done before breakfast. If it didn't get started soon, the chore would drag on until suppertime.

I needed to finish it all today because Mutter, Aenti Nell, and I planned to go to a frolic at Aenti Pauline's the next day to finish a quilt she would sell at a local shop. Her quilts were beautiful, although not quite as amazing as Aenti Nell's. Still she earned a fair amount of money for them. Being a Mamm didn't leave her a lot of time for handwork though, so having help made all the difference for her. My maternal grandmother, who lived in the *Dawdi Haus* behind Aenti Pauline's, would be home from her visiting and would be there too. We were taking sticky buns. Surely Mutter would release me to make those.

Once they let me out of my room, I'd humble myself and ask their forgiveness for going behind their backs. I'd tell them I felt bad about the whole thing with Phillip, that all along I wasn't sure he was the right one but I'd hoped I'd come to love him, but now I knew I never would.

I'd tell them I had feelings for Jonathan and that he and I both, more than anything, wanted the grudge between our families to end. But for that to happen we needed to know what it was all about. Maybe Aenti Nell could help me make Mutter and Daed understand. Surely my parents wanted what was best for me.

My stomach growled. I stretched out on my bed, wishing I'd eaten a piece of ham while I was cooking.

Closing my eyes, I heard the creak of the stairs.

A moment later there was a loud knock.

"Who is it?" I rose to a sitting position, expecting Aenti Nell.

Timothy's diabolical laugh came through the door. "Learned your lesson?" He snorted. "You'll never be allowed to court a Mosier. They'll have you married off to Phillip before Christmas."

My head landed back on my pillow as his footsteps fell back down the hall. A few minutes later the back door slammed again.

I must have dozed, because I awoke to Joe-Joe and Billy's voices outside my door.

"Mamm said not to," Billy said.

My doorknob turned.

"But I want to," Joe-Joe answered.

Billy must have pulled Joe-Joe's hand away. "Come on," Billy said. "She'll be out later. When she's ready to do a better job listening to Daed."

My heart broke a little bit at Billy parroting what Mutter, most likely, had said.

"Addie," Joe-Joe wailed.

Billy's voice was firm. "Come on!" Clearly he had taken charge.

After a scuffle across the wood floor, they left too.

It wasn't until midmorning that Aenti Nell opened my door, waking me again. "Come on," she said. "I need help or I'm never going to get the wash done."

"Did Mutter send you?"

"Jah," she answered. "Your Daed said it was all right."

"Will they listen to me?"

"Ach, Addie. Don't bother. There's no way this grudge is going to end by you pleading with them. We'll have to figure out another way."

I scrambled to my feet. "Jah, about that grudge. Tell me how it started."

"Later." She sashayed back out the door, the back of her kerchief bobbing up and down. "Come on. I'm buried in your work, and your Mamm's done nothing but cry all morning."

I flooded the wringer washer in the basement. Then after getting the whites started, I accidently splashed bleach on a good dress of Mutter's, one that still fit. And by the time I had the first load on the line, it was past time to start scrubbing the potatoes for lunch.

We ended up eating late, which didn't escape Daed's notice. "Ach, Addie," he said, "I thought pigs would fly before you'd be tardy with a meal."

I kept my face stoic and unresponsive, but inside I frowned. He couldn't send me to my room for the morning *and* expect me to get my work done.

The meat was dry, the potatoes undercooked, and I'd forgotten to add butter to the green beans, the way Daed liked them, but thankfully, he didn't say another word.

Near midafternoon, I took the whites from the line, folding each item and dropping it in the basket as I did, putting off going back into the house as long as I could. I breathed in the warmth of the sun and the sharpness of the bleach still lingering on the fabric, thinking of Jonathan as I did. Despite the frustration of the morning, remembering the night before made me smile.

I turned toward the willow tree and thought of Jonathan kissing my cheek. Holding a worn pillowcase in my hand, the last item off the line, I pulled it to my face, pressing the crisp fabric against my skin. I felt freshly laundered too as an odd mixture of both hope and satisfaction, as real as the lingering scent of bleach, filled my soul.

Jonathan and I were meant to be together.

A pinecone landed in the laundry basket, startling me.

"Daydreaming?" Timothy stood between me and the barn.

I folded the pillowcase, even though it needed to be ironed, and dropped it in the basket. "No," I retorted. "I'm working. How about you?" I didn't wait for him to respond but, leaving the pinecone, picked up the basket and marched to the house.

Mutter managed to iron the small items at the table, while I manned the board and finished up the sheets. She cried a little more, including over her dress I'd ruined.

After I put everything away, Mutter sat in the living room, her feet up on the couch. I'd asked her several times to sort through the stack of *Budget*s, the national Plain newspaper, and the back issues of *The Connection* magazine we subscribed to and that she tended to save, but since she hadn't for the last couple of months, not even when tidying up for the barbecue, I doubted she would today.

Aenti Nell said she planned to quilt for an hour or so, and I followed her into the sewing room, asking her to tell me the story about the grudge. "In a minute," she said. "First let me give you something to work on."

It wasn't until she'd given me the pieces of a block to stitch together that I remembered the money Jonathan had given me. I pulled it out of my apron and extended it to her. "Here," I said. "Don't tell Timothy, but Jonathan gave me back the money I paid him for the mantel."

She cocked her head to the side, the back of her kerchief dangling at an odd angle. "Why?"

"He said he fixed it."

She held up her hand. "Well, well," she said. "He's a gentleman. I'm not surprised."

"Take it," I said.

"No, you keep it. Those were old potholders. I probably wouldn't have sold them anyway."

I gave her a questioning look.

She shrugged. "Think of it as my gift to you in these trying times." Her mouth turned downward.

She settled into her chair and picked up another stack of pieces.

"Tell me," I said.

She glanced toward the open door and lowered her voice. "They want you to marry Phillip more than anything else in the world right now."

"You were going to tell me about the grudge."

"I didn't say that."

"You said 'later.' "

Maybe I needed to warm her up to the idea. I told her my intention to humble myself and apologize to Mutter and Daed and then explain my feelings for Jonathan.

"I can't marry Phillip." My voice was firm.

"I know," she said, her voice tender. "But don't tell your parents that yet. I told them this morning that I thought you'd get over Jonathan."

I began to shake my head as I opened my mouth to speak.

She held up her finger to shush me. "I said he's not your type. That your feelings won't last more than another day or so."

I gasped, "That's not true."

She nodded. "I know."

"Then why did you say it?"

"To slow them down. To free you from your room. To give you more time to figure all this out. So don't go telling them how you really feel about Phillip—not yet."

I was surprised she would deceive my parents for me but grateful that she'd intervened. I leaned forward. "Will you help me?"

"I don't know if there's much I can do. . . ."

"You can start by telling me what the feud is all about."

"Feud." She tilted her head. "That's a strong word."

"And accurate."

She sighed and then stood and closed the door. "Just in case your Mamm's hearing is better than I think."

When she sat back down she turned her chair toward me. "Don't tell your Mamm or your Dat what I'm going to tell you."

I nodded in agreement. I wasn't in the habit of talking deeply with my parents. I couldn't imagine not being able to keep Aenti Nell's secret.

She took a deep breath, as if to build her courage, and then said, "When your Mamm was your age she courted Jonathan's father—Dirk."

I gasped.

She took a raggedy breath. "Actually, there's a story before that but I'm not going to share it . . . and one after it."

"Aenti Nell?" I said, puzzled even more.

She ignored me. "The families back then were from the same district, and the households were very much alike. Both full of fun and laughter. The children were well disciplined. The grown-ups, hard workers." She paused. "And Dirk and your Dat were the very best of friends, straight from the cradle."

I could scarcely believe what she was saying. "Oh . . . goodness."

"Exactly. And they stayed that way, day in and day out. Dirk is the one who gave your Dat the nickname Cap. And it stuck."

My father's given name was David, but I'd never heard anyone call him that.

"We all thought your Mamm and Dirk would marry—but then they quit courting. Laurel wouldn't tell us why. A few people speculated but no one seemed to know for sure." Aenti Nell stopped for a moment and rubbed her temple.

"Then Cap started taking Laurel home from singings."

"Oh . . . and that made Dirk mad?"

Aenti Nell shook her head. "No, that was the funny thing. Dirk seemed fine with it. He and Cap stayed best friends. All seemed well."

"So what happened?"

"Laurel started receiving anonymous letters. The first one said that Cap was trouble and she shouldn't be courting him. The second said she'd be miserable if she married him. They went on and on, probably five at least. Finally she showed Cap. He was certain the handwriting was Dirk's."

"Was it?"

"It seems so. Everyone thought so. But he denied it." Her eyes drifted toward the window.

I waited for her to continue.

Finally she did. "Dirk had quite the temper, and he exploded one night after a party." She paused again.

"Were you there?"

"Jah." She sighed.

"What happened?"

"Dirk said horrible things to your Mamm and then left for Big Valley the next day. He came back a couple of times but didn't have any further contact with your parents. He didn't come to their wedding. He didn't try to patch things up with your Daed."

"When did he marry?"

"Several years after your parents did. Mary is her name." She sat up a little straighter. "But that's neither here nor there. What's important is what Dirk said after Cap confronted him at the party."

"Which was?"

"That your mother was a she-devil and would destroy the entire community if she wasn't stopped. He said the worst year of his life was when he was courting her and that your father was a bigger fool than he'd ever suspected and would live in misery if he married her. Then Dirk stormed off."

I had to agree that Mutter was a bit of a manipulator, but what Dirk said seemed over-the-top harsh. No wonder Mutter and Daed were angry with him.

"The thing was," Aenti Nell said, "his words seemed to draw your Mamm and Daed even closer. They married three months later."

I wrinkled my nose. "And that started the problem between the two families?"

"Jah. Not between the Mosiers and the Cramers so much, not back then. Old man Mosier and your Dat's parents all continued on with their friendship, which made your parents angry. But my parents, well, my mother in particular, was very offended and couldn't let it go."

I could see that. My grandmother, Gladys Yoder, did tend to hold a grudge, and probably without intending to, encouraged her daughters to also. Although Aenti Nell didn't seem to. Not even against the Mosiers.

"Then your Dat's father died and then his mother too, and Dirk's Dat became more lost in his own world."

I wasn't as concerned about the oldest generation. "Does Mutter still have the letters?"

Aenti Nell blanched. "I wouldn't think so. I can't think of why she would have kept them."

I raised my eyebrows. "She keeps everything."

"She wouldn't have kept those." Nell shook her head as she spoke.

I wasn't so sure.

"She wouldn't need to. She let the memory of them fester all these years," Aenti Nell added. "That's what's kept the whole thing going."

"But Onkel Bob seemed to want to patch things—he invited our family and Mervin and Martin's family to dinner—remember? Just over a year ago?" Aenti Nell hadn't gone.

"Jah, Bob and the twins' Dat, Amos, are friends. And the twins worked for Bob. Did your Mamm and Dat behave themselves that day?"

I nodded.

"Well, Amos is quite a bit older than Dirk. And he was never as hotheaded. But now Timothy's all worked up and only making things worse."

I sat forward in my chair. I needed to get the dough started for the sticky buns for the next day's frolic. But I had one more question first. "What should we do?"

"Don't try to meet him tonight."

I swallowed hard, not sure I could do that.

"Addie, listen to me. Your parents will know if you go out. And they won't assume it's with Phillip. I'll send Danny on a buggy ride with a message—in a sealed envelope—over to the Mosiers, telling Jonathan not to come."

"If you think it's for the best . . ." Danny was the only one we could trust.

Aenti Nell gazed beyond me again, out the window. "And then how about if I visit Jonathan's grandfather before the frolic tomorrow? Bring up the relationship he had with your grand-father? See if he can talk to Dirk?"

"All right." I wasn't sure if it would help or not, but I didn't see how it could hurt.

Foolish me.

Chapter 7

ᔕᕴ

Aenti Pauline's kitchen was the biggest in the county, I was sure. New cabinets and counters lined the room, and the white linoleum floor sparkled in the morning light coming through the wall of windows at the far end. The quilting frame stood in the center, with all of us women seated around it in perfectly matched chairs. My Onkel had done quite well for himself and his family raising horses.

My cousins had pushed the table to the end of the room. The sticky buns I'd made and a bowl of blueberries were set out for a morning snack. A pot of coffee simmered on the stove.

Mammi Gladys, the matriarch of my Mutter's clan, was taking a break for the moment, a cup in her hand, watching the rest of us. She wore a black dress and apron. She'd always been tiny, but lately she seemed to be shrinking. However, she was one of those small women whose presence grew more powerful with every year. The older I grew, the more I realized the influence she carried over her daughters.

She had no sons.

And those daughters all had only daughters, except for Aenti Nell, who had never married, and my Mutter. Ours was the only "boy" family.

Mutter, Aenti Pauline, and Aenti Nell all lived in Lancaster County. My two other Aentis had both married and moved away, one to Ohio and the other to Indiana.

My grandfather had died two years before, and my grandmother still dressed in mourning attire, which seemed oppressively hot, especially on a mid-July day that promised to be a scorcher.

Once I learned English, I thought it odd my grandmother's name was Gladys. She was anything but glad. Quite the opposite, in fact.

"Where's Nell?" she asked, as if just realizing she was missing.

"Running an errand," Mutter answered. "She'll be here soon."

She was going to the store to buy some thread, but she also planned to stop by Old Man Mosier's place. Of course, Mutter didn't know that.

"Where's Hannah?" my mother asked.

Aenti Pauline shifted in her chair. "Resting."

"So early in the morning?" Mutter's head shot up from her stitching. "What's the matter with her?"

"She hasn't been sleeping well," Pauline answered. "She'll be down soon."

My grandmother frowned and then said, "Well,

if she didn't eat so much she wouldn't be so tired. Five pancakes for breakfast would put anyone to sleep."

Aenti Pauline didn't respond.

My mother and her Schwesters had grown up with their mother talking about their weight. Their father had been on the plump side, and they all took after him, my mother even more so than the rest. He'd been a jolly man, though, and used to humor my grandmother. Now that he was gone, she seemed to be growing more sour by the day.

Generally, we Amish women don't worry about our weight or how we look, at least not compared to Englisch women. We dress the same. Wear our hair the same. Cover our heads. We don't have to worry about makeup and beauty products. We don't read magazines with fashion models or watch TV or movies, so we don't compare ourselves to others the way I've heard Englisch women do. But in Mutter's family, because of pressure from their mother, there was more of an awareness of first being a little plump, then heavy, and then downright overweight.

Aenti Nell stayed plump, probably because she never had the additional stress to her body of having babies. And Aenti Pauline ended up heavy. But Mutter was definitely overweight—and knew it.

Now it seemed Mammi Gladys was starting in on Hannah.

Thanks to Daed's side of the family, I wasn't plump at all. It wasn't that I was skinny, but I was lean and fit. It wasn't because of how much I did or didn't eat though. It was just the way I was made.

My grandmother turned to me with the hint of a smile on her face.

It surprised me and I smiled in return.

"I heard you're sweet on Phillip Eicher," she said.

My smile vanished. Besides feeling free to speak about people's weight, she also had no problem being blunt concerning other topics.

I blushed.

"Good family, that one. You couldn't do better."

"Jah," Aenti Pauline said. "I hope my girls will follow your example." She had seven daughters—from Hannah, the oldest at nineteen, to Maggie, the two-year-old. Deborah—who was four years younger than Hannah because Aenti Pauline had lost a set of twin boys before her and then had some other problems—was next oldest, then Sarah, who was almost thirteen, Katie, Lydia, and Cara. "I hope," Aenti Pauline continued, "that they'll do as well as Phillip Eicher."

"Well, they won't," Mammi Gladys said, "if you don't rein Hannah in now." She blinked hard as her eyes locked on my Aenti's. "They'll all follow her example."

"Now, don't start on that," Aenti Pauline said.

155

"You've said your piece—more than once." She pushed back her chair and stood. It was obvious the subject had been discussed before.

"Where are you going?" Mammi Gladys asked.

"To check on the little girls." They were jumping on the trampoline out in the side yard with Joe-Joe. Billy had stayed home to help Daed.

Mammi Gladys said, "Have Sarah check."

Both Deborah and Sarah had joined us for the quilting frolic, but so far they hadn't said a word. They were both ones to listen and take everything in—and were so quiet that the older women usually forgot they were around. At the mention of her name, Sarah's head popped up and the look on her face was one of concern, as if she were in trouble.

"Go," our grandmother said to her.

"No," Aenti Pauline said. "I'm doing it."

As Aenti Pauline headed for the back door she shot my Mutter a desperate look. I wondered if she expected sympathy. I was pretty sure, inside, Mutter was gloating. It was as if she'd totally forgotten my declaration about Jonathan the day before. Mutter's powers of denial, a term I'd learned from Cate, were incredible. That, or Aenti Nell must have done a convincing job assuring Mutter and Daed that in no time I'd lose interest in Jonathan.

Mammi Gladys must have sensed Mutter's

smugness. "How are those boys of yours doing?" I did not want the conversation to turn to my Bruders.

"Joe-Joe's outside with the girls."

"I mean your older ones. Why didn't you tell me Samuel and George moved into a trailer?" Mammi Gladys kept stitching, her eyes on the quilt as she spoke. "I heard it from Hannah's friend Molly." I could imagine how badly that encounter embarrassed my grandmother.

Before Mutter answered, Aenti Pauline came through the back door with little barefoot Maggie high on her hip. My youngest cousin wore a miniature apron, a *Schatzlin*, and a *Kapplin*. Underneath, her blond hair, too fine to stay in a bun, was in two thin braids. Her chubby hands rested on Aenti Pauline's shoulders. My Mutter said Aenti Pauline, because she'd lost the set of twins and then wasn't sure she'd ever have more children, babied her girls, which wasn't the Amish way. Children were valued but never idolized. I thought Mutter was wrong, but still, Aenti Pauline looked at little Maggie as if she was a miracle, perhaps one who could, at least at this moment, do no wrong.

"Laurel," Mammi Gladys said. "I asked about Samuel and George."

Mutter sighed. "They're fine. They're both working." Mutter shrugged. "There's nothing to tell." I knew she was trying to put up a good front.

Aenti Pauline, who was usually sweet, said, snidely, "Offspring reflect their parents, jah? Your boys are taking after Cap's wild ways."

Mutter's voice fell in volume. "You're carrying this one awfully low. Perhaps he'll be a boy. And then you'll have to eat your words." The story was that Aenti Pauline's husband, Onkel Owen, had quite a running around time too.

Aenti Pauline looked as if she'd been struck. I'd had no idea she was expecting another Bobli, and by the look on Deborah and Sarah's faces, they didn't either.

Pauline didn't say another word and headed down the hall with Maggie. But Mutter had successfully deflected the topic from her husband and sons, and a slight smile spread over her face as she concentrated on her stitches.

Seconds later, however, Mammi Gladys tenaciously took up the topic again. "Speaking of the father of your unruly sons, I heard Cap's old friend Dirk Mosier is back."

At the mention of Jonathan's father, I glanced at Mammi Gladys out of the corner of my eye, trying my best to be inconspicuous.

"I wouldn't know," Mutter said.

"Oh? Well, does Nell know?"

I inhaled sharply. What did Aenti Nell have to do with Dirk Mosier?

"Dirk is married, remember? For the last twenty or so years."

"Of course I remember," Mammi Gladys said. "I was just wondering what Nell's reaction was to him moving back to the old Mosier place."

"Why don't you ask her?" Mutter said.

My grandmother snorted, sounding a lot like Timothy.

Mutter didn't respond, and the rest of us stayed quiet until Hannah entered the room and broke the silence. A strand of hair she hadn't bothered to secure fell against her face, and her steps were slow, as if she had to work at keeping her balance.

"It's about time," Mammi Gladys said.

My Mutter surprised me by considerately asking, "How are you feeling, Hannah?" Mutter, with her own problems with insomnia, actually appeared somewhat sympathetic to my cousin's plight.

"Fine." Hannah settled into the empty chair beside me.

I patted her arm and handed her a needle that had already been threaded. She took it from me, holding it in midair for a moment before plunging it into the penciled-in outline on the fabric.

Aenti Pauline came back into the kitchen from down the hall, still carrying her littlest one. "Deborah, take Maggie back outside."

Deborah responded straightaway, standing and taking the child in her arms.

After they left, Aenti Nell arrived. She was wearing her best blue dress and a Kapp, which I didn't see her in much since around the house she wore her old dresses and kerchiefs. Her face was flushed and her eyes bright. Her dimples flashed when she saw me.

I couldn't help but smile back and hope I'd soon know what she'd found out at the Mosier place. I pulled up another chair for her, in between Hannah and me, just in case Aenti would be able to talk, but she didn't try, which was probably wise.

The morning progressed uneventfully, and I did my best to concentrate on my stitching, half listening to the others. Mammi Gladys gossiped about their new neighbors, an Amish couple with ten children between the ages of twenty-two and ten. They'd moved to Lancaster County from Canada.

"Those kids of theirs are hog-wild," she said. "The oldest boy came home with a car yesterday. I could hear the mother screeching at him clear over in our backyard."

Mutter didn't respond, and Mammi Gladys kept talking.

"Joseph and I wouldn't allow it. I don't know what's wrong with parents these days that they just don't say no."

Some people might have intervened at this point, telling Mammi Gladys to be more considerate of my mother. The truth was, because Mammi Gladys never had a boy, she couldn't

160

know what it was like to raise a bushel of them. Sure, sometimes a girl raised Amish bought a car, but it was mostly the boys. The running around years seemed to offer more temptations for Plain boys than girls.

When Aenti Pauline got up to start setting out the lunch things, a wave of relief passed over me. Finally I'd be able to speak to Aenti Nell. But once the sandwiches were made, Pauline sent Hannah and me outside to help the little ones with their lunch.

Afterward, I settled Joe-Joe down on the couch for a nap, and by the time I rejoined the women, Mammi Gladys was ready to go out to her Dawdi Haus to rest. "I expect to hear about your wedding being published soon," she said to me. Then she turned to Hannah. "No matter what your parents allow, you need to stop running around. You hear? That's not the way to find a good husband."

Hannah pursed her lips but didn't say anything. As much as it was the Amish way to have grandparents live with one of their children, I felt sorry for Aenti Pauline's girls to have Mammi Gladys around all the time.

If I didn't have so many Bruders, she might have moved in with us.

Mutter surprised me by standing and saying she thought we should go too. "It's too hot," she said, dabbing at her neck with her apron. "I need to go rest too."

I pretended to concentrate on my work. "Could I keep quilting and go home with Nell?"

"Why?" Mammi Gladys turned toward me from the doorway. "You haven't done more than ten stitches the whole time you've been here."

I did my best not to be defensive. "Well, that's why I should stay. To earn my keep for the day."

Mutter shook her head. "I don't feel well. Come along."

"What about Joe-Joe? He just fell asleep."

Mutter turned toward Nell.

"I'll take him," my Aenti said. "I won't be long." But she seemed so engrossed in her quilting that I wasn't sure she even remembered she needed to talk with me.

In the buggy on the way home, Mutter didn't speak at all. As I drove, she closed her eyes, her head bobbing along to the beat of the horse's hooves, until we heard the clopping of a horse's hooves behind us. She turned on the bench seat.

"It's Phillip," she said.

"Shouldn't he be at work?"

Mutter swatted her hand toward me. "He said he might come by today."

I groaned inwardly, but the expression on my face must have given me away.

"Addie." She shifted on the bench and glared at me. "What has gotten into you?"

I forced my face to slacken, hoping she wouldn't

persist in her questioning. Obviously she hadn't taken me seriously yesterday.

Cate and Pete stood at the edge of their garden, chatting as we passed by. They waved and I waved back, but Mutter stared straight ahead. I let her out near the back door and then went alone to the barn, except that Phillip stayed right behind me instead of parking his buggy at the front of the Haus, where our visitors usually did.

"I'll do the unhitching," he called out. "I think your mother needs some help."

"Denki," I said, shading my eyes. Sure enough Mutter was sitting on the bottom step to the back door, waving at me, her face beet red.

By the time I reached her, she had calmed down some. "I twisted my knee. Get me into the house. I'll rest on the couch for a while. You go on with Phillip."

"Go on where?" I asked as she clutched my arm and I helped her stand. But I knew. He wanted to take me to the farm he hoped to buy. I'd forgotten all about him mentioning it at Molly's market.

Instead of answering me, Mutter winced as we made our way up the steps. Finally she said, "He'll tell you."

The day had grown even worse. But maybe it would get better if I told Phillip how I felt about him—I cared about him, jah, as a person, but I couldn't continue this façade of courting.

But if I told him, he would tell my parents,

who would then grow even more suspicious of Jonathan.

I pushed open the back door and guided my mother inside. It would be best, for now, if I followed Aenti Nell's advice and kept my mouth closed.

After I settled Mutter on the couch, I ventured back outside. Phillip ambled toward me, a grin on his face. "Today's the day."

"Oh?" I shaded my eyes against the burning sun, pretending to have no idea what it might be.

"To tour the farm."

Obviously, since Mutter already knew about this, I didn't need to tell her where I was going. Still, I glanced toward the house.

"We won't be gone long," Phillip said.

Even though we lived in different districts, our farm was on the edge of the boundary and not far from Phillip's home—and his prospective farm.

"Come on," he said, reaching for my hand. Thinking I might as well get the visit over with, I moved quickly down the steps, as if I didn't realize his intention.

By the time I reached his buggy, he was right behind me. Stepping to my side, he extended his hand again. I took it and scampered up, releasing it as soon as I could.

We rode in silence down the lane until another buggy forced Phillip to pull to the side and stop.

It was Aenti Nell with Joe-Joe curled up on the seat beside her. My Aenti slowed her buggy, a surprised expression on her face. "Where are you going?"

"To see my farm," Phillip announced.

She looked straight at me. "I thought we were going to talk."

I nodded. "We are. As soon as I get back."

She pursed her lips, clucked her tongue, and started the horse on its way without saying good-bye.

Phillip didn't comment on her odd behavior and most likely hadn't noticed as he urged his horse along. We didn't talk the rest of the way. I mulled over Aenti Nell's strange response. She appeared as alarmed as I felt about my going off with Phillip.

Already hot and sticky after the ride from Aenti Pauline's, I was now very uncomfortable as sweat trickled down the back of my knees.

Thunderclouds billowed on the horizon. We needed a good fall of rain to break the heat.

Phillip sat statue-still, staring straight ahead. As we passed his farm, his mother waved from the clothesline, where she was adding a tablecloth to a row she'd already pinned. Phillip nodded as we passed by, and I offered up a half wave. At the end of the Eicher's yard, the bishop was pushing an old gas-powered mower. He didn't notice us as we passed.

A minute later we turned down the next lane.

The rambling barn came into view first. Its corrugated tin roof needed repair, the exterior needed a fresh coat of paint, and the silo beside it seemed to lean a little to the left. A small group of dairy cows huddled around the barn door, ready to be milked.

"The herd's included," Phillip said.

The lane curved, and a large Haus came into view. It needed painting and roof work too, but the structure looked sound.

Phillip said, "There's room for lots of kids."

My face grew even warmer than it had been, and the hollow feeling returned at the thought of being intimate with him. I didn't respond.

Phillip stopped the buggy at the hitching rail in front of the house, jumped down, and tied the horse. I jumped down before he could come help me.

"Hello," a voice called out.

I startled.

"Over here." An old woman, stooped and wrinkled, shuffled toward us from the garden, a basket full of greens looped over her arm.

Phillip stepped toward her, offering to take her basket, but she shook her head and held onto it tightly. Phillip turned back toward me. "Addie, this is Elsie Lehman," he said.

She smiled, showing several gaps in her teeth. "So you're going to have a look-see?" she said to me.

I nodded, feeling like a fraud.

"It's a *gut* place," she said. "Although in need of more than we can give it now."

I glanced around.

"A little work will do the trick," Phillip said.

Elsie motioned for us to look around. "Mister's in the barn," she said. "Make sure he knows you're here." She stepped toward the porch. "Before you leave, knock on the door and look around the house too."

After saying hello to Mr. Lehman, Phillip showed me around the barn and the corncrib, and then led the way to the chicken coop, then the pasture, and back to the garden. He talked non-stop as we marched along, spewing his ideas for each structure and site, elaborating on each task he had in mind.

Along the way, I kept encouraging him to keep moving.

"If we're going to look at the house," I finally said, "we should go now. I need to get home and start dinner."

I followed him up the steps to Elsie's back door. After he knocked, she opened it immediately and welcomed us in, where it was even hotter than outside. I knew older people didn't mind the heat as much, but the interior of the house was stifling. The smell of kraut, an odor I didn't usually mind when it wasn't so hot, added to the suffocating atmosphere.

The spotless room was small, and there was only one cabinet. The stove was propane, and I didn't see a refrigerator. A tiny table without any leaves sat in the center of the room.

I took several shallow breaths and leaned against the doorframe, trying to fill the empty feeling growing inside of me.

I could see into the living room from the kitchen. And down the hall.

"There are two bedrooms and a bathroom on the main floor," the woman said. "And two more bedrooms upstairs."

"A bedroom for us," Phillip said. "And three more for our children. We'll build on when we need to." He smiled at me.

"I need to go," I whispered. The air in the room was so thick I could hardly breath.

"But we haven't seen everything."

I pointed to Elsie's clock on the wall. It was a quarter past four. "I need to feed everyone in an hour."

Phillip let out a sigh and said good-bye to Elsie.

"We're looking forward to turning our home over to a young couple," she said, a twinkle in her eye. "I'm sure you'll be as happy here as we've been."

I thanked her and numbly followed Phillip out to the buggy. Getting out of the house brought a little relief but not much. By the time Phillip turned onto the highway, I was damp from a cold sweat, ill at the way I was leading him on.

As we rode home he rambled on again about what a great property it was. He was right, it was a nice place. The sick feeling made its way up to the back of my throat.

"It's what I've always dreamed of," he said. "To have a farm close to my parents'."

I didn't answer.

"And we'll be close to yours too," he said.

I swallowed hard.

He chattered on the rest of the way until we approached a tall man carrying a fishing pole and whistling.

My heart sped. It was Jonathan. I waved as we passed by. And I looked back to see Jonathan smiling and waving back. He motioned toward the creek. I blushed and shook my head. There was no way I could get away before dinner, during dinner, or after dinner. Perhaps after my parents were in bed, but I doubted Jonathan would still be fishing by then.

Phillip snorted. "That's Mervin and Martin's cousin, right?"

I nodded.

"Wasn't he at your place? Playing volleyball?"

I nodded again, wondering if Phillip was playing dumb. Or maybe he hadn't been as aware of Jonathan as I'd been. Perhaps he would have been that possessive of me regardless of whom we'd been playing against.

"He doesn't seem very serious, not like he should be. And I hear he's artistic—too much so. My Dat's concerned he's pushing the *Ordnung* with his carvings." That was the unwritten code that governed every aspect of our lives, from what we wore to the work we did.

"Oh?" I tried to keep my voice even. "Doesn't he sell mostly to the Englisch?"

"Still . . . he shouldn't be overdoing it with the fancy work."

I didn't respond. Phillip began talking about the farm again, how he planned to put in a new fence as soon as he could and then paint the barn. "The other buildings can wait," he said, "for a year or so."

When we reached our house, I told him he could let me off. "There's no need to come in," I said.

"Then I'll see you soon," he answered.

He turned his buggy around as I walked up the steps. I spun around and waved, doing my best to be polite, and then opened the back door, stepping into the kitchen.

When I reached the counter, I slumped against it.

"Are you all right?" Mutter asked from the end of the table.

"I'm not feeling well." I pressed my hand to my side.

"Lovesick?" She laughed.

"No. Dehydrated, I think." I turned on the tap,

retrieved a glass from the cupboard, filled it, and then downed it.

"Where's Aenti Nell?" I asked.

"Resting. Until dinner."

I'd have to wait even longer to find out what she'd learned at the Mosiers'.

I drained another glass of water, deciding as I did to make taco salad for dinner. Daed liked that sort of meal even less than spaghetti—said it wasn't a "man's meal." But it was the best I could come up with. The kitchen was too hot, and I was too tired and distraught to do anything else.

Chapter 8

ᓀᏉᎥ

It wasn't until I had the little boys in bed that Aenti Nell and I finally had a chance to talk. Daed had lit the lamp in the kitchen so Mutter could see as she wrote out one of her lists.

"Come help me with my oven mitts, Addie," Aenti Nell called out from the sewing room. "You can do the price tags."

I left the door open behind me, but we moved our chairs to the far corner of the warm room. All the windows were open, in anticipation of the coming rain. The sky was entirely gray, but still no precipitation had fallen.

Aenti Nell had changed back into a work dress and her kerchief. She handed me a stack of mitts, the price tags, and a ballpoint pen.

"The usual?" I asked.

She nodded.

She sold them at a friend's shop during the summer tourist months and had been charging seven dollars per oven mitt for as long as I could remember.

As I worked, she leaned forward and spoke softly. "So, I talked to Old Man Mosier. He agrees this grudge has gone on long enough. He says he can't even remember what it was all about." Her eyes twinkled. "So I didn't remind him. I told him that you and Jonathan had met. He wanted to know all about you. I said you were friends with Mervin and Martin, but Jonathan was the one who interested you."

I blushed, something I'd been doing a lot lately.

"Anyway, then he got up and told me to follow him. So I did." She paused.

"And?"

"He took me out to the shop, where Jonathan's been working."

"Was he there?"

"No," Aenti Nell said. "He was off on a delivery, but my, oh my."

"What?"

"He's good. I've never seen anything like it."
She leaned away from me for emphasis and
stopped talking.

"Do tell."

She whispered, "Well, it's all a little fancy but
very beautiful."

"Really?"

She nodded. "And good, really good."

"How so?"

"He adds little embellishments. The mantels
have a design carved into them. So do the hope
chests. Mostly flowers but some trees. A few with
stars and moons."

I smiled, remembering his words.

Aenti Nell said, "I can see what you like about
him."

I sighed.

"He's gifted, jah, with his work," she said. "But
it's more than that. He's sensitive. Caring. You can
see that in his work too. And the way he talked
about you."

The pen clattered to the floor. "What?"

"He came back while I was still there." Aenti
Nell's eyebrows shot up, and her eyes brightened
even more.

My heart raced as I picked up the pen. "What
did he say?"

"That he's never met anyone like you. That
you're the kind of girl he's always wanted to
marry. That he can think of nothing but you."

I gasped as I straightened up, clasping the pen.

"Jah." Aenti Nell grinned at me. "You can't marry Phillip. Not when you have someone who adores you the way Jonathan does. To be loved is one thing—to be adored, that's more than most people can ever hope for." She had a faraway look in her eyes.

"What did his grandfather say?"

She focused on me again. "He slapped him on the back and said, 'You are blessed.' "

"Ach." I knew then I would adore his Dawdi. "What about his parents?"

Aenti Nell's face fell. "They've gone back to Big Valley for a few days to settle some things and put their land up for sale. Then they'll return."

"What did the grandfather think their response would be?"

She shook her head. "Not good. He said Dirk will absolutely forbid any sort of relationship. And . . ." She hesitated.

"Go on," I urged.

"Amos . . . Mervin and Martin's—"

"Dat." I knew.

"Jah." She frowned. "He stopped by while I was there. Seems he'd heard about you and Jonathan being together at the barbecue."

I groaned. "Will he say something to Jonathan's parents?"

"I don't know," Aenti Nell said. "He seemed torn as far as what he should do. He said he wanted the grudge to end too, but he's worried about the way Timothy's been treating Mervin and Martin. He wants that to stop before something happens."

No wonder. If I were him I'd be worried too. Timothy was a big problem in all of this. "So what do we do?"

Aenti Nell wrinkled her nose. "Pray. Talk to someone who can give you good advice—both about stopping Timothy and about your relationship with Jonathan."

"Such as?"

"How about your Onkel Bob?"

I pondered that idea a moment. It wasn't as if he'd be able to sway Jonathan's parents, but he might have some influence over my Daed and Amos—and Mervin and Martin. "Did you mention Onkel Bob's name to Jonathan?"

"Jah, I did. He said he'd talk with you about it. He hoped to tonight."

"I saw him headed to the creek to fish this afternoon." I didn't bother explaining I thought he wanted to see me there.

"He said he'd stick around until late, in case you can sneak away."

I couldn't help but smile. I could tell him about the letters his Dat had written my Mutter all those years ago. And we could make a plan to talk with Onkel Bob and ask for his help. The smile stayed on my face until I remembered what Mammi

175

Gladys had said about Nell being interested in Dirk's return.

"I have a question for you," I said.

She stuck a couple of pins in her mouth as she nodded.

"Mammi wondered today if you knew Dirk Mosier had moved back to the old Mosier place."

Aenti Nell wrinkled her nose.

"Why would she ask that?"

She pursed her lips around the pins.

"Aenti Nell?" I whispered.

Her eyes clouded over as she shook her head. Then she turned away from me and pawed through a stack of quilt squares on the table.

"What is it?"

The back of her kerchief shook a little.

"Are you all right?"

Her head nodded up and down as a knock rapped against the kitchen door. In my hopeful state, I imagined it being Jonathan, coming boldly to the house to ask for me.

But then Mutter called out, "Phillip! What are you doing here?"

Aenti Nell turned back toward me, the pins still in her mouth, as a wave of panic seized me. I sat frozen, unable to move. Why had he come back?

"I was hoping to speak with Addie," Phillip said, his voice low and somber.

"Oh goodness, it's late," Mutter replied. Of

course she was only trying to appear to be concerned. She didn't care how late it was.

"I won't be long," Phillip answered.

I thought of Jonathan going down by the creek. Surely he wasn't still there.

"She's in the sewing room." Mutter's chair shifted on the wood floor. "Addie!"

"Go," Aenti Nell whispered. "Say you're tired. He knows you've had a busy day."

She nudged me to my feet, and I managed to make it across the sewing room, out to the kitchen.

"There she is!" Mutter announced, as if Phillip couldn't see.

I stopped in the doorway, feeling as hollow as the sycamore tree my little Bruders played in.

Mutter laughed. "Look, she's so smitten the cat's got her tongue." She tilted her head and smiled at me, then added, "I have to say, my heart still stops at times when I look at Cap, but I'm never at a loss for words."

I cringed. I certainly didn't feel my heart stop around Phillip. Right now it was more like it had crawled out of my chest, leaving an empty spot.

But I hadn't felt my heart stop with Jonathan either. It was as if it had felt content for the first time in my life. Safe. Like it had finally found a home.

"Would you like to go for a walk?" Phillip stood by the back door, his arms crossed.

I couldn't speak.

"Go along before the storm starts," Mutter said. "Go show him the garden. The celery patch in particular."

I willed her to be quiet. Some Amish families planted more celery if they expected a wedding the coming year, because many of our traditional dishes called for the late vegetable. Mother had actually made me plant more in the spring. I should have known she was up to something then.

Phillip opened the door for me, and I slipped through first and down the steps. He caught up though and led the way—but not toward the garden, toward the creek.

"There are mosquitoes down there," I stammered. "How about if we go this way?"

I headed toward the orchard. "Why did you come back?" I asked.

"I'd gone to the gas station to fill up my Dat's can—he ran out earlier."

"Oh?" I still didn't understand.

"I ran into Timothy, gassing up his car." Phillip yanked a blade of tall grass from a clump along the lane.

"Oh." This time it wasn't a question.

"He told me something that I can't believe. That's why I needed to see you." He led the way along the trail. I followed, feeling like a traitor walking the same route as I had with Jonathan just two nights before, wondering now if perhaps Jonathan was below us along the creek, able to hear every word we said.

"Is Timothy trustworthy?" Phillip twirled the long blade of grass through his fingers.

"It depends," I answered.

Phillip gripped the grass, holding it still now. "I don't think he is."

I fell another step behind. "What did he tell you?"

"That you're interested in someone else." He stopped and turned to look at me, his expression full of pain.

"Ach, Phillip," I said, overcome with compassion. "I never meant to . . ." My voice trailed off as I thought of Aenti Nell's warning.

Thunder rumbled in the distance.

"But your Mamm and Daed like me a lot." He dropped the blade of grass.

"Jah, they do. And it's not that I don't like you. But not enough to spend the rest . . ." Again my voice trailed off.

A puzzled expression settled on his face. "What are you saying?"

My brow wrinkled, and I clasped my hands together.

He whispered, "Addie, every couple is bound to have a spat or two."

The word *couple* echoed in my head. This was my fault. I had led him on, as a sort of backup. I'd wanted so badly to get away from home—and please my parents—that I'd allowed myself to use him.

And going to the farm with him when I knew I had no intention of ever marrying him had only compounded things.

"I'm sorry," I said.

"But the other day your Dat said you are as fond of me as I am of you."

"I am fond of you. . . ." That was when it hit me. He didn't love me either. Sure, he was fond of me because he wanted a hardworking wife. But he didn't want me any more than I wanted him. He just hadn't realized it yet.

I took a deep breath as I opened the gate and held it for Phillip. He took it from me, motioning for me to go first, brushing his arm against me. I flinched, realizing I hadn't known until being with Jonathan what I felt for Phillip—nothing. At least nothing that would build a marriage and a life together.

I waited until he hooked the latch to say, "I'm sorry. I didn't mean to be dishonest."

He shook his head. "I think you just have cold feet. That's normal too."

I wrinkled my nose. More thunder crashed, but this time closer.

"This Jonathan has nothing to offer you. No job. No farm. Only a struggling business. You'll come to your senses, jah?" He nodded solemnly.

I took a second deep breath and this time held it for a moment, trying to find the words I needed as more lightning flashed across the darkening sky.

I heard a splash below us in the creek, but Phillip didn't seem to notice it. "It's late," I said, turning back toward the house, tearing ahead of Phillip. I hoped Jonathan had hooked a fish—not fallen into the creek—and was going to head home to beat the storm.

"So all is well, then?" Phillip called out, struggling to keep up with me.

I marched faster, calling over my shoulder, "Not in the way you hope."

He didn't respond for half a second, but as his steps gained on me, said, "But you could, jah? All you need is a little time?"

I shook my head. "No, that's not it at all." Hadn't he heard a word I'd said?

He was beside me now, his face contorting just a little, but then he seemed to rally. "Ach," he said, "don't be so pessimistic."

Feeling as if he'd just knocked the air out of me as I reached the garden, I opened my mouth to respond when Timothy's Bronco came barreling down the lane.

Someone was in the passenger seat. Relieved it wasn't Danny, I strained to see who it was in the waning light. Timothy stopped just before the garden, and the passenger door popped open.

Hannah climbed out, her Kapp pushed back on her head.

Her red-rimmed eyes met mine. "Can I spend the night?"

"Jah," I answered, alarmed. "Do your parents know where you are?"

She shook her head.

"We should tell them."

"Will you call?"

I nodded.

"I guess I'll go," Phillip said.

"It seems that would be best." I met his eyes for a brief moment. "Good night."

He said the same and started toward his horse and buggy. Although I was unsettled by Hannah's bizarre arrival, relief washed over me to finally have Phillip on his way.

"I'll be home later," Timothy called from his open window. I didn't bother to respond, which didn't matter to him. He turned his Bronco around and buzzed back up the lane.

I suggested Hannah sit on the back stoop, and then I turned toward the barn, to where our phone was, to leave a message for Aenti Pauline. I supposed, once she figured out Hannah wasn't coming home, she might check her machine.

As I spoke on the phone I heard the clippity-clop of Phillip's horse's hooves fade off down the lane. When I finished, I stepped out of the barn and squinted in the dim light toward the creek.

An owl hooted, and then another flash of lightning struck. I counted to ten before the thunder crashed. I took a step in the opposite direction of the house. I couldn't leave Hannah, not in the state she was in, but I longed to see Jonathan. It had been forty-eight hours since we'd spoken. It felt like forty-eight days.

I heard the hoot again. Perhaps he was headed home too and simply wanted to let me know. My heart jumped at the rustling in the brush past the willow. Up popped Jonathan's head.

I shook mine. I didn't want Hannah to see him. He nodded and blew me a kiss.

"Come back tomorrow night," I whispered, not sure whether he'd be able to make out my instruction in the dim light. He disappeared again, and by the movement of the brush on my side of the trail, I knew he'd headed back down to the creek.

Another flash of lightning . . . and then more thunder, but this time I counted to twelve. He would be fine going home.

I turned back toward my cousin, aching for Jonathan's embrace, for the brush of his lips against my skin. But even more for how it felt to be heard by him. I had so much I wanted to say.

Hannah leaned her head against my shoulder. We'd scooted back under the porch roof, side by side, the sky now pitch-black, the rain falling around us. A shroud of clouds covered the moon.

"What's going on?" I asked.

She hiccuped. "My Mamm and I had an argument."

"About?"

"She doesn't want me to go out anymore. She says that's why I'm so tired and lazy. But I'm so tired because I hate being at home. I'm fine when I'm out with friends."

Hannah's parents were far more lenient than mine were with me. Not more than mine were with my Bruders though.

"She wants me to join one of those youth groups that just sings and plays volleyball." There were groups of Youngie like that who didn't do any of the usual Rumschpringe activities. The parents decided what was allowed and somehow they made the kids stick to it.

Hannah continued. "My Mamm thinks Molly is a bad influence." She hiccuped again. "We fought about it tonight, and I stormed off, then called Timothy to come get me."

I pulled her closer, knowing there was no reason for me to speak now. We sat in silence for a minute as the freshness of the rain swirled around us. Then she said, "I don't want your Mamm to know I'm here. Not until tomorrow morning."

"She's probably already gone to bed."

"Could you check?"

"Jah." I stood. "I'll be right back. Stay here."

The kitchen was dark when I stepped inside. Relieved, I was starting back out when Mutter asked, "Is he still here?"

I twirled around, seeing now that she was still sitting at the table. "Who?"

"Phillip." She laughed. "Who do you think?"

"No," I answered.

"Oh." She pushed herself up to a standing position. "I thought maybe you were going to go back out to spend more time with him."

I shook my head. "I forgot to make sure the chicken coop is secure." That was true.

"I was waiting up to tell you how pleased I am," she said. "Your Daed too. A son is a son until he takes a wife, but a daughter is a daughter for life. You're the only one we have. Who you marry means so much to us, far more than who the boys choose. Phillip will stand by you through the years as you care for us." She put her hand on her hip. "I know you had that . . . episode earlier in the week. But we knew you'd get over it and see things our way. It shows us how much you care—how much you honor us."

I bristled. Caring about them was one thing. Marrying Phillip was entirely another. "Mutter," I said, my voice as calm as I could keep it. "I don't love Phillip."

Even in the darkness I could make out a look of surprise on her face. "How could you not love him? He's all any girl could want."

I shook my head. Speaking the truth to Phillip had given me confidence. It was time for me to be honest with my parents too. "Not me. He doesn't make my heart stop—or do anything at all except make me feel hollow, as if I'm not even myself around him."

"Oh, Addie," she said. "It works differently for different people. Those feelings will come in time, to be sure. It's fate for the two of you to be together."

"No it's not. If I was going to feel that way about Phillip Eicher, I would have by now."

She slumped forward, grabbing the chair.

I paused, a feeling of regret coming over me. What had I just said to my Mutter? What if it caused her to have some sort of an attack?

She began waving her hand at me, and I stepped to her side and took her arm. "Are you all right?"

"Help me to the stairs," she said.

I did, without saying a word.

When we reached the staircase, she said, "I'm okay now. Go take care of the chickens."

I watched her taking the stairs one at a time. Halfway up, she turned and said quietly, "Don't tell your father. It will break his heart. And I'm guessing you'll change your mind anyway. Who would pick Jonathan Mosier over Phillip Eicher?"

She waited for me to answer, but when I didn't she added, "Only a fool."

Shaken, I slipped back to the kitchen. I didn't

want to hurt my parents, but I wasn't going to change my mind. Daed would find out sooner or later. I stepped out the back door. "Come on," I whispered to Hannah. "Follow me."

I led the way to the coop through the rain, easing up the latch and then directing Hannah to go in first. The hens had all settled down for the night, but a few squawked from their roosts at the far end as we stepped across the cedar shavings that I'd spread the week before. The half-grown chicks we were raising to sell as fryers huddled together as we approached. I wiped my hands, wet from the rain, on my apron and then turned on the battery-operated heat lamp, even though it was already humid and stuffy in the coop, to give us some light. Several of the chicks awoke. I picked up one and sat down on the shavings, feeling the warmth of the creature in my hands as I drew it closer. Hannah did the same.

"There's something I've been wanting to ask you," I said.

She kissed the top of the chick's head and then looked up at me, her brown eyes heavy. "Jah?"

"Are you interested in Jonathan Mosier?"

She smiled a little. "Who wants to know?"

Not sure if she was teasing or not, I decided to be straightforward. "I do."

"Why?"

I narrowed my eyes and smiled a little. "Why do you think?"

She smiled. "I'm not interested in him. But what about Phillip?"

"Ach, Phillip, Phillip, Phillip. That's all I hear. What a great catch he is. What a good husband he will—"

Hannah took over. "How handsome he is. How buff—"

"Hannah!"

"It's true." A sassy expression settled on her face.

"Perhaps you would like to court him."

She shook her head. "But I know who would."

I leaned toward her. "Who?"

"Molly."

I leaned back. "That's perfect!" She'd make him notice her. "If you're not interested in Jonathan, then who do you want to court, Hannah?"

"That's part of my issue with Mamm." She stroked the chick's head as she looked up at me. "I like Mervin."

"Oh," I said, surprised.

My cousin continued. "But my Mamm says there's no way she'll allow me to go out with a Mosier. That's why she wants me to go to the youth group. She says I'm not to go to the parties anymore."

"Oh," I said again.

"Your parents will never let you court Jonathan either, you know."

I sat up straighter. "Aenti Nell thinks maybe

they will." But she'd also instructed me not to talk to Phillip or my parents about how I really felt—and I'd just done both. Ignoring my fear that I'd blown it, I continued. "Aenti said Jonathan and I should talk to my Onkel Bob, that maybe he can help us straighten everyone out."

"Good luck." Hannah hiccuped and then closed her eyes, leaning her head against the worn plank of wood behind her, her shoulders slumping.

"You okay?" I inched toward her, the cedar chips bumpy under my dress.

She shook her head. "I feel so sad. . . . Unless I'm riding my horse or out with friends." She opened her eyes. "I don't mean to say I feel bad being with you."

"Don't worry," I said. "I understand."

"I'm tired of being bossed around," she said. "And the thing is, my Mamm and Dat wouldn't come up with this plan to confine me on their own. It's Mammi Gladys who's behind it. It's like she's so miserable she wants everyone else to be too." Her eyes watered. "This is our Rumschpringe. After we join the church and marry, we'll have to obey all the rules. But we're supposed to have some freedom now, right?"

I swallowed hard, not knowing what to say.

"Sure, we have freedom, as long as we don't court any Mosiers. Or go anywhere they'll be." She stood and put the chick back with the others.

I didn't want to leave the coop, the one place I felt we could talk, but Hannah seemed to be exhausted. She needed to get to bed.

"Let's go," I said, running my fingers down the back of the chick's head. We needed to get as much sleep as possible. Aenti Pauline was apt to be in our kitchen tomorrow morning soon after I was, if not before.

Chapter 9

ಬಬ

Aenti Pauline didn't beat me to the kitchen—she didn't show up until after breakfast. Mutter and Aenti Nell had both stayed at the table to quiz Hannah after Daed and the boys had all gone out to the field. And I was relieved that my cousin's presence took Mutter's attention off me.

Aenti Pauline didn't knock, but she didn't exactly march right in either. She looked a little tentative as she opened the door, squinted as her eyes adjusted to the dimmer light, and then said, "Hannah, are you all right, then?"

I felt sorry for my Aenti.

"Jah," Hannah said. "I just needed some time."

"Are you ready to come home?"

Surprised she didn't simply order Hannah to go with her, I glanced at my cousin's face.

She appeared relieved. "Could I stay another day? I got up early and helped Addie with the chores. I'm feeling better."

Aenti Pauline turned to Mutter. "Is that all right with you?"

"Goodness, Pauline," Mutter answered. "Just tell her to go home with you."

"Then you mind if she stays?"

"Of course not." Mutter exhaled. "Just don't let her decide." My Mutter had a covert way of criticizing other people's parenting. I think it made her feel better about her own.

Aenti Pauline turned back to Hannah. "Laurel and Cap are much stricter than your Dat and I, at least with Addie." I wasn't the only one aware of my Mutter's hypocrisy.

"I know," Hannah answered. "But it helps to be with my cousin."

Aenti Pauline turned toward Mutter, who shrugged and then said, "Addie, start weeding the garden, and take Hannah with you."

A few minutes later, the hoe looped through my arm so it wouldn't fall to the muddy ground, I swatted at a fly buzzing around my face and then wiped my forehead with my apron. The rain from last night had given way to another day of humidity.

"I should have gotten a glass of water," Hannah said.

I pointed to the hose.

She wrinkled her nose.

"Go back into the kitchen, then."

"No, I don't want to get in the middle of the Schwesters." She took a deep breath.

We worked for an hour—me at twice Hannah's pace—and then decided to take a break. The Schwesters had had enough time to talk. We leaned the hoes against the garden fence and headed to the back porch, kicking our shoes off and then entering the kitchen. It was empty, but I heard voices in the sewing room. I stopped at the door. Aenti Nell and Aenti Pauline were talking, but Mutter wasn't in sight.

"Where did she go?" I wondered if Aenti Pauline had upset her.

"Who?" Nell asked.

"Mutter."

"Oh, I think to rest," Aenti Pauline answered.

"She must be upstairs," Aenti Nell added.

"Did you all talk things through?"

Aenti Pauline gave me a puzzled look.

"About Hannah staying."

"Jah . . ." Aenti Pauline glanced at Aenti Nell and shrugged. "There wasn't much to talk about. . . ."

"When did Mutter leave?" It wasn't like her not to be with me, or Nell, during the day. If for some reason Nell was gone, Mutter would sometimes sit in a chair while I weeded the garden to keep from being alone.

"Oh, a while ago." Aenti Nell's gaze drifted into the kitchen. "Before we came in here."

"I'll check on her," I said. I hoped I didn't appear alarmed, but I feared she might have fallen or that perhaps she was sick. I hurried up the stairs. She wasn't in her room or in the little boys', which I didn't expect because she hadn't done any cleaning in there in years. Next I checked the bathroom. She wasn't there either.

I heard a bump above. The ladder to the attic was in Timothy and Danny's room, so I pursed my lips and headed down the hall, opening their door. Danny's side of the room was tidy, but a tumble of blankets covered Timothy's bed, and heaps of clothes, both Englisch and Amish, were scattered around his floor.

The ceiling of the room appeared as always— the ladder in place. I heard another bump then and my mother's voice calling out my name.

"Mutter!" I reached up to the rope dangling from the ceiling and yanked. The ladder popped down, followed by a wave of heat, and then my mother's face appeared.

"What took you so long?"

"I had no idea you were up here."

"Someone raised the ladder on me."

Timothy probably returned to get something. "He must have thought it had been left down by accident." I started up toward her. "Can you get down on your own?"

She shook her head.

"Okay . . ." Why, with a bad knee, had she ventured up? "What were you doing?" I asked as I reached the top, overcome with worry.

"Pauline mentioned something this morning. I wanted to look for it."

I sighed. She was forever misplacing things. Bills. Paperwork. Books. Mementos. Doilies. Handwork. "Let's get you down from here." I coached her then, step by step, and held on to her thick waist to steady her. By the time we reached the bottom, she was shaking and collapsed on Danny's bed with a bounce.

I hurried to the bathroom to get her a glass of water and brought it back for her, waiting for her to catch her breath. I'd felt responsible for her for years. Never had I neglected her so.

After she drank the water, a sip at a time, I helped her up and then down the hall to her room. After she collapsed on her own bed, she lifted her head. "I think you just need some time away from Phillip. To clear your mind."

I didn't answer her, not wanting to upset her, and hurried back down the stairs to talk with Hannah. When I reached the kitchen I was surprised to find her sitting at the table with

Timothy. Both had empty glasses in front of them.

I filled a glass with water and sat down too.

"I'm going to go home," Hannah whispered, nodding toward the sewing room, indicating Aenti Pauline was still talking with Aenti Nell. "Timothy said there's a party tonight. I'll have a better chance of going being at my house than staying at yours." She smiled.

"You said your Mamm didn't want you to go." I held the cool glass against my face. The summer parties seemed to be heating up—here it was only midweek.

"I think she'll change her mind. Or I'll ask to stay at Molly's tonight."

Before I could respond, she hurried up to my room to collect her things.

"I'm going too," Timothy said. "And I promise I won't drink. Want to go? Phillip won't be there." He smirked.

I didn't dare ask if Jonathan would.

I'd been a good girl all through what should have been my Rumschpringe, not going behind my parents' backs, not going to parties, not running around in any way. It wasn't that I thought going to one party would make me a bad girl, it was just that it went against what I'd been raised to do.

"Jah," I answered my brother. Armed with my growing confidence, I decided it was worth the risk. By this evening, it would be seventy-two hours since I'd seen Jonathan. Going to the party was my best chance to spend some time with him.

I scrubbed out the stainless steel kitchen sink, working wide circles with the cleanser and the sponge, as I waited for Timothy. Mutter and Daed had headed to bed soon after Billy and Joe-Joe had settled down, as was their usual routine, and Aenti Nell had soon followed to her room. Timothy had told me after dinner we'd leave for the party as soon as everyone had gone to bed, but then his cell phone rang. He'd said he'd be right back, hurried out to his Bronco, sped down the lane—and hadn't returned.

I turned on the faucet and began rinsing the sink, splashing water up on the sides. I'd accepted it wasn't meant for me to go to the party after all, when I heard Timothy's Bronco coming back up the lane. I stopped the water and dried my hands quickly, leaving the towel on the counter in my hurry to get out the back door. I dashed toward the car, holding on to the top of my Kapp, hoping to stop him before he got to the house and drew more attention to us.

Waving, I sprinted around to the passenger side as he braked.

"Thought I'd forgotten you, jah?" He began cranking the wheel to turn around before I had the door closed.

As I clicked my seatbelt, I noticed his wasn't on. "Fasten up," I said.

He grunted.

"Timothy."

"Stop bossing me around."

"Let me out, then."

"All right, all right," he said, grabbing the belt as he drove. Too many Amish youth were badly injured in car accidents because they didn't wear safety belts. The car drifted, the fastener clicked, and he planted his hands back on the wheel.

I let out my breath, slowly, and we rode in silence until the stop sign at the end of our lane.

That's when I heard the beer bottles clink behind the driver's seat.

I craned my neck.

"I only had one," he said, turning right.

"There are four empty bottles."

"George had three."

I eyed him for a moment but couldn't tell if he was being truthful or not. "If you can afford beer, why can't you afford to pay me back?"

"What are you talking about?"

"For the mantel you destroyed."

He smirked and said, "I forgot all about that."

"Obviously." I wasn't about to tell him Jonathan had returned the money. If by some chance Timothy did pay me, I'd tell him then. "Where is George?" I asked.

"At the party already. With Sadie."

"And where is it?"

"Down by the Susquehanna." He braked for a curve.

I relaxed a little.

But the next one he accelerated for. "Timothy!" I squealed. He laughed as the Bronco veered onto the shoulder and then straightened out again.

"There could have been a buggy on the curve!"

"There wasn't," he answered.

We were on a straight stretch now, buzzing along. "How many beers did you really have?"

"Maybe more than one. I lost track." He shot me a grin as he crossed the center line into the other lane, which was clear, to pass a buggy.

I turned to see if it was anyone I recognized but couldn't make out the man's face.

I shifted in my seat toward Timothy. "We need to go back to the house."

"Nah, I'm fine."

"You're not fine."

He ignored me.

"Turn around," I said.

He ignored me again.

"Stop!" I commanded.

He continued to ignore me until I yelled, "Now!"

He slammed on the brakes, stopping the car in the middle of the road, the beer bottles clattering in the back again.

"Now go back to the house."

"Fat chance," he said. "You can walk back if you need to run home to Mamm."

"You said you wouldn't drink."

He shrugged. I weighed my options—it took me half a second. "Okay." I opened the door handle. "I'll walk."

"Don't get hit by some crazy Amish kid," he said as I climbed out.

"You're an idiot." I slammed the door.

He sneered and then accelerated, making me jump back onto the narrow shoulder.

The moon rose over the hill behind me, and I began walking back the way we'd come, chastising myself for having believed Timothy in the first place.

He was the least trustworthy person I knew.

I looked across the plowed field, squinting in the dim light. The farmhouse in the distance was Old Man Mosier's. Getting there by the road would be a long, long walk. I stumbled over a rock, catching myself before I fell. To cross the plowed field, as much as I wanted to, would be quite the ordeal. Besides, what would I find when I got there? Jonathan gone to the party? That would only add insult to injury. I was so close to where Jonathan was living—but he was most likely not there.

I began humming as I walked, a nonsense tune that I sometimes sang to Joe-Joe at bedtime. In the distance, car lights came toward me. I stepped beyond the shoulder to the edge of the field, well out of the way. The car zoomed by too fast. I didn't recognize the Englisch man driving.

A pickup passed a few minutes later with a dog in the back. It barked and lunged as the vehicle zoomed by. I stayed on the side of the field, my shoes filling with dirt from the tilled soil.

When I reached the crossroads, I turned to the left. A few minutes later, I could heard the clippity-clop of a horse's hooves and then the whir of wheels on the pavement, but a turn in the road prevented me from seeing the buggy.

I could make out the faint sound of singing. " 'When through the woods, and forest glades I wander, And hear the birds sing sweetly in the trees. When I look down, from lofty mountain grandeur . . .' "

The voice sounded familiar—or was I just hoping beyond hope it would be Jonathan?

It wasn't until the chorus that I recognized the song as "How Great Thou Art," an Englisch hymn Aenti Nell sometimes sang. She told me it was from singings she attended as a girl. Certain it was a song Jonathan would sing, I began jogging.

As I came around the bend, there he was, his face lit up in the moonlight—until he saw me.

"Whoa!" He pulled the horse to a stop, his lantern swinging back and forth, casting a wide shadow. "Addie?"

"Jah," I said.

The look on his face, under the wide brim of his hat, was a mixture of joy and confusion. "What are you doing out here?"

I could feel my face light up, nearly as brightly as the moon, as relief and a sense of safety flooded over me. "It seems . . . finding you." I climbed into his buggy before he had the chance to ask me to.

As I dumped the dirt from my shoes, one after the other, over the side onto the pavement, I explained to Jonathan why I was walking alone, in the dark.

"I don't know why I ever trusted Timothy," I said, putting my second shoe back on. "Well, actually I do." I looked up at Jonathan shyly. "I was hoping you would be at the party."

He grinned. "Mervin and Martin asked me to go, but I didn't think you would be there."

I leaned back against the bench, pleased.

"I'll take you home," he said.

"There's no hurry."

He stopped at the crossroads instead of turning the buggy around. "Want to come look at my shop?"

"Are your parents home?"

He shook his head. "Not until tomorrow."

He urged the horse forward, toward Old Man Mosier's place. We rode in silence for a moment, until I thought to ask what he was doing out so late, if not going to a party.

He laughed a little. "Well, I was headed over to someone's house, hoping she could sneak away for a quick ride. But about ten minutes ago, I saw her fly by in a yellow Bronco."

"Oh no, that was you? I couldn't see your face."

"I turned away on purpose, so Timothy couldn't see me."

"And you were going to our place?"

"Jah. I'm not sure what I planned to do. Maybe knock on your door." He grinned.

Knowing how that would have gone over, I was happy with the way things turned out, except for Timothy being out on the road.

Old Man Mosier's house was one of those that sat just a few feet off the road. But in the early 1800s when it was built, most likely around the same time our house was, there was only the occasional horse and buggy or wagon. One didn't have to worry about kids spilling out onto the busy road.

As Jonathan turned the buggy into their short driveway, two barking hounds lunged out from beside the house.

I must have looked worried, because Jonathan said, "Dawdi is practically deaf. That's why the dogs are so loud." Then he laughed, and I couldn't help but chuckle at his joke too.

Because he would soon be taking me home, Jonathan tied the horse to the hitching post instead of taking it to the barn. I started to jump down, but before I could, he told me to wait. "Let me help you," he said.

In a moment, he was looking up at me, reaching for my hand. I offered it to him, and he took it tenderly, sending a jolt straight to my heart. As I stepped down, he put his other hand on the small of my back.

"Denki," I managed to breathe out as I took a step toward him, our shoulders practically touching. Our eyes met, and he smiled, again, but then stepped away, even though I longed for him to hug me the way he had the first night down by the creek. He headed toward the house, not letting go of my hand as he led me toward the back door.

"I want to introduce you to Dawdi first. And my cousin Tabitha. Then I'll show you the shop," Jonathan said, opening the door.

A young woman, a year or two older than me, stood at the kitchen sink, washing beans. She smiled shyly. When Jonathan introduced us, after I said hello, she asked if I was Timothy's sister.

"Jah, I am." I braced myself for her reaction.

"Is he doing all right?" she asked. "I only met him the one time, but he worried me."

It wasn't the response I'd expected. "Jah." I sighed. "He worries me too."

"He seemed as if he might be nice enough," she said. "But I couldn't really tell."

"He can be nice," I said. "And not so nice too."

She nodded. "That's what I was afraid of." She didn't bring up his drinking, but it was implied. "It's great to meet you," she said. "I hope the best for the two of you."

"Denki," I answered, wishing Timothy was worthy of a girl like her. Not that he wouldn't be someday, but he had a lot of changing to do first.

Jonathan took my hand and pulled me along toward a faint light from another room.

"Is your Dawdi in bed?" I whispered.

"No. He hardly sleeps."

Jonathan led the way toward the light. We rounded the corner and into the living room. In the far corner in a rocking chair, under the light of a lamp, sat an old man with thick snow-white hair and a beard down to his waist. He wore a dark blue bathrobe and leather slippers. His head was bent forward as if he were sleeping, but then I saw the book in his lap.

"Dawdi," Jonathan said.

The man raised his head, a smile spreading across his face as he did, his pale blue eyes dancing.

He struggled to his feet, tucking the book under his arm.

"This is Addie," Jonathan said.

His Dawdi extended his hand to me. I took it, clasping the bony fingers and paper-thin skin. "*Willkumm*," he said.

"Denki," I answered.

"Cramer, right?"

I nodded, bracing myself.

"Ach, I'm thinking my prayers are working." His eyes lit up as bright as the lamp beside him. "I can't tell you how much I've missed your Dat all these years. He used to be like my own son. . . ." His eyes watered, and then he let go of my hand.

He reached for Jonathan, wrapping his arm around his shoulder. "It's late—take her home so her parents don't worry. But bring her back sometime when we can visit." He plopped back down into the chair.

"Come on," Jonathan said to me.

I stalled, gazing at his grandfather a moment longer. He opened the book back up, and I realized it was a Bible.

I waved at him—although he didn't see it because he was reading again—and then I followed Jonathan back through the kitchen, saying good-night to Tabitha, and out to the shop. I could smell the spicy sweetness of pine before we entered. Once we stepped through the side door and he flipped on a switch, a wonderland of wood greeted me, all illuminated by electric lights. Obviously the shop was wired, probably mostly for the tools Jonathan used.

"Solar power," Jonathan explained. I nodded. Several businesses and even some homes had the panels on their roofs, including Onkel Bob's shop and showroom.

Bookcases, benches, butcher blocks, bowls, bookends, mantels, and, jah, hope chests filled the room. All had some sort of carving on them. A single flower. A shaft of wheat. A name. A star. A moon. All reason enough to make Bishop Eicher concerned, I was sure. I stepped closer to the first hope chest. *Sarah* was carved into the wood with forget-me-nots around it.

"This must be for an Englisch girl," I said.

Jonathan stepped beside me. "An Amish woman ordered it. For her daughter." He lifted the lid. The inside was carved with forget-me-nots too. "The girl's turning thirteen."

I swallowed hard. "Was the woman over-weight? With dark hair?"

He nodded.

"And named Pauline?"

"Jah."

Tears stung my eyes.

"What is it?"

I shook my head. It wasn't that I was jealous of my cousin—I was happy for her. And not surprised. Hannah and Deborah both received a hope chest when they turned thirteen too, although not as wonderful. I just felt the pain of not having been given one of my own. "It's beautiful—that's all."

I could tell by the expression on his face he knew it was more than that, but he didn't press me.

"All of it is incredible, every single piece."

"Ach, Addie. Don't say that." Jonathan's eyes fell to the concrete floor covered with sawdust.

"What? You don't think it is?"

"Jah, some of it. But I have so much to learn. So much to improve."

I couldn't see that. All of it looked perfect to me, but I was sure, as a craftsman, he saw flaws I couldn't.

"That might be," I said, full of enthusiasm. "But still it's the most amazing carpentry I've ever seen."

"Don't, Addie."

I stepped toward him. "It's true. Now show me everything."

He did, talking about the different kinds of wood. Maple. Oak. Hemlock. Pine. He touched each piece tenderly, running his hand along the grain. He told me if the wood was hard or soft and if soaking it before carving worked better or not and if he joined the wood with glue or dowels.

He showed me his tools. His saw and sander. His lathe and planer. "Dawdi convinced my Dat that the solar electricity would be okay. This shop is so much better than the one in Big Valley."

"So you must be staying, considering you moved everything down?"

"Jah, that's the plan. Although my Dat's still not convinced I can make a living with my woodworking. He says I'm too passionate to run my own business—and not organized or level-headed enough. He says I'll turn into one of those 'starving artists.' " Jonathan made quotation gestures with his fingers. "That's why he wants me to help him farm. He's thinking about buying a dairy herd."

"You wouldn't have much time for your work then."

He nodded, sadly.

"What does your Dawdi say?"

"He stays out of things when my Dat's involved."

"Ach, Jonathan," I said, my brain whirring around and around. "I'm organized. And level-headed. I know Cate would teach me about running a business."

"Are you saying you'd be my business manager?"

"Jah." I couldn't think of anything I'd rather do than partner in life—and business—with Jonathan. It was another reason for us to be together. So he could succeed as a carpenter. But it would use my strengths too. Both of our gifts could work together to make it a success— something neither of us could accomplish on our own.

"You'd be willing to live with my passion and all?"

"Jah," I said again. Perhaps that passion made him rash, but it also opened a new world to me —one of beauty and God being present and hope. "And promote your work. No matter what you believe, I think it's amazing. All of it."

He picked up a small box from the worktable. "Here," he said. "I made it for you."

I took it from him. It had forget-me-nots carved on the top, similar to the ones on Sarah's chest.

I wrapped my hand around it and held it to my heart. "Denki," I whispered. I shivered, amazed that I'd only known him for three days.

I was about to tell Jonathan that when we both turned to the sound of a vehicle. It sounded as if it was just outside the shop.

Then a door slammed.

Jonathan's voice was low. "I'll check and see who it is."

I stepped to the side of one of the bookcases as he opened the side door. I waited a long moment, watching his back. When he turned toward me I knew it wasn't good.

"It's my parents," he said. "They came back early."

Chapter 10

ಬಾ

I wasn't tempted to hide or flee, but the only thing I could do was walk out at Jonathan's side with my head held high and meet the two people responsible for his life.

He searched my eyes for a long moment. I nodded toward the door and then stepped beside him. He led the way. A van was parked in the driveway, the interior lights and the headlights on. A Plain man, Dirk I assumed, stood straight and tall, broad shouldered and bulky—nothing like his son—facing the side door of the van. He had a long, full beard, a head of dark hair under his black hat, and a burly look about him. An Englisch man walked around the van, no one I knew, probably from Big Valley. Neither man noticed us, but the Amish woman did as she came around the back of the van, carrying cloth bags in each hand. She stopped immediately, but instead of being angry, a smile spread across her face.

"Jonathan," she said. "Who do you have with you?"

He spoke clearly. "This is Addie."

Before Jonathan could go on, I knew by the look on his father's face he knew who I was.

"Addie Cramer," Jonathan said.

"Jah," his father said, his voice full of disappointment. "That's what I thought."

"Oh, Jonathan," his mother moaned. "So what Amos called about is true?"

I exhaled slowly, disappointed in Mervin and Martin's Dat. Was I really so bad?

Jonathan stepped forward. "I was showing her my work."

"Why?" His Dat's eyes drilled us both. "Out of all the girls in the county, why a Cramer?"

"Maybe it's not what we think," his mother said. "Right?" She turned toward Jonathan and me.

My heart raced. Jonathan shook his head.

His mother's mouth turned downward, and she placed the bags by the back door and spun back around to the van.

"We'll talk about this later," Dirk said to Jonathan. Then to me he said, "You go along now."

"I'm giving her a ride," Jonathan said, gesturing toward the horse and buggy.

His Dat froze.

Jonathan took my hand and pulled me toward the buggy.

"Son!" Dirk called out. "Randall can take her home."

The driver, who had gone around to the back

211

of the van, appeared, carrying two suitcases, nodding his head.

Jonathan thanked the driver and then said, "There's no need. I'm taking her."

His mother slammed the side door to the van shut as the back door to the house opened. Dawdi Mosier stepped out, his white beard caught by the slight breeze, looking like Moses on Mount Sinai. "Welcome home," he called out. Then he looked beyond his son and daughter-in-law and said, "Jonathan, it's late. You hurry Addie on home. Remember, I said we don't want her parents to worry."

Jonathan nodded.

I looked over my shoulder, wanting to communicate my thanks to the old man, but he'd stepped down and was collecting bags.

Jonathan's mother made a shooing motion with her hand, willing me to disappear, I was sure.

By the time we reached the buggy, I was trembling. I'd never felt so rejected in my entire life. As Jonathan turned the buggy around, I held out my hand to show it was shaking. He reached for it and held it until it stopped.

"Is this how you feel around my house, jah?"

He shook his head. "Your folks were nicer."

"Timothy hasn't been. And none of them would be if they knew we were . . ." I stopped, searching for the right word.

"Courting?" Jonathan interjected.

"Is that what we're doing?"

"Jah," he answered. "It is. We're officially, for us, courting."

I nodded. I liked the sound of his words immensely.

We needed an advocate. Someone from the older generation to broker a deal with our parents. That's what happened in the classic novels I sometimes had a chance to read. One person would talk to another who would talk to another. Then everthing ended up being a bigger mess than at the beginning, but by the end of the story everything was sorted out. I hoped we could skip to the end and avoid the bigger mess in the middle, though.

"Does your Dat know my Onkel Bob?" I asked.

"Jah. I don't think well, but they're acquainted. When I cited your Onkel as someone who has made a living off carpentry, my Dat knew who I was speaking of."

"My Aenti Nell thought he might be able to help us. I was going to talk with you about it last night." I scooted my hands under my thighs. "Maybe you and I could talk with my Onkel about approaching our parents to try to put an end to the grudge. I'm sure your Dawdi would try to help too."

"Jah," Jonathan said. "I think it's worth a try."

Then I told him what Aenti Nell had said, about the letters his father had sent my mother all those years ago.

"That's strange," Jonathan said when I finished. "I've never known my Dat to send a letter. He hates to write."

I pondered that as we rode along. Maybe those letters were the reason he hated writing. Who wouldn't after destroying a relationship with their best friend?

We decided to meet at Onkel Bob's the next afternoon at two o'clock. At one fifty, Joe-Joe still hadn't settled down for his nap and was sitting on the couch, making monster noises inspired by a library book I now regretted checking out for him. Mutter had fallen asleep upstairs, and Aenti Nell was dozing in her chair in the sewing room, sending soft snores into the kitchen.

Deciding it was too late for Joe-Joe to nap now anyway, I motioned for him to follow me. With a smile on his face, he did. We tiptoed through the kitchen, but by the time we reached the back door he started to whine that he was tired. I put my hand over his mouth and pulled him outside and down the steps.

"Why didn't you take a nap, then?"

He rubbed his eyes. "I wasn't tired."

I scanned the barnyard for Billy but couldn't see him. Daed, Timothy, and Danny were repairing the south fence today, and I imagined Billy had tagged along.

I couldn't leave him unattended at the house.

Even if I woke Aenti Nell to watch him, it wouldn't be long until he woke Mutter. Then she would wonder where I went.

"You're going over to Onkel Bob's with me."

Joe-Joe smiled. He liked Cate.

"Come on." This way I could honestly say Joe-Joe and I went on a walk. Or to pick blackberries along the creek.

"Wait a minute," I said. "I'll be right back."

I hurried into the house and grabbed an empty ice cream bucket from the counter. We used them for all sorts of things—compost, slop, and berry picking mainly.

I handed Joe-Joe the bucket, and he swung it around as we walked. I kept a look out for Billy as we rounded the willow tree and then started down the trail, instantly feeling the drop in temperature as we neared the creek.

Joe-Joe, barefoot, splashed into the water. I wore my flip-flops and crossed on the stones— until Joe-Joe slipped and fell, plopping onto his side.

"Hop up," I said.

He turned up toward me with startled eyes, the bucket handle still in his hand. By now his pants and most of his shirt were soaked. I wadded my skirt, holding it above my knees with one hand, stepped into the water, and pulled Joe-Joe up with my other hand. Together, we waded across the creek. When we got to the other side, he scampered up the trail, digging his toes into the mud.

He'd definitely be staying outside when we reached Onkel Bob's.

He left my sight for a moment at the crest of the trail. A moment later a screech from him made me increase my stride. When I reached the top, I found Joe-Joe sitting in the middle of the trail next to a rock, holding his foot, his bloody big toe pointed upward, the bucket off to the side.

"Did you stub it?"

"Jah."

"Well, come on." Stubbed toes were a part of every Amish childhood.

His eyes filled with tears. "It hurts."

I grabbed the bucket and pulled him to his feet; he hobbled along for a few steps, obviously in pain. Then he stopped. "Can you carry me?" he sobbed.

I handed him the bucket and swung him up into my arms, feeling his weight in my lower back. His foot brushed my apron, leaving a muddy mark, and then he wrapped his legs around my waist, the bucket banging against my thigh. I walked along the edge of the sycamore grove and then through the gate to Onkel Bob's property. I'd heard my Daed say several times that he could have used the ten acres his sister and Onkel Bob were given. I'm sure he could have, but I was thankful to have such kind relatives next door.

What Onkel Bob ended up with wasn't prime

farmland anyway. It was good land for his show-room and shop, and of course the house and barn he built too. And for the few steers he raised for beef.

"Addie!" It was Jonathan's voice, but I couldn't see him.

"There he is." Joe-Joe pointed toward the barn.

Jonathan stepped out of the shadows and started to jog toward us. When he reached us, he took Joe-Joe from me.

"What happened?" he asked.

Joe-Joe held up his mud-covered and still-bloodied toe.

"Let's see if you can walk." Jonathan slid Joe-Joe to the ground, leaving a muddy streak down the side of Jonathan's white shirt.

Joe-Joe handed me the bucket and took a few steps.

"And run!" Jonathan took off at full force. Joe-Joe barreled after him.

I shook my head. I'd been duped.

Joe-Joe stopped at Betsy's rose garden, out of breath, and collapsed onto the grass beside it.

When I reached the garden, I bent down to smell a peach-colored rose. My parents felt roses were too fancy to grow. I always envied my cousin's bushes.

"It's the pinnacle of God's beauty," Jonathan said. "Don't you think?" Then he chuckled and said, "Except for you."

I stood up straight. "Don't be ridiculous. I'm no beauty."

"Ach, but you are," he said.

Joe-Joe groaned in our direction and crawled to the bench of the picnic table.

Jonathan took out his knife and cut the stem of the flower, handing it to me. I raised my eyebrows as I took it.

"Your Onkel won't mind," he said. "Smell it."

I breathed deeply, soaking in the heavenly scent.

"Now touch a petal."

I lifted it to my face, rubbing the blossom against my skin.

"If you don't think you're far more beautiful to God than that rose, then you need to get to know God better."

His voice was full of kindness, but still his words embarrassed me—his claim that God found me beautiful and that he did too, and his admonishment.

I turned away. "I'll go see if Onkel Bob can talk with us," I said.

"I already asked," Jonathan answered. "He'll be out in a few minutes."

I nodded toward Joe-Joe. I didn't want him to overhear the conversation.

"Hey." Jonathan sat down beside him. "How about some shade?"

"And some lemonade?" Cate stood behind me holding a tray with four full glasses.

"Ach," I said. "Denki."

She put the tray on the table and picked up two of the glasses. "Better than the shade, Joe-Joe, how about if you come in the house with me? I was just taking a reading break. Want to join me?"

He seemed torn about leaving Jonathan.

"It's nice and cool in the living room," Cate said. "Plus I have some sugar cookies I made this morning."

He broke into a smile and scampered off the bench.

"He's really muddy," I said.

"I'll help him clean up," Cate answered.

I changed the subject. "Tell me about Betsy before you go."

"She thought she was in labor yesterday, but it turned out to be false. It should be any day though."

I searched Cate's face, wondering if she felt even a hint of jealousy. All I could see was joy, mixed in with a little bit of worry.

"Come on," she said to Joe-Joe as she carried one glass back toward the house. She'd never seemed very fond of children—until she married Pete.

It would have seemed like a long time waiting for Onkel Bob—wondering how long Cate would keep Joe-Joe busy, wondering if Mutter had woken up yet and realized I was gone—

219

except that I was sitting next to Jonathan.

I hardly noticed the heat. Or the horse flies buzzing around. Or the thunderclouds building again on the horizon.

"I prayed about all of this," Jonathan said. "This morning."

"Denki," I said, a little embarrassed I hadn't thought to do the same.

A moment later Onkel Bob joined us, apologizing profusely. "A customer called."

He sat down across from us. I slid the third glass of lemonade toward him. The ice had melted, and the condensation was thick on the outside. "Cate brought these out."

Onkel Bob drained it. "Ach," he said. "That's much better. It's so muggy today. We can go into the house. Somehow Cate manages to keep it cool."

"Joe-Joe's in there with her," I said.

Onkel Bob nodded, as if he understood.

"We won't be long," Jonathan said. "We're hoping for your advice—and maybe your help."

Onkel Bob met Jonathan's gaze and then mine. "I can guess what this is about—but why don't you go ahead and tell me."

"We're courting," Jonathan said. "But our parents don't approve."

"And you want to figure out how to get around that?"

"No," I said. "We want to figure out how to stop

this grudge between them. It's been going on too long."

"I agree," Onkel Bob said. "I thought we made some progress at the barbecue."

I wasn't sure how to say my parents only behaved because they cared what other people thought. "I don't know that there have been any lasting changes."

"And my parents are stubborn too," Jonathan added. "Although my grandfather wants to see it end, as he has from the beginning."

"Jah," Onkel Bob said. "That's always been my impression too."

"Plus, I'm afraid if something isn't done, it will explode with our generation," I said. "I don't think Martin and Mervin will do anything, but Timothy is likely to."

Onkel Bob nodded, but he didn't say anything.

"So what should we do?" Jonathan asked.

Onkel Bob took his hat off and then put it back on. "Well," he finally said. "Don't go behind your parents' backs. That will only lead to more hard feelings."

My face fell. I wouldn't be able to see Jonathan at all if we didn't sneak around.

Onkel Bob's expression was sympathetic. "I'll talk to all of them," he said. "Soon."

"When?" I couldn't help but ask.

"Within the next couple of days, God willing."

"Denki," Jonathan said.

"Just remember, go slowly. You're bound to stumble if you run too fast." Onkel Bob started to stand, asking as he did, "Anything else?"

"Jah," Jonathan said. "Are you hiring?"

Onkel Bob swung his leg over the bench. "Not right now, but in a few weeks or so I will be. Check back then."

Jonathan's face hid his disappointment—he'd probably be locked into farming by then—as he too stood. "We appreciate your help. We really do." He extended his hand.

Onkel Bob clasped Jonathan's hand with both of his and then let go, reaching to pat my shoulder. "I'd do anything I could for Addie," he said to Jonathan. "I trust her as a judge of character when it comes to you. She's always been a wise soul, along with being a hard worker."

I blushed at his compliments, unusual in our community. But Onkel Bob had always been extra positive. All my life I'd tried not to be jealous of Cate and Betsy and the relationship they had with him, reminding myself they didn't have a mother. But the thing was, I did have a mother, and a live-in Aenti, but I still didn't have the encouragement Cate and Betsy had always had.

My family, from my maternal grandmother on down, could be negative with subtle put-downs and not so subtle criticisms, but Onkel Bob and Cate and Betsy were the opposite. Even when

Cate had been rough around the edges, she still had an enthusiasm for others, especially for Betsy, and even for me. There was a sense of gratitude in their family that I hadn't experienced in mine.

I glanced at Jonathan. I felt the same optimistic attitude from him.

"Something will work out," Onkel Bob said, yanking me out of my thoughts. "Come back if you need more advice, but right now I'd best get back to work."

We bid him good-bye, and then I started toward the house to collect Joe-Joe.

"Do you have a minute?" Jonathan asked.

I nodded, even though I didn't.

"I have something for you in my buggy." He took my hand. "It's in the showroom parking lot."

I followed him, wondering what he had for me and marveling at his generosity, but stopped when I noticed Pete standing in the open door-way of the showroom. He worked part-time for Onkel Bob and part-time in the publishing business he and Cate had become involved in after they moved back to Lancaster County from New York, not too long after their wedding.

"Just trying to catch a breeze." Pete mopped his forehead with a handkerchief and then around his beard, a mischievous smile on his face. "What are you two up to?"

Jonathan made a funny face, and Pete smiled

and then winked as Jonathan pulled me along to the rear of his buggy. He let go of my hand and unlatched the back. There was something pretty large but covered. It wasn't for me—I was certain my gift was something small, like the bookmark or box.

Jonathan pulled the horse blanket off, revealing one of his hope chests.

"Nice," I said. Perhaps Onkel Bob had ordered one for Cate. It wouldn't surprise me if she'd refused one when she was thirteen. "Who is it for?"

He folded the blanket in half, catching it under his chin. "You," he answered, folding the blanket again.

"Me?"

He nodded, placing the blanket back into the buggy.

My heart raced. How did he know I'd wanted one of my own more than anything else in the world?

He pulled the chest toward us, balancing it on the edge. "Can you help me?"

"Jah." I hurried to the other side. "Jonathan, I can't tell you how much this means . . ."

He grinned. "It's your anniversary gift."

I laughed. "Jah, it's been all of four days."

He tilted his head toward me. "It feels like four years. I can't wait until it's been forty."

We lifted the chest together, carrying it to the

sidewalk in front of the showroom, and then put it down, the front facing me. Jonathan stepped backward. I gasped.

Carved into the front of the chest was my name—*Adelaide*—with a willow tree on one side and cattails on the other. Above shone the moon and stars.

"Oh, Jonathan." I stepped forward and lifted the lid. Inside were more carvings of the orchard and the creek tumbling along with the sycamore grove above the bank. "It's beautiful. When did you have time to do this?"

"The chest was already made—but I started carving it Sunday night. And finished it an hour ago." He yawned, and for the first time I noticed how tired he looked.

"Did your parents see it?"

He shook his head.

"Where was it last night?"

He smiled. "Covered up. Just in case."

"In case I visited your shop?"

He nodded. "Or in case my parents snooped around."

I stared inside, inhaling the sharp cedar scent, imagining all of the things I'd made through the years that I'd be able to store safely inside. "Denki," I whispered, stepping back and taking his hand again.

He put his arm around me in a half hug. "Are you sure you like it?"

"Of course!"

He stepped forward and rubbed his hand along the side. "The varnish isn't quite right here."

"Stop it." I couldn't see a thing wrong with it.

He pointed to the carving of the moon. "I slipped a little here."

"It's perfect," I said. "No one has given me anything so wonderful in all my life."

"Ach, Addie," he said. "I don't believe you."

I grabbed his shirt and pulled him close, looking up into his blue eyes. "Believe me." I nearly burst into tears.

"All right." His eyes searched mine. "I do."

"I can't take it home today though," I said. "I won't be able to until I can sneak it into the house."

"I figured that," he said. "I asked Pete if you could leave it in the showroom."

I nodded, grateful for his foresight. We each picked up an end and headed toward the door.

I might not have a Daed like Onkel Bob, or a Schwester or a Mutter who listened. But I had Jonathan, and I'd never felt so cherished in my entire life.

How ironic that he was the one person I wanted to be with but couldn't, starting now, if we followed Onkel Bob's advice.

Chapter 11

ထ

By the time Joe-Joe and I returned to the house, our bucket full of blackberries, Mutter was in the sewing room with Aenti Nell, with an iced tea in one hand and a fan made from a newspaper in the other.

"Where have you been?" she called out.

I scooted Joe-Joe toward the sewing room with the bucket so she could see for herself.

"Oh, goodie," she said. "It looks like we'll have a cobbler for dinner."

"Good thinking," I said.

"It feels like it's going to storm again," Aenti Nell called out.

"Jah," I answered. "Soon, I think."

"Hopefully it will break this heat," Mutter added.

I took the bucket from Joe-Joe, shooed him outside to find Billy, and busied myself making the topping for the cobbler. I already had two fryers marinating in the refrigerator to barbecue —Danny said he'd do it. I'd been hoping to keep the kitchen from getting too hot, but because I was going to bake the cobbler anyway, it didn't matter.

Some Amish families had a summer kitchen in the basement or on an enclosed porch, but we didn't. We did try to barbecue often though, and during canning season I'd set up an old portable camp stove outside that Daed used to take hunting.

As I worked, my mind fell back to the hope chest. I wanted it in my room as soon as possible and wished I could go get it after supper and sneak it up after Mutter and Daed had gone to bed, but it would be too likely that Timothy would see it.

I needed Mutter, Timothy, and Daed all out of the house to pull it off—that was certain.

As I was putting the potatoes on to boil, Danny came in for a drink of water before starting the milking. After he drained his glass, he ran water over his hands and wiped them along his hair-line, from his forehead to the nape of his neck.

"Mamm has a phone message," he said.

"Go tell her." I nodded toward the sewing room.

He wrinkled his freckled nose but did as I said. I stopped working, listening as hard as I could.

"Aenti Pauline left a message wanting to know if you and Aenti Nell could help her tomorrow," Danny said.

"Help her with what?" Mutter asked.

Danny hesitated. "Something about the girls' room. Painting and things."

"She knows I don't paint."

"There was other stuff too. Making curtains, maybe. Something like that. She wants you to come over in the afternoon."

"Probably while the younger ones are sleeping," Mutter said. "What do you think?" she asked, I assumed of Aenti Nell.

"Sure, we can help."

"Call her back," Mutter said to Danny. "Tell her we'll be there."

Danny came back into the kitchen and started filling his glass again. "Will you?" he asked me.

"Will I what?"

"Call Aenti Pauline back?"

"Sure," I said, smiling, happy to do my part to get Mutter out of the house tomorrow. Now I just needed to make sure Timothy wouldn't be lurking around. And then I'd recruit my younger Bruders to help me carry the chest up the stairs.

For a moment I felt a measure of chagrin for sneaking around my parents' backs—but although I would be sneaking around with something he had made, it wasn't as if I were sneaking around with Jonathan.

When Daed had Timothy drive him across the county to look at a bull he was thinking about purchasing the next afternoon, I knew my chance had come to bring my hope chest safely home. I recruited Billy and Joe-Joe to ride along with me.

We harnessed the pony to the old cart, because Mamm and Aenti Nell had taken one buggy and Daed had the wheel off the other one, for some sort of repair. We'd started down the lane when Danny began waving from the field. "Where are you going?" he yelled.

"Just over to Cate's."

"In the cart?"

"I need to get something," I replied, urging the pony to keep going.

"What?" Danny, out of all of my Bruders, was usually the least nosy.

I pretended I hadn't heard and continued on.

"What *are* you getting?" Billy asked.

"You'll see," Joe-Joe said, snuggling up against me, his body heating mine up even more. "Jonathan made it." He'd seen it in the show-room the day before.

"Another fishing pole?" Billy looked befuddled. "Why would you need the cart for that?"

Joe-Joe grinned, happy to know something Billy didn't. "You'll just have to wait and see."

Billy glared for a minute but then became intent on tapping out a rhythm with his bare foot as we rolled on down the lane. It hadn't rained the night before after all, and the humidity had continued to grow worse, until the air felt thick enough to eat. By the time we reached Onkel Bob's, Joe-Joe had fallen asleep against me and I was soaked with sweat. I pulled around to the showroom parking lot and up to the hitching post. Billy jumped down and ran over to my side, taking the reins, and then winding them around the pole.

I eased away from Joe-Joe, lowering his head to the bench so he could keep sleeping, and wiped the trickles of perspiration from rolling toward his eyes.

"Are we going up to the house?" Billy started that way.

"No. It's in the showroom."

He scowled but then turned and pushed through the door. I followed him. Pete leaned against the counter, flipping through a binder. He greeted us warmly, as if overjoyed to see other living souls on a hot and lazy afternoon.

"Everyone who has come in has commented on your hope chest," he said. "I think Jonathan will get a few orders out of leaving it here. I'm going to suggest he bring another one by and a stack of cards."

Billy was staring at the hope chest. "This is for you?"

"Jah," I answered. "There's my name."

"Ad-e-laide," Billy sounded out. "Who's that?"

"Me, silly." I tousled his hair.

He frowned. "You're Addie."

"It's a nickname for Adelaide." No one at home ever called me that—except Aenti Nell every once in a while. I liked it though. It sounded old country and made me think of high mountain meadows and peaks. It felt extra special that Jonathan had put it on my hope chest.

"We brought the cart for it," I said to Pete.

"I'll help load it." He grabbed the handle on one end and I reached for the other, but Billy grasped it before I could. I opened the door for them, and they passed through with Pete's end quite a bit higher than Billy's.

I followed them, freezing as I looked at the buggy. Joe-Joe was gone. I didn't panic though. He'd probably gone up to the house to see Cate, looking for a cookie and a glass of lemonade.

"Put it in the back, okay? I'm going up to the house to look for Joe-Joe."

"Cate's in her office," Pete said.

When I rounded the corner of the showroom, I spotted the two of them at the picnic table. Joe-Joe was showing Cate the toe he'd stubbed the day before.

"Hey," I called out, walking toward them. "We're about ready to go."

Cate waved, and when I reached her, I gave her a quick hug. "Is your Dat around today?"

"Jah," she said, nodding her head. "Over there."

Onkel Bob stood near the rose garden, with Nan Beiler at his side. I glanced toward the driveway. Sure enough her car was there.

She wore a lavender print dress and sensible shoes. She and my Onkel appeared to be deep in conversation. Cate had told me Nan left the Amish church in New York years before, and now she was a run-of-the-mill Mennonite, not Old Order, and drove a car and all. And, of course, the bookmobile too. I couldn't imagine my Onkel Bob ever leaving the Amish, which meant if they wanted a future together Nan would have to rejoin the Amish. Still, some saw it as scandalous that Onkel Bob spent time with her.

However, their challenges paled compared to what Jonathan and I faced. All Nan had to do was rejoin the church. They didn't have to challenge fate and family.

Even though I'd hoped Onkel Bob was over at the Mosiers having a heart-to-heart with Jonathan's parents, I knew he had his own concerns. His relationship with Nan. His first grandbaby on the way. Perhaps he had too many of his own issues to deal with Jonathan's and mine too.

Joe-Joe tugged on my sleeve. "Did you get the big box?"

I nodded.

"What are you going to do with it now?" Cate asked, standing.

"Put it in my room."

"What will your parents say?"

"They won't notice," I answered. It was hard to explain. They wouldn't possibly think anything in my room would pose a problem—it was the things outside my room that worried them.

"How will you get it up there?"

I shrugged. "I'll figure out something." I didn't want to share too much with her that revealed my deceit—nor did I want Joe-Joe to figure out I needed the hope chest to be a secret. If he did, he was bound to mention it to others.

I gave Cate a hug. "Come over and see me sometime."

"I will," she answered and then yawned.

"Tired?" I asked.

"Jah," she answered.

Joe-Joe yawned too and then said, "I'm not."

Both Cate and I laughed, and then she said, "I spent half the night at Betsy's. It was a false alarm again."

"Ach, that's too bad," I responded. "Hopefully, it will be soon."

Cate nodded, pulling Joe-Joe close in a tight hug. "I'm hoping for a nephew who's just like you."

He leaned into her in appreciation, and then we all walked toward the showroom parking lot. When we arrived, Pete was tucking the horse blanket around the hope chest.

When he saw Cate, holding Joe-Joe's hand, his face lit up. I turned toward my cousin. She smiled back at her husband, a knowing expression on her face. I could only guess at what their exchange was over—could Cate be expecting?

The whole encounter made my heart ache

though. Would I ever be allowed the future Cate had found—happily married, but with Jonathan?

That was what I wanted—and soon.

"Tell Onkel Bob I said hello," I said after Joe-Joe scampered up onto the cart bench. I could only hope my greeting would remind him of the urgency of Jonathan and my situation.

Cate said she would. "As soon as Nan leaves," she said, glancing toward the garden.

My thoughts stayed on Jonathan as I drove the cart home. Joe-Joe snuggled against me again, as warm as any heater, while Billy leaned his head over the side of the cart, seemingly intent on the rows of corn in the field.

"Are you counting them?" I asked.

He held up his hand and nodded yes, obviously not wanting to be interrupted. Billy was as determined to be a farmer as Jonathan wasn't. How ironic that as an only son, Jonathan might inherit the family farm, while Billy, as one of six boys, would be far less likely to.

The wind rustled through the corn, and a horsefly buzzed by.

As I came around the curve to our farm, I spotted a buggy by the barn. It was as if the orange triangle on the back shouted out a warning. For a moment I hoped it was Jonathan's—but knew it wasn't when Phillip stepped out of the shadows by the barn.

"Hot enough for you?" he called out.

I pulled the cart over by the tool shed, away from his buggy, feeling as if the hope chest in the back had a neon sign on it too—except that Pete had covered it.

I climbed down in a hurry, pulling Joe-Joe into my arms. "Can you unhitch the pony?" I asked Billy. "Make sure and water and feed him."

Billy nodded.

Phillip had almost reached the cart, so I hurried toward him. "How about a glass of lemonade?" I knew I was being nicer than I should, probably giving him the idea I didn't mean what I'd said the last time we saw each other.

"Ach, Addie. How did you know what I needed?" he answered.

"How about you, Billy? Would you like a snack after you're done out here?"

He bent down to pick up a rock and tossed it above his head, catching it. For a moment I thought he might say something about the chest and Jonathan, but instead he tossed the rock toward the barn and then said, "Nah." He headed around to the pony.

I lifted Joe-Joe higher in my arms so his head rested on my shoulder and led the way. Anyone but Phillip would have asked where we'd been and what was in the cart, but he chattered away alongside me about cleaning out the irrigation pump at the farm he worked on as I calculated how I was going to get the hope chest up to my room now, especially if Mutter got home from Aenti Pauline's before Phillip left.

Phillip didn't offer to carry my sleeping brother, but he did open the back door for us. I headed straight for the living room, slipped Joe-Joe onto the couch, and hurried back to the kitchen, trying to be as quiet as possible, hoping to encourage Phillip to keep his voice low.

We chatted as I pulled ice from the freezer and then filled up the glasses. He acted as if nothing had happened, as if I'd never told him I wasn't interested in him and never would be.

As I bent the tray of ice to release the cubes, one popped onto the floor and skated across the floor. For some reason Phillip found it amusing and burst out laughing. I quickly scooped it up, hoping he would stop. At the same time a car door slammed in the driveway.

Daed and Timothy were home. I groaned out loud.

"What's the matter?" Phillip asked. "Are you afraid they'll mind that I'm here?"

If only.

I hurried to the back door, deciding the best thing to do was distract my father and brother. "Want some lemonade?"

"Sure," Timothy said. "It's too hot to work right now."

Daed shook his head in disgust but followed

Timothy into the house anyway. I knew I was only stalling. I wouldn't be able to keep all of them in the kitchen forever.

I pulled more ice from the freezer, filled three more glasses, and then poured the lemonade, passing it around the table. As I did, the sound of a horse's hooves beat across the driveway and then stopped. After a long moment they started up again.

A few minutes later, Mutter opened the kitchen door, ecstatic to see Phillip and me together, not even attempting to hide her emotions. I poured her a glass of lemonade too, asking her about her day. She started in on a story about Maggie and a baby lamb at Aenti Pauline's.

That got Phillip started about sheep and the latest shearer the farmer he worked for had used. The discussion shifted to the price of wool as the front door opened.

"Addie," Mutter said, "go see who's there."

I stepped quickly, sure it was Joe-Joe trying to sneak out to find Billy. It wasn't. My baby brother was still asleep on the couch.

It was Billy coming through the front door, carrying one end of my chest with the horse blanket still draped over the top. Danny had the other end and they both had their lips pursed together in shushing gestures, as if they needed to tell me not to say anything. Aenti Nell tiptoed behind them.

"Denki," I mouthed.

They all smiled and started for the staircase. Billy tripped and banged against the newel post. Danny grimaced and made a circular motion with his head, indicating he needed to go first up the stairs. Aenti Nell waved her hands above her head.

I stepped forward to take Billy's end, but just then Mutter called out, "Addie, who is it?"

"The boys," I answered.

"What in the world are they doing?" she yelled.

Joe-Joe stirred, flopped to his stomach, and then settled back down.

Danny motioned with one hand for me to go back in the kitchen.

I did, slowly.

"Addie!" Mutter yelled again.

As I stepped through the archway, I said, "They're just taking a box upstairs."

"A box!" Mutter hooted. "Is it full of crickets? Or snakes?"

"It's empty," I answered. "But who's to say what they'll fill it with when they get the chance."

Mutter shook her head. "Phillip, I'm sure you never tormented your mother the way my boys do me."

I filled another glass with lemonade, for me, not bothering to put ice in it.

"Right?" Mutter was still trying to get an answer out of Phillip, probably wanting to empha-

239

size to all of us, again, what a good catch he was.

Phillip grinned at her, and then said, "Speaking of my mother, I'd better get on my way home. I was just passing by and thought I'd say hello."

He sure seemed to pass by our house a lot. Granted, it was on his way home from work—except for the detour up our lane. Still, I couldn't imagine anyone as persistent as Phillip, although I certainly hoped Jonathan would be—once he had the chance.

Chapter 12

I made chocolate cream pie for dessert that night as a special thank-you to Billy and Danny. With whipped cream dripping down his chin, Joe-Joe asked what happened to the box, and I answered that the boys had put it upstairs.

Joe-Joe seemed satisfied. Billy and Danny kept their eyes on their slices of pie, seconds for both of them, but no one else seemed to have even heard Joe-Joe's question. Timothy and Daed were arguing about the workload for the weekend, and Mutter and Aenti Nell were talking about Hannah. After Danny finished, he pushed back his plate.

"Ach, Addie," he said. "I just remembered.

Hannah telephoned you today. She left a message."

"What did she say?"

"Something about you visiting her. Spending tomorrow night, I think. And then going to church with her on Sunday." Aenti Pauline and Onkel Owen were in a district to the north of us.

Mutter and Aenti Nell stopped talking.

Mutter's jaw jutted toward me. "What do you have planned?" Her voice held a hint of suspicion.

I stood and began collecting dirty plates. "I'm not sure." Hannah and I hadn't talked about my spending the night at her house.

"Addie, we can manage without you." Aenti Nell's voice sounded upbeat.

Mutter added, "Barely."

Aenti Nell winked at me. "You should go."

Hannah clearly liked Mervin. That meant there might be a chance I could see Jonathan. Sure, Onkel Bob had told us not to go against our parents' wishes, but we couldn't help it if we bumped into each other.

I put the dishes in the sink and turned back toward the table. "Mutter? What do you think?"

Aenti quickly added, "It would be good for Hannah."

Mutter crossed her arms on top of the table, grasping her elbows. "I suppose . . ."

"Go give her a call," Aenti Nell said. "The boys can clear the table."

Timothy sprang to his feet. "I have work to do."

241

Billy and Danny groaned.

Joe-Joe climbed from his chair and grabbed his own plate. "I'll help," he said. "I like doing the dishes." Sure he did. Standing on a chair and splashing water around was an adventure, not a chore.

"Denki, Joe-Joe," I said. "I'll be right back to help."

At least spending the night with Hannah would give me something to look forward to—besides filling the hope chest that was now in my bedroom.

After I left a message for my cousin, I put away the food the boys had piled up on the counter and then rinsed and dried the dishes Joe-Joe was washing. Next I spent an hour outside weeding the garden, and then I read Joe-Joe and Billy three library books, tucked them into bed, and started to close their door gently behind me.

Finally, it was time to fill my hope chest.

"Addie!" Mutter's voice startled me, and I ended up yanking the little boys' door closed with a bang. "Come here a minute."

I followed her voice into her room, where her bed was covered with stacks of papers and books. "Help me put these away." Her fingertips pressed against her temples. "I'm too tired."

Several boxes littered the floor.

"Where did these come from?" I picked up a stack of yellowed notebook paper.

"My closet." Red rimmed her eyes.

It appeared to be a scholar's papers. I looked more closely. *George* was written in the upper right-hand corner of the first one. I thumbed through the stack. It was a collection of essays, probably from his eighth grade year.

"How about if we get rid of these?" I put it in a box and picked up another stack. *Sam* was written on the top of it. "And these too."

"Oh, no," Mutter said. "I'm saving those."

I frowned.

"Don't do that," she said.

"Do what?"

"Judge me. Just put all of this back in the boxes on the floor." She put her hands over her face, muffling her voice. "I want to go to bed."

I began scooting stacks of papers into the boxes. "What are you looking for?"

"Something I saved from when I was a girl." She spoke through her fingers.

"Anything in particular?" I asked, looking up at her.

She shook her head. In another minute, she sat down on the edge of the bed and turned away from me. I finished the job and pushed the boxes up against the wall.

"Anything else?" I asked.

She shook her head, her eyes on the boxes, but then she said, "Nell was so stubborn. She could have had lots of other suitors. She should have married one of them instead of reminding me every day what she gave up."

"Mutter," I said, stepping closer. "I don't know what you're talking about."

Her head jerked up, a puzzled look on her face. "What was I saying?"

"Something about Aenti Nell not marrying."

She shrugged. "It was her choice, jah? No matter what everyone said."

"I don't understand. . . ." I wrinkled my nose.

Mutter yawned. "That's just it. I never did either."

"Are you all right?" I sat down on the bed beside her and took her hand. My mother could be moody, but this was different. She wasn't making sense.

"I'm fine." She yawned. "Just tired. You go on. Let me go to bed."

I told her good-night and left the room, nearly bumping into Aenti Nell in the hall.

I put my finger to my lips and dragged her down to the end of the landing by the window. "Mutter was just rambling on about you being too stubborn to marry. What was she talking about?"

Aenti Nell shook her head. "Who knows?" But her words didn't convince me.

Since she wouldn't answer that question, I tried another. "Do you know what she's searching for? She won't tell me."

Aenti Nell shrugged. "Pauline said something

about the letters. That's what sent your Mamm up to the attic the other day."

I kept my voice low. "*The* letters?"

"Jah." Aenti Nell whispered much more loudly than I did. "Pauline asked what the story was way back when, about the letters Dirk sent."

I froze. Of course that's what she was looking for. I managed to say, "Jonathan doesn't think his father wrote the letters."

"Dirk always claimed he didn't." Aenti Nell wrinkled her nose. "I wondered at times too."

"Once Mutter finds them, we should know more, right? Dirk can look at them and say he didn't write them. We can figure out who did and put an end to the grudge."

Aenti Nell exhaled. "I doubt it will be that simple. Or that she would show them to you."

"Why?"

"It's complicated, jah?"

I nodded. "But not hopeless."

She turned her head toward the window and gazed out over the yard, toward the barn. "Don't ask her about the letters."

I didn't answer my Aenti. I couldn't promise I wouldn't, not if the opportunity presented itself. I didn't tell her I'd told both Mutter and Phillip what my true feelings were, but I did tell her what Onkel Bob had advised. She squeezed my hand. "It will all work out. Just wait and see."

Sensing the need to change the topic, I said,

"Denki, for getting the boys to carry the hope chest up."

"Jah." She put her hands to her bosom as she continued to look out the window. "It's beautiful. I'm happy for you."

I gave her a quick hug and retreated to my room, closing the door firmly behind me, and then lifted the blanket from the chest. I ran my hands over the smooth wood, stopping at the carving of my name, admiring Jonathan's work, knowing his thoughts were on me every second as he carved it.

It didn't take me long to transfer the things I'd been saving from the hamper to the hope chest, breathing in the scent of the cedar lining as I did. I put the first quilt I'd ever made—lap size designed from simple blocks—in first and then the one I'd finished in the spring—a log cabin pattern made from my Bruders' old shirts. Next I put in pillowcases, sheets, towels, doilies, potholders, and oven mittens, filling the chest halfway.

As I closed it, there was a knock and Mutter called out my name. I quickly placed the blanket back over the top.

"Are you in there?"

I hurried to the door and opened it.

"I need your help again." She pointed to the linen closet at the end of the hall. The cupboard doors were wide open and sheets, tablecloths, and towels littered the floor below.

"I thought you were going to bed." I followed her toward the closet.

"I am—now. Would you put that all back in? And reorganize it. It was such a mess I couldn't stand it any longer." She seemed sincere, but I couldn't imagine why it would bother her now when it hadn't for the last decade. Especially when she'd been exhausted fifteen minutes before.

She continued on to her room, shuffling along, favoring her bad knee, her skirt shifting back and forth across her hips.

I refolded each item and then stacked the sheets all together, twins on one side and doubles on the other, along with the pillowcases and then the towels.

I knew Mutter wasn't in a cleaning mood. She was definitely looking for something. I could only hope it was the letters and that Aenti Nell was wrong—I still hoped Mutter would be willing to show them to me.

Saturday after supper Timothy drove me to Hannah's. There seemed to be an unspoken agreement between Daed and the older boys—he wouldn't say anything about their cars as long as they provided rides for the rest of us, when needed. And although I'd sworn off riding with Timothy, I decided, since he hadn't been drinking, to accept the ride.

As we drove down the lane, I noted that Nan's car was at Onkel Bob's again. I sighed out loud. That meant my Onkel wouldn't be calling on my parents tonight either.

Cate stepped onto the porch and began waving.

"Stop," I said to Timothy.

He grimaced but obeyed.

Cate came running toward the Bronco, to Timothy's open window. She leaned against the door, speaking to me. "Betsy's at the hospital. She's really in labor this time."

"Are you going?"

Cate nodded, her face as bright as I'd ever seen it. "Nan is taking all of us."

I was a little surprised to hear that. Technically, because Nan had left the Amish church, none of them should be riding with her, but maybe because she was originally from New York and it was so long ago, the bishop hadn't given it a thought.

I shuddered. It wasn't like me to track that sort of thing—that was something my parents would do. I was certain my Onkel knew what he was doing.

"I'm praying for Betsy," I said. "And her Bobli."

"Denki." Cate's voice gave away her gratitude. I thought of their mother dying after Betsy's birth and how that must weigh on all of them now.

Timothy tapped on the steering wheel. "Can we go?"

Cate patted him on the shoulder. "At least you stopped." She stepped backward.

Pete called for her as he walked toward Nan's car.

"Let us know when the Bobli comes!" I shouted as Timothy accelerated.

"I'll leave a message!" Cate called over her shoulder, jogging toward the car.

As I offered up a silent prayer, Timothy said, "You should just hang out with me tonight."

I didn't know what made him think I'd want to do that, but I didn't ask. Instead I said, "I told Hannah I'd come over."

"She's going to the same party I am. We'll just meet her there."

I wrinkled my nose. "I'm spending the night with her. I told Mutter and Daed that's where I was going. She didn't say anything about a party." Which was true. I'd just assumed there might be one she planned to go to, if her parents let her.

"That's not what I heard," Timothy said.

"What did you hear?"

"That Hannah's about ready to go stir crazy."

"That's why I'm going over."

Timothy smirked and then turned on to the highway, speeding along. "She wants to hang out with Mervin."

Everything was working as I'd hoped. Perhaps I'd see Jonathan after all.

"Those Mosiers are all such losers," Timothy

said. "Especially Jonathan. It's like he's from another planet."

"He's an artist."

"He's a sissy."

"He's kind."

"He pretends to be."

I didn't answer.

"Don't be swayed by his acting," Timothy said. "Phillip might be boring, but Mutter and Daed are right. He'd be much better for you to marry."

I crossed my arms.

"It's not like you to be so stubborn," Timothy said.

"It's not like you to care about my life," I shot back.

He didn't answer. We rode in silence—me fuming, him taking the curves too fast. He slowed, barely, as we sped through Paradise, then took a sharp turn down the road to Hannah's farm on the other side of the highway. He slowed as he turned into their drive, past the sign that read *Paradise Stables*. Onkel Owen trained and boarded horses.

"I'll see you soon," he said as he stopped in front of her house.

"Don't count on it," I shot back, opening the car door and darting away from him. He screeched out of the driveway as I hurried up the front steps.

The house was less than ten years old with a wraparound porch and a wide front door.

Aenti Pauline answered when I knocked,

pointing to the staircase after she said hello. "Go on up," she said.

I could hear voices by the time I reached the landing and then all-out laughter by the time I stood at Hannah's door. She didn't sound depressed.

I knocked.

"Go away!" It was my cousin's voice all right, but I could scarcely believe her words.

"Hannah?"

More laughter. "Sorry!"

The door swung open, and there stood Molly, brushing her long blond hair, her apron off. Hannah stood behind her, a grin on her face.

"We thought you were Deborah and Sarah," she said. "They keep trying to spy."

"What are you up to?" I stepped into the room, and Molly pushed the door shut behind me with both her hands.

"Getting ready." Hannah lifted her dress to show a pair of jeans, the pants legs rolled up.

"To go . . . ?"

"Out."

I turned toward my cousin. "Your parents are letting you go to a party?"

"They think I'm going over to Molly's."

"And me too?"

"Jah."

"Won't they check with Mutter and Daed to see if it is okay?"

"Nah," Hannah said, blushing a little. "I told them we're not spending the night."

"Oh," I said, trying to keep up with the plan.

"Mervin and Martin are coming to get us," Molly interjected, scooping her hair up in her hand and twisting it into a bun.

"In their buggy?"

"No." Hannah laughed at me. "They're borrowing a friend's car."

I knew Mervin and Martin hadn't joined the church, but I'd never known them to drive. I wondered if they were getting wilder as they grew older—instead of the other way around.

"Does one of them have a license?"

"I think Martin does," Molly said, looking at Hannah as she pinned her hair.

She shrugged.

"I don't know about this," I said.

"We're going over to Jonathan's," Hannah said. "To pick him up."

I sat down on her bed. That only made it more complicated. It wasn't that I didn't want to see him, but I did want to be mindful of Onkel Bob's advice. And I didn't think bumping into his parents again would help the situation any. "I shouldn't go," I said.

"Why not?" Hannah pulled a tube of mascara out of the top drawer of her bureau.

"Because I came over here to hang out with you. Remember? You said you were depressed in the message you left and that having me around would help you feel better."

Hannah glanced at Molly, who was positioning her Kapp on her head and didn't seem interested in us in the least. Hannah turned back toward me. "I'm feeling better. Molly's been here for a couple of hours."

"But I can't come back and spend the night," Molly chimed in. "My parents want me home."

Molly tended to be a go-about—that was for sure. Her parents were old, close to Mammi Gladys's age, it seemed, and I could see them wanting her at home every once in a while.

I stood and walked to the window. A sedan turned into the driveway.

Molly must have heard it because she stepped to my side. "They're here," she said, pinning her hair.

Mervin and Marvin wore baseball caps instead of their straw hats. I guessed they had on Englisch clothes too.

I could stay at the house with Aenti Pauline or go with Hannah.

I could stay in the car, in the back seat, when we picked up Jonathan. His parents would never know I was there.

The good news was, I would get to see him. The bad news was, Timothy was most likely right. We were probably all headed to the same party.

• • •

Mervin, wearing jeans and a T-shirt, stepped into his grandfather's house as the rest of us waited in the car for Jonathan. A couple of minutes later, Mervin appeared and then stepped into the shop.

Martin's voice held a hint of frustration as he spoke. "Jonathan is always late. He gets caught up in his work and forgets everything else."

I wondered if he would have lost track of time if he'd known I was coming along. Finally, Mervin appeared, followed by Jonathan, who wore his Amish clothes and dusted his hands off each other as he walked. Then the back door to the house opened and Dirk Mosier appeared, catching up with his son and nephew.

I held my breath.

"I just want to say hello," he chided Jonathan as they all neared the car. He appeared even bigger than he had earlier in the week, and I marveled at how dark his hair and beard were—so different than my Daed's. I didn't stare long though, and turned my head so he couldn't see my face. Hannah did the same.

Martin clamored from the car, calling out a hello to their Onkel before he got any closer.

"Who do you have with you?" Dirk asked.

Molly rolled down her window. "Just a few of us girls," she said. "My last name is Zook. We have the farm with the nursery stock on the other side of Paradise."

"Sure," Dirk said. "Where the Youngie farmers' market is."

"That's right." Molly's voice surged with enthusiasm. "Jonathan's done really well there."

I couldn't see Dirk's face, but by the long pause, I gathered he didn't agree with her.

"We should get going," Martin interjected. The twins blurted out good-byes to their Onkel, and then Mervin asked Jonathan if he wanted to drive.

As he climbed into the driver's seat, he saw me and broke out into a big smile. After he fastened his seatbelt, he reached back and brushed my leg. My heart swelled. I grabbed his hand and gave it a squeeze, which he returned.

I smiled and then stole a glance toward the house. His father was standing at the back door, his arms crossed, his feet apart. Dusk was falling, so I couldn't see his face, but I sensed a frown on it.

"Hello, Molly and Hannah," Jonathan said as he backed up the car, looking over the driver's seat. Then his gaze fell on me for a long moment.

"Do you have a driver's license?" Molly asked.

"Who, me?" Jonathan turned forward, put the car in Drive, and pulled up to the highway.

"Jah—who else?" Molly seemed a little flirty.

"I got it back home." He turned left. "I did deliveries for a local carpenter for a while—a retired Englisch pastor."

I kept my eyes on the back of his head, on the brim of his straw hat, as he drove, wanting to ask why he quit working for the man, but guessing his Dat forced him to. There was a lot, granted, I didn't know about Jonathan.

"So where are we going?" he asked.

"To the river," Martin answered.

"There's a big party starting up. With kids from all over." Mervin pulled down on the bill of his cap. "Take a right at the next intersection."

The twins directed Jonathan, arguing now and then about the next turn. Molly chimed in often, but Hannah and I stayed quiet. I didn't like sharing Jonathan with everyone, and Hannah seemed to be sliding into one of her moods. However, whenever Mervin looked at her, she smiled and perked up.

The sun set behind us, casting a golden glow into the car, but by the time we turned toward the river, darkness covered the countryside.

Martin directed Jonathan to follow a pickup down a dirt road. He slowed to a crawl, but still the three of us girls bumped along in the back seat, jarring into each other. Molly and I began to laugh but Hannah stuck out her elbows, forcing us back against the doors.

The lights of the car bounced along the field of stubble on either side of us. Soon there was a car behind us, and one behind that.

"I heard kids from all over the state will be

here," Martin said. "And even as far as Ohio."

I couldn't help but think it was crazy for Youngie to travel so far—for a party.

"Of course there will be lots of locals too," Mervin added. He shot another glance at Hannah. "But just so you three girls know, we're not after any trouble. Isn't that right?" He turned first to Martin and then to Jonathan.

"Of course we aren't," Jonathan said. "We're looking to mend things. Not make them worse."

Ahead, I spotted George's blue pickup. Next to it was Timothy's yellow Bronco.

"Turn right," I stammered. "Park down that way." I could only hope there would be so many teenagers and young adults that Timothy wouldn't even see Jonathan, Mervin, and Martin. It was a nice delusion to hold on to—at least for a short time.

Chapter 13

Hannah and Molly took off their Kapps in the back seat, and as soon as the boys climbed out of the car, the girls started to wiggle out of their dresses too. Eager to give them more room, I climbed out, closed the door firmly behind me, and stepped around to Jonathan's side. He took my hand in his rougher one and held it tenderly. I leaned against him.

When Hannah and Molly finally appeared, they were wearing jeans, tight fitting tops—Hannah in a red one and Molly in a sparkly silver one—and strappy sandals. They ran their fingers through their hair, raking it out over their shoulders. Hannah's dark curls fell midway down her back, while Molly's straight blond hair nearly reached her waist.

I glanced down at my dress and apron, then touched my bun, tucked under my Kapp.

"You look nice," Jonathan whispered into my ear. "I like what you're wearing much better."

"Denki," I whispered back, even though I didn't quite believe him.

Martin and Molly fell into step with Mervin and Hannah, leading the way to the crowd gathered closer to the river. The air grew cooler the farther we walked.

Mervin reached for Hannah's hand, and they walked in step for a bit, but then he put his arm around her and drew her close.

"Ach," Jonathan said. "They make a sweet couple."

At least I wasn't the only girl in my extended family now interested in a Mosier boy. But the truth was, although the adults in the families wouldn't be thrilled, they wouldn't be as upset about Hannah and Mervin as they would about

Jonathan and me. It was our fathers, Cap and Dirk, who were at the heart of the problem.

Martin stopped at a group of guys gathered around the trunk of a car. A few of them slapped him on the back and then Mervin too. Beers were offered around, but Mervin and Martin declined. The guys offered Hannah and Molly each a beer, but they giggled and refused.

Jonathan put his hand on my back and directed me around the group and away from the cars and headlights.

"It looks like there's a trail over here," he said.

I followed him through beaten-down grass, still holding his hand. The terrain began to slope a little, and soon we began sidestepping down a slight hill that led toward the riverbank.

I asked about Tabitha, if she'd thought about coming along tonight.

Jonathan shook his head. "She said she's not going to any more parties around here. She doesn't like what goes on." He paused for just a moment and then added, "I understand what she means. I think this will be my last one."

I nodded. There was too much tension in the air for my liking.

Jonathan let go of my hand as the slope increased and took my elbow, leading me along. I'd never felt so cared for. So cherished. A new hope hung over me, as promising as the canopy of the night sky twinkling above my head.

In the background the hum of voices grew louder, and someone shouted, "Look who's here!"

But it wasn't just someone. It was Timothy.

"Your brother?" Jonathan clasped me tighter as the slope grew steeper.

"Jah," I said. "Timothy the Terrible."

Jonathan grinned. "Do you have names for the other Bruders too?"

"Of course." I smiled back.

He cocked his head.

"Samuel the Simple. George the Generous. Danny the Dependable." I took a breath.

"Let me guess. . . ." He inched a little closer to me. "Billy the . . . Brave."

"How'd you know?"

He smiled. "Billy told me. He really likes it that you call him that."

I sighed. "Well, Timothy and Samuel don't know what I call them. I only share the positive ones."

"That's wise, "Jonathan said. "And what about you? What do they call you?"

I squirmed a little. "Just Addie."

"How about . . . Addie the Adored."

I sighed again. "Hardly."

"What? How could you say that? Everyone adores you."

"Not in my family."

"I think you're wrong." He met my eyes. "You know I adore you, right?"

"Stop."

"No. I will adore you my entire life. I promise." He tilted his head toward the sky. "As sure as the moon rises and the stars shine, even when we're old and gray."

I groaned. "Please stop."

"Oh, no. I'm just starting. We have so much to look forward to. So much God is going to give us." He reached his hand that wasn't holding mine high above our heads. "We'll set our sails by his direction."

Timothy shouted again.

Jonathan grimaced. "But tonight our course is away from your brother."

"Hopefully, no one will tell him we're here."

Jonathan let go of my arm and pointed to a boulder. I sat and he leaned against it next to me, his leg pressed against mine. On the other side of the vast inky river, lights fell across the water. Above our heads the cool breeze danced through the leaves of the trees.

Jonathan scooted back a little and put his arm around me, tilting his head heavenward. "Isn't it amazing?"

"Jah" was all I managed to say.

"I read somewhere that there are eight thousand stars visible at any one time but more than four hundred billion stars in the Milky Way alone." Jonathan tilted his head back even farther. "It's impossible to comprehend, isn't it."

I nodded. "It makes me feel so small." Sure, I felt hopeful because of Jonathan, but not even that could shake my feelings of insignificance.

"Really?" Jonathan turned his attention to me. "It makes me feel so chosen. So designed. Such an important part of God's world—not special, mind you, not more valued than anyone else he's made. But definitely as if I have a purpose."

It was easy for him to feel that way. He was made to see the positive—and had a personality to appreciate beauty. Plus a gift to create incredible things.

"Addie?" he said.

"Jah?"

"What are you thinking?"

"That I wish I could talk about God the way you do."

He leaned his shoulder against mine but stayed silent.

"I guess I should say 'feel' about God," I clarified.

"What do you mean?"

"You speak of him with such certainty." I realized that didn't sound as I meant it. "Not certainty that he exists—I know that. But certainty that he cares about you."

"Jah, I know he does. And he cares about you too. Don't you feel it?"

I took a deep breath. How could I explain to Jonathan that I didn't? What I did feel was that I was a disappointment to God, and that I'd never measure up to what he wanted from me, just like I felt as if I'd never measure up to what my parents wanted of me either.

"But God adores you, Addie. Far more than I even do—which is saying a lot. Don't you see? He wants you to abide in him—to talk with him and follow his teachings. It's as simple as that."

He smiled. "Although, *simple* doesn't always mean *easy*. I worry sometimes—I even ended up with a stomach problem a while back from stress. And sometimes I'm not mindful of others, like with being late."

I nodded. He had been late a few times, including tonight. His face was inches from mine as he spoke. "And as you know, I sometimes lack confidence about my work."

I nodded again. I'd seen that firsthand.

"And my Dat and I don't have a great relationship, but I keep trying to talk things through with God—I keep trying to live by faith, bit by bit."

I did like the way he spoke about God.

We both watched the sky, leaning against each other. I also liked having him so close. I nuzzled my head against his, and he turned toward me.

"How about another holy kiss?" he asked.

I leaned toward him. "How about a real kiss?" The scent of wood that hung on his clothes grew stronger.

Downriver, it sounded as if someone threw a

rock into the current, followed by laughter. Timothy again, I was sure.

Jonathan put his hand on the small of my back, drawing me closer. I raised my face to his.

There was another splash, then a girl's voice —Molly's?—yelled, "Knock it off."

"Make me!" That was definitely Timothy. He laughed again, this time in a jeering way.

I took a deep breath, wishing I could make my oh-so-terrible brother disappear.

"He'll stop soon," Jonathan whispered, his nose touching mine.

I shivered. "He's probably had too much to drink. I hope he doesn't hurt anyone."

"Jah, it's troubling, isn't it." Jonathan's breath warmed my face.

There was another outburst—Timothy again, yelling, "Prove it."

Then a scream, most likely from Hannah. Then Molly yelled, "Timothy Cramer, you're going to get it."

I froze as Jonathan turned his head toward the ruckus.

It sounded as if there was a scuffle going on and then there was another splash, but this time it didn't sound like a rock.

"Mervin?!" Martin's voice relayed both uncertainty and fear.

"He went under the water!" This time I was sure it was Hannah.

Jonathan let go of me and dashed toward the trail before I registered what had happened, but once I did I sprinted behind him.

"Who has a flashlight?" Molly yelled.

A beam appeared in the distance, most likely an app on someone's phone.

"Mervin!" Panic filled Martin's voice.

There was another splash. We were close now, close enough to hear Molly say, "I'm calling 9-1-1." She sounded sure and calm, but Hannah began to scream.

Jonathan ran, with me struggling to keep up, urged on by my cousin's wailing and the thought of Mervin drowning in the Susquehanna River.

By the time I reached Hannah, Jonathan had jumped into the water. Though Martin seemed to be thrashing about, Jonathan made his way straight out. There was now a crowd gathered around, shining flashlights and cell phones onto the surface of the river. I searched the group for my Bruders but couldn't find any of them—not even George, whom I assumed had come with Sadie.

It didn't surprise me that Timothy would run off, but it wasn't like George to be a coward.

Standing back from the crowd, Molly spoke into her phone.

I pulled Hannah close as soon as I reached her. "Shh," I whispered. "Jonathan and Martin need to be able to hear each other." I wasn't sure if what I said was true, since Martin was still thrashing around, but I didn't think Hannah's noise was going to help anything.

Jonathan turned back toward the shore, stood, and bent over. I imagined him methodically sweeping his arms back and forth under the water. After a few steps he reached deeper. He didn't shout or call out. He simply pulled, yanking Mervin to the surface, and started moving toward the bank. Mervin's body flopped forward like a rag doll. Water poured from his hair and down his face.

Hannah's hands flew to her eyes, and she screamed again. That got Martin's attention, and he stopped thrashing around and floundered toward Jonathan, grabbing Mervin's other arm. Together they dragged him to the bank as Mervin's head lolled forward.

Other young men stepped forward and grabbed Mervin, pulling him out of the water and up the slope of matted-down grass onto level ground. Jonathan knelt and bent over Mervin, scooped his finger in his mouth, and then leaned down and breathed. Then he began compressions on his chest. As he worked, he spoke to Martin, who moved closer to Mervin's head and took over the breathing. Jonathan kept up with the compressions.

Hannah stepped backward to the edge of the

crowd, and I moved with her, grabbing her hand, praying silently for Mervin as I stood beside my cousin. Seconds dragged on like hours as Jonathan and Martin continued working on Mervin. The crowd kept stepping in closer and closer until Jonathan shooed them all back. Molly, still on her phone, started jogging toward the parking lot. She looked like an Englisch girl—her hair long, her jeans tight, her demeanor confident and sure. No one would guess she was Plain.

In the distance a siren wailed.

The crowd broke in two then, with half the kids hurrying back to their cars. Motors revved to life. Lights came on. Beer cans flew out of windows. A few cars sped away, but most left slowly, one by one. Those Youngie who didn't leave congregated at the far end of the field, away from the river. I guessed those were the ones who hadn't been drinking. And a small group stayed in a semicircle around Mervin.

The sirens grew louder, and a fire truck turned off the road into the field, followed by an ambulance. Molly directed them to the edge of the field. The lights blinded us as the emergency vehicles turned toward the river, their red-and-white lights falling on the twins and Jonathan.

The engines continued to idle as fire fighters and EMTs climbed out, collecting their equipment. A police car, its blue lights flashing, bumped onto the field in the distance.

The firefighters reached Mervin first and then the EMTs. Jonathan and Martin stood and stepped backward. I realized then that neither had their hats, and of course, Mervin didn't have his either.

Perhaps I was trying to distract myself, but I began searching the water, which was nearly pitch-dark now that the flashlights and cell phones had left with their owners.

God, I prayed, *if only I can see their hats, even one of the hats, then I know everything will be okay.* It was a silly prayer, a "fleece," some would call it, but it was the best I could do.

Just then a figure moved along the bank, headed downstream, a stick in his hand. He squatted and reached out, fishing out one straw hat and pulling it in. When he stood I realized it was George—with Jonathan's hat, since Mervin and Martin had both been wearing baseball caps.

George continued downstream, disappearing into the dark.

I turned then toward the group that remained, looking again for Timothy as two police officers climbed out of the car, its lights still flashing. They stopped a young Amishman I didn't recognize, but he shook his head. They made their way around the group that had been pushed farther from Mervin by the firefighters.

I pulled on Hannah, tugging her back more, away from the officers, but one of them headed straight toward us. He had a small notebook in his hand.

"What happened?" he asked.

"I was upstream," I answered. "I didn't see it." I felt sick to my stomach, sure the problem was Timothy.

"How about you?" the officer asked Hannah.

She leaned against me, nearly pushing me over.

"Miss," the officer said, "are you all right?"

She was slumping, and her weight was nearly more than I could bear. I had no other choice but to wrap my arms around her and let her weight pull both of us to the ground.

Hannah's eyes remained opened and focused, but she wouldn't talk to me. She leaned against me as we both sat in the flattened grass, which was easier for her in her jeans than it was for me in my dress.

"Is she diabetic?" the officer asked, kneeling beside us. "Or epileptic?"

"No," I answered, with my arms still around her. "I think she's just distraught."

"Maybe a panic attack?" He stood.

"Jah." I'd heard of those but had never seen one.

"Is she Amish?" he asked.

That stopped me a moment until it registered that in her Englisch clothes Hannah looked anything but Plain. "Jah," I answered.

"Has she been drinking?" he asked.

"No," I said. "She hasn't." I couldn't smell anything on her breath, and I hadn't seen her take a beer earlier.

"I'll ask one of the EMTs to check her out," the officer said. "Perhaps she should be transported too, along with the young man."

I didn't know what good that would do. Once we knew Mervin would be okay, I was certain Hannah would be too.

"Can you find out how Mervin is doing?" I asked. "And let us know? That will help more than anything."

He turned toward the group hovering around Mervin. Jonathan stood behind them, his head bowed, while Martin stood beside him with tears rolling down his face.

The officer said, "I'll see what I can do."

As he walked away, I squeezed Hannah's shoulder. "It's going to be okay." I hoped I'd told the truth.

A sob welled up inside of her and shook her whole body.

"We should pray," I said.

Her head bobbed up and down as another sob shook her.

We both bowed our heads, saying our silent prayers. I asked God to please spare Mervin's life and heal him. And for peace between our families—between the Cramers and Mosiers.

And that Hannah would be all right too. After a minute, I said amen and opened my eyes.

My cousin kept hers closed and leaned against me even more.

"Addie?" George knelt beside me with Jonathan's hat still in his hand. "Are you two okay?" Sadie, wearing a dress, apron, and Kapp, stood behind him.

"Jah, I'm okay." I glanced toward the officer, who was talking to an EMT and pointing our direction. "But Hannah's having a hard time."

Just then the other EMTs began transferring Mervin onto a gurney. I stood quickly, pulling Hannah up with me, and George hopped up too. Hannah turned her back to what was going on, which was too bad because Mervin had a mask on his face and, although it looked scary, he seemed to be alive.

Two of the EMTs carried the gurney toward the ambulance, and the officer and the third EMT came toward us.

I pulled Hannah back around.

As the officer approached she said, "I'm o-o-kay."

"Is he a friend of yours?" the EMT asked.

Hannah nodded, tears welling in her eyes.

The EMT stepped closer to Hannah. "He's breathing."

I couldn't help but exhale in relief.

The EMT continued, "We'll transport him to the hospital, and they'll do a thorough exam. He has a bump on his head."

"Do you know anything about that?" the officer interjected. "Did someone strike him?"

"I don't know," Hannah whispered.

"You were with him though?" the officer persisted.

She nodded.

"But you didn't see what happened?" the officer asked.

She shook her head.

The officer turned toward George. "How about you?"

George put up his free hand and shook his head.

"Not a thing?" The officer crossed his arms and looked at Sadie. She shook her head too.

George nodded. "I had my back to the river when it all happened."

The officer didn't respond for a long moment, as if hoping to draw more out of George.

Finally my brother said, "Sorry, Officer."

The man let out a long sigh. "I've heard that more times than I can count," he said, flipping through his little notebook and looking down. "One person did mention someone named Timothy." He looked up. "That he might be involved. Any of you know him?"

I glanced at George, whose face was blank.

"Jah," I answered.

"Did you see him near the river tonight?" The officer made a sweeping motion with his free hand.

I looked around the diminishing crowd. "No."

"Did you see him earlier?"

I nodded. I wasn't going to lie.

"When?"

"Well, at our house . . ."

The officer cocked his head.

"He's my brother," I explained.

"Oh."

"And then here, when we first arrived. Out by the cars."

"But not before the incident."

"I was upriver, like I said. But I heard him yelling . . ."

George stepped away from me as the officer jotted something down and then asked, "And what's your name, miss?"

"Addie," I replied. "Addie Cramer."

As he wrote that down, I realized George and Sadie were walking toward Molly, taking Hannah with them. I looked beyond them to the ambulance. Martin climbed into the passenger side as the EMTs loaded Mervin into the back. Jonathan stood off to the side.

The officer cleared his throat, and I focused on him again.

"Where do you live?"

I gave him our address, my heart sinking as I did, wondering how furious my family would be with me.

His eyes met mine. "Anything else you can tell me?"

I shook my head.

Then he nodded toward Hannah, "Does she have a ride?"

"Jah," I answered. "I'll get her home."

I motioned to George and Molly, who hurried over to us. "Sadie needs to get a ride with someone else," I said to George. "You need to take Hannah and me to her house."

George seemed grateful to have me take charge.

I turned to Molly. "You go with Jonathan in the car we all came in," I said, as much as I hated to. "Stop and get Mervin and Martin's parents. Once you're at the hospital, call George on your cell as soon as you know how Mervin is. He can let Hannah know."

Molly nodded in agreement as Jonathan started toward us. He stopped beside me. I reached for his hand and squeezed it and didn't let go. If George noticed he didn't let on.

"Molly's going with you," I said to Jonathan.

He gave me a puzzled look.

"I need to go with Hannah," I added.

He nodded then and tightened his grip on my hand, stepping closer to me until our shoulders touched and I could feel his soaking wet shirt through my sleeve and against my skin.

"Have you tried calling Timothy?" Jonathan asked George.

He shook his head.

"Someone should. The police will probably be after him."

"Jah," George said. "Addie ratted him out to the officer."

I bristled. "I wasn't going to lie," I said. "He would have found out who Timothy is eventually. And it's not like I saw anything." I turned to Molly. "So what did happen?"

"Timothy chased him into the water—that's all I know for sure." She flicked her hair over her shoulder. "There was some sort of a struggle, but it was too dark to see exactly what happened."

Hannah sucked in a raggedy breath.

"We'd better go," I said, letting go of Jonathan's hand. His eyes met mine for a moment.

"I need to find my purse." Molly searched around, holding her cell tightly in her hand. She scurried over to a rock closer to the river.

George handed Jonathan his hat.

"Denki," he said. "I thought it was a goner."

"Jah," George answered. Then he extended his hand, saying "Denki" as he did.

Jonathan clasped it as he continued to hold on to me with his other hand, and the two shook but neither said another word.

After a moment George stepped away and said to me, "Over this way." He led us toward his pickup, away from the direction Jonathan and Molly headed.

As we walked along, Hannah between us, George said my name quietly.

"Jah?" I whispered back.

"I'm grateful to Jonathan—I can't imagine the heap of trouble we'd all be in if he hadn't saved Mervin—but don't think I didn't see you holding his hand."

"Leave it be, George." I kept my voice firm and quiet.

"There's already enough trouble without—"

Hannah sobbed again.

"—all of you acting like idiots," I countered.

"I haven't done anything," he said.

"Exactly," I said. "If you'd stopped Timothy, Mervin wouldn't be on his way to the hospital now, would he."

Chapter 14

രൂ

We sat with Hannah between us in the cab of George's truck. He kept bumping her leg as he shifted, making her whimper. As he wound his way over the country roads, he drove more cautiously, I was sure, than he or my other Bruders ever had.

"Stop here," Hannah said, about a half mile from her house.

George glanced at me. I shrugged my shoulders, not sure what to do. "Why?" I cooed to Hannah.

"Until Molly calls." She'd be calling George's phone, since neither Hannah nor I had one.

"That might be a long time," I said.

"Then will you come in and wait with us at the house?" she asked George.

He pulled over to the side of the road. "Let's wait here."

"Won't Aenti Pauline be worried?"

"She'll just think we stayed out late."

George stopped the car.

"Are we all the way off the pavement?" I craned my neck, trying to see in the dark.

"Close enough," George said, turning off the engine. He settled against the headrest.

"Is your ringer turned up?"

"Jah," he answered.

Hannah snuggled closer to me. George sighed, and then his breathing changed, as if he'd fallen asleep already. I tried to stretch out my legs, but the cab was cramped with Hannah turned toward me.

A car's lights filled the back window and then zoomed by, going too quickly, I was sure. I must have dozed too, because I awoke to the jangle of George's cell.

Trying not to wake Hannah, I shook George's shoulder. "Your phone," I said.

He stirred, then started shifting around as if looking for it. Finally he muttered, "Hello."

Whoever had called was doing all the talking until George said, "Where are you?"

It definitely wasn't Molly.

"Jah, the police were asking about you—that's true." George shifted in his seat and mouthed *Timothy,* as if I couldn't guess with that last piece of information, as he continued to listen.

Finally he said, "Molly's going to call and tell us how he is. I'll let you know." Then he said good-bye.

"Where is he?" I asked.

"At the house."

"At least we won't be there when the police arrive."

"Jah," George said. "Daed's going to be furious."

"Did Timothy say what he did?"

"What do you mean?"

"How Mervin got hurt." I was trying to keep my voice low, but Hannah stirred again.

"He said he must have hit his head on a rock."

"Did Timothy push him though? That sort of thing."

"He didn't say."

And of course George didn't ask.

The cell phone rang again, and this time George answered it right away, and with "Hello,

Molly." I hadn't realized she was programmed into his phone—but then again she hadn't asked for his number. I was sure I was the only Youngie without a cell, besides Hannah.

George listened, saying jah a few times.

"Oh," George said. "Betsy's there?"

I gasped. I'd forgotten all about Betsy.

After a moment he said, "Denki. I'll tell Addie. And Hannah—both of them—about Mervin. Bye, Molly." George ended the call.

My cousin opened her eyes and sat straighter. "What did she say?"

"It seems like he's okay."

Hannah began to cry.

"They're doing a whole bunch of tests though, just to be sure, and they won't have the results for a while. But he's conscious and talking. Molly hasn't seen him, but his parents have."

I wondered if Jonathan had.

"It sounds like his Daed is angry with Timothy. And with our whole family. Jonathan's Daed is at the hospital too."

Hannah started sobbing again. I glared at him.

"Ach, don't do that," George said, patting Hannah's leg as he gave me a helpless look. "I shouldn't have said anything."

I undid my apron and handed it to her to dry her eyes, but instead she buried her head in the fabric and sobbed more.

I almost asked if she wanted to change before

we went back to her house, but then I remembered that her bag was still in the car the twins had borrowed.

"What about Betsy?" I asked.

"Oh, jah," George said. "She had a baby boy tonight. Molly ran into Cate and Pete. Cate left a message on our phone, but Molly thought we'd like to know sooner."

"And Betsy's okay?"

George shrugged. "Jah. Why wouldn't she be?"

"Well, you know. Childbirth and all."

He shook his head. "Women have babies every day."

I sighed. Betsy and the Bobli were fine. That's what mattered. I couldn't imagine how excited Cate and Onkel Bob were. It had been so long since there had been a Bobli in that family—since Betsy. They had to be beside themselves.

"We should get going," George said, turning on the engine. Behind us, lights filled the rear window again. This time the vehicle's horn blared as it sped by.

A few minutes later we turned into Aenti Pauline and Onkel Owen's driveway. George pulled up by the back door.

"Help me get her inside," I said.

"Nah," George answered. "You're on your own for this one."

"Come on."

He shook his head. "I'm going to stop by the

folks' place and see Timothy. Hannah will be okay."

Disappointed not to have his help, I opened the truck door, climbed out, and reached for Hannah's hand, pulling her along. She kept one hand on the apron, still holding it to her face. By the time we reached the door she was sobbing uncontrollably.

I gave George a pleading look, but he was turning the truck around, oblivious to us.

"We don't want to wake your parents," I whispered as my brother sped away.

That only made her cry more loudly.

I wasn't sure if we should stay in the kitchen until she calmed down or hurry upstairs. Her Mamm and Daed's room was on the main floor, not too far from the staircase. "Hannah," I cooed, hoping to distract her. "Do you need a drink of water? Something to eat?"

Her sobs grew louder.

"Take a deep breath," I whispered. "Let's get you upstairs." If we stayed down, her parents would be sure to hear her.

She did as I said, even lowering the apron. Her eyes were rimmed with red and had the same vacant look as they'd had down at the river.

"Come on." I took her arm and we made our way through the kitchen to the hallway. At the end was the staircase. I hurried, pulling her along, sure we didn't have much more time until she began crying again. I breathed steadily, as I sometimes did with Joe-Joe, hoping she'd follow my example.

Once we reached the stairs, I pushed her forward to go first. She took the first couple just fine, but then she stumbled. I steadied her body— but could do nothing about her spirit. She began to cry again and then wail. She collapsed in a heap on the staircase, her forehead pressed against a wooden step.

"Hannah," I coaxed, tugging on her.

It did no good.

A moment later a door opened. Another wail from Hannah blocked out any sound of footsteps, but I could imagine they were coming.

"Hannah?"

I turned toward my Aenti Pauline, standing at the bottom of the stairs in a long-sleeve white nightgown, her hair hanging loose down her back. It was obvious, now, she was expecting.

"Addie, what's going on?" she asked.

Hannah stopped crying, but she didn't look up. It was as if she'd frozen in place.

"It's kind of a long story," I answered.

"Have you two been drinking?"

"Oh no," I said. "Of course not." Suddenly I wondered if Hannah had other times though.

"Is Hannah all right?"

I shook my head. I'd been hoping she was, but I couldn't pretend anymore. She clearly wasn't.

It sounded as if Mervin was going to be okay, but I wasn't so sure about my cousin.

Aenti Pauline didn't say a word about Hannah's jeans and skimpy shirt, her uncovered head, or her strappy sandals. Instead she led her into the room Hannah shared with Deborah and Sarah and sat her down on Hannah's double bed. When Aenti Pauline lit the lamp, the younger girls woke up in their double bed, wide-eyed. Their mother shook her head and told them to go back to sleep. They both rolled toward the wall and didn't look our way again.

Aenti Pauline helped Hannah undress as I took a nightgown from the top drawer of her dresser.

"Hannah," Aenti Pauline said. "I need you to talk to me."

My cousin shook her head.

Aenti Pauline slipped the nightgown over her oldest daughter's head. I picked up her clothes and folded each item.

"Put them in the bottom drawer," my Aenti said. Surprised, I did as she said, thinking my mother probably would have burned them if they belonged to me.

Hannah allowed her mother to pull her to her feet, to let the nightgown fall down around her legs. Then Aenti Pauline pulled back the covers, plumped her pillow, and motioned for Hannah to lie down. She tucked her in then, kissing her on the forehead. "Addie will be in shortly," she said.

Hannah closed her eyes and didn't respond.

I wasn't sure we should leave her, but Aenti Pauline motioned me to follow her, so I did, pulling the door shut behind me.

"What happened?" she whispered, leading me down the hall to the window at the far end.

I explained about the accident and the ambulance taking Mervin to the hospital.

There was enough moonlight that I knew Aenti Pauline was growing more concerned with each twist of the story.

"She started sobbing, uncontrollably. She stopped when a police officer came over with an EMT to check her out. She said she was fine. But then she started again. Then, even after we knew Mervin was better, right before George dropped us off, she started up again." I searched my Aenti's face. "I'm sorry."

"It's not your fault," she answered. "And it's nothing new. The circumstances are—the accident and all—but she's been crying a lot. She's been inconsolable, some. We've been worried about her the last few months. The only time she seems happy is when she's riding her horse."

I tilted my head. "So it's been more than just her feeling unsettled? Like what she told me when she came over last week?"

"Jah," Aenti Pauline said. "We don't know what's going on. I took her to the doctor, and everything checked out okay. He said to make sure she got plenty of sleep, exercise, and good food—and to come back if she didn't get better."

"It looks like it's time to go back."

Aenti Pauline nodded, her shoulders slumping. "I'll make an appointment on Monday." Gravity seemed to be tugging at her face, her shoulders, and her swollen belly. Her mouth turned downward and her eyes weighed heavy.

"You should get to bed." I touched her arm.

"Jah," she answered. "You too." She turned toward the staircase but then stopped. "Addie?"

"Jah."

"Denki," she said, facing me again. "For taking care of Hannah."

"You're welcome."

By the time I closed the door to the girls' bedroom, my Aenti's footsteps fell on the stairs.

I changed into my nightgown as quietly as I could and slipped into bed beside Hannah. She stirred in her sleep but didn't wake. Later during the night, with her back toward me, she whimpered, but I patted her as if she were Joe-Joe, and she settled back down and went to sleep.

Sometime after dawn, I opened my eyes to Aenti Pauline waking up Deborah and Sarah, but I immediately went back to sleep and didn't wake again until well past seven, alarmed. If we didn't hurry, we'd make the whole family late for church.

"Hannah." I shook my cousin's shoulder. "We should get up."

When she didn't respond I spoke louder. The third time I shook her a little harder.

Finally her eyes fluttered and she muttered something.

"What did you say?" I asked.

Her eyes closed again, her eyelids nearly translucent in the bright morning light, and she rolled over. When I shook her again she didn't respond.

I dressed quickly and hurried down the stairs, finding Aenti Pauline in the kitchen drying the breakfast dishes. Onkel Owen was sitting at the table, his big hands wrapped around his coffee mug, reading *The Budget.*

Aenti Pauline mouthed, "How is she?"

Sensing she didn't want her husband to know what was going on, I motioned toward the stairway.

"What's going on?" Onkel Owen asked.

"Hannah's not feeling well," I said.

"'Course not. You two stayed out too late."

"Jah," I answered. "And I think we learned our lesson."

Aenti Pauline put the towel on the hook and dried her hands on her apron. "It's not just that, Owen. You know she hasn't been well."

"Then she shouldn't have gone out last night."

Aenti Pauline nodded. "I can see that now."

"Go tell her to get ready. We're going to be late."

I followed my Aenti up the stairs.

The light from the window fell across the shadow quilt covering Hannah, who was folded into a fetal position, her head tucked against her chest, her long curly hair wound into a nest.

Aenti Pauline sat down beside her daughter. "Talk to me, Hannah," she said.

Hannah didn't stir.

Aenti Pauline shook her shoulder.

"Go away," Hannah muttered.

"That's enough, young lady." My Aenti's face grew red.

Hannah rolled away from her mother. Aenti Pauline seemed more like my own mother now than the long-suffering person she usually was. Clearly she was reaching the end of her patience. She stood, didn't say a word, and left the room, her steps falling heavy on the staircase.

If there was something I could have said to my cousin to make her feel better or get her out of bed, I would have. But I couldn't think of a thing that would make a difference. We hadn't heard anything more about Mervin and probably wouldn't for another few hours, until Molly or George left a message or stopped by.

But the truth was, I didn't think being worried about Mervin was at the root of Hannah's problem. This despondency she was feeling seemed critical to me. Even dangerous.

I knew my cousin. She wasn't faking it.

Heavier steps, Onkel Owen's I presumed, fell on the stairs, following Aenti Pauline's lighter steps.

She led the way into the room, but it was Onkel Owen who spoke first. "Hannah, this has gone on long enough. Get up and get ready for church."

When she didn't respond, he grabbed her arm and yanked her up like a rag doll. She let out a wail, flopped to the side, and began sobbing again.

Onkel Owen let go of her arm as if he'd been shocked and stepped back. His eyes fell on me as if seeing me for the first time. "What do we do?" he asked.

I stepped forward and sank to the bed beside Hannah, trying to put my arms around her, but she curled into a ball again, like a potato bug.

I found my Onkel's eyes. "Call someone and get some help. Maybe one of the bishops or preachers will know what to do."

My Onkel stepped toward my Aenti, but instead of speaking they both simply nodded at the same time.

"You should call someone right away," I said.

"Will you stay with her?" Aenti Pauline asked me.

I nodded. "Could you leave a message for Mutter and Daed too?" They'd have already left for church but they'd get the message when they got home, about the time they'd be expecting me. "So they know I'll be late."

My Aenti nodded.

After they left I sat beside Hannah again and sang songs to her, starting with "How Great Thou Art."

A half hour later Deborah brought me a mug of coffee and a slice of buttered bread. "Here," she said. "Mamm asked me to bring this up for you." She paused and stared at Hannah.

"Tell your Mamm I appreciate it," I said. When Deborah didn't move, I added, "Denki to you too."

She must have realized she was staring because she started walking out of the room backward, saying, "Dat said you and Hannah stayed out too long last night."

"That's not why she's like this."

"Why is she, then?"

"I don't know."

Deborah turned around and fled the room.

I drank my coffee and sang more, working my fingers through Hannah's hair as I did, pulling the tangles out. I got my brush from my purse and worked on it some more. A few times when I pulled too hard she whined, but besides that she didn't respond.

It was a full two hours later that I heard horse's hooves in the driveway. I stepped to the window but then retreated with a gasp. Onkel Owen and Aenti Pauline had reached a bishop.

Phillip and his father climbed down from their buggy. Bishop Eicher wasn't their bishop, but he was respected throughout the whole area. It wasn't a surprise he'd been summoned.

Chapter 15

೧೫

I was relieved that Phillip didn't come up to Hannah's room, but Bishop Eicher did, following Aenti Pauline and Onkel Owen. When Hannah wouldn't respond to his questions, the bishop said, rather loudly, "You have two choices. If you can get Hannah moving, hire a driver and take her to that clinic I told you about. If you can't, call an ambulance and have them haul her down the stairs and to the emergency room."

He paused, as if waiting for a reaction from Hannah. She didn't move.

"I'll go call for a driver," Onkel Owen said. "Pauline, get her ready to go."

I wanted to ask Bishop Eicher to pray with us, to pray for Hannah, but instead he left the room.

Suddenly I ached for Jonathan. He would have

prayed. He would have spoken gently to Hannah.

Aenti Pauline stayed by the wall, frozen, so I sat back down beside Hannah. "Sweetie," I said, "we need to get you dressed, but first let's ask God to help us." I reached for her hand and prayed silently, hoping perhaps she was praying too. After a few minutes I opened my eyes to find her looking at me.

"We're going to get you help. Can you get dressed?"

She nodded.

"I think we can handle this," I said to Aenti Pauline.

She nodded and started to leave but stopped at the door. "There was a message on the phone machine from Molly. She said Mervin was discharged this morning. He's fine."

"Denki," I said, speaking both to God and to my Aenti, who was out in the hall now.

"Did you hear that, Hannah?" I asked, pulling back the quilt. "Mervin is going to be all right."

She rolled toward me and nodded, just a little, but then she started to cry again.

"Jah," I said. "How you're feeling is more than just that. I know. So do your Mamm and Dat."

I wondered if Molly knew anything about Timothy—if the police had gone out to our house yet—but she probably wouldn't have mentioned that in a message. I pulled a dress and apron from a peg on the wall and put them on the end of the bed. I'd find out when I finally got home. I collected Hannah's underthings from her top drawers and placed them on the end of the bed too.

"Come on," I said, taking both of her hands and pulling her to a sitting position. "Let's get you dressed."

By the time I got Hannah downstairs, a baby step at a time, Phillip and the bishop were back in their buggy ready to leave, and the hired driver was waiting in a minivan.

Phillip acknowledged me with a nod, but the look on his face was as self-righteous as I'd ever seen as I struggled down the back steps with Hannah clinging to me. Her Dat stepped forward to take her the rest of the way. Phillip motioned to me, and although I wanted nothing more than to ignore him, it wasn't in my nature. I stepped toward the buggy.

"What happened last night?" His tone was uncharacteristically harsh.

His father sat beside him, staring straight ahead.

"It's a bit complicated." I switched my overnight bag to my other shoulder.

"You were out with her, jah?"

I nodded.

"And Mervin Mosier got hurt?"

"Jah."

"Why were you with all of them?" The harshness in his voice now paled in comparison to the sharp tone of judgment.

I didn't answer.

"Addie?"

"Leave her be," his father said.

Phillip stared at me. I stared back.

"Speaking of the Mosiers, isn't that one coming this way?" Bishop Eicher pointed toward Onkel Owen's horse pasture. A tall man was marching across it. *Jonathan.*

I couldn't help but rush toward him.

As soon as he saw me, he began to run too. We met at the end of the pasture and clasped hands.

"Is she okay?" he asked.

"We're taking her to get some help," I answered. "We heard Mervin went home."

Jonathan nodded. "He's worried about Hannah."

"Addie?" It was Aenti Pauline.

"Coming," I yelled, and then quietly I said, "Do you know if the police went after Timothy?"

"They didn't. Mervin wouldn't give them any information. He didn't want Timothy arrested."

"What about his Dat? And your Dat?"

Jonathan put his hand against his stomach. "They're upset, jah. But they decided not to involve the police."

I wasn't sure if I was relieved or disappointed. A visit from the officers, at least, might have been good for Timothy.

293

I couldn't help but notice Jonathan's hand, pressing now against his middle. "Are you all right?"

"Jah, just a little pain." He dropped his hand to his side. "I had this back when my Dat and I weren't getting along."

I remembered him mentioning a stomach problem.

"I think I have some pills left from the naturopath," he said, "or I'll get some more."

"Addie!" This time my Onkel called for me.

"You should go," Jonathan said.

"When will I see you again?" I asked, trying to push away Onkel Bob's warning.

Jonathan hesitated but then said, "Tonight. Meet me down by the creek at nine—if you can."

I squeezed his hand and, even though Onkel Bob had told us not to meet, said, "Until then."

Aenti Pauline yelled for me. "Addie! We're going!"

Jonathan let go of my hand. "Hurry," he said.

I turned my back to him just as Phillip drove his buggy by. He stared straight ahead, as did his father, not glancing my way. My face grew warm as I hurried toward the van. I knew the *Shahm* I felt coming to me from Phillip wasn't deserved, but still my face burned.

Perhaps he understood now though. No matter his reasoning—even if it was because he'd decided I wasn't worthy of him—I'd be blessed to have him finally comprehend we didn't have a future together.

I climbed into the van and scooted to the seat in the back, behind Hannah. Aenti Pauline sat beside her and Onkel Owen sat up front.

Mammi Gladys appeared at the door of her Dawdi Haus. My Onkel rolled down his window and instructed Deborah, who held Maggie in her arms, to go tell our grandmother what was going on. I didn't envy my cousin one bit.

As we passed the horses in the pasture, Hannah began crying again, softly. I patted her shoulder as I looked out the window, down to the oak at the fence line. Jonathan had stopped and was staring up at the tree. I imagined he was calculating how many hope chests he could make from the wood —or maybe he was just appreciating the underside of the canopy.

Or perhaps he was praying.

Jah, that was what he was doing. Praying for Hannah. And Mervin. And me.

Onkel Owen and the driver chatted about the hot weather and the crops as we rode along. Hannah had her head against the window and her feet on the bench seat, her knees pulled up to her chest. Aenti Pauline twisted around in her seat so she could look at me.

"Bishop Eicher called ahead. It's a place that works with Plain people, both Old Order

Mennonite and us. It doesn't have electricity—just lamps, like at home. And no artwork on the walls. Or any Englisch magazines like at the doctor's office." She sighed. "They have a bed available." She glanced at Hannah and lowered her voice more. "He said he couldn't know how long she'd be there but probably a few days, at least."

I nodded. She'd been off track for a while. It would probably take a little time to get her moving ahead again.

We rode along in silence. The air-conditioning was on in the van, but it was clearly growing warm outside. The Englischers we passed were wearing shorts and tank tops. A crowd was gathered outside a church, the women in short-sleeved dresses and the men wearing summer shirts. A few doors down, a little girl ran through a sprinkler, wearing a bathing suit.

The driver turned onto a busier highway and then a freeway. He pulled around a truck, accelerated, and then a few minutes later exited and turned onto a country road. After a while he turned down a driveway. At the end was a parking lot and then a house.

The driver stopped the van in the first space.

Onkel Owen opened the door.

"I'll wait," the driver said.

"Denki," Onkel Owen said as he opened the side door for Aenti Pauline, who stepped down.

Hannah scooted across the seat and climbed down too, with her father's hand supporting her.

I followed them up the walkway into the house. There was a foyer area with a desk and to the right a living room. A middle-aged woman wearing a Mennonite Kapp greeted us. Clearly she'd been expecting Hannah.

She handed Onkel Owen a clipboard with papers attached and motioned down the hall. "We have a private admittance room this way," she said. "Follow me."

"I'll wait here," I said, stepping toward the living room.

Hannah gave me a look of panic. I gave her a hug and whispered, "This is a good thing. You'll be better soon."

She hugged me back.

Then I watched her shuffle after the woman down the hallway, Aenti Pauline on one side, her head bent a little, her maroon dress wrinkled in the back and her apron coming untied. Onkel Owen was on the other, his black hat in one hand and the clipboard in the other. My Aenti and Onkel looked old to me for the first time, nearly as old as my own parents, who had already been worn down by their children.

I wondered at Aenti Pauline having another Bobli, thinking about all the years ahead of her, worrying about her girls going to parties and growing up, hoping they'd join the church, marry, and settle down. That was every Amish parent's dream.

Except for my parents. Their one desire was that I'd marry Phillip. Maybe, after today, he'd set them straight for me.

When the driver dropped me off at home, Aenti Pauline said, "Tell your Mamm and Nell I was too tired to come in."

"Should I say what happened?"

Aenti Pauline glanced at Onkel Owen. He shrugged his shoulders. "Better they hear it now from Addie than later from someone else."

Aenti Pauline's eyes welled. "Tell them not to spread it around, jah? That will only make it harder for Hannah."

"Of course," I said. "Let me know how Hannah is, and if there's anything I can do."

Aenti Pauline nodded.

I watched the van turn around and go back up our driveway, then trudged up the stairs and into the kitchen. Mutter sat at her usual spot, but all around her were boxes and stacks of papers.

"What are you doing?" I asked, without even telling her hello.

She looked up. "Oh, just trying to sort through some things. I found my old school papers in the closet in Billy and Joe-Joe's room."

I couldn't keep silent any longer. "Mutter, are you looking for the letters?"

"What letters?"

"The ones supposedly from Dirk Mosier."

She dropped her eyes as she fanned her face with a piece of paper. "I don't know what you're talking about." She shifted in her chair, away from me, and said, "Betsy had her Bobli."

"I heard," I answered.

"Oh." Clearly she was disappointed she wasn't the one to tell me. "Well, did you have a good time last night?"

I shrugged.

"Tell me all about it." She seemed unaware that I was down.

"It's a long story," I said, placing my overnight bag on a chair at the end of the table. "Did you get the message from Pauline?"

"Just to say you'd be late." She sat up a little straighter. "Who brought you home?"

"Aenti Pauline and Onkel Owen's driver."

Mutter's face grew concerned. "What's going on?"

I told her what had happened with Hannah, leaving out what transpired at the party, but including the trip to the clinic.

"Oh goodness, I'd better tell Nell," Mutter said, pushing back from the table.

"Don't tell anyone else," I said. "Aenti Pauline doesn't want to make this any harder on Hannah."

"Oh," Mutter said, her face shifting a little. "I'll

tell Nell to keep it quiet." She pushed herself up from the table. "When she gets up from her nap. She hasn't been feeling well."

"Oh?" I said. "Since when?"

"The last couple of days," Mutter answered, stepping away from her chair. "I told her I'd do some piecing for her this afternoon."

I hadn't seen much of Aenti the day before. And when I had, she'd been quiet. I hoped she was all right.

There was a stack of pancakes on the counter. "Who made breakfast?" I asked.

"Danny."

Realizing I was famished, I grabbed a pancake, rolled it into a tube, and took a bite. It was dry but edible. I swallowed, gulping it down. "Is Timothy around?"

Mutter shook her head, starting toward the sewing room. "He spent the night at George and Sam's."

"Do you know that for sure?" I asked.

She stopped. "Well, he's not here." Her face reddened. "That's where I'm assuming he is."

I sighed. He must have driven over after George stopped by.

"Why?" Mutter asked.

"No reason." I took another bite.

"Don't go anywhere." Mutter started toward the sewing room again. "There's someone here to see you."

"Who? Where?" I looked out the kitchen window, but all I saw was the courtyard.

"Guess. He's out back with your Daed."

Phillip. I hadn't expected him so soon. He must have parked his buggy on the far side of the barn.

I finished the pancake and headed toward the counter. The breakfast pans were soaking in the sink. I undid the plug, letting the cold, greasy water drain.

Fortunately for me, the family had eaten lunch with our district after church. Otherwise I'd have even more to clean up.

"You should go on out to Phillip," Mutter called from the sewing room. "You can clean up later."

"I'm sure he'll be in soon enough," I answered.

After I'd scrubbed the griddle and dried it, the back door opened. Daed stuck his head inside. "Come on out here a minute, Addie."

I dried my hands and headed outside. Daed and Phillip were now sitting at the picnic table under the elm tree. Billy was sitting on one of the limbs, and Joe-Joe was trying to catch a lower one to pull himself up.

"You boys run along," Daed barked.

Billy dropped to the ground and searched my eyes.

"Go," I said. "You too, Joe-Joe. But stay in the shade. It's getting too hot to be out in the sun." I sat down on the same side of the table as Daed, across the table from Phillip.

My father turned and straddled the bench so he faced me. His eyes narrowed as he spoke. "So Phillip says you were at a party last night. And one of the Mosier twins ended up in the hospital, and then Hannah did something—or something was done to her—that led to some sort of breakdown."

That was exactly what I feared people would say. I glared at Phillip.

"That's how my father summed it up," he said.

"Nothing happened to Hannah last night."

Daed's voice curled with scorn. "She wasn't drinking? Or compromised?"

"No."

"But you were at the party last night?" Daed demanded.

"Jah."

"Are you intending to break your Mamm's heart?"

"Of course not." But I knew I was going to.

"You've been such a good girl." Real pain filled Daed's eyes.

"I still am," I said. "Although I am a woman, if you haven't noticed."

"Jah. That's what I'm worried about." His face hardened.

"There's nothing to worry about." I found his questioning my virtue, at the urging of Phillip Eicher, insulting.

"I'm disappointed in you," Daed said.

302

I cocked my head.

"That you were at a party at all. Clearly something happened that affected Hannah—something that made her feel guilty, perhaps?"

I shook my head. "She's been feeling despondent for weeks. Depressed. Aenti Pauline had already taken her to the doctor."

"But then last night, she was with that boy, Mervin Mosier, the one I steered you clear of," Daed said.

I took a deep breath.

"And it sounds as if you were with someone too." He tugged on his beard.

I stared at him, not breaking my gaze.

"Jah, she was," Phillip said. "And like I said, my Dat and I saw her with him again this morning, at Owen's place."

I didn't respond.

"I want you to know . . ." Phillip said, speaking to me now. "Like I told your Daed, I can forgive you—no matter what happened—this one time."

I wondered if he fancied himself to be some kind of long-suffering biblical hero—and me, a fallen woman. My face grew warm as anger welled inside of me. I wanted to jump up from the table. How could Phillip's denial run so deep?

How could my own Daed have no idea who I really was or what I wanted out of life?

But if I told them what I really thought, Daed would only come down on me all the more, and any chance of settling the grudge between the Cramers and Mosiers would be gone.

Daed cleared his throat. I knew he expected a response from me. I silently prayed that God would give me the right words, or better yet help me to keep from speaking at all. I turned my head toward the trunk of the tree beside the table, concentrating on the rough bark, tears stinging my eyes.

Finally Daed cleared his throat. "Addie?"

I kept my eyes on the tree.

"I'm a patient man." Phillip leaned forward on the table. "We can talk more about this later."

"What do you have to say for yourself?" Daed bellowed. Clearly he'd had enough.

I turned away from the tree, toward my Daed, blinking away the tears and shrugged.

"Go to your room," Daed barked. "I'll talk with you later."

I didn't bother to say good-bye to Phillip. Instead, I stood and marched away, holding my head as high as I could.

I hoped to get a nap, but Mutter sent Billy up to tell me to come down and finish cleaning the kitchen. I told him to tell Mutter that Daed had sent me to my room. Billy sighed and shuffled out of my room. Ten minutes later he returned.

"Mutter said to come down anyway," he said.

I complied, of course, trudging down the steps,

my bare feet against the cool wood. Just the feel of the oak beneath my soles made me long for Jonathan.

Mutter was still sitting at the table, yawning as I entered the kitchen. "Oh, there you are," she said. "Carry these boxes back up to my room."

"Don't you want to get rid of some of it?"

She shook her head. "Not yet."

"Mutter," I said. "You just went through all of it. Surely most of it can be burned. Your room can't hold all this junk."

"Just take it to my room like I asked," she said.

I picked up a box, reading the top piece of paper. It was a receipt for hay. I scooted it over. Next was a tax form from a decade before. I groaned. Underneath were her old school papers —from thirty years before.

By the time I cleared everything off the table and cleaned the kitchen, it was time to start supper.

Once the meal was over it was time to clean up again. I busied myself with the task, all the while thinking about Jonathan and then Hannah and then Mervin and then Jonathan again. As I finished, I heard a knock on the screen door.

"Come in," I called out.

The door pushed open, and Onkel Bob appeared, his hat in his hand.

I congratulated him on his new grandson.

He beamed. "Betsy and little Robert are doing great."

"Ach, named for you?"

He blushed.

"Of course." I smiled. "A double congratulations then."

He said that Betsy would spend the night at the hospital, and then she and the Bobli would head home in the morning. "She'll be ready for visitors soon," he said.

"I can't wait," I said.

"Are your parents around?"

Relieved, I said, "Jah." How kind of him, in the midst of becoming a grandfather, to remember my ordeal, although he spoke as if I didn't have any idea of the purpose for his call. "They're out on the front porch."

He nodded. "I'll go around the side of the house," he said, stepping back out the door.

"You should know, more has developed," I said.

"Jah," he answered. "I saw the Mosiers last night, at the hospital."

I gave him a quick nod.

"Do your parents know?" he asked.

"Daed does—not about Timothy's involvement, though. At least I don't think so. Mutter knows about Hannah, but I think that's it."

He nodded. Obviously he'd heard about Hannah too. "All right, then." He turned back toward the door. "Say a prayer."

"Jah," I answered. "Good idea."

As soon as he left, I scurried up the stairs to Billy and Joe-Joe's room. Through their window, which I'd opened to cool off their room after dinner, I might be able to hear the conversation below.

I arrived as Onkel Bob made his way to the front porch.

"Bob," Mutter said, "how nice to see you! Congratulations on your grandson." My mother was always on her best behavior around my Onkel. She hadn't been as fond of my Aenti when she was alive, or at least that's the impression I'd gotten through the years. My guess was she'd been jealous of her.

"Thank you, Laurel. I'm humbled by God's blessing." He paused a moment and then said, "Cap, good to see you." The fall of Onkel Bob's boots reverberated up the worn stairs and then across the porch to the corner where my parents sat in their favorite chairs. "How are you tonight?"

"Fine, just fine," Daed responded. "What brings you over this way?" There was an edge of defensiveness in his voice that made my pulse race.

"Oh, just had a few things on my mind."

"Have anything to do with what happened with the Youngie last night?"

I couldn't hear Onkel Bob's answer, and then my mother said something I couldn't hear either. I moved closer to the window, kneeling down on the floor.

"Like I said, I've been meaning to talk with you for a few days. I just wish I had before last night."

"What's going on?" Mutter asked. "Is this about Hannah?"

Daed's voice grew in volume. "You think it would have made a difference if you'd talked to us sooner?"

"Perhaps. It might have stopped Timothy—"

"Timothy? It's those Mosier boys who've stirred things up. Especially since that cousin of theirs moved here."

"Those Mosier boys are good kids," Onkel Bob said. "Jonathan too."

"You know that for a fact?"

"Jah," Onkel Bob said. "I've had a chance to talk with him."

"One talk will do it, then?" Daed continued without giving Onkel Bob a chance to respond. "Because two decades wasn't enough for me to know the character of his father."

"Cap, that was years ago."

"Not so many," Mutter said.

"How old is Samuel?" Onkel Bob said. "Seems he's Cate's age. So looks as if it's been more than twenty-five."

"I'd appreciate it if you'd stay out of our business," Daed said.

"This is the community's business," Onkel Bob replied. "Someone is apt to be hurt even worse than Mervin was last night—not to mention the ones who have already been hurt emotionally. Plus, you could be standing in the way of God's will."

"How about you go talk to Dirk about all this? Then let us know what he says."

Onkel Bob's volume fell, and I could barely make out him saying, "I already did."

Daed boomed, "And?"

I lifted my head a little, hoping to be able to hear my Onkel.

"He said he'd be interested in knowing what you had to say."

"Seems to me," Daed said, "you have enough of your own worries right now. I heard that librarian gave you a ride to the hospital last night. I thought she'd been shunned."

Onkel Bob didn't answer.

Mutter's shrill voice piped in with, "How's that?"

"She used to be Plain," Daed answered.

"My goodness, Bob Miller!" Mutter exclaimed. "Are you getting serious about her?"

There was a long pause, and then Onkel Bob said, "I came to talk about the Youngie."

A chair scraped against the porch and footsteps came toward me. "What I'm interested in right now is why my Youngie—my daughter, to be exact—is eavesdropping."

I froze. How did he know I was listening?

The footsteps stopped. "Bob," Daed boomed, "maybe you can tell me why Addie is so interested in this conversation."

"Addie?" It was Onkel Bob's voice, louder now but calm. "You need to move along. Let me talk with your parents in private."

I stood, slowly.

"Do you hear me?" Onkel Bob called out.

"Jah," I answered.

"Young lady," Daed growled, "I'll talk to you later."

"Jah," I said and then under my breath murmured, "I expect you will." In the last week, I'd gone from never once causing my parents a worry to being the biggest problem in their lives.

Chapter 16

෩

I couldn't wait in my room—if my parents barged in, they might see the hope chest—so I trudged down the stairs to the dim kitchen. I would round up Billy and Joe-Joe and send them up to bed on their own tonight because I couldn't very well go back in their room now. Then I hoped

310

to slip down to the creek. I was in trouble as it was. I might as well hang out down there until it was time to meet Jonathan.

"Addie."

I jumped.

Timothy laughed. He was sitting at the table, in Mutter's chair, eating a piece of pie.

"What are you doing?" I asked.

"What do you care?" His eyes hung heavy in the dim light. "You're the one who turned me in."

"I answered the officers' questions."

He snorted. "Even the Mosiers have more sense than you."

I headed toward the door. "I'm going to call the boys in for bed," I said.

"Sure you are," he answered.

I ignored him.

"Jonathan's not coming tonight," Timothy called out.

I stopped, my hand on the handle of the screen. "What are you talking about?"

"You know exactly what I mean."

I put one hand on my hip. "I have no idea." I wasn't lying. I had no idea how he could have found out. Unless he tortured Jonathan. "What have you done?"

"Nothing." He stood. "He's just not coming."

"You're bluffing."

He laughed. "So he is planning on coming, then?" He headed toward the counter. "It's as clear as mud you and Jonathan asked Onkel Bob to help you. Even Daed has to know that."

I opened the screen.

"It's only going to make things worse, you know, to have Onkel Bob meddling."

I stepped out on the stoop and yelled, "Billy! Joe-Joe! Time to come in!"

Timothy burped and then, as he put his plate in the sink, said, "Molly went and saw Hannah today."

I spun around. "When?"

"About an hour ago."

"How was she?"

"Better than last night." Timothy shrugged. "Personally I think she's faking it. And it's just making the whole 'Martyrs "R" Mosiers' story way more dramatic than it needs to be. And you being with Jonathan in front of everyone isn't helping either."

I narrowed my eyes. I was certain he hadn't seen me with Jonathan last night. Molly must have told him.

"And just so you know, once I found out you'd ratted on me, I was so upset I hit a pole on the way to George and Samuel's last night."

"You mean you were so drunk."

"Ach, Addie, you're always jumping to conclusions."

"At least you didn't hit a buggy."

He ignored me and leaned against the counter.

"Had to get towed. It will be a while till I can get it fixed. George had to give me a ride back here. So," he said, "I won't be paying you back for that stupid mantel anytime soon."

"You never intended to pay me back at all."

"Well, now I can't. And it's all your fault."

I crossed my arms. "It doesn't matter. Jonathan returned the money to me the next day."

Timothy jerked his head back, his eyes wide open. "That only proves he's even more of a fool than I thought."

"No, it shows what a gentleman he is."

"Well, my gain." Timothy yawned. "Except you took mighty long to tell me. Oh well. Looks like I'm totally off the hook."

Joe-Joe and Billy scurried around me into the house just as Daed bellowed, "Addie!"

Timothy smirked.

"Go wash your feet," I said to the little boys. "And then get your pajamas on."

"Addie!" Daed yelled again. I shooed the boys along to the hall and headed to the front of the house, dread permeating my entire being.

When I stepped onto the porch, Daed was waiting for me, standing tall, his broad shoulders squared and his arms crossed. "I already had it from two sources, and Bob just confirmed it. How dare you associate with Dirk Mosier's son after we told you not to?"

Onkel Bob stepped toward me. "Now, Cap, we

can all discuss this. You know as much as anyone that Addie didn't seek Jonathan out because he's Dirk's son. These things happen. And like I said, this grudge—mutual, sure—has gone on long enough. It's time to put an end to it."

It was as if Onkel Bob hadn't spoken—or at least as if Daed hadn't heard a word of it. "What do you have to say for yourself?" His eyes bore down on me.

Mutter shuffled over from her chair, her face growing redder with each step. "Answer your Dat."

"Jonathan is kind and true and wants to please the Lord," I said. "There's nothing about him that should bring you any concern."

"Except that he's Dirk's son," Daed bellowed.

"And that he's not Phillip," Mutter wailed.

I groaned.

"Phillip's spoken for you," Mutter said, her voice full of hurt.

"No one ever asked me how I felt about Phillip Eicher. Neither of you, nor Phillip."

"Of course we did," Mutter said.

I shook my head.

"There's no reason to talk about Phillip right now," Daed boomed.

Onkel Bob stepped in front of Daed. "Cap, let's wait and discuss this tomorrow. After you've had some time to think about it."

Daed shifted slightly toward his brother-in-law. "There's nothing to discuss—not with you."

"Then how about if Addie goes home with me tonight? She can spend some time with Cate."

Daed sneered, just like Timothy. "Why would I send her over to your place? She belongs here. With her family."

Onkel Bob didn't seem offended. "Sometimes a break is a good idea. We can take a fresh approach in the morning."

"I don't think so, Bob," Daed said. "I don't want her sneaking out tonight to meet that Mosier boy."

I held up my hand. "Denki," I said to Onkel Bob. "I'll be all right."

Perhaps Onkel Bob was afraid Daed would explode once he left and take it out on me, but I couldn't imagine he would. I could imagine, however, if I tried to sneak out of the house, that he would follow me and take it out on Jonathan.

"Good night," I said to Onkel Bob and slipped into the house before any of them had a chance to say another word. I raced through the house to the back door. As I expected, being sure Daed wouldn't want to talk anymore, Onkel Bob had nearly reached the driveway.

I hurried out the door and down the steps, meeting Onkel Bob at the walkway, but before I could ask him to meet Jonathan for me and tell him I wasn't coming, Daed rounded the corner of the house.

"Denki" was all I could manage to say to my Onkel.

I sat in my room, running my finger along the letters of my name, thinking about Jonathan carving the *A* and then the *D* and on and on, when I heard the hoot of an owl.

The house had been quiet, except for Daed's snores, for more than the last hour, meaning even Timothy was asleep. My heart racing, I stepped to my open French doors.

Under the elm tree stood Jonathan, his hat in his hand.

How I longed to be with him.

Daed let out another snore. It was well past eleven. At first I'd thought Jonathan was late again, then not coming at all. I'd been both disappointed and relieved. Still, I hadn't changed out of my dress and apron.

Perhaps I could sneak out after all. I pointed toward the creek and tiptoed to my door, pushing against it to keep the latch from squeaking. Then I tiptoed down the hall. Daed's snoring stopped for a moment and I froze. But then, in another beat, he started up again, and I moved to the stairs and tiptoed down. I avoided the loose boards in the living room and kitchen, stooped to pick up my flip-flops, and shot out the back door. Jonathan stepped toward me, but I waved him away, toward the creek, and followed at a distance.

Jonathan darted in front of the willow tree and disappeared down the trail. An owl hooted again.

I quickened my pace, fleeing to the willow. The weeping branches tickled my face and neck as I ducked beneath it. I slowed as I reached the path, finding my footing.

"Take my hand."

I jumped and then relaxed, reaching for Jonathan. Silently, holding onto me, he led the way to the creek, over the stepping-stones, and to the sycamore grove, where we stopped near the hollow tree.

He wrapped both arms around me and drew me close. I breathed in his spicy smell of pine and rested my head against his shoulder, letting out a shudder of relief to be with him again after the last twenty-four hours of turmoil.

"I stopped by your Onkel Bob's earlier. He told me about his meeting with your parents. I'm sorry—that's why I waited so long to come over tonight."

I exhaled. "He didn't say much about his meeting with your family—just that your father wanted to know what my Dat said."

"Ach, well, that was the nicest thing he had to say to Bob. The rest was one long complaint against your parents."

I pulled away a little, tilting my face toward his. "What are we going to do?"

He shook his head. "Talk to the bishop in your

district? Or run away? Elope, maybe?" He smiled. "Go to Atlantic City to marry? Or how about Las Vegas?"

He had me smiling at the image of two Amish Youngie getting married in a little white chapel halfway across the country. Not that it couldn't happen. It just wouldn't happen with us.

He pulled me close again, held me tight, and whispered into my ear, "What if I just came by tomorrow afternoon and addressed this with Timothy and your Dat. What if we stopped sneaking around? I'll tell your Dat I'm crazy about you."

I shook my head.

He continued. "That I want to court you."

I shook my head again.

"I won't say I want to marry you—that might seem a little soon. Right?" He grinned. "But I'll make my intentions known."

"Jonathan," I said, pulling away again.

"Why not? Isn't honesty the best policy?"

"Ach, it should be. But it doesn't seem to work with our families. But we do need to figure something out."

It didn't feel as if we had much time.

"Just let me talk to Timothy," Jonathan said, "about what happened to Mervin. Then maybe we could all play a game of volleyball. Or baseball. The Cramers against the Mosiers. Just the men. Whoever wins the game wins the grudge."

Jonathan was a dreamer—that was for sure. "I don't think that would work," I said.

"But isn't it worth a try? I'll stop by tomorrow."

"Jonathan," I said. "I don't see how that will possibly help anything."

He put his finger under my chin and lifted it until our eyes met. "Not doing anything isn't helping either." Even in the darkness his eyes shone bright. "What other options do we have?"

I wasn't sure, since even Onkel Bob struck out. "We need a plan," I said.

"You sound like my father," Jonathan said.

"I don't think it's wise to approach my Dat so soon, but we can't just let fate decide."

"But we could trust God."

I bristled.

Jonathan raised his eyebrows.

I sighed. "We could move back to Big Valley," I said. "Or somewhere else."

"That's an idea . . . if it's God will."

By the tilt of Jonathan's head I could tell he would consider it. "Is that what you want?"

I paused for a moment. As much as my family demanded of me, I couldn't imagine living so far away from them. I shook my head. "What I want is for us to court and marry here."

He nodded. "My business would do better here too. There's not as much of a tourist market in Big Valley."

"So what now?" I said, glancing across the

creek at the sound of a rustle in the bushes, wanting more than anything for him to kiss me. I'd been waiting oh, so long.

"I'll come by tomorrow afternoon."

"Are you sure?" The tone of my voice confirmed my own doubt that it was a good idea.

"Jah," he answered, wrapping his arms around me, pulling me close. "I've been praying about it. I think it's the only thing I can do."

"Addie!"

I startled and then focused on Aenti Nell at the water's edge, wearing a dress and a Kapp she hadn't taken the time to pin but no apron. "Your Dat's looking for you. Come now."

Jonathan squeezed me tight and then released me. "Go! I'll see you tomorrow."

I waved to him as I rushed down the path. As I crossed the creek I slipped, sending my foot into the water. I hopped from stone to stone the rest of the way, my flip-flop slapping against the sole of my foot, onto the far bank. In the distance I could hear my father yelling.

"Come on," Aenti Nell said, giving me a gentle shove. "You go first."

I hurried up the path, slipping a few times. At the steepest part I reached down for my Aenti, taking her hand and pulling her up. Her Kapp had slid back on her head, and once she landed beside me, I straightened it for her. "Denki," I said.

"Go," she replied, nearly out of breath. "Tell him you couldn't sleep—or something."

I ducked under the willow tree and into the pasture. Daed stood at the fence, the moon illuminating his bare head and gray beard. Both appeared bright in comparison to his weathered face.

"Here I am," I said.

"Where were you?" His suspenders hung down, as if he'd been in too much of a hurry to loop them over his shoulders.

"Down by the creek."

"Alone?"

"No," I answered.

"With Phillip?"

"No."

He stepped away from the fence and jerked his hand toward the house. "I forbid you from going farther than the garden without my permission."

I stalled a moment, waiting for Aenti Nell to catch up.

"Do you hear me, Adelaide Cramer?"

"Jah, I hear you," I said, falling into step with Aenti Nell.

"And you." Daed pointed to my Aenti. "What's your involvement with all of this?"

"She has none." I moved in front of her. "She simply came to say you were calling for me."

"That's hard for me to believe." Daed stepped forward and glared down at me.

"It's true," I answered.

Aenti Nell grabbed my arm, pulling me beside her. "Cap Cramer, my involvement in this is that I think you've all been fools long enough. It's one thing to limit your own life but quite another to box up your children."

"Box up my children? I'm protecting my daughter."

"No, you're teaching your boys—or at least one of your boys—to be small and petty. And you're teaching Addie to sneak around."

Daed snorted. He pointed to Aenti Nell and then the house in a sweeping motion. "I've had enough of this tonight!"

He marched ahead of us. We followed. When we reached the back door, he swung it open, ushering us inside. As we entered the kitchen, Mutter turned in her chair at the end of the table.

"What in the world is going on?" She dabbed at her eyes with a hankie as she spoke.

"We'll talk about it tomorrow," Daed said, his voice tired. "Now, everyone go off to bed." It was as if the fight, at least momentarily, had left him.

As I climbed the stairs behind my parents and Aenti Nell, for a fleeting moment I felt hopeful —that perhaps Jonathan could talk some sense into Timothy and Daed. And I felt grateful that my Aenti, even though she'd been feeling poorly, still stuck up for me.

• • •

It was midafternoon when I heard Daed yelling from the barnyard. I hurried to the back door and flung it open. He stormed toward the house with Jonathan following him.

"Addie!" Daed bellowed.

"Let's not involve her," Jonathan said. "The two of us should talk it through."

Daed stopped and reeled around. "You don't seem to be much like your father."

Jonathan hesitated and finally said, "No. I'm not."

All I could see was Daed's broad back. He took his hat off and swiped his hand through his hair, then pulled the hat back on his head. "Not that it matters. You're still not courting my daughter."

Without missing a beat Jonathan said, "Then do you mind if I talk with your son?"

"Which one?"

"Timothy."

Daed snorted. "Why?"

"If I can't sort things out with you, I'd like to try with him."

Daed laughed. "Do you want to get hurt? Because *you* may not be like your father, but Timothy's a lot like me—and your father. Or at least like we used to be."

"I don't think he'll hurt me."

Daed snorted again. "He's in the north field. Give it a try if you'd like."

"I would," Jonathan answered.

"At your own risk," Daed added.

"Exactly." Jonathan tipped his hat.

I slipped back into the kitchen and toward the front door, determined to get to the north field before Jonathan.

Billy was working a puzzle on the living room floor as Mutter dozed on the couch. Joe-Joe had only been down for his nap for an hour—he had at least another thirty minutes.

"Where are you going?" Billy whispered.

"To check on Timothy," I said softly. "You stay here."

He shoved the puzzle to the side and stood, saying in a normal voice, "I'll go with you."

"No," I whispered. "I need you to stay here in case Joe-Joe wakes up." I put my finger to my lips. "Don't wake Mutter."

He sank back down to the floor, obviously displeased. "I should go with you—because I'm brave," he said.

"Oh, I know you are," I said. "Just be brave in here now, jah? I'll be right back." We had to end the grudge. I didn't want to lose Billy and some-day Joe-Joe to the bitterness that had consumed my parents and was now eating away at Timothy too.

But first I had to protect Jonathan.

I flew out the door and down the worn front steps, around the far corner of the house toward the windbreak of poplar trees. Jonathan walked ahead of me in the middle of the pasture. Daed trailed him.

I cut around the other side of the trees and began to run, my stride as long as my dress would allow, the ties of my Kapp in flight behind me, my bare feet hitting the uneven ground, rolling with each landing. Once I reached the field I darted back through the trees.

Somehow Jonathan stayed ahead of me. Timothy continued to drive the team of mules forward as Jonathan stepped over the cut hay.

Daed had lagged behind.

I stepped to the side of a poplar. There was nothing I could do but watch.

"Timothy," Jonathan called out in a firm but kind voice. "We need to talk."

The team kept coming straight at Jonathan, and Timothy, a smirk on his face, acted as if he hadn't seen or heard a thing.

Jonathan swept his hat off his head and began waving it. The mules balked and one by one, in a clumsy motion, veered to the left but kept on going.

"What do you think you're doing?" Timothy bellowed. "Get off our farm."

I lunged forward, away from the tree, into the field.

Now at the edge of the hay, Daed yelled, "Addie, go back to the house." Both Timothy and Jonathan glanced toward me.

I stepped back again, this time behind the tree, out of view. Which meant I didn't see what happened next.

When Timothy shouted, "Whoa!" I stepped back into the shadow of the tree, where I could see Jonathan, my brother, and the team. The mules weren't easily spooked, but they were as strong as oxen, so when they took off, away from me, the cutter swung wide.

It appeared as if the breeching strap came unbuckled from the shaft, sending Timothy flying. He was holding the reins in his hands one moment and in the next they were whipping through the air as he flew beyond them.

Jonathan grabbed for the harness on the lead mule and yanked the team to a stop as Timothy landed on his side in the cut grass. I wasn't surprised when he didn't get up right away. He rolled onto his back, holding his right arm in his left hand, rolling his legs back and forth.

"You all right, son?" Daed ran, moving faster than I'd seen him go in years.

Jonathan held onto the lead mule, straining his head to see Timothy. "Are you hurt?" he asked.

"Jah," Timothy barked, still writhing. "I am."

"You'd best be on your way," Daed said, reaching the scene. "You've done enough."

As he knelt beside Timothy, Daed looked back over his shoulder at Jonathan. "The mules are fine. You go on, like I said." Then he looked straight at me, squinting against the light. "Addie, you come get the reins," he said. "And finish up the cutting since you have so much time on your hands. Buckle the strap—that's all that's wrong."

Jonathan took a step toward me, as if it were instinctual, his hand still on the mule's harness. I shook my head as I came out of the shadows and walked toward them. I stepped around Timothy, pulled back on the strap to reposition the mules, and struggled to rebuckle it.

Jonathan extended his hand to help me.

"Go now," Daed said to Jonathan, his voice as harsh as I'd ever heard it.

Jonathan dropped his arm to his side. "I'd still like to speak with Timothy, about the other night." He looked straight at Daed. "And speak with you again too."

"Go!" Daed bellowed. "Now!"

I nodded at Jonathan, sure his sticking around was only making things worse.

He put his hat back on his head, tipped it toward me, and started for the far side of the field, most likely to take the shortcut to his grandfather's place.

Daed helped Timothy to his feet.

"I'd better get it X-rayed," Timothy said.

"Let's put some ice on it and decide," Daed answered.

"We could send the ER bill to the Mosiers," Timothy said.

Daed smiled a little at that. Neither said anything to me as they passed by. I realigned the mules and started them back to the cutting. It had been a few years since I'd driven the team, but it came back to me. Thankfully, Timothy had already done three quarters of the field.

As I turned the mules around at the end of the field to go back, I could see Jonathan watching me at a distance, from Onkel Bob's property. He waved his hat at me, boldly, still appearing to be full of optimism.

But I wasn't so sure anymore.

Chapter 17

Timothy hadn't broken a bone, but falling on his wrist had sprained it. Daed ended up taking him to our regular doctor instead of to the ER, which annoyed Timothy for some reason.

He was still seething as the three of us traveled along in the buggy on the way to Bishop Eicher's place. That was the reason Daed brought him along, I was sure. Timothy was one piece of powerful evidence, and somehow I was another, as to why the bishop needed to intervene—and soon—when it came to Jonathan Mosier.

As we turned into the Eichers' driveway, I spotted Phillip standing at their horseshoe pit, his father at the other end. Both started toward us, like a set of bookends marching to the driveway, one older than the other, sure, but with the same build and looks, just one with a white beard and the other without one at all.

"Good evening," Bishop Eicher called out.

Daed nodded and then said, "We've come on serious business, I'm afraid. About a family in your district."

Bishop Eicher's face grew bleak. "Hitch the horse and come on up to the porch. I'll have the missus bring us some lemonade."

I followed the men up the steps, trying to keep as far away from Phillip as possible, and sat in the white rocker at the edge of the group of chairs, hoping no one would ask me any questions. Phillip sat beside me. Once Patty Eicher brought out the glasses of lemonade and a plate of oatmeal raisin cookies, Daed cleared his throat.

"We've come to discuss Jonathan Mosier. He's brought enough trouble to my family and this community. It's time to talk about him going back to where he came from."

"That sounds awfully harsh," Bishop Eicher said. "Have you taken your grievances to him? And his parents?"

"Jah," Daed said.

I sat up straight, sending the sticky lemonade

over the rim of the glass onto my hand and down on to my dress, which I blotted with my apron.

"How'd that go?"

"Not too well."

Daed was slyly claiming Onkel Bob's conversation with Jonathan's father as our family approaching theirs.

"I know about the incident the other night with Mervin Mosier. Is that what you're referring to?"

Daed's face reddened. "No." He nodded to Timothy, who pointed at his sling with his good hand. "Tell them, son, what happened today."

Timothy took a deep breath and hesitated just a moment, then he said, his voice wavering a little, "What happened Saturday night was an accident —what happened today wasn't. Jonathan came over to retaliate—and he did."

I leaned forward. "Timothy . . ."

My brother ignored me. "I was cutting grass this afternoon when Jonathan confronted me. When I resisted, he stepped wide and slapped two of the mules, one with each hand. They balked." He pointed to the sling with his good hand. "And look what happened."

I shook my head.

My brother glared at me. "What's worse than my injury is how he's hurting my Schwester." Timothy turned his gaze to me, and his eyes actually watered. "He's deceiving her." He looked at Phillip now. "Attempting to steal her away from one who truly cares about her." Next his eyes landed on Bishop Eicher. "It's been one thing after another since Jonathan Mosier arrived in Lancaster County. None of the Youngie are safe."

I shook my head in disgust. At the time of the accident, I hadn't been sure of what Jonathan had done. But now, based on Timothy's dramatics, I was pretty sure my brother had made up Jonathan slapping the mules. Most likely Timothy just hadn't fastened the belt tight enough.

"Addie?" Bishop Eicher scowled at me. "What do you have to say?"

Daed cleared his throat. "I'll speak for my daughter."

"No, I'd like to hear from her." Bishop Eicher's eyes remained on me.

I leaned forward again, looking around Phillip, straight at his father. "Jonathan Mosier is the kindest, most thoughtful, most Christ-loving, God-fearing person I've—"

This time it was Daed who interrupted me by jumping to his feet.

But I wasn't deterred. "—ever met. You should be thinking about how to encourage everyone to end this grudge in a nonviolent way, not considering how to banish Jonathan from Lancast—"

"Do you see what we mean?" Daed was beside me now, pulling me to my feet and wrapping one arm around me, clutching me against him. He patted Phillip on the shoulder with his other hand. "Don't worry—she'll come back to her senses as soon as Jonathan is gone. She'll remember what it means to honor her parents again. It's as if he's put a spell on her."

"A spell of goodness," I said, pulling away from Daed. "True, I didn't see exactly what happened today. But I know Jonathan's intention wasn't to hurt Timothy."

I couldn't stand to be a party to Timothy and Daed's scheming for another moment, so I fled the porch, hurrying down the steps to the buggy. As I climbed in, I noticed Phillip standing on the far end of their porch, his arms crossed, a scowl on his face that rivaled his father's. I was pretty sure he finally understood my feelings for Jonathan.

My Daed didn't say a single word the whole way home, but Timothy wouldn't stop. After chastising me, he predicted Jonathan Mosier would be gone from our lives by the next day. Two at the most.

"I never liked Bishop Eicher until tonight," Timothy said. "Having Phillip interested in you is going to work to our advantage."

I bit my tongue.

"There's no doubt he's going to influence his Dat. He looked like he was going to cry when you spouted off like that." Timothy turned toward me. "Did you do that on purpose?"

I stared straight ahead.

"Maybe you should go into acting." He laughed.

Finally unable to contain myself, I asked calmly, "What do you care?"

"What do you mean?"

"This is some sort of game to you, right? A win-at-all-costs competition." I locked onto his eyes. "But it's my life. And you're ruining it."

His pupils flickered, but then he seemed to brace himself again. "Get over yourself," he said. "It isn't about your life, Addie. It's about us. The Cramers."

Daed shifted in his seat.

"What's best for our family," Timothy jeered.

"That's enough," Daed said to him, sharply. And then, as if he regretted his tone, he added, "I've had all I can take for one day."

The sun set as we continued on, sending streaks of pink and orange across the gray-blue sky. A flock of starlings flew for home. A calf called for her mother. By the time we turned down our lane, dusk had fallen, darkening my spirits even more.

"Addie," Daed said as he stopped the buggy by the back door. "It goes without saying that you won't be sneaking out tonight. Is that understood? I'll sleep outside your bedroom door if I need to."

For a moment I contemplated slipping out onto the balcony, but sneaking around at all had only gotten us into more trouble. We should have heeded Onkel Bob's advice, entirely. "Understood," I said.

As I climbed down from the buggy, I felt as

heavyhearted as I ever had. Never before in my life had I loved someone the way I did Jonathan. Never before had I known such generosity and kindness. Never before had I wanted to be with someone the way I wanted to be with him.

I truly didn't contemplate sneaking anywhere until Aenti Nell shook me awake and whispered, "He's leaving."

"What?" I struggled to a sitting position.

Her hand hovered close to my mouth. "Whisper," she hissed. She was wearing her dress and Kapp and must have stayed up late quilting, as she sometimes did.

I bolted out of bed. "What's going on?" I had to see him.

"He's down in the sewing room. He saw me through the window and climbed into the room so your Dat wouldn't be awakened by the door."

"He's here? Now?"

She nodded.

"What do you mean he's leaving?"

"He'll tell you," Aenti Nell answered.

"Is Daed in the hallway?"

"No. He's snoring away in his room."

I swung my feet over the edge of the bed, and Aenti Nell handed me my robe. By the time I stood, my heart began to race. I tiptoed after my Aenti, out my open door, and down the hall. I took the steps one at a time, but when I reached the living room I ran, skipping over the creaky boards and then doing the same in the kitchen.

I opened the door to the sewing room quickly but didn't see Jonathan until he stepped from the far corner, out of the shadows.

I flew into his arms.

"Where are you going?" I cried.

"Hush," he said. "It's all right."

"No," I said. "It's not. Nothing is all right."

He pulled me down into Aenti Nell's chair, turning me on his lap, and then our arms intertwined. "Bishop Eicher came out to Dawdi's tonight."

I clung to him. "Did Phillip go too?"

"Jah . . ."

"And?"

"Bishop Eicher said I needed to leave the community, but before he finished, Dat said I was going back to Big Valley, that we all were, that he wasn't going to have his son railroaded by lies the way he had been."

"Your Dat said that?" I leaned my head back, getting a clear view of Jonathan's face.

"Jah, fancy that, he stuck up for me, but not in the way that I'd hoped. I want to stay here. But he let his pride get in the way, again. He's taking our farm up there off the market."

"What about your Dawdi? What did he say?"

"He scolded Dat and Bishop Eicher, saying Youngie need models more than critics."

I smiled. That was something I'd heard my Onkel Bob say too.

Jonathan sighed. "He said if he wasn't so old he'd turn them both over his knee—and your Dat too."

I shivered. "I like your Dawdi."

"Jah, me too."

"But who will take care of him now?"

"Tabitha is going to stay on for now. We'll see what happens in time."

"What about your shop?" I leaned against him.

"Ach." Pain filled his voice as he spoke. "Dat said he's not paying to have it moved back to Big Valley. He's going to sell it and put the money toward our home up there, to fix it up. He says he and I are going to make another go of farming at our old place."

"Oh, Jonathan. I'm so sorry." Life would be miserable for him without his woodworking. "So what now?" I whispered.

"I wanted to tell you happy birthday."

I shook my head. "It's not today—it's the day after tomorrow," I said. I'd forgotten about my nineteenth birthday and no one had mentioned it.

"Jah, I know." He remembered from our one conversation about it. "I have something for you."

I couldn't believe he'd remembered my birthday. "You already gave me the hope chest."

"That was a just-because gift," he said, pulling a

336

bookmark from a paper bag on the desk. "This is for your birthday."

I took it from him. Instead of a picture there was a reference, carved into the wood: Revelation 21:5. "What's the verse?" I asked.

" 'Behold, I make all things new,' " Jonathan quoted. "Remember that—because . . ." His face grew serious.

"What is it?"

"I'm praying God will make all of this new. That this won't be good-bye for long."

I sank against him. "Don't go." I nestled my face into his neck, drawing comfort from the warmth of his skin.

"I'll come back," he said. "When things calm down. Unless you need me sooner." He handed me a slip of paper. "This is the number of the retired pastor I used to work for. Leave a message. He'll come get me right away."

I took the slip of paper and slid it into the pocket of my robe.

He reached for the bag again, this time taking out a rose—a peach one, obviously from Onkel Bob's garden. Immediately the sweet smell filled the room.

He handed it to me.

I took it, holding it tenderly.

"You think it's beautiful, jah?"

I nodded.

"One of God's most amazing creations?"

I nodded again. He'd said the same thing in Onkel Bob's garden.

"Know you are so much more amazing. When God holds you—as he does every day, all the time—he feels a thousand times more pleased than you do right now."

"Ach, stop, Jonathan." We weren't brought up to think highly of ourselves. I could only take so much of his talk.

"It's how he feels about all of us," he said. "It's how you feel about Joe-Joe, but more so. And the sycamore grove. And your dreams. It's okay to value life and see the value in ourselves."

I held the rose high on the stem, my fingers far from the thorns. Not knowing what to say, I said nothing. He pulled me closer, touching my hair, my face, and then my chin, tilting my face toward his.

He kissed me then, his soft lips on mine. He smelled of the warm night, of sadness, of longing, all mixed with the scent of wood and sweat. His rough hand held my face. I kissed him back, and as I did, tears began flowing down my face.

"Ach, Addie," he said, brushing my cheek with his hand.

"I'm sorry."

"Don't be," he said.

"Don't go," I whispered. I pressed my wet face against his, thinking of Hannah and her despondency. Perhaps I had a glimpse of how she felt. Jonathan and I had only had eight days together—and now we were being forced apart. How would I go on?

But still, I felt anything but hollow, even in my grief. In fact, I'd never felt so alive.

There was a soft rapping on the door, and Aenti Nell hissed, "Someone's up. Go now!"

Jonathan and I clamored to our feet as one, and then he embraced me before he scooted toward the window. I dropped the rose onto Aenti Nell's table as he swung his legs through. He sat on the sill for just a moment, waved one last good-bye, and then jumped down as Aenti Nell opened the door.

I collapsed into her chair the moment Daed appeared behind her.

"What's going on?" he demanded.

"I couldn't sleep," I said.

"Go back to bed, Cap," Aenti Nell said. "I stayed up quilting and Addie is keeping me company. Everything's fine."

He left, stopping at the sink for a glass of water. When he was done, the floor in the kitchen creaked, then the board in the living room.

Aenti Nell collapsed in the chair across from me once Daed was on the stairs.

"Ach, Addie," she said. "I'm too old for this."

"Denki," I said. I touched my lips.

"Jah, I know you needed to see him, to say good-bye, but . . ." She sat up straight, unpinning her Kapp as she spoke. "This needs to end."

"What?" I couldn't believe her words.

"It's too much, Addie. You're tearing your family apart. You didn't follow Bob's advice or mine not to see Jonathan. Now you need to sacrifice for the greater good, like I did."

I shook my head. "What are you talking about?"

"I cared for Dirk Mosier—as he did for me. But then your Mamm pursued him, and it seemed he cared for her, for a short time."

"Aenti, I'm so sorry," I said.

"And then he wrote—or someone did—those horrid letters and everything got worse."

"Jonathan hasn't written any horrid letters. Or done anything else wrong."

"But your pursuing him is tearing your family apart." She stood, holding her Kapp in her hands, unwinding her dark hair. "Your parents have aged a decade in the last couple of weeks." She sighed. "Phillip really is a fine young man."

I shook my head. "He's self-righteous. And self-absorbed."

"Addie!"

"It's true."

"He'll be a good provider. He cares for you."

"But he doesn't love me."

Now she shook her head. "I think I helped put ridiculous ideas in your head. I'm sorry. Forget Jonathan. It's never going to work. We all need to make the best of things. That's what I did."

"By never marrying? By living with your sister —who hardly even appreciates you—all these years?" I stood. "I'm not going to follow your example."

"Of course not," she said. "You'll marry Phillip."

I rushed past her, grabbing the rose from her table, my other hand clutching the piece of paper inside my pocket.

The next afternoon, standing under the clothes-line, I pulled a bed sheet from the basket at my feet and flung it over the wire. Taking a pin from my mouth, I clipped it and then, scooting the near-empty basket along with my bare foot, clipped the other end. Then I picked up one of Daed's T-shirts to pin next.

"Addie!"

I turned. Cate, appearing weary, walked toward me across the lawn, a casserole dish in her hands. "I brought you a lasagna."

I shook my head. "Your family is the one with the new Bobli. Why are you bringing us food?" It wasn't as if anyone was sick or injured—except for Timothy's silly sprain, which didn't count.

"I thought it might help you out a little. I know things have been stressful the last few days." She stopped beside me. "Have you heard?"

"What?" I whispered, still hoping it wasn't true.

She tilted her head, a look of concern spreading across her face. "That Jonathan left this morning for Big Valley."

Even though I knew that was the plan, the T-shirt fell from my hands. Cate stooped and plucked it up, holding the casserole dish with one hand.

"Who told you?"

"Mervin and Martin. They stopped by this morning."

"How is Mervin?"

"Fine." Cate shook her head a little. "Still a little shaken, though."

I swallowed hard. "What did your father say when he heard the news?"

Cate looked around and then whispered, "That foolish people do foolish things. Meaning all involved, except Jonathan. And you, of course."

"And there's nothing your Dat can do to help?"

Cate took a deep breath. "He said he'd keep trying."

"Tell him I appreciate it." Although at this point I couldn't think of anything he could do. I hung the T-shirt and then pulled another from the basket. "How is Betsy?"

"Good. She's at our house. Come over and see her and little Robbie. He's a sweetheart."

"I'm sure he is," I said, "but I can't." I motioned with my hand to the fence. "Daed's forbidden me from going any farther than the garden."

"Oh dear," Cate said. "Maybe he'll change his mind with Jonathan gone."

"Maybe," I echoed, but I doubted it, unless it was to go on a date with Phillip.

I heard a rustling behind me and spun around, expecting Timothy. I let out a sigh of relief at the sight of George.

He smiled and stepped between Cate and me, forming a little circle. "This is about the stupidest thing I've ever heard of." He nudged me. "I think even Timothy is feeling bad."

"I doubt it," I said, grabbing another T-shirt.

"I've got to go," Cate said.

I gave her a one-arm hug. "Denki," I whispered, taking the casserole from her.

"Come see me when you can," she said.

After a final good-bye, she turned and made her way slowly toward the willow. George and I watched her until she ducked down to the creek.

Then he turned toward me. "It will all work out," he said. "You'll see."

"Maybe if I run away to Big Valley . . ."

"Don't do that," he said. "I have an idea."

I crossed my arms.

"But that's not why I came out. Mutter wants you."

"Why? So she can lock me inside the house?"

He shook his head. "Aenti Nell is going to see Hannah. Mutter doesn't feel up to it, but she wants you to go along."

"At the clinic?"

"No, she's home. Aenti Pauline left a message."

"Does Hannah want visitors?"

He shrugged. "It sounds as if she wants you."

I wrinkled my nose and handed George the casserole. "Tell Mutter I'll be right in."

Daed agreed to let me go, and Aenti Nell and I stopped at Onkel Bob's on the way, rushing in to tell Betsy hello and see the Bobli. Betsy, happy to see us, showed off Robbie, but she seemed extra tired. So did Cate—more so than when she'd visited earlier.

"I took a couple of turns with him last night," Cate said, as if that explained it.

Betsy and Levi still lived with his parents, so I wasn't surprised Betsy felt more comfortable with the Bobli at her old home than at her in-laws. Although Levi's mother had lots of experience with babies, it was probably easier for her to ask Cate for help.

But now Cate appeared worn out—more so than even Betsy. I followed her into the kitchen. "Are you sure you're all right?"

Her violet blue eyes filled with tears.

"What is it?" I asked.

She shook her head. "Don't tell Betsy. She didn't know . . ."

"What?" I prodded.

"I miscarried. Only Pete knows. And now you."

"Ach, I'm so sorry." I wrapped my arms around her, pulling her tight. So much joy and heartache, all wrapped together. I admired my cousin for her sacrifice, for not sharing her pain that would mar Betsy's joy. Cate was the most generous person I knew. I was sure I could never be as selfless.

"I can't believe you brought us dinner. . . ."

"I made it yesterday," she said. "Before I knew."

"When did it happen?"

"This morning." She pulled away and dabbed at her eyes with her apron. "I wasn't very far along."

"You still need to rest," I said, amazed she was able to think of me in her grief.

"I'm going to now," she said. "And you should get going."

Once we were back in the buggy, Aenti Nell clucked her tongue and said she didn't think Betsy had what it took to be a mother.

"Of course she does," I said.

"She's been too pampered," Aenti Nell said. "And leaving Levi's parents to stay with her family . . . That's bound to cause hard feelings."

"Please don't say that to anyone," I pleaded. "That would only get a rumor started."

"Your mother's right. Bob's spoiled those girls."

I shook my head. "No, he's loved them. And still does. He was patient with them. And it paid off."

She clucked her tongue again, indicating she didn't agree, as we rode along. I focused on the fields—the corn stood nearly waist high now.

The alfalfa was ready for a second cutting. The soybean plants had grown thick across the ground.

Granted, things were strained between Aenti Nell and me since her declaration against my relationship with Jonathan last night, but I'd never known her to be so quiet. I gathered she didn't like my not agreeing with her that I needed to go "back" to Phillip or about her view of my cousins.

Once we reached Aenti Pauline's, Aenti Nell oohed and aahed over Sarah's hope chest that had just been delivered, while I acted as if I hadn't seen it before. It was Sarah's thirteenth birthday, and she was pleased with her gift. She'd been born the day before I turned six. I remembered it well. I was so sure, after holding her, my next sibling would be a girl.

I had to wait three long years to find out I was wrong. But once I held Billy, I didn't care. And when it was time for Joe-Joe to come along, I just expected he'd be another boy.

Hannah and I slipped out the front door, over to the swing hanging from the oak tree in her yard.

Deborah and Katie were on it, but when they saw us coming Deborah said, "Hannah, do you want the swing?"

Hannah simply nodded and the girls scurried away, as if they were frightened by their oldest Schwester.

346

We barely fit on the swing, but still we sat together.

"Molly stopped by. She said Mervin is fine," Hannah said.

"Jah," I answered. "That's what Cate said too."

"And that Jonathan's been sent away." Her head bumped against mine.

I wasn't sure if Molly needed to tell Hannah everything. "Jah," I replied again.

"I'm sorry," Hannah said.

"Things will work out," I said, trying to sound confident.

"That's what my counselor keeps telling me."

"Will you keep seeing her?"

"Jah. Mamm and Dat saw her with me yesterday. And we're all going again next week."

"Really?" I couldn't imagine Onkel Owen agreeing to that.

"She told them their support would help me get better."

"Did she say what's wrong?"

"Jah. It seems I have a genetic predisposition toward depression. Mamm told them about your mother. And our grandmother too."

I sat up a little straighter. "Did they prescribe something for you?" Perhaps Mutter's moods could be helped too.

"We'll talk about it if counseling doesn't help. But in the meantime, I'm to get enough sleep— they gave me a tincture to help with that—and get enough exercise. So I have a good excuse to ride as much as I like. And I need to eat right. All of the things my Mamm told me to do that I wasn't doing before."

I stood. "Let's go for a walk, then."

Hannah started to laugh.

"I'm serious," I said and then smiled. "Let's go down to the end of the pasture. To the blackberry bushes."

As we walked along, five of the horses began to follow us. Hannah cooed at them and rubbed their necks, one by one. I did too, but not with as much enthusiasm as Hannah. She finally pulled away, but the horses continued to follow us.

When we reached the fence line she said, "It wasn't that bad at the clinic. Everyone was really nice. Sometimes I felt as if my parents didn't care much, but now I think they do."

I nodded. I was sure her parents cared too.

"The counselor helped me see that I'm having a hard time becoming my own person."

I reached for a blackberry that was nearly ripe and plopped it in my mouth as I thought about what Hannah had said.

She continued. "She said I need to figure out how to grow up safely, by not putting myself at risk."

"Just how bad were you feeling?" I ventured.

"Ach, Addie." Tears filled her eyes. "There were times I didn't want to live. Times I even thought about . . ." Her voice trailed off. "But I talked that through with the counselor. That helped. If I have a bad spell again, they'll try some medication—more than what they gave me at the clinic —if the talking doesn't help."

Hannah turned toward the field. "Another interesting thing the counselor said was that generous people are less likely to be depressed. She encouraged me to give to others—to play with my little Schwesters and read to Mammi Gladys, to not just think about myself."

I plopped another blackberry in my mouth, mulling over what my cousin had said. One of the horses nudged me, so I gave her a blackberry too and then giggled as her wet mouth nuzzled my palm.

Mutter was one of the least generous people I knew. Plus, she had little empathy for others and seemed oddly competitive, mostly with Aenti Pauline. I was sure Mammi Gladys's criticism of her daughters had contributed to my Mutter's selfish behavior.

George the Generous, on the other hand, was never depressed. He was always thinking about others. And so was, so far, Billy the Brave.

Did Timothy have bouts of depression? Was that why he drank?

I couldn't help but wonder what came first— my mother's depression or her lack of generosity.

Unaware of my racing thoughts, Hannah

continued. "Talking honestly with my Dat and Mamm helped—a lot. The counselor said they're trying to do their best and that a lot of parenting is experimenting. That made me think of your parents."

I bit into another berry. "Why?" It was a sour one, and I made a face.

"Addie." Hannah's voice sounded like my Mutter's. "They do care about you."

I spit out the berry. "They care more about how things look than about me." I sputtered, getting the rest of the seeds out. "They think my pleasing them is the same as my honoring them."

Hannah held up her hand. "But they're doing what they think is best for you."

"Maybe if they educated themselves a little . . ."

"Exactly," Hannah said. "Hopefully, my Mamm will tell yours about the genetic predisposition. Maybe she'll get some help. And I'm hoping my Mamm will say something to yours about girls our age needing to become our own person—individuals—even though we're Amish and told being part of a community is more important. We can do both."

I shook my head. My mother would never believe it.

Hannah picked a blackberry and held it between her thumb and index finger. Her expression darkened. "I still don't see why you don't just marry Phillip."

"Hannah!" I balked. "How can you say that?"

"Sure we can become our own person, but it's not like we have a lot of choices, not in the long run, not as far as marriage."

She was contradicting what she'd just said. "Of course we do," I responded. It wasn't like the Amish had arranged marriages or anything. I didn't know anyone who'd been forced by their parents to marry someone they didn't love—although I was sure my parents wanted me to be the first.

Hannah sighed, still holding the berry. "But we really don't. We're limited to an Amish beau, and someone we've met, right? Most likely someone who lives nearby. And then if our parents don't like his family—say if he's a Mosier—then that's out of the question. Or if he decides not to join the church. Or if he—"

"Hannah, you've said this before. I halfway believed you then but not anymore. It's not hopeless. Not for you. Not for me. I assure you, I'm going to marry Jonathan Mosier. If you have your heart set on Mervin, it will work out."

She dropped the blackberry on the ground and stepped on it, then lifted her foot, looking down at the purple mess of pulp. She stepped away from it. "We'll see, won't we? For both of us."

I smiled sympathetically, even though I had a hard time empathizing. I knew exactly what I wanted.

To me, that seemed better than being

despondent and unsure. True, I didn't know how to get what I wanted. As much as I'd wanted Jonathan to come up with a plan, I knew all we could do now was wait for God's leading. However, knowing God was in control gave me confidence to carry on. And that knowledge had come directly from Jonathan's words. Honestly, I was surprised by my optimism—and pleased.

"I don't mean to sound simplistic," I said to Hannah, "but have you been able to pray about how you're feeling? Ask God for direction? For his reassurance?"

"My counselor talked about that," Hannah said. "I've tried, but I don't feel like he's listening."

I nodded. "I feel that way sometimes. Or that he's listening but with his hands on his hips, tapping his foot, fed up with me." Looking a lot like Daed.

Hannah smiled for the first time all day. "Jah," she said.

"But that's not how he sees us," I said, pulling three long blades of grass from along the fence line. "Think about how your Mamm looks at little Maggie."

"Like she can do no wrong?"

"Exactly," I said, tying a knot at the end of the blades of grass.

"But we do wrong." Hannah's eyes were big.

"That's right, but he forgives us. And sees the good in us." I began braiding the grass together.

"He's not mad and ready to pounce. He sees our potential, what he made us for."

She was frowning now. "How did you know I felt that way?"

"Because I've felt that way too, for a long time. But it's changing." I surprised myself that I could feel so optimistic, even with Jonathan so far away. I was trying so hard to be brave, trying to abide in Christ's teaching, trying to let God's love—and Jonathan's—change me.

Hannah stood statue still for a long moment and then said, "I'm tired. I'm going to go take a nap."

As we walked back through the pasture, the horses following us again, I finished braiding the blades of grass, knotted the end, and handed it to Hannah. She dangled it for a moment and then held it against her face.

"Denki," she said. "And not just for this, but for the words too. I'll think about it." Her eyes teared as her gaze met mine. "I'm sorry about Jonathan leaving."

"Denki."

She shook her head. "Molly said she's really sorry for what both you and Jonathan have had to go through."

"He'll be back."

"Molly doesn't think so. You really should go back to Phillip. If you don't, you'll be stuck in your parents' house forever."

"Ach, Hannah, don't say that. You just said we

need to become individuals, to have a say in our lives."

"Well, your parents will only allow that to a certain extent," she said. "Everyone thinks you should marry Phillip. Your parents, of course. My Mamm. Molly. Phillip. Everyone."

Even Aenti Nell. "And you too." My voice wavered, "Jah?"

Hannah bowed her head. "There's nothing else for you to do, Addie. It's inevitable."

Chapter 18

ᏃᎤ

I'll never know if Mutter had already seen the hope chest Jonathan made me and found an excuse to get me out of the house, or if she just found it that afternoon.

In the long run, the sequence of events didn't matter. Perhaps this too was, as Hannah had pointed out, inevitable when it came to what I couldn't control in my life. Or as Mutter believed, fate had destined it to happen.

No one was around, not even the little boys to run out to greet us, when Aenti Nell and I arrived back at the house. She stopped the buggy, handed me the reins, and stepped down. "Go take care of the horse," she said. "I need to go cool off." She waved her hand in front of her face as she turned toward the house.

I urged the horse forward.

Aenti Nell stopped halfway to the back door and pointed toward an object on the lawn, beyond the courtyard. "What is that?"

I gasped. It was my hope chest. "Help me get it back in my room," I said, setting the brake and then jumping down from the buggy.

The front door screen banged, and Aenti Nell's face fell.

Mutter marched down the steps, yelling, "Leave it there." She continued on once she reached the yard, straight toward me. "How dare you take such a gift from him," she said. "And after we forbade you to see him."

Without answering, I rushed to the side of the hope chest.

"Don't touch it," Mutter said.

Aenti Nell stepped between the two of us. "Laurel, it's only a wooden box. Addie's wanted one for years."

"She has mine."

"That's just it," I said. "It's yours."

From the barnyard, Daed called out, "Addie, leave it be."

Aenti Nell nodded at me, turning to whisper, "Do as they say."

I stared at it, longingly. "What did you do with my things?"

"They are in the hope chest in your room. The one we wanted you to have." She shook a finger at me. "You leave this one alone—it's right where I told Timothy to put it. I'll have him move it in the morning."

"Where?"

"Back to the Mosier place."

"They're gone," I said. "Except for Jonathan's Dawdi."

Her face twitched, as if she couldn't decide whether to smile or frown. "Well then, it seems our troubles are over. You'll never see him again."

I took a deep breath but didn't respond.

She turned then, toward the house, and marched back the way she'd come, her arms swinging back and forth as she limped along. Aenti Nell followed Mutter.

On the porch, Billy and Joe-Joe peered through the slats of the railing. Behind them, at the door, stood Timothy, his arm still in the sling. I wondered if he'd taken it off to carry the chest down. A shadow passed over Billy's face and he turned away from me. Mutter must have made him help. Perhaps Timothy had been able to manage with one arm and a conscripted ten-year-old.

Poor Billy. It went against his nature, I knew.

I sat down on top of the chest, rubbing my hand over the wood, again.

From the barn, Daed said to someone, "Leave her alone." He was either talking to Danny or George, whose pickup was still parked in the driveway.

I stayed put. Daed didn't say anything to me when he headed toward the house a half hour later. Not too long after that, both George and Danny sauntered toward me, stopping and positioning their backs to the house when they reached me.

I turned to George and whispered, "Will you help me get this over to Cate's tonight? After everyone is asleep?"

He nodded.

"I'll help too," Danny said. "And we've come up with a plan to get you out of this mess." Danny the Dependable glanced up at George. "Haven't we."

My generous brother nodded. "Just wait and see. Everything is going to be all right."

That night, after everyone had gone to bed, I stood by my open French doors waiting to see the lights of George's pickup coming down the lane. Ten o'clock passed. Then eleven. At eleven twenty, thunder crashed in the distance, then again a few minutes later, much closer. The smell of rain and ionized oxygen filled the air coming through the doors.

I needed help—now. I tiptoed down the hall to the older boys' room, eased open the door, and made my way to Danny's bed. He was sleeping on his stomach, one arm dangling over the bed. I shook his bare shoulder.

Lightning flashed, sending a bolt of light through the window, followed by another peal of thunder. Timothy stirred across the room. I stood statue still.

After the darkness returned, I shook Danny's shoulder again. He didn't stir. Nor did he when I shook him a third time. So much for Danny the Dependable helping me. Or George the Generous. Maybe their intentions were good, but their follow-through was lousy.

There was no way I could get the hope chest to Cate's or back up the stairs or even into the house by myself. But I could drag it into the barn.

Lightning flashed again, this time followed by rain pelting the roof. And then a crash of thunder.

I fled the room and hurried down the stairs, hoping the beat of the rain would mask the sound of my steps and the door opening. Through the living room, the kitchen, and out the back I hurried, dashing into the pitiless rain barefooted. By the time I reached the hope chest, it was covered with water.

With rain dripping down my face, I tugged on it, yanking it along the grass. Hopefully in the morning I could scrub the stains from the bottom.

Another flash of lightning cut through the sky. This time the thunder crashed immediately. I pulled harder as the rain soaked through my dress. Wet hair fell out of my bun and into my face as I jerked the box, as heavy as my grief, along.

When I reached the barnyard, the going got better, although the soil was already turning to mud and sticking to the bottom. I would have dirty grass stains to scrub in the morning. I'd get up early and see to it before Mutter was out of bed.

Lightning flashed again—this time in the south field, as the immediate thunder rocked the ground. I began to pull with all my might. Thankfully, the next strike was farther away, to the north.

When I reached the barn door, I leaned against it. Unlatched, it creaked open.

I pulled the chest inside, making a screeching noise on the concrete floor. One of the horses snickered. I aimed for the empty stall at the very end. As I moved along, the mules raised their heads and one of them snorted. Ahead a starling fluttered toward the rafters.

The patter of the rain drummed on the tin roof, masking some of the sound of the wood against the floor. Once I reached the stall, I pulled the chest all the way to the end. Bending down, I rubbed straw from the floor around the sides, hoping to wipe off the mud. But it was too dark to see if I'd succeeded or not. Then I tucked a horse blanket over the top and sides, securing it in the back.

I latched the barn door behind me and sprinted back to the house. Already as wet as I could be, I stopped before the back porch and held my hands up to the sky, letting the rain fall on my muddy skin. I scrubbed my palms together, but even the downpour wasn't enough to wash them clean.

Once in the kitchen, using soap, I washed them properly and then grabbed a dishtowel to dry them, my face, and hair, thinking about what my chances were of rescuing my hope chest.

Pretty slim, I knew, but it was still worth waking up before the crack of dawn to see what I could do next. There were many things in life I was not willing to fight for. This wasn't one of them. The hope chest was all I had left, for now, of Jonathan.

Tears started to flow down my still-damp face. The chances of saving it, at this point, were better than my chances of rescuing my relationship with Jonathan. Grief grasped my heart. Were my earlier words to Hannah worthless? I'd give up the chest in a moment if it meant having a future with Jonathan.

I stumbled through the house to the stairs and up to my room, thankful for the continuing fall of the rain on the roof. Still crying, I stripped off my dress, pulled my bath towel from the hook on the back of my door, and dried off. Then, after slipping on my nightgown, I crawled into bed, pulling my quilt to my chin. Shivering, I began to sob.

Why couldn't my family see what I needed for once? And I didn't mean the hope chest.

If they would only recognize Jonathan was best for me, I'd never need anything from them again. But instead I was completely alone. No Jonathan. No support from my parents. No help from my Bruders, who had promised it. Even Aenti Nell had turned her back on me.

Feeling utterly unloved, I curled in a ball, sure I finally comprehended what Hannah had gone through.

I awoke late, past six, to rain still falling on the morning of my nineteenth birthday. The endless beating of the drops and the darkened sky had lulled me into thinking it was earlier than it was. I dressed quickly and hurried down the stairs, horrified to find another set of boxes on the table. Mutter was already up and going through more of her junk—but she wasn't anywhere in sight. Neither was anyone else. I grabbed a slicker from a hook by the back door, wondering why I hadn't thought of it last night—I must have been more distraught than I'd realized—and rushed out into the rain.

Maybe everyone had gotten up late. Perhaps Daed and the boys were doing the milking. Maybe Mutter had been up long enough to search another couple of boxes and then had gone back to bed.

Danny stood in the doorway of the milking barn but turned away when he saw me. My heart raced. Something was up.

I headed toward the horse barn. As I reached it, the sound of an axe splintering wood rang out, as loud as the thunder from the night before. Feeling sick to my stomach I opened the door and raced over the concrete, slipping on fallen straw but catching myself, then making my way to the last stall as the axe fell again.

"Stop!" I cried out as I reached the stall.

Mutter stood with the axe above her head, my destroyed hope chest all around her in bits and pieces.

"No!" I shouted.

Her eyes met mine. But instead of the anger I expected, a wave of regret spread across her face.

"You defied us," she said, her voice barely a whisper.

"You were unreasonable."

" 'Children, obey your parents.' "

" 'Parents, provoke not your children.' "

"I'm done," she said, lowering the axe toward the floor.

I stared her down. "So am I." I didn't know exactly what I meant, but for a moment, anyway, saying it made me feel better.

She placed the axe next to the wall, the head

against the concrete. "You have dishonored us over and over."

I didn't answer her.

She stepped through the stall gate and passed me, her rubber-soled shoes making a slight padding noise against the concrete, her gait veering to the left, favoring her bum knee.

Before she reached the barn door, I stepped into the stall. I didn't cry this time. I simply knelt and picked up pieces of wood, turning them over and then putting them down until I found the ones with Jonathan's carving. I found part of the tree. The letter D. Then an E. And the A. I kept looking until I found all the letters of my name. All of the pieces were sharp and jagged with splinters on the sides and ends, in contrast to the varnished fronts. I made a basket with my apron and loaded the pieces, holding the ends of the fabric out as I walked through the barn and toward the house.

Daed stepped out of the cow barn as I passed. I held my head high and aimed straight ahead. Billy and Joe-Joe stood on the front porch, but instead of running out to meet me, they stayed put. Mutter hadn't latched the back door, so I poked it open with my foot. She sat at the table, the clutter around her. She turned toward me, but I didn't meet her eyes.

When I reached the stairs, Aenti Nell was coming down.

"Good morning," she called out. But her tone

changed when she saw what was in my apron. "Oh, Addie. Look at what all this has led to."

I shook my head. I let her pass, and then I trudged up to my room, my heart as broken as the bits of wood I carried.

Chapter 19

ཥ

I didn't go down to fix breakfast, and no one came up to demand I do so. Instead I arranged the pieces of wood on my bare floor, spelling out my name, and then sat on the end of my bed and stared at the letters.

After a while, I smelled bacon frying and then heard the clatter of dishes and the scrape of chairs against the floor. Aenti Nell must have taken over. I wondered if someone had cleared Mutter's mess or if they would eat around it.

I stood at the French doors as Daed and the boys headed out to the fields, Billy and Joe-Joe tagging along but then veering off toward the creek. After a while they appeared carrying fishing poles— new ones. They stopped in the backyard and held them up to me, and Billy shouted something I couldn't understand.

I opened the French doors but didn't step out onto the balcony. "What?" I called out.

"Jonathan left these for us," Joe-Joe said.

"How do you know?"

Billy held his up higher. "Our names are carved on the handles along with the moon and stars."

I gave them a thumbs-up, and they smiled, then turned away toward the tool shed. A minute later they headed back toward the creek with a shovel, most likely to dig for worms.

After a while I heard footsteps on the stairs and then a soft rap on my door.

"Come in," I said, expecting Aenti Nell.

It wasn't—it was Danny.

He stood in his stocking feet, his straw hat in his hands, his hair flat against his head. "Why didn't you wake me last night?"

"I tried. You wouldn't budge."

"Didn't George come?"

I shook my head.

"Maybe his pickup wouldn't start—or something."

I nodded. *Or something.* Maybe he'd decided I should give up on Jonathan and marry Phillip too.

Outside, Daed yelled for Timothy. Then he bellowed, "Danny!"

"You should get going," I said.

"George does have an idea. . . . But he needs to reach Jonathan, run something by him. Do you have his number?"

"What's his plan?" I reached for my robe on the end of my bed.

"I'm not sure," Danny said. "But we can't sit around and do nothing." His face reddened. "Not you. I don't think there's any more you can do. But maybe George can do something. . . ."

I pulled the piece of paper from my robe and grabbed a small notebook and a pen from the bottom drawer of my dresser, quickly copying down the number in case I needed it.

"Here," I said, handing the scrap to Danny as Daed yelled his name again. "It's his old boss's number. Jonathan said the man would get him a message right away."

Danny clutched the paper and turned to go, waving his hat at me as he hurried from the room.

A few minutes later, Aenti Nell stepped into my room, brusque and businesslike, as if nothing had happened, holding a dishtowel in her hand. "Come on down and help your Mutter. She's been weepy all morning."

"No wonder," I said. "She did a terrible thing."

"She knows what she did was wrong."

I exhaled. "I'll believe that when she tells me."

"You know she won't admit to it." Aenti Nell headed for the door. "But still, she needs your help. She found another box she's going through." She stepped into the hall, her voice trailing behind her. "The whole house is a mess. . . ."

I put my head in my hand. "I can't help her with

this house any longer. I think I'm going to move to Big Valley."

"With no money? No connections? No family?" She stepped closer to me. "Listen, Addie, we don't always get what we want in life. I know that better than anyone. But you make do. Besides, Jonathan was nothing but trouble." She snapped the dishtowel in my direction. "Just like all those Mosiers. The more I hear about Dirk Mosier and see the problems he's created, the more thankful I am that neither your mother nor I married him. And you shouldn't be thinking about marrying a Mosier either. You're a Cramer—it's up to you to keep peace in this family. You could do a whole lot worse than"—I covered my ears with my hands, pressing the palms against my Kapp—"Phillip Eicher. . . ." She glared at me and threw up her hands.

"Aenti Nell," I said, my hands still over my ears. "Why have you turned on me?"

"Why? Because you're pushing everyone to the brink."

"You could go live with Mammi Gladys."

Aenti Nell wrapped her arms around herself. "I'm afraid that's where Cap is going to send me if things don't get back to normal around here."

I flinched but didn't verbally respond, and she stormed out of my room.

I walked to the French doors. The rain had stopped, and steam rose up from the manure pile by the barn. Daed and the boys headed to the pasture. Danny carried the posthole digger. Timothy followed him, his arm still in a sling. Daed turned around and lumbered back toward the barn, probably for another tool.

He didn't look angry at that moment. Just old. And tired.

I sighed and headed downstairs to help Mutter with her papers. This time she'd come across more old Plain magazines—some that were no longer in print. There were more school papers and certificates. One was hers, from over thirty years ago.

Of course she still wouldn't let me throw any of it away, so I took the whole mess up to the attic, where I doubted she would go again—not by herself anyway.

The boys all avoided me throughout the day—even Billy and Joe-Joe, except when they brought the three fish they'd caught in to be cleaned. Then they were happy for my help.

There was no mention of my birthday—not even at the evening meal. After I'd finished the supper dishes, I ventured out to the garden to weed. Thunderclouds billowed on the horizon again, and it looked as if we were due for another storm. When dusk began to fall, Daed ambled over from the porch where he and Timothy had been sitting.

"About done?" he asked.

"I thought I'd work until it's dark."

He appeared suspicious. "You won't be able to see but for a few minutes more. Why don't you go on in."

I pointed to the end of the row of carrots. "I just have a couple of feet to go. I think I'll get it done."

He crossed his arms. "Then I'll say my piece out here."

I stood straight and turned toward him, looking him straight in his tired, faded blue eyes.

"A child—especially a daughter—is meant to obey her parents. And honor them. You know what it says in Scripture." His eyes narrowed. "I've had enough of your stubbornness. Maybe we've been too strict and this is your way of getting back at us. Maybe you think you could follow your Bruders' examples, but the truth is you've done far worse. None of them have betrayed your mother and me the way you have. It's time to stop. It's clear as mud."

He paused for a moment as if waiting for me to respond to his nonsensical statement.

I didn't.

He continued. "I left a message for Phillip and the bishop. They'll be over in the morning. We'll all discuss your future then."

I continued to stare at him, clenching my jaw as I did. Anything I said would only make it worse.

He turned toward the house, but then, over his

shoulder, said, "You're not to go anywhere tonight. Come in as soon as you're done."

I bit my tongue. Sure, I wanted to get to Big Valley, but not tonight.

I turned my attention back to the garden. It was completely dark when I reached the end of the last row. I leaned against the hoe for a moment, feeling sticky in the thick humidity, when I heard the rattle of a vehicle. Its headlights bounced up and down the lane.

It was George's truck. I waited until he parked to walk toward him.

He jumped out.

He spoke quietly but with excitement. "Danny left a message for me, with the number in Big Valley. I've taken care of everything. Jonathan's probably on his way back already."

"What are you talking about?"

"Plus, I called Molly around noon and told her you were having a hard time, worse than Hannah even. That you weren't leaving the farm—barely leaving the house. And if Jonathan didn't come soon, I imagined you'd soon be hospitalized. I told her we're all afraid you might hurt yourself."

"George." My heart fell. "That's not true."

"It doesn't matter. The whole county will think it is, including all the Mosiers. So eventually Jonathan's parents will hear it too. They'll realize how badly they've treated you and feel bad about it—don't you think?"

"No!"

"You don't think they'll feel bad?"

"No—they won't. It's a horrible plan."

"Ach, Addie. It's working perfectly. Molly called up there to Jonathan too. He's frantic about you. He said he'd leave as soon as he could."

"George, this is terrible." What if something happened to Jonathan on his way down? What if he truly believed I was distraught, that I might harm myself?

"It's going to work, Addie. You'll see. I'm going to go talk to Onkel Bob and tell him Jonathan's on his way back, and I'll assume Dirk Mosier will soon follow. Onkel Bob can arrange a meeting with all the parents."

I brushed a trickle of sweat from my temple. "Daed has Phillip Eicher and his Dat coming over in the morning."

George grimaced. "Let me think about that."

"And what about Timothy? Does he know Jonathan is coming back?"

"No."

"But he will, right? If Molly and everyone else knows."

Obviously George hadn't thought about that either. "I'll talk to him," he said.

I shook my head. "That will only make it worse."

"What will make it worse?" a voice behind me asked.

I spun around.

Timothy leaned against the tailgate of George's truck, his baseball cap on his head and a smirk on his face, the sling no longer on his arm.

I didn't answer him.

"No need to be evasive," he said to me, "since you two aren't any good at being secretive. I heard you say the bit about Jonathan being on his way." He rubbed his hands together. "But don't worry—I had a call about it earlier today. You're right, Addie, I am still out to get him. And I'll be waiting. . . ." He leaned back farther. "I'm guessing he'll come here first."

I grabbed George's arm and pulled him toward the barn. "Call Molly and tell her to get a message to Jonathan. Tell him to stay put. I'll find a way to get to Big Valley."

"Ach, Addie, you can't do that." George's voice was louder than it needed to be. "You don't know anyone there."

"You could take me," I said. "Tonight. Please."

"Please." Timothy followed us, mocking me.

"Go away," I hissed.

"Oh, I will," he said, stopping in his tracks. "Straight to Daed." He spun around and headed to the house.

"Now you've done it," George said.

"What does it matter to you?"

"I was hoping to move home—you know, to save some money and join the church." He blushed. "So Sadie and I can get married."

I was thrilled, really, but the most I could muster was "Congratulations."

"Jah, that's why I can't take you anywhere tonight. I can't jeopardize Dat not letting me move home." He threw his keys up in the air, caught them, and turned back toward his pickup. Obviously his generosity had its limits. "I need to get going," he said. "But I'll stop by Onkel Bob's and tell him what's going on."

I sighed. He could do what he wanted. I just couldn't imagine what difference it would make in the long run.

I stepped from the dim kitchen into the dark living room, expecting that everyone had gone up to bed, but startled when Daed said my name. I squinted toward the couch. He and Timothy were sitting on opposite ends with Mutter in the middle.

"You're not to go anywhere tonight," Daed said. "Do you understand?"

"Jah," I answered, overcome with frustration.

"This is out of your hands," Mutter added. "There's nothing you can do."

"Jah," Timothy chirped.

I fled to the stairs, away from all of them, up to my room. I lit my lamp and began pacing around and around. About ten minutes later, a knock came on my door. It wasn't Aenti Nell. It was Daed asking, "Are you in bed?"

"Getting there," I said, trying to decide what I should do. Maybe I could hitchhike to Big Valley—but I would most likely pass Jonathan on the way. Maybe I could hitchhike to Molly's house. She would have an idea.

I grabbed a jacket, the flashlight from beside my bed, and my purse. I had the money Jonathan had returned to me—but that was all.

I extinguished the lamp and turned the knob slowly, pushing open the door as I did.

"Addie." It was Daed's voice, coming from the floor of the hall.

I stepped back.

"I'm staying out here until I know you're asleep."

I pulled the door shut, imagining him sitting with his back against the door in the dark. It was the most I remembered him doing on my behalf in all my life, although it was exactly the opposite of what I wanted him to be doing.

I sank back down to the bed, feeling as if I'd consumed two pots of strong coffee even though I hadn't had a sip since breakfast. Desperation overtook me and my eyes landed on Mutter's old hope chest. I didn't want my things in there. I didn't want them at all if I didn't have a future with Jonathan. As I opened it, thunder crashed in the distance.

I used the flashlight to peer in. Mutter had folded everything neatly, a first for her. I pulled out pillowcases, taking the stack to the French doors and opening them all the way.

"What are you doing?" Daed called out, as if he were speaking into the crack between the floor and the door.

"Just getting some fresh air," I replied, stepping onto the balcony for the first time in my life and flinging a pillowcase over the railing. It floated down just as the rain began to start.

"Go to bed." His voice sounded as if he were half asleep.

I flung another pillowcase over the railing, and it caught for a moment in the air, like a cloud of hope, but then the rain pelted it to the ground. I threw the rest of the stack over, hurried back to the chest, grabbed a set of sheets, and returned to the balcony.

They didn't sail as far and landed in the flower beds below.

I spun the potholders with a flick of my wrist like Frisbees and they went farther, although I couldn't see how far in the dark. Next went the dishtowels and then the bath towels. I placed my quilts on my bed and kept digging.

It only took me a few minutes until I pulled the last item out of the chest, or so I thought. As I yanked up the linen table runner I'd embroidered when I was eleven, my hand brushed against what felt like paper.

It was a business envelope, wedged upright

against the inside bottom of the chest, flush with the corner. I pulled it free. It was addressed simply to *Laurel*. My heart raced as I opened the flap that had been tucked inside and then pulled out a packet of papers.

Sitting down on the bed, I unfolded it and began to read the first one.

LAUREL, it read, all written in capital letters.

I MUST WARN YOU AGAINST DATING DAVID CRAMER. No one called my father by his given name.

HE'S A LIAR AND A CHEAT. I bristled at anyone calling my father that. He was a harsh man, true, but I'd never known him to lie and certainly not to cheat anyone.

YOU CAN DO MUCH BETTER.

I began to feel sick to my stomach, and it was from more than just the content of the letter. It was the writing, the capitals, in particular. Mutter wrote all of her lists in caps.

I patted my apron pocket, feeling the paper inside and pulled it out. It was a list from the day before.

LAUNDRY
WEED THE GARDEN
MEND DAT'S WORK SHIRT
CLEAN THE FLOORS

The handwriting wasn't identical. The list had a shaky appearance, but her hand wasn't as steady as it used to be. I'd noticed that for a few years now.

I kept reading the letters. Each one was more of the same, until the last one.

I KNOW YOU'VE GUESSED WHO'S WRITING THESE. AND SO HAS EVERYONE ELSE. KNOW I ONLY HAVE YOUR BEST INTEREST IN MIND. I MEANT NO HARM— JUST WANTED TO WARN YOU AGAINST MAKING A MISTAKE THAT WILL LAST A LIFETIME.

I shook my head. If Mutter wrote these, what was her purpose? Was she trying to make Daed jealous? Draw attention to herself? Or make him value her love all the more because there appeared to be someone who clearly didn't think he was worthy of her?

I placed the list on top of the letters, clutched them in one hand and the flashlight in the other, and headed toward the door. Opening it, I almost kicked Daed with my foot. He was asleep, sprawled out on the hard floor, guarding my door.

He stirred.

"Daed," I said, stepping over him and then bending down by his head. "I have something to show you."

He sat up with a jerk, a stunned look on his face.

"Everything is all right. I just want to show you some things." I sat down beside him and shone the flashlight on the letter and then the list. "Do you think there's a chance Mutter wrote the letters instead of Dirk? Because it looks a lot like her handwriting." I shifted the flashlight to her list and then shuffled through the letters to the last one, sure if I could show him that his fallout with Dirk was one big mistake, then we could put an end to the grudge between the Cramers and the Mosiers forever.

He took the letters from me, and I handed him the flashlight too. He read the last one, then thumbed through back to the first and read them one by one. "Where did you find these?" he finally asked.

"Mutter's old hope chest."

"Ach," he said, rising to his feet. "I'll ask your mother." He patted my shoulder. "But not tonight. Tomorrow. Now go to bed, for sure."

"Jah," I said, certain we'd turned a corner. "And then we can talk about Jonathan."

He exhaled slowly and then said, "We'll see."

It was the best answer I could hope for. "Good night, then," I said, taking my flashlight from him and stepping back into my room, pulling the door shut behind me. I waited, listening for his steps going down the hall. When they didn't come, I sat down on my bed, puzzled.

A moment later he stepped away from my door. It took another moment for me to realize he wasn't going toward his door at all but down the stairs.

I stood, listening for a moment, until it came to me what he was up to.

"No." I rushed from my room, down the stairs, the flashlight still in my hand. When I reached the kitchen, I turned on the beam, shining it on the woodstove. Daed stood in front of it, the door open, striking a match against the side of the box.

He looked up at me as he flung the flame into the stove, followed by the letters.

"No," I cried out again.

"Go back to bed," he said, his voice heavy with exhaustion. "I'll explain in the morning."

He didn't care about the truth, but worse, he didn't care about me. Not about what I needed. All my parents cared about was their own pride. About exactly what, as Amish, we were supposed to deny. I couldn't depend on them. I couldn't depend on my Bruders. I couldn't even depend on my Aenti.

I couldn't depend on Jonathan. I was utterly, completely alone.

I turned and ran, not out the back door or out the front, but up to my room. When I reached it, I shut my door tightly. But I felt no relief. I was trapped. And tomorrow I'd be forced to court Phillip Eicher. I flew to the French doors, flinging them open again, stepping out onto the balcony. My Bruders used to climb down the trellis just over the side. Why couldn't I?

I had to take charge, to at least get to Molly's house.

I eased my leg over the railing of the balcony

and scooted all the way to the side, grabbing the trellis. I tugged on it. It seemed secure. The rain had slowed to a drizzle, but everything—the balcony, the railing, the trellis—was slick. I swung one foot onto it, testing to see if it would hold. It did. Then I placed my other foot on it. Daed had built it to be secure, although I was sure he never guessed his daughter would use it to flee. I swung my body off the balcony and onto the trellis.

Tightening my grip, I paused for a moment.

"Remember, God is always present," Jonathan had told me. *"Just like the stars, even when we can't see them."*

In my angst, I'd forgotten to pray. I'd forgotten God cared.

He didn't have any pride he needed to protect.

"Dear God," I whispered.

I took another step down.

"Please help—"

Chapter 20

ᎣᏣ

Daed knelt beside me. Timothy stood behind him, talking on his phone. The wail of a siren grew closer.

I must have blackcd out again, because the next thing I remembered was pain radiating from my head. The EMTs, one woman and one man dressed in dark pants and white shirts, stooped beside me as Daed stepped backward. Behind Timothy I could see Aenti Nell in her nightgown and robe, a Kapp placed haphazardly on her head.

The woman asked me how I was feeling.

"Fine," I answered. "I'm okay." I tried to sit up, but the woman told me not to.

She asked me a battery of questions. Could I move my hands? I did. My feet? Ditto.

The man pulled out a penlight and had me follow it with my eyes.

Then the woman slipped on a pair of latex gloves and felt under my head. "You've got quite a goose egg," she said. "And some blood."

I rolled my head to the side a little, orienting myself. The flower bed, lined with rocks, was only a couple of inches from my face. It appeared I'd hit a rock when I landed. I rolled my head the other way. Across the courtyard, in wet lumps, were my linens, towels, and runner—all that used to represent what I hoped for.

"We'll have to transfer her," the man said, looking up at Daed. "Probable concussion. Possible neck injury."

"I'm sorry," I whispered to Daed.

He didn't seem to hear me.

The woman pulled a white collar from the box beside her and slipped it around my neck, while the man headed back to the ambulance. A moment later he returned with another man carrying a yellow board. Together the three of them carefully rolled me onto my side, slid the board under me, and rolled me back onto it. Then they strapped me to the board, pulling one of the straps snug against my forehead.

Timothy said good-bye to whomever he was talking to, and George stepped forward, patting my arm. "It will be okay," he said. "We still have a plan."

I groaned. "Don't do anything stupid."

"Not like you did, I promise." He grimaced. "By morning all will be well. Just wait and see."

I tried to shake my head, but the collar and strap prevented it from moving.

"Find Jonathan and tell him the truth. That I'm not depressed."

"But you are going to the hospital." George smiled, just a little.

"Tell him why. Don't make him think I'm unstable."

George looked toward the house, up at my window. "But you are. Don't you think?"

I started to say I wasn't, but the female EMT broke up our conversation. "Who's going with her?" she asked.

"I am," Daed answered, without hesitating. For a moment I wondered why Aenti Nell wasn't, but she wasn't dressed. Besides, Dacd would need to fill out the paperwork. "Go get my hat," he said to Timothy. "And my wallet."

"I'm sorry," I said to Daed, tears stinging my eyes.

"Ach, Addie . . ." He shook his head as if, for once, he didn't know what to say.

The male EMT jumped into the back of the ambulance, still holding onto the board, and then all three slid me onto some sort of platform. If I didn't hurt so bad, I'd have been mortified that an ambulance had come for me.

Aenti Nell stood at the open doors, with Daed behind her. She held her hand out to me, a befuddled look on her face.

"I'm okay," I called out. "Tell Mutter."

She nodded.

Timothy came running—with Daed's hat and wallet, I presumed—and stuck his head in the back of the ambulance. "Get better real quick, Toad."

I tried to smile at his childhood nickname for me, but even with the brace on, it hurt. Still, he hadn't called me that in years.

He stepped closer, where I could see his brown eyes, the same color as mine. They were bright and caring. He hadn't been drinking tonight. Hopefully he wouldn't.

But a moment later, as the boys all took off in the direction of George's truck, I feared that Timothy was trying to trick George—and that it was working. Someone still might get really hurt.

The driver slammed the back doors. A moment later first one of the cab doors shut and then the other.

The male EMT hit a switch that raised the platform I was on. Then lights filled the back window. My brothers were following in George's pickup. When we reached the highway, though, they turned to the left after the ambulance turned right.

I could only guess where they were going. But I couldn't imagine that they would find Jonathan, not if he'd already left. But if they did, having Timothy the Terrible along would only lead to even more trouble.

There wasn't a radiologist working to read the X-rays, so the ER doc made me keep the neck brace on and ordered me to spend the night. He also said I had a concussion, a pretty bad one. The nurses gave me medicine to stop the nausea I was feeling and kept the lights turned low.

I told Daed he should go on home.

"She'll be fine," the nurse said. "Come back in the morning."

"I don't have a ride," Daed said.

"You could call Samuel," I offered.

Daed shook his head. "He has work in the morning."

"A taxi?" I closed my eyes. My head pounded.

"One of our aides is getting off soon," the nurse said. "Where do you live? I'll ask if he's going your way."

Daed thanked her. "You'll be okay?" he asked.

I nodded, my eyes still closed. Actually I'd be better off alone.

Maybe Daed sensed that, because he didn't say any more until the nurse came in and said she'd arranged a ride for him.

"Good night," Daed said to me.

I opened one eye. "See you tomorrow?"

"Jah."

Once my earthly father left, I remembered my unfinished prayer to my heavenly Father, the one I'd started as I'd stepped out onto the trellis.

"Be with Jonathan," I whispered now. I felt God's comfort as if he were beside me. *Denki, for your care*. I didn't have the energy to speak out loud any longer. *And that I'm really never alone.*

I dozed after that, but a nurse awakened me a little while later to give me another medication. After that I slept soundly, although my dreams raced from one thing to another. I was in the woods with Jonathan, but then he turned into Mutter. She climbed a tree. Jonathan's father started to chop it down. Daed pushed him away. Mutter fell anyway, and I caught her, but she turned into Aenti Nell by the time she landed in my arms. Joe-Joe fell in the creek. I stooped to scoop him out, but Jonathan caught him on one of the fishing poles he'd carved. Jonathan pulled up blades of grass and started twisting them. The braid grew longer and longer and longer until it landed in the creek and flowed along like water. It was only then I realized I'd been dreaming.

It took me a minute to remember where I was when I awoke. Light streamed through the crack in the window covering, where it hadn't been pulled shut completely. The soft blankets touched my chin, as if someone had tucked me in.

It was then that I sensed someone else beside me—a weight against the bed. Perhaps Daed had returned already. I started to turn my head, but the pain increased and I stopped for a moment, until my eyes fell on a bottle on the little table scooted partway over the bed. Why would the nurse leave medicine out like that? I shifted an inch more.

Jonathan was sitting in a chair pulled next to the bed, his head on the edge of the mattress, his hand extended toward the bottle.

I gasped, which made my headache worse. I closed my eyes against my fear.

My brothers hadn't found Jonathan. Somehow he'd known to come to the hospital anyway and found me as bad off as George and then Molly had warned. Perhaps he thought I'd jumped from a building or maybe a bridge. Surely, looking at me he thought I'd tried to take my life. Maybe he'd thought I was comatose or even brain dead.

And now there was a bottle of pills. He was passionate yes, but I hadn't thought he was stupid. Could it be . . . ?

I struggled to open my eyes again, to turn my head directly to look at him, but couldn't. Instead I sank back against the pillow, my heart racing, praying I was having another dream.

When I heard my mother scream, I knew for sure I wasn't.

"Addie!" Mutter bellowed like a cow that had lost her calf.

My eyes flew open. Jonathan stirred beside me.

"Thank you, Lord," Mutter and I groaned in unison.

She collapsed on the end of my bed, Daed right behind her, as I reached for Jonathan's hand, patting the bed until he grabbed mine.

"I thought you were—" Mutter gasped—"both dead."

Jonathan leaned over me, and I could finally see his face and the questioning expression on it.

I pointed. "The bottle."

Mutter gasped again. "I thought you'd both overdosed."

"We wouldn't do that," Jonathan said, but then gazed into my eyes. "Would we?"

"No," I whispered. It hurt my head to talk. "I fell. Climbing from my window. Trying to get to you."

"Jah," he said. "That's what the nurse said, but I needed to know for sure."

I pointed, as best I could, to the bottle. "Are those yours?"

He nodded. "From my naturopath. My stomach hurt worse once I got back to Big Valley. I called Molly when I arrived in Paradise. When she told me what happened to you, that you were here, it flared up again. And worse once I made it to the hospital. That's all." He picked up the bottle. "I put one under my tongue. . . ."

I would have laughed—if I could have.

Daed stepped closer to me, ignoring Jonathan. "Are you better?"

"Jah," I answered, "I think so." The truth was, I felt worse, but that was to be expected. The doctor said even if there was no permanent damage to my neck it would hurt for several days.

"The radiologist is looking at your X-rays now," Daed said. "They'll let us know."

I touched my forehead.

Mutter noticed. "Is everything all right?"

In some ways things were all right. I had no desire to please my parents at that moment, and funny thing, for the first time in forever I knew my parents did care about me. My father riding along in the ambulance and coming right back this morning. My mother screaming at the thought of me appearing to be dead.

Neither of those reactions were because they cared about what others thought.

And now, flat on my back, helpless, unable to do anything, I felt God's love for me in a way I never had before. He didn't care how capable I was. He cared how dependent I was on him. I felt as if, finally, I was getting to know him better.

In that sense, things were all right.

But what wasn't right was that my parents were pretending—now that he was obviously okay too—as if Jonathan didn't exist.

"Actually . . . everything's not okay." I closed my eyes.

"Should I ring for the nurse?" Daed asked.

"No. You should acknowledge Jonathan. Pretending he's not here won't make him go away. Avoiding the fact that we care for each other won't make us stop." I continued to keep my eyes closed.

No one moved, as far as I could tell. No one said a word.

Finally, Jonathan said, "I know this is hard on the two of you, but we should try to work things out."

As difficult as it was not to open my eyes—especially after Mutter gasped again—I kept them closed, until I heard Timothy call out, "How is she?"

My lids flew open. He rushed into the room, followed by George and Danny. All three were wearing the same shirts as the night before, now wrinkled, and looked as if they hadn't slept. Jonathan stood.

I put my hand out, as if I could stop Timothy.

"Man," he said to Jonathan, "we've looked everywhere for you. And here you are with Toad."

There were more footsteps in the hall and someone—Mervin?—yelled, "Wait up!"

Martin scooted into the room first, followed by Mervin.

"What's going on?" Daed asked.

George was out of breath as he spoke. "We couldn't find Jonathan last night so we went and got Mervin and Martin this morning—and then decided to come here."

"So"—my eyes found Timothy—"you're all friends now?"

He shrugged. "Well, I was still thinking about

getting even last night, even after you were hurt. But we hashed it out when we grabbed these guys." He jerked his thumb toward Mervin and Martin. "It was a misunderstanding, really."

"Jah," Mervin said. "At that party when we told him to leave Tabitha alone it was because he'd been drinking, but—"

Timothy interrupted. "I thought it was because I was a Cramer."

I wanted to shake my head in disbelief, but the neck brace stopped me.

"Jah," Martin said, stepping forward where I could see him. "We're really sorry for the part we played in all of this. And that you got hurt, Addie."

"But there's still the problem with our Dats, jah?" Timothy turned toward Daed.

"And your drinking," I said.

Timothy shook his head.

"No, it's true." My voice grew stronger. "You have a problem."

He crossed his arms and the room froze.

"Addie . . ." Mutter said.

But Daed said, "Son, your Schwester is right. It's time we sought some help. I'm afraid where this might end if we don't."

"You don't know what you're talking about." Timothy's eyes narrowed.

"Listen to your Dat," Mervin and Martin said in unison.

"Jah," George said. "You're lucky you didn't hurt someone when you had your accident. You've got to stop."

Danny, Mervin, Martin, and George all started talking at the same time as Timothy backed away from the foot of the bed.

"Quiet!" I didn't recognize the voice, but then a new nurse, middle-aged with short dark hair and a scowl that rivaled Mutter's, appeared behind Timothy. "What happened to you all being a peaceful lot?"

Before anyone could answer, she put her hands on her hips. "Everybody out!" she ordered.

"Everybody?" Mutter said.

"Addie can choose one of you to stay."

Jonathan stood.

"No," I said. "Don't go."

He shook his head. "I'll come back. I should go talk this out with your Dat and Bruders. And with Mervin and Martin too."

"Good," Mutter said. "Because I'm staying."

The men filed out as the nurse said, "There's a conference room to the right you can use."

"Denki," Jonathan said, the last to leave.

Mutter closed the door behind him and settled down on the edge of the bed. "You've really made a mess of things," she said.

This time I kept my eyes open. "All these years I felt as if what I wanted didn't matter—as if what I needed didn't matter. But I finally found something that matters more than being who you want me to be."

She inched closer to me. "The Lord says to honor your parents."

"Jah, but pleasing isn't honoring."

"What do you mean?"

"You've been trying to manipulate me all along when it came to Jonathan Mosier. And now I know why."

Her face reddened.

Before I could say more, my door flew open again—Dirk Mosier stood with his hat in his hands.

His face fell. "Addie. Laurel. Sorry," he muttered. "I thought Jonathan was here."

"He is," I answered. "In the room next door."

He closed the door quickly.

Mutter's face had turned from red to white as the door closed. "What do you mean," she said, turning to me, "that honoring your parents isn't the same as pleasing them?"

"Honoring you means to respect you—which I do. But it also means putting my trust in God, not in you and Daed." I took a deep breath. "Pleasing you means to make you happy. That's not up to me."

"Who told you that?"

I hesitated and then said, "I came up with it on my own. But the ideas came from a conversation with Hannah."

Mutter rolled her eyes. "I knew they shouldn't have taken her to that place."

"It probably saved her life."

Mutter shook her head.

"Back to what I was talking about before we were—"

Someone knocked on the door, and Mutter bounced from the bed and hurried to open it.

"I came as soon as Nell told me." It was Onkel Bob's voice, but I couldn't see him. "How is she?"

Mutter opened the door wider. Onkel Bob, his face full of concern, stepped to the end of the bed, followed by Aenti Nell.

"I'm fine," I said to my Onkel, wincing a little as I spoke. "But we need your help. Daed and Dirk and all the boys are in the conference room next door. Could you join them?"

Onkel Bob glanced at Mutter, who was back at my side. She shrugged. I nodded, as best I could with the neck collar on.

"Jah," Onkel Bob said. "I'm happy to do what I can."

"Denki," I whispered, waving my hand at Aenti Nell and then closing my eyes against the throbbing in my head.

"You should wait in the hall," Mutter said to my Aenti. I didn't have the energy to say it was okay if she stayed in the room.

I sensed Mutter settling into the chair against the

wall, keeping her distance from me. "I'll let you rest," she said.

Sleep sent me back down to the creek, this time at night, chasing fireflies with Jonathan.

Mutter's plan to let me rest—and my dream—lasted until Dirk Mosier's voice startled both of us.

"Let's ask Laurel," he said from the hall.

I opened my eyes.

"I'll get her." It was Daed, stepping into my room. "Come with me," he said to Mutter, as serious as I'd ever seen him.

"No." It was time for me to take charge of our two chaotic households. "Tell the others to come back in here." I struggled to sit up a little more in the bed.

Daed gave Mutter a questioning look. She shook her head. "I'll go with Daed."

"No." My voice was firm.

"Addie, this is too much stress," Daed said to me.

"It will be more stressful if you don't."

It sounded as if Mutter sat back down in the chair, but I didn't try to turn my head to make sure. Daed's footsteps fell across the linoleum.

The boys came in first. Timothy, George, and Danny stopped at the end of my bed, while Jonathan stepped to the side closest to my head, followed by Mervin and Martin.

Onkel Bob entered next and stood next to Martin, followed by Dirk, and then Daed, who stepped to the side by Mutter. Finally Aenti Nell came in, stopping at the wall beyond the end of my bed.

Onkel Bob cleared his throat. "It seems as if it's time for me to meddle." He paused for a moment. "We'll start with the question Dirk has for Laurel."

I couldn't see any of them, just my Bruders at the end of the bed.

"Why did you blame me for those letters?" Dirk asked.

Mutter's voice sounded teary. "I didn't. Others did. Because of the words. And the handwriting. Cap was sure it was you."

A bolt of pain shot through my head.

"There's no use rehashing all of this," Daed said. "It happened years ago."

"I was wrongly accused," Dirk said. "And the one person who could have spoken up for me didn't." He glared at my Daed.

I turned my head as much as I could toward my parents. "Mutter," I said. "Daed already knows. So do I. We read the letters."

Her face grew as white as the sheets on my bed.

"Go on," I said. "We both still love you. But you should tell the truth."

She opened her mouth and then gulped, as I

imagined someone about to drown might do.

Daed put his arm around her.

She patted her apron pocket and slipped her hand into it, taking something out. When she unfolded it, I realized it was the empty envelope from the night before.

"I found this in your room," she said. "This morning. On the floor. I searched all over for the letters. When I couldn't find them I hoped I'd destroyed them years ago."

I turned my gaze to Daed.

"I did, last night," he said.

Mutter's voice was barely audible. "So you believe I wrote them, then?"

Daed didn't answer.

She held up the envelope, turning it first to Onkel Bob and then to Dirk. "Jah," she said. "I did. But I didn't mean to implicate Dirk. I didn't know he wrote like that. I just wanted to get Cap's attention because it seemed, once he got to really know me, he was slipping away, just as Dirk had. I thought if I received these letters saying how I shouldn't marry him, but he saw me only growing more committed to him, it would win his heart."

Daed grimaced.

Mutter folded the envelope and slipped it back into her pocket. "But it wasn't until everyone assumed Dirk was writing the letters that my plan began to work. Cap was furious with you."

She was looking straight at Dirk now, or so I assumed without being able to turn my head. "And even more so after you said those horrible things that night at the party."

She swiped at her eyes. "I never meant for it to get so out of hand." She turned to Daed. "To ruin your friendship with your best friend. Everything snowballed."

"Why didn't you speak up?" Daed asked, his voice raw with pain.

"And lose you?" Mutter shook her head. "After a while I started to believe the lie myself, and it was easier to blame Dirk for the pain I felt in ruining your friendship than myself. Then when Dirk came back for Nell—"

I gasped, "What?"

My Aenti's hand flew to her face.

"Jah, but I convinced her not to marry him. I begged her to put our family first. It would have added insult to injury to have Dirk as a brother-in-law. But then, as the years went by and she didn't marry anyone else, I felt worse and worse about what I'd done. That was when I started to feel so sad."

"Mutter," I whispered.

Aenti's hand slid from her face to her throat, an expression of pain covering her face.

"I'm sorry," Mutter said. "If I'd only known then how far-reaching the consequences would be . . ." She looked directly at me.

"You could have said something a few weeks ago," I said. "Before Timothy hurt Mervin. Before Jonathan was banished."

"Ach," Mutter said. "I wanted to. I just couldn't." She stepped backward and stumbled. Daed caught her arm and helped her find the chair. She sat down abruptly, her thick-soled shoes flopping out in front of her. "I hope all of you can forgive me, in time. You too, Nell."

No one said a word, but in an instant Jonathan had left my side. A moment later he was giving my Aenti a hug, and was then beside my mother, extending his hand to her.

"I forgive you, Laurel," he said.

She grasped his hand and held on to it tightly. "Denki," she whispered, not letting go of him.

She seemed so vulnerable, more fragile than ever.

"So do I," I said.

She nodded.

"Don't worry about it," Mervin and Martin said in unison.

George and Danny both shrugged, but Timothy crossed his arms. I couldn't tell if he was unwilling to let the grudge go or if humiliation might now fuel his anger.

"Timothy?" Mutter pled.

"Jah," he said. "I don't really understand all of this, but I won't hold it against you."

Onkel Bob stepped to the end of the bed. "All

you boys, except Jonathan, go along now. Get something to eat. Or wait in the lobby."

They filed out one by one, each one telling me good-bye and that they hoped I'd be better soon.

I waved, grateful they were leaving, but then I tensed as I heard Bishop Eicher's voice outside the door.

"I heard we might be needed here," he said.

"Jah," Phillip piped in. "We came to help."

I groaned. Daed's heavy footsteps fell across the floor. In a calm voice he said, "No need. Bob's handling it."

"We'll stop by your place later, then," Phillip said.

"I'll be in touch," Daed answered, closing the door.

I couldn't help but notice Phillip hadn't asked about me. It filled me with relief. No one could possibly think he really cared for me—not even my Daed, not compared to Jonathan anyway.

Before Onkel Bob could say anything, Dirk spoke up. "Could we wrap this up? Jonathan and I need to get back to Big Valley."

Onkel Bob crossed his arms. "Laurel hasn't gotten what she asked for yet, Dirk. From you or Cap. And there's the matter of the ruined friendship between the two of you too, and the relationship between these Youngie." He nodded at Jonathan and then at me.

"Forgiveness is one thing," Dirk said, nodding

at Mutter and then at Daed. "And jah, I extend that. But joining our two families is quite another matter." He turned to Aenti Nell then, and she nodded her head to acknowledge him, but that was all. He stepped to the edge of my bed and pointed to Jonathan. "Come along, son. We never should have returned to Lancaster. We're going home."

Chapter 21

ഇയ

When Jonathan didn't budge, Dirk stepped to the end of the bed and shook his finger at his son. "We'd best be going. Now."

"Jah," Daed said. "That's what we want too. For you to go." He tugged on his beard. "We appreciate your forgiveness, but past that we're in complete agreement," he said. "We don't want the two to marry either. Go along, Jonathan. All of us need to get back to how things were two weeks ago. Addie has a beau waiting for her answer."

I groaned. "Daed."

He looked at me, a befuddled look on his face.

In a pleading tone that surprised me, Mutter said, "Cap—"

But he interrupted her with "You've done quite enough as it is. Let me handle this." He turned to Jonathan. "Go on."

Jonathan didn't budge. "No," he said. "I won't. We want to court."

"I feel the same," I interjected.

Jonathan continued. "We hope to marry." He turned to me. "If you'll have me."

"Jah, of course," I whispered.

Both Daed and Dirk stepped toward him, but Mutter stood, stopping them as she positioned herself in front of Jonathan. "You two, listen." First she looked at Daed. "Don't think it's escaped me that you haven't offered your forgiveness. Nor should you yet. I know we have a lot to work out. But that doesn't mean we let all of that get in the way of our daughter's happiness. I already ruined Nell's life—I'm not going to ruin my daughter's too."

My eyes grew wide.

"And you, Dirk Mosier. Maybe you want to see us hurt—maybe even see our daughter hurt—but don't hurt your son. He's kind and generous. Good to Addie and her Bruders. He's the one who has tried to mend things all along. He's a good friend—unlike all of us were to each other." She planted her hands on her hips and widened her stance. "Treat me how you like, but don't ruin things for these young people."

I couldn't see Jonathan's face, but I could see

his father's, and it was without expression. Beyond him Aenti Nell smiled.

Daed hung his head but said, "Now, Laurel, we don't need to meddle in Dirk's family business."

"No," Jonathan said. "She does." He stepped around Mutter and toward his father, stopping just an inch away. "I can't change whom I love."

His father continued to glare.

Mutter spoke up again. "He's like Jonathan in the Bible—a good friend."

At that Dirk's face softened a little. He exhaled and said, "That's who I had in mind when I named him. I wanted him to be a good friend—unlike I was to David." He was looking at my father now. No one ever called him David anymore. Not even Mutter.

"I always wondered if you got tired of the name Cap after you were grown and married." Dirk turned toward Daed.

"Nah," my father answered. "It's suited me just fine. You named me well."

"Why did you name him that?" I asked.

"We were four or five, I think. Somewhere he'd gotten an orange hunting cap that I wanted."

"It was the brightest thing we'd ever seen." Daed paused. "And the first time you pounded me."

"But not the last." Dirk sighed. "You never would let me borrow that cap. You lost it somewhere along the way, and I started calling you Cap in memory of it." He chuckled a little. "Stupid, huh?"

"Jah," Daed said. "But you were more like family to me than my own brother."

"And then you bought me that hunting cap when we were in our teens. Do you remember?"

Daed nodded.

"It was as bright as could be." He met my father's eyes then. "I still have it. Still wear it . . ." Dirk exhaled slowly. "That's why it hurt so much when you stuck by Laurel instead of me."

"What else could I do?" Daed tugged on his beard. "I loved her."

"I thought you knew me better."

"I'm sorry," Daed said as the nurse entered the room.

"What's going on?" she barked.

"We're leaving," Onkel Bob answered. "How about a cup of coffee?" he asked Daed and Dirk.

The nurse smiled. "I was teasing. Actually the radiologist cleared her. There's no permanent neck issues—just whiplash. She can be released in about an hour to a dark room at home. No screen time though." She laughed. "Which won't be a problem for you. You can read if it doesn't make your head worse. Get lots of sleep. No outings or work for a week. Boring, I know," she said. "But it's what's best."

It didn't sound boring to me.

"But hire a driver," the nurse said to Daed. "Or

get one of those boys with a car to drive her home. A buggy ride's a little rough for a while."

"Will do," Daed said. "They're probably in the cafeteria." He turned to Dirk. "How about that cup of coffee?"

Dirk didn't respond. Instead he turned to Aenti Nell and took her hand. She smiled at him but that was all. A moment later, he followed Daed out to the hall, without demanding Jonathan come along. As much as I felt sorry for Aenti Nell, I was relieved she hadn't married Dirk. If he hadn't ended up with Mary, Jonathan wouldn't exist. Still, I wished Aenti would have courted and married someone else and had a family of her own.

When Onkel Bob reached the door, he turned to Jonathan. "If you decide to stay in Lancaster County, come see me about a position. I'm pretty sure I have an opening now."

"Denki," Jonathan said. "I'll be out right away." He moved around to the other side of the bed, slipping back into the chair and taking my hand, holding it without saying a word as Mutter and Aenti headed toward the door too.

"So you're staying?" I whispered, turning my head as best I could. I'd known him eleven days, a lifetime to be sure.

He smiled then, that light-up-the-sky smile I'd been missing. "Jah," he said.

He leaned toward me, his lips brushing mine

just as the nurse came back into the room. She clasped her hands together and said, "I so like happy endings." But then her voice grew harsh again. "But none of that now. Wait until she's better."

If Jonathan and I had starring Englisch roles in a Hollywood movie, perhaps we would have married immediately.

After all, we now both believed in love at first sight, or at least nearly so anyway.

But that wasn't the way our community did things. We had a plan to follow. One that had proven true over many centuries.

Within a week, I was back at my old tasks but with a new vigor. After Dirk and Daed patched things up, they gave Jonathan and me their blessing. Dirk and Mary decided they liked Big Valley better than Lancaster County and moved back for good, but Jonathan stayed on with his Dawdi, with Tabitha running the house. He worked for Onkel Bob during the day and kept up with his own carpentry during the evening, after he made me a new hope chest, this time with both of our names engraved on top.

On the weekends, he and I sold his hope chests and mantels, bookends and trivets at farmers' markets. I kept track of the inventory and pricing, expenses and profits, grilling Cate over and over on business practices. Both Jonathan and I lived out our gifting—his of dreaming and creating, mine of organizing and orchestrating. We saved everything we could, from both of Jonathan's jobs.

And of course we began to court, something even Phillip Eicher finally accepted when Jonathan and I showed up at our first singing together at Molly's parents' place. Phillip nodded at me from a distance and then followed Molly around for the rest of the evening.

Hannah came in late that evening with Mervin and Martin. She was definitely doing better, although I couldn't be sure that she was fine. Only time would tell.

Soon after that, Jonathan and I started classes to join the church.

My parents seemed too careful with each other for several weeks after the revelation in my hospital room—then not careful enough. I could hear them arguing long into the night—for them at least, meaning way past nine thirty—on several occasions.

And then, without telling us where they were going, they started disappearing one afternoon a week. They didn't even tell Aenti Nell what they were up to, but Hannah figured it out. She said Aenti Pauline had told Mutter about the counselor at the clinic and urged her to go.

I don't know what exactly my parents learned, but it seemed to help. They stopped arguing. They started sitting on the couch before dinner, holding hands and chatting. Mutter stopped talking about "fate" and seemed to become more thoughtful. A few times I found her at the table by herself, her head bowed in prayer. And at bedtime, she took over reading to Joe-Joe, starting with a book of Bible stories. Soon Billy was listening too.

And Daed put his foot down with the older boys, saying, when George asked to move back in, that he only could if he got rid of his truck. Then he started taking Timothy to see a counselor one afternoon a week too. I could only guess on that one. But it seemed Timothy suffered from the same melancholy as Mutter and Hannah, only in him it came out as anger instead of depression. Perhaps that was why he drank.

He cut back, with Daed's intervention, but he wasn't willing to stop altogether, not even with the prospect of courting Tabitha if he did. Nor was he willing to get rid of his Bronco, which he'd since gotten repaired. Timothy ended up moving in with Samuel when George came home.

But Timothy did seem to be changing, slowly, and I was certain it had started that night I fell, when it seemed he finally cared more about someone else—me—than himself. And then it continued when he realized that Mervin and Martin had been opposed to his drinking, not to him. I hoped in time he'd come all the way around and get lasting help for his problems.

As they addressed their own issues, my parents seemed to care less about what other people thought. Sure, they still held to the Ordnung and honored the church and all it stood for. But they relaxed. I overheard Mutter sharing her frustrations about the boys with Aenti Pauline instead of saying everything was fine. The flip side was, Mutter stopped gossiping about other people, and one time I overheard her ask Aenti Nell, kindly, not to share her opinions about Onkel Bob and his relationship with Nan.

Soon after that I began calling Mutter and Daed *Mamm* and *Dat*—the more familiar terms. They'd earned the endearments.

And around that time Aenti Nell took a job at a quilt shop out on the highway. She said she needed a life of her own. And she was right. She'd given far too much of her life to us already.

The week after Jonathan and I were baptized, we wandered down to the creek on the afternoon of my parents' annual barbecue. Mamm oversaw the food table while Aenti Nell stood ready to help with the cleanup, allowing me some time with my beau. We stopped, hand-in-hand, at the edge of the sycamore grove.

Betsy and Levi, who carried Robbie, rounded the corner of the trail from Onkel Bob's place, calling out a greeting. The little one was nearly a year old and as cute as could be. It looked as if perhaps Betsy was expecting again.

As far as I could tell, sadly, Cate wasn't.

But the family had other news. Nan was considering giving up her car—and her job. It wouldn't be long, it seemed, until she and Onkel Bob were officially courting.

We chatted with Betsy for a minute, and then Jonathan pulled me close and stood beside me until my cousin was out of sight, following Levi up the trail to our pasture.

In the distance we could hear the little boys splashing in the creek. Above us, the branches of the sycamore trees swayed in the breeze. A toad croaked on the far bank.

"Come on," Jonathan said, taking my hand, pulling me along the path past the grove, toward Onkel Bob's.

He didn't say another word until he stopped at the rose garden. The sweetness of the flowers surrounded us. This time he didn't cut a bloom with his pocketknife. Instead he got down on one knee and took both my hands.

"I've waited an entire year for this day," he said. "As much as I wanted to be rash back then, I wanted more to do things right." He smiled as sweetly as the roses swaying in the breeze. "Will you marry me?"

I knelt beside him and simply answered, "Jah."

And so we were married in my parents' house the next November.

Mammi Gladys was there and Dawdi Mosier,

along with Tabitha, who would be returning to the other side of the county now that I would be moving into the old Mosier place. All my Bruders were there, of course; plus Aenti Pauline and Onkel Owen, their one-year-old son, and their daughters; and Mervin and Martin and their parents, who were now my Onkel Amos and Aenti Eliza.

Aenti Nell, Onkel Bob and Nan, Cate and Pete, Betsy, Levi, and Robbie, and Dirk and Mary were all there too.

Plus my Mamm and Dat, of course.

Even Phillip Eicher came, and not surprisingly with Molly. Although Hannah assured me, as she sat beside Mervin, that Phillip and Molly were only friends. Still, it did me good to see him with someone else.

As all the Cramers and all the Mosiers supported us as one, the grudge between the two households was finally, and entirely, mended.

Acknowledgments

ଦ୍ଧ

Numerous people supported me as I wrote this novel, contributed in some way, or helped shape the story. I am very grateful to all of them! My husband, Peter, and children, Kaleb, Taylor, Hana, and Thao, are at the top of my list. God has greatly blessed me in giving me all of you as my family.

My siblings, Kathy Fink, Kelvin Egger, and Laurie Snyder, also continue to bless me, along with our father, Bruce Egger. It was my mother, Leora Houston Egger—who is now in heaven— who first introduced me to God's grace and to Shakespeare's plays. I am forever grateful for her continued influence on my life each day.

First readers of this story include Libby Salter, Laurie Snyder, and Tina Bustamante (so grateful!) and critique group members Melanie Dobson, Nicole Miller, Dawn Shipman, and Kelly Chang (thank you!).

Those cheering from the sidelines, whose encouragement and prayers mean more than I can ever express, include Kate Commerford,

Becky Berg, Holly Frakes, Jan Puntenney, Marilyn Weisenburg, Renee Naslund, Rod and Ruth Ann Richards, Denise Capps, Ann McGraw, Fran Heinith, Julie Johnson, Mary Hake, and the good people who belong to Oregon Christian Writers, along with all my wonderful readers. Thank you! I'm also grateful to Lynn Ferber and Alan Rosenfeld for their support and for, again, providing me with a writer's retreat to finish this story.

A special thank-you to my agent, Chip MacGregor, to Mindy Starns Clark (for all she's taught me about the Amish), and to those in the Plain community who have shared their stories with me. Any mistakes in this novel are mine alone.

I can't thank Bethany House Publishers enough for all of their support, including editors extraordinaire Karen Schurrer and Dave Long. It's been a delight to partner with everyone at Bethany on THE COURTSHIPS OF LANCASTER COUNTY series.

About the Author

꼬

Leslie Gould is the coauthor, with Mindy Starns Clark, of the #1 CBA bestseller *The Amish Midwife*, a 2012 Christy Award winner; and the author of ECPA bestseller *Courting Cate*, first in THE COURTSHIPS OF LANCASTER COUNTY series; and *Beyond the Blue*, winner of the Romantic Times Reviewers' Choice for Best Inspirational Novel, 2006. She holds an MFA in creative writing from Portland State University and has taught fiction writing at Multnomah University as an adjunct professor. She and her husband and four children live in Portland, Oregon.

Learn more about Leslie at
www.lesliegould.com.

Center Point Large Print

600 Brooks Road / PO Box 1
Thorndike ME 04986-0001 USA

(207) 568-3717

US & Canada:
1 800 929-9108
www.centerpointlargeprint.com